The Iris Deception

■ ■ ■

Western Literature Series

The Iris
Deception
■ ■ ■

BERNARD SCHOPEN

University of Nevada Press
Reno   Las Vegas

Western Literature Series

University of Nevada Press, Reno, Nevada 89557 USA
Copyright © 1996 by Bernard Schopen
Manufactured in the United States of America
Cover design by Erin Kirk New

Library of Congress Cataloging-in-Publication Data

Schopen, Bernard.
The iris deception / Bernard Schopen.
p. cm. — (Western literature series)
ISBN 0-87417-286-1 (pbk. : alk. paper)
1. Private investigators—Nevada—Reno—Fiction.
2. California, Northern—Fiction. I. Title.
II. Series
PS3569.C528141I7 1996
813'.54—dc20   96-14575
CIP

The paper used in this book meets the requirements of American
National Standard for Information Sciences—Permanence of Paper
for Printed Library Materials, ANSI Z39.48-1984. Binding
materials were selected for strength and durability.

05 04 03 02 01 00 99 98 97 96   5 4 3 2

To my daughters,
Laura and Rachel,
and
To their friend and mine
Michael Binard

CHAPTER ONE

Mid-October, midmorning. In the California Avenue office I'd leased nearly a year before, KUNR was playing Dvořák and I was playing lawyer, roughing out a brief for an attorney down the hall. Then I sensed a presence, glanced up.

I didn't know how long she'd been standing in the shadowed doorway. I did know that everything about her was wrong. Everything she wore said style, ease, wealth. Everything she wore it on said desert, sweat, work.

A white cashmere sweater and a well-cut beige dress softened the hard lines of her big, raw-boned, rangy body. Her tendony forearms ended at large knobby hands that clutched a dainty suede purse. Her graying light brown hair was stylishly tinted and cut, her face cruelly cut and tinted by the desert.

I knew the face, but I couldn't give the woman a name until she took a hesitant step out of the shadow and I saw her eyes—the deep dark blue of the wild iris, beautiful, unforgettable.

1

Stunned, I rose from my chair. "Mrs. McLeod?"

She gave me an uncertain desert squint, as if she, or I, were in the wrong office. "Never would of figured you for a place like this, Ross. The slick gitup, neither."

My vested gray pinstripe blended with the decor—off-white carpet, chromium and smoked glass and gray leather furniture, computer workstation, abstract paintings that looked like flowers and bones and wounds, it had all come with the lease. The only things of mine in the room were the books on the shelves and the portrait of my daughter atop the filing cabinet.

I smiled. "It's been a long time, Mrs. McLeod."

She squinted down at her own slick gitup. "I know. Things change. I—you still a private detective?"

"Yes ma'am."

"Got a minute?"

In fact I didn't. I had a brief to finish, and a cross-examination strategy to outline. I had a report to write informing an attorney that her client wasn't who he said he was. I had one witness to locate for an attorney in a vehicular homicide case, another for an insurance company. I had a check to run on a woman being considered for the comptroller job at a Tahoe casino.

"Have a seat," I said, as the New World symphony ended. "I've got fresh coffee."

"Black'd do me." She stepped inside, her gaze drifting. For a moment it fastened on something on a bookshelf and brightened, for another fixed on the picture of my daughter and softened.

I turned off the radio, pressed the computer's Save button, went to the coffeemaker and poured Patsy McLeod a black cup and turned to find her holding a book.

"You read this?" *Squaring the Circle: Settling the American Desert*, by a Stanford history professor named Draine.

I nodded, set her coffee on an end table. She sat on the edge of the couch, her work-scarred thumbs absently stroking the book's bright jacket. "So?"

She wasn't asking about the book. In the oblique desert way, she was asking about me. Things change. Maybe people too.

I nodded at the dustjacket photograph: a sagging old piñon-pole and barbed-wire fence dangled over a wide dry wash, fencing in blue sky, air, nothing. "Revisionist stuff, the New History."

"How's that?"

"You know. We white people came to the desert and tried to make it fit ideas and values that we'd devised in a different land, a different culture, but all we've done is destroy the desert, and our values, and maybe ourselves."

She gave me her deep-seamed desert squint. "You buy that?"

"The idea isn't really new." I sat at my desk. "There's something to it, but not as much as he wants to make."

The creases around her big fine eyes smoothed. "I heard professors talk. Plenty of notions how things oughta be done, but hardly a doin'-callus in the bunch."

She stared at the book in her hands, but she didn't seem to see it, or the stroking of her doin'-calloused thumbs. "They think I should hire you to look for Heather again."

When I didn't answer, she slowly looked up at me.

Patsy McLeod had never been pretty. Her features were too broad, her bones too heavy. But her eyes were beautiful. I watched them as I tried to think of a way out.

"Who are *they*, Mrs. McLeod?"

She opened the book, showed me the small, fuzzily focused photograph on the back flap: a man, fortyish, bespectacled, bearded, thinning hair curling over his collar, in a tweed jacket with leather patches.

"Him, Professor Draine, an' his wife. I work for them, take care of the house and kids up to Tahoe."

A Stanford professor with a house at Lake Tahoe might have explained the cashmere.

"Mrs. McLeod," I said quietly, "Heather disappeared—"

"Eighteen years ago," she said curtly, "I know. You won't find her. She's dead."

I thought so too.

Her gazed drifted to my daughter's portrait. "But the professor an' Rosetta think you should try."

"Why?"

"To . . . put her back in the grave."

"What brought Heather out of the grave, Mrs. McLeod?"

She put down the book, opened her purse, withdrew a business card, handed it to me. Martha Reedy, Private Investigations, a Berkeley address and phone number. "She come up last night. She's looking for her."

"She thinks Heather's alive?"

"Hopin', mostly, I think. Hard to get much outta her."

She picked up her coffee, sipped, set it down. "Alls I know is what she said, and it don't make much sense. Said Royce is dying, which I knew. But he won't make a will, an' this outfit wants to find Heather before Royce goes, make a deal with her for the place in Beulah Valley, cause Heather'd get it if she—"

She gave me her seamed and lidded squint. "You're a lawyer too, they say. Is what she says right?"

I played lawyer for her. "Pretty much. The will doesn't matter. If he dies intestate, the county will establish and attempt to locate the legal heirs."

Her squint deepened. "In-tes-tate, huh?"

I grinned. "Heather would be the only heir?"

In the silence, dark currents stirred in her blue eyes. "We had a son. Mal. Malcolm. He never come back from Vietnam."

"Yes, ma'am, I remember," I said. "Your ex-husband never remarried?"

"Couldn't find another total idiot, I guess."

I ignored that, nodded at the card. "Did this Martha Reedy say who she represented?"

"En-vi-ra-men-tal-ists." Her voice etched each syllable of the word as if with acid.

I thought about it, still looking for a way out. "What doesn't make sense, Mrs. McLeod? That he refuses to make a will?"

"Be just like him. Contrariest man in Washoe County. They say he's even shooting at folks who come try to help him." Something different drifted into her eyes then, a kind of aching bewilderment.

"He's just lettin' it go to ruin, settin' there waitin' for a bad spring to wash it all out onto the alkali, all we worked so hard to hang onto. . . ."

Her hands clutched the book, her thumbs stroked its glossy surface. "But it ain't Royce. It's the money. A couple hundred thousand dollars, she says, maybe more. It ain't worth that. There's nothing but the canyon now—can't ranch it anymore. You'd have to start all over—been nothing but lease land for years."

"Land is worth what somebody will pay for it, Mrs. McLeod." But the money wasn't the only thing that didn't make sense. "Did this Martha Reedy say exactly why the environmental group wants to find Heather?"

"So they can make a deal with her for the place. They say she—that ain't right?"

I shrugged. "After your ex-husband's death, if the county can't locate the heirs, they'll auction the estate and hold the proceeds in trust. Anyone, including environmental groups, can bid. There's no need for the heirs to be involved in the sale."

"You're saying them wanting to find Heather don't fit?"

I sipped my coffee. "I don't know enough about the situation to say that. Did this Reedy woman say anything else?"

She shook her head. "Alls she said was she wanted to help."

I dropped the card on the desk, changed the subject. "Mrs. McLeod, is it possible that Heather has tried to reach you and couldn't, that she didn't know you were in Tahoe?"

She shook her head. "Till a couple years ago it was all the same phone book. Alls anybody'd have to do is look."

"Has her father seen or heard from her?"

"Wouldn't know. I ain't talked to Royce in twenty years."

I didn't say anything.

She didn't say anything.

Finally I sighed, said something. "Mrs. McLeod, do *you* want me to look for Heather again?"

She looked down at the book, at her smoothing thumbs. "I . . . told the professor an' Rosetta I'd see what you said."

I told her what she wanted to hear. "Heather is dead, Mrs. McLeod. She's been dead a long time."

She nodded, thumbs stroking. "I know."

I told her what she didn't want to hear. "If she isn't dead, there's a reason she hasn't contacted you all this time. Probably you don't want to know what that reason is."

"No, it ain't that." She focused fiercely on my daughter's smile. "She's dead, Ross."

"Yes ma'am. But trying to confirm that will be expensive, and after all this time there's next to no chance we'd learn anything. You'd be wasting your money."

Silently she opened her purse, withdrew a wallet, removed some bills, and spread them on my desk. Ten of them. Hundreds.

"They pay me too much, the professor an' Rosetta. And give me things." She looked down at the expensive cloth cloaking her breasts. "Nothin' to spend money on but the grandbabies."

I was confused. "You have grandchildren?"

She shook her head, almost smiling. "Just pretend. The Draine kids ain't got grandfolks, we unofficially adopted each other. They got somebody to call Nana. I got somebody to . . ."

The word she didn't say was "love."

I looked at the money, thought of another thing that didn't make sense. "In any case, if this Martha Reedy can find Heather, or learn what happened to her, it won't cost you anything."

"A girl detective?" She snorted. "What can she do?"

"The job," I said. "If they're any good at it at all, women are usually better investigators than men."

"May be. If Royce don't shoot her." But she was dubious. "Anyhow, she ain't working for me. No reason for that little Reedy girl to tell me anything."

That didn't really make sense either.

But then, it didn't have to make sense. None of it had to. Patsy McLeod knew it, and I knew it.

I sighed again, frustrated. "I couldn't find Heather eighteen years ago. Why do you think I could find her now?"

"I don't."

"Then why—"

"She's dead." She looked at my daughter's portrait as if it were the only real thing in the room. "But you'll do your best. And when you don't find her, I can put her back in the grave."

I had been subtly trying to dissuade Patsy McLeod from hiring me. I tried less subtly. "I don't involve myself in personal or family matters anymore, Mrs. McLeod. I work only for attorneys or corporations these days."

She looked at me. "This ain't a these days affair, is it?"

As I tried to think of something else to say, Patsy McLeod turned back to the photograph. "Your daughter?"

At my nod, the tears suddenly welled up, spilled, slicked her desert-scarred skin.

"The thing is . . . I dream about her. But in my dreams she ain't the way she was then, a kid, she's the way she would be now if... And she's in trouble. And she's mad at me for not helping her."

Grief dreams. Guilt dreams.

"A lot of parents of missing children have that dream, Mrs. McLeod," I said quietly. "It doesn't mean anything."

She brushed the back of her hand at her shimmering eyes.

"Maybe not," she said, "but I'm gonna keep having it till I know for sure."

CHAPTER TWO

Patsy McLeod wanted to hire me not to find her daughter. And I was going to let her.

Heather McLeod was long dead, but I was going to look for her, even though it wasn't what I did these days. Because it wasn't a these days affair.

I'd go through the motions. Check the file, looking for something I'd missed eighteen years before. I wouldn't find anything. Run Heather McLeod's name through all the record systems I could bribe and cajole and suborn and flatter my way into. I wouldn't find anything. Talk to the contrariest man in Washoe County, now dying. If he didn't shoot me.

"All right, Mrs. McLeod." I started to take out a contract, looked at her, stopped. It wasn't a contractual affair, either. "I'll give you a receipt for—"

She waved a hand. "Don't bother. Fact is, I owe you money. You never billed me from before."

"I didn't do you any good," I said. I didn't say anything else. I didn't want to think about what I *had* done.

She seemed to have forgotten that. "Did the best you could, Ross."

I shrugged, tapped the bills into a stack. "I'll give it three days, Mrs. McLeod. If I haven't come up with a substantial lead by then, I'll refund what's left."

She was silent for a moment. "Three days ain't very long."

"Long enough." I jotted down her address and phone number on the back of Martha Reedy's business card. "Which environmental group is she working for?"

It came like a desert wind, hot, harsh. "One of them liberal scavenger outfits Rosetta keeps giving money to so they can buy out ranchers that the feds and the bankers get together and make go bust. Des-ert Con-ser-van-cy."

"I know it," I told her. What I didn't tell her was that I'd given them money myself.

A nonprofit organization with little overhead and a mostly volunteer staff, Desert Conservancy collected money to purchase ecologically sensitive or threatened land in the Great Basin and the Sonoran Deserts, set up income-producing accounts to pay the taxes, and let the land sit.

"Martha Reedy was going to Beulah Valley this morning?"

"Said so. I gave her directions. Don't mean she found it. She—that what you're gonna do, go see Royce?"

"It's a place to start," I said, rising.

She set the book on the end table, rose, almost smiled. "First time you were out there you were looking for a girl too, remember? One of them pond hippies, called herself . . . ?"

"Gentle," I said.

"Gentle." She shook her head. "Poor little thing, all them awful scars. Wanted to go to San Francisco, wear flowers in her hair. That's where you and your granddad took her, wasn't it?"

I nodded. We had taken her there, even if the San Francisco she wanted to go to no longer existed, if it ever really had.

"What happened to her, Gentle, you know?"

I did. "She owns a bookstore over in Sparks."

Patsy McLeod shook her head again. "Things sure do change."

Little else about Gentle had changed. But before I could say so, another woman appeared in my office door.

Nothing about her was wrong.

She was small, slim, had lovely features, lovely skin, dark brown hair, dark brown eyes, wore pearls at her ears and throat and a pale green silk suit and a paler green silk blouse. Her mouth was tinted bud pink, spread as she smiled.

"I don't mean to interrupt." Her voice fit her smile; both were soft, with a warmth slightly sexual but mostly just human.

Patsy McLeod's cheeks cracked like mud-caked playa under the desert sun as she smiled. "You ain't. We're done."

The woman stepped briskly up to my desk. Her small hand was smooth, her grip firm. The faint lines around her eyes and mouth said she was in her late thirties.

"I'm Rosetta Draine, Mr. Ross. Have you agreed to help?"

I nodded.

She turned, slipped her arm around Patsy McLeod's. "I'm happy for you, dear."

"Nothin' to be happy about yet," Patsy said brusquely, but she smiled, seemed to be happy for herself.

"Is there anything you need, Mr. Ross, any way we can help?"

I shook my head.

"If something should arise, anything—oh!" She hugged the older woman gently. "Patsy, I left a manila envelope on the seat of the car. Would you mind getting it for me?"

The ploy was obvious, but Patsy McLeod didn't seem to notice or, if she did, to care. "Sure," she said.

Rosetta Draine watched her leave. Then she turned back to me. "Poor dear. Can you find Heather, Mr. Ross?"

I cleared my throat. "Heather's dead."

She nodded her approval. I began to understand why she was there. "We think so too. The envelope Patsy's getting contains the report of a private investigation agency we hired several years ago. When Bill and I learned about Heather, we thought we might be able to help. I'm afraid nothing came of it. We didn't tell Patsy about the investigation, we didn't want to raise her hopes in case . . . but maybe it can be of some use to you."

"I'll give it a look," I said.

She settled onto the couch, tucked back her slender legs, brushed the pale green cloth over her knees. She noticed the copy of *Squaring the Circle,* picked it up, smiled.

"You've read Bill's book? He'll be pleased. He's afraid his only readers are other academics."

"With hardly a doin'-callus in the bunch."

She laughed softly. "As you might guess, Patsy and Bill have some intense conversations."

I didn't respond. Something about Rosetta Draine bothered me.

She looked around the office, then at me in frank appraisal. "You're . . . not quite what we expected, Mr. Ross."

I didn't respond to that either. I thought I knew what she had expected—everything I was working hard not to be anymore.

She straightened her slim back, folded her hands as if calling a meeting to order, taking charge, control.

"This morning we went to the address listed in the phone book and found the new St. Mary's parking garage. When we phoned, we got the office of Rondo and Keene."

I nodded, sat down. "When I got evicted, Wally Keene told me about the extra office here, so I leased it. I have a private line, but it rings at the law firm when I'm not in."

"So you are not associated with Rondo and Keene?"

"I contract some simple legal work for them and do most of their investigations, but I'm my own boss, if that's what you're asking."

She smiled. "I like to know whom I'm doing business with."

I smiled. "I'm not working for you, Mrs. Draine."

Her smile flickered, then held. "I'm sorry, I misspoke. Your business is with Patsy, of course. But you understand that we are concerned for her welfare."

"You seem to be," I said. "Hiring detectives on behalf of your employees is a remarkably generous policy."

"Patsy's not really an employee, Mr. Ross. At least we don't think of her that way. She's part of our family."

I didn't say anything.

Her smile might have tightened a notch. "My husband and I are very busy—he's always down at the university or working on his books, and I have a number of family financial matters to oversee. Patsy's become our ground, our rock. We're all very fond of her, and we couldn't be a family without her."

"She's fond of you, too," I said, "even if you keep giving money to them liberal scavenger outfits like Desert Conservancy."

She laughed her soft laugh. "She doesn't hesitate to express her views, does she?"

"No reason why she should."

"Indeed." She was silent for a moment, again frankly appraising me. "You perhaps share those views?"

"I don't share anybody's views. There are good arguments and well-meaning people and hypocrisy and hucksters on both sides."

"Unfortunately." Then she smiled. "We disagree with Patsy, Mr. Ross, but we respect her opinions, and the fact that she came by them honestly."

I was having big trouble with Rosetta Draine. Her beauty was natural, her intelligence obvious, her personality warm, her attitude enlightened. But something about her bothered me.

I was also having trouble connecting her with Patsy McLeod, or at least with the Patsy McLeod I had known. "How did you come to hire Mrs. McLeod?"

"Through an agency here in town." She smiled wryly. "I know she seems a bit odd for a housekeeper. We interviewed women with wonderful credentials, but—Patsy was rough and ungrammatical and inexperienced, but she was also refreshingly real compared to the smarmy competence of the others. She wanted out of casino work, and we liked her, so we took a chance. It was the best decision we ever made."

It sounded reasonable enough. But there was something else that still didn't make sense to me. "Why urge her to see me when another investigator's looking into Heather's disappearance?"

"Patsy trusts you," she said. "If you learn nothing, she'll be convinced that her daughter is dead."

"She is," I said.

She nodded. "We think so too. But we also think that there are two other reasons why you should take the case. You looked for Heather before, interviewed people. When you reinterview them, you'll be able to note any discrepancies in their statements."

"After eighteen years, Mrs. Draine, there'll be half as many people and half a sackful of discrepancies."

She smiled. "But one or two might be meaningful."

It made sense. It also suggested that Rosetta Draine and her husband had thought this all through, very carefully.

"The second reason is that if someone knows something about Heather's disappearance, he or she may do something unusual when Ms. Reedy asks questions. That might give you a lead you wouldn't otherwise be able to get."

That too was reasonable. It was also highly contingent, wholly improbable. She knew it, smiled wryly. "That's our theory, at any rate."

Rosetta Draine had all the answers, could explain everything. But I was still having trouble with her, maybe because she had all the answers, could explain everything.

Or maybe because of my growing awareness of the small, slim body under the pale green blouse and suit, the slender legs like succulent spring shoots, the hint of sexual warmth in her smile, in her voice.

I didn't have time to worry on it. Patsy McLeod returned, handed Rosetta Draine a thick manila envelope. "Here you go."

Mrs. Draine rose from the couch, patted Patsy McLeod's hand, placed the envelope on my desk. "Thank you, dear. This is some material Bill and I put together, hoping it might help Mr. Ross."

I noticed how what she said was both true and not the truth.

Both women looked at me expectantly, but I had nothing to give them.

I stepped out from behind the desk, toward the door. "I'll walk you out."

I led them down the hall, past a bathroom outfitted with lockers for lunchtime joggers, a kitchen converted to a casual conference room, a pantry filled with shelves of paper and forms surrounding a huge copier, a library from which voices droned legalese. In what had once been the foyer of the house, the receptionist sat surrounded by computer equipment, phones, and huge potted plants.

Patsy McLeod squinted at the plastic and veneer and all the electronic accoutrements of high commerce. "Musta been a real nice home once, when folks really lived in it."

Many of the once-grand old stone and brick and wood houses in the neighborhood had been sheetrocked and carpeted into cubicles for lawyers, dentists, and accountants.

"It was," I said. "A brick-for-brick reproduction of a home in Philadelphia. A fifty-year-old Reno banker built it to woo the nineteen-year-old Philadelphia girl of his dreams. Alas, he built it with depositors' money, which was discovered after he blew his brains out with a Colt hogleg, which he did after the girl of his dreams ran off with a florist."

Rosetta Draine smiled in amusement. Patsy McLeod's brow furrowed like a desert dune after a hard rain. "Forgot that about you, Ross, how a body never knows if you're joking or not."

"I only joke about things that are true, Mrs. McLeod."

"I—is that a joke too?"

"Alas."

Rosetta Draine laughed. Patsy McLeod snorted, shook her head, stepped through the door.

The mid-October air was August hot, softened by sprinklers that illegally greened the lawns and parking strips on California Avenue, sweetened by the beds of marigolds that lined the walk. Street traffic was light, soughed against the sounds of the city muted by the huge old elms that dropped a few dying leaves along the sidewalks and on the houses lining the street.

I turned to Rosetta Draine. "Nice confirmation of your husband's thesis, isn't it? Here in the high desert, in the big drought, this enclave of lawns and trees and houses you could plunk down in the middle of Chicago and nobody would notice the difference."

She smiled. "You agree with that thesis?"

"Some of it."

A large dark green Mercedes stood at the curb, absorbing the sunlight, turning glare into glow. Crunching through a thin layer of leaves, Rosetta Draine moved around it to the driver's door. I opened the other door for Patsy McLeod.

Seated, she looked up at me. "S'pose you could do something for me, Ross?"

"Yes ma'am."

"After you see Royce, could you let me know how he's doing?"

"Yes ma'am."

She squinted, smiled almost shyly. "And you ain't a kid anymore. S'pose you could call me Patsy?"

I grinned. "Thank you, Patsy."

Then her eyes went solemn, still. "Things change, Ross, but people don't, not really."

I thought I understood what she was telling me. She was telling me about herself, and I thought that was the truth.

She was also, perhaps, telling me about myself. I hoped that wasn't the truth.

I closed the door.

Over the rich dark gleam of the Mercedes top, Rosetta Draine was smiling again.

"It was nice to meet you, Mrs. Draine," I said.

Her smile deepened. "Not at all what we expected, Mr. Ross."

CHAPTER THREE

Back in my office, I shut the coffeemaker off and the computer down, switched the phone over to the reception desk, picked up the manila envelope, and headed out.

Wally Keene stood in the conference room door, his Dartmouth ring flashing as, with broad theatrical swoops, he stirred the coffee in his Stanford mug. "Can I buy you a cup, Jack?"

"I'm about coffee'd out." I waved the manila envelope. "And I've got work to do."

"If it concerns Rosetta Draine," he said, still stirring, "I might be of some assistance."

"On the other hand," I said, "one more cup wouldn't hurt." The old kitchen had been gutted, outfitted with a veneered mahogany bar, a small new refrigerator, and a microwave oven. A beautiful old maple table dominated the room. Wally sat at it, carefully hitching up the pant legs of his eight-hundred-dollar suit.

"Quid pro quo?"

I poured myself a cup of coffee, wondering at his interest. "Not much I can tell you, Wally."

His ring flashed with his grin. "Tell me what you can. You never know what might be important."

His grin was oversized. All Wally Keene's gestures were large, as if he were always playing to an audience. His gestures succeeded, the record showed, with both clients and juries. They also succeeded, bar talk had it, with women.

"You first," I said. "How do you know Rosetta Draine?"

"I really don't know her so much as know about her. She operates in circles to which I still aspire." He grinned, sipped at his coffee, gave it an exaggerated frown, set the cup aside. "I'm guessing you don't know who she is."

I studied his lean, handsome face. But for the deepened creases around his nose and mouth, it hadn't changed since we'd been classmates, first at Reno High, later at Stanford Law. Neither had his dark, shrewd, ambitious eyes.

"I guess I don't," I said.

"Try a different name," he said. "Say, for instance, a name like Mercer. As in Mercer Foundation."

I'd heard of it. A San Francisco philanthropic organization, the Mercer Foundation used the profits of the American Security Bank to support environmental groups, fund private inner-city rehabilitation projects and social service agencies, provide scholarships for ghetto kids, and subsidize artists of promise.

"Rosetta Draine is connected with the Mercer Foundation?"

"Not connected. Rosetta Draine *is* the Mercer Foundation. At least now."

"Now?"

"For years the foundation wasn't much more than a tax dodge old Claude Mercer set up so he'd have free seats at the opera and the symphony. His kids kept it that way while they stewed themselves in nouveau-riche dissolution. Then fifteen years ago, Rosetta Draine took it over and started actually doing something."

Which meant that the "family finances" she oversaw amounted to a million or so dollars a year. "She'd be family then. What, the granddaughter of—"

"Wife of," Wally said. "Her husband is the great-grandson of old

Claude Mercer, last of the really big-time Nevada conmen."

I smiled at the irony. Professor William Draine, who wrote revisionist history attacking the men who had ravaged the West, was the heir of a man whose mining enterprises had left the Nevada landscape pocked with gaping, ugly holes as empty as the pockets of the people he more or less legally bilked out of a fortune.

"But she runs it?"

"Heads the foundation, chairs the board of American Security. He's mucho ivory tower—books, ideas, all that life of the mind stuff. At least since he met her." He grinned. "Gossip has it that he led the wild youth of the spoiled rich kid—sex, drugs, and rock 'n' roll—until she straightened him out."

"How did she do that?"

"The usual way, I'd guess." His grin became a mock leer. "I know she could straighten me out fast." He began humming the opening bars of "The Impossible Dream."

"I assume that means she's faithful?"

"Devotedly. And smart. She's old Bay Area money, I think I heard, but she picked up a degree in econ from Yale while he was working on his Ph.D., then later an M.B.A. at Cal. She's liberal but no bleeding heart, and as tough as she needs to be."

"Impressive," I said.

He grinned his leer. "The star of every Yuppie's wet dream."

When I didn't respond, Wally leaned back in his chair. "It helps to know who you're doing business with, Jack."

"She thinks so too," I said. "But I'm not doing business with Rosetta Draine. I'm working for one of her employees, on a missing person case. Mrs. Draine was just checking me out."

"The employee would be the Wild Horse Annie in cashmere?"

When I nodded, he began to study his Dartmouth ring. "I thought you weren't going to do that kind of work anymore."

"I'm not. This is just . . . unfinished business."

He cocked an interrogatory eyebrow.

"It was a long time ago," I said. "Patsy McLeod and her four-teen-year-old daughter were living in Sun Valley. Then the daughter disappeared. I'd run into the mother two years before, when I found a runaway out in Beulah Valley living with a bunch of hippies—"

"Hippies?" Wally shook his head, reached for his coffee cup. "Jesus, Jack, how unfinished is this business?"

"The daughter disappeared eighteen years ago." I jumped over his objection. "I know. I won't find her."

He tested his coffee again, again frowned and pushed it aside. "Then why pick it up now?"

"She hired me to find her daughter. I didn't."

"Eighteen years ago." He shook his head. "I don't get it. This girl can't be the only missing person you never found."

"I didn't just not find her." I too pushed my coffee aside. "The girl was gone, Wally, and her mother was suffering everything the parent of a missing child can suffer. Instead of helping her, I made it worse."

Wally watched me. "What happened?"

I slumped in the chair, explained to him, to myself, why the fact that none of it made sense didn't matter in this case.

"We had nothing. Neither the sheriff nor I could come up with a lead. Finally I found a postman who'd seen a tall bearded cowboy driving a beat-up old Chevy pickup away from their trailer the morning the girl disappeared. Then I found a kid who might have seen the girl in a pickup that day."

Wally nodded. "So you checked it out."

"We couldn't find a single connection between the girl and anybody who fit the description. Then it turns out that the postman isn't sure it was a Chevy or if it was coming from their trailer. And the kid never was sure he'd seen the girl in a pickup."

I really didn't want to go on.

"And?"

"I—you need to understand about the mother. She grows up in the desert, marries at seventeen, spends the next twenty-odd years working like a dog to hang onto a piece of land. Then everything falls apart. Son goes to Nam and doesn't come back. Husband goes to prison for manslaughter. Finally she sees she can't run the ranch alone, goes to see her husband in prison and he says he's divorcing her, and lays a nasty load on her in the bargain."

"So," Wally said, "you feel sorry for her."

"It's not that," I said. "It's—look, she's forty, she's lost her life and her family and her sense of herself. She and the daughter end up in Sun Valley, she's carrying change downtown, the daughter's gone wild. She feels guilty, she's lonely. She's not pretty or young, but she's got a big, strong body and some half-baked ideas about love she picked up from the hippies. And she doesn't have a clue. You can imagine what happened."

It didn't take much imagination, if you knew the kind of men who hunted in downtown Reno.

Wally did. "The coyotes cut a cripple out of the herd. But what's that got to do with her missing daughter and a cowboy?"

I shifted uncomfortably in the chair. "We can't connect him to the girl. He has to be one of the mother's boyfriends, right?"

"Apparently not," Wally said. "But where's the problem?"

I took a deep breath. "I was going to connect the cowboy and her pathetic love life if I had to tear her to pieces. I did. And there was no connection."

Wally studied his ring. "If I understand what you're saying, Jack, you simply explained the facts of life to her."

"And took away the only hope for a life she had left. For nothing. Because I couldn't admit I had nothing."

Wally frowned. "Some people would say you did her a favor."

"They didn't see her face." I was seeing it then, a desert face uglied by anguish, beautiful blue eyes muddied by shame.

"She seems, however, to have survived quite nicely."

I didn't say anything.

"How did she end up arm in arm with Rosetta Draine?"

I told him what Mrs. Draine had told me. He nodded, brushed at his jacket sleeve. He was, I could see, no longer interested in Patsy McLeod or her daughter. The story I'd told him had told him nothing useful about Rosetta Draine.

He had something else on his mind now. "Maybe when you finish this you'll be ready to talk seriously about my offer?"

I didn't want to talk about his offer.

"You've got the background and brains, Jack. The other partners agree. We could make a lot of money together."

I'd always known how ambitious Wally was. When we were boys, Rondo and Keene had been a joke—Rum and Coke, a pair of alcoholic ambulance chasers. Wally had suffered it, vowing that the jokes would stop, that someday he would transform Rondo and Keene into the most respected and profitable law firm in the city. It wasn't that yet, but it was getting there.

But I hadn't understood how shrewd Wally was until I moved into my new office and, because he was understaffed and because I had time, I'd helped prepare a few criminal cases for trial. I discovered that I was good at it. I discovered that I liked it.

Neither discovery, it turned out, surprised Wally. He made his offer. I would investigate and prepare all criminal cases, assist in the courtroom if I chose, try cases if I wanted to.

I was as surprised by the offer as I was by my response. I told him I'd think about it. I was still thinking about it.

Now I tried to grin him off. "I work for attorneys, Wally. I already make more money than I know what to do with."

He didn't grin. "That's because you don't *do* anything except work, and putter around that dump of yours."

I ignored that. "You said you wouldn't press. Don't."

He shrugged elaborately. Then he grinned. "All right, Jack. But do me a favor, will you? Make Wild Horse Annie happy. Even more important, make Rosetta Draine happy, so happy that she'll toss some Mercer Foundation business to the firm of Rondo and Keene, with which you will soon be associated."

I rose from the chair. "Look, Wally . . ."

He stood up, carefully shooting his cuffs. "There's a lot of work there, Jack—honest, easy, lucrative work. Somebody's got to do it. If you want to use that fancy legal education your grandfather sweated blood to help you get, it could be . . . us."

He grinned, patted the envelope in my hand, and walked out.

CHAPTER FOUR

I went down the hall and out the back into the swelling and unseasonable heat. To the west, the Sierra Nevada rose through a heavy blue haze, the pine dark mountains asplatter with groves of turning aspens, like huge marigolds. Below the treeline, new homes scabbed slashes on the foothills. Below the houses, the city spewed pollutants, sucked water, flashed neon, chased money.

In the parking lot, my boxy aging Wagoneer stood amid the sleek new German and English and Japanese beauties like a Clydesdale in a chorus line. I climbed in and drove home.

Home was a small three-bedroom in a forty-year-old housing tract across from Rancho San Rafael Park. It was the first house I'd ever owned, the first home I'd ever had that didn't include my office.

A year earlier, it had been a dump. I'd given the shingle siding a good coat of red paint, the trim a coat of white. I'd put on a new roof. Then I'd put in a patio and Xeriscaped the rest of the lot with

22

redwood chips and river rock and native shrubs and wildflowers with a drip system to water them.

Now, from the street, the house looked like something a normal human being might live in.

Pulling under the old mulberry tree shading the driveway, I parked and went inside. Chipped paint, crumbling sheetrock, ragged and stained green carpet. I'd cleaned it all, but the only really habitable space was a back bedroom and bath I'd patched and painted for my daughter to use on her overnight visits.

My grandparents' heavy old furniture, many of my books and records, and things I'd hauled in from the desert over the years clogged the living room. In the bedroom I was using, a converted single-car garage off the kitchen bathroom, I changed into boots, jeans, a blue shirt, and my old Harris tweed, then went into another bedroom and sat at my grandfather's old oak desk.

In the bottom drawer, under the teakwood box that held my grandfather's .38 Smith & Wesson, lay a thin stack of folders.

Unfinished business. Cases that, over the years, I hadn't been able to finish or to let go. People I hadn't found. Kids, mostly. I carried them with me the way I carried my daughter's photograph in my wallet, out of sight but not out of mind.

I pulled out the McLeod file, then opened the envelope that Rosetta Draine had given me. The twelve-year-old report had been prepared by a large San Francisco agency, had cost the Draines about what I had earned that year. Professionally detailed and documented, it began with a photocopy of the Washoe County Sheriff's Office report paper-clipped to a photograph.

The girl in the school portrait half hid behind hair the color of a weathered haystack. Her hazel eyes were dreamy, her mouth sullen, her features somehow her mother's and somehow not.

Missing. Heather Alice McLeod, 428 Quail Run, Sun Valley. Fourteen, female, Caucasian, five-eight, one-thirty, brown and hazel, no IMOS, no SSN, no DMV record, no juvenile record.

NOK mother Patsy McLeod, same address, forty-one, divorced, club worker; father Royce McLeod, forty-nine, state penitentiary, manslaughter, three to five. No living siblings.

Average student, some extracurricular music and drama.

Indication sexual activity, indication substance abuse, indication social maladjustment.

Neighbors, friends, teachers knew nothing.

Possible runaway. Possible abduction.

No further action.

Fourteen-year-old Heather McLeod had no social security number, and extensive and expensive record checks by name were negative, so the head of the agency had sent teams of operatives back to Sun Valley.

I started to read, then to skim the report.

What the agents found behind the low barren hills north of Reno was depressing, the Romance of the West trapped and gnawing on its own entrails—weathered trailers and junk-strewn lots, shaggy horses and shiny Harleys, Stetsons and tattoos, ADC and unemployment compensation, drugs and booze, grand schemes and petty cons, scarred angry men and bruised angry women and dead-eyed children.

What they learned about the missing Heather McLeod was equally depressing—she was just one more Sun Valley teenager who would escape reality through sex and chemicals and fantasy and thus ensure the perpetuation of that reality and her future in it.

I found myself thinking about the Heather McLeod I had met, briefly, twenty years before, when I traced the girl who called herself Gentle to the hippie camp in Beulah Valley.

At twelve, Heather McLeod had been awkward and gangly as she began to grow into her mother's big body, but she was friendly, smiling, eager for school to start so that she could get back into her singing and dancing classes.

The Heather McLeod who disappeared from Sun Valley was a different girl. I'd never understood what had happened to change her.

The report didn't say. All it said was that, finally, no one knew what had happened to Heather McLeod. There was no mention of a tall thin bearded cowboy in a Chevy pickup.

The agency had determined that no further investigation was warranted. They would keep the file open, reexamine it quarterly, cross-index it with other cases. Something might turn up.

I put down the report, stared out the window. Dark treetops, tar rooftops, neon flickering palely in the sun, the city oozed like an oily, iridescent sludge toward the brown ranges that bunched up against the empty sky and hid the desert beyond.

I hadn't been to the desert in a long time.

I stuck the photograph of Heather in my shirt pocket and put both reports back in the drawer under my grandfather's .38.

Then I hauled a couple of jugs of water out to the Wagoneer, checked my supplies and tools, climbed in, and went looking for it.

CHAPTER FIVE

Twenty-five miles and most of an hour from Reno, I was still looking for the desert.

Highway 395 had tugged the city with it as it four-laned up out of the Truckee Meadows to a rolling sage plain under Peavine Mountain and a new shopping center and new black roads arcing off to valleys stuffed with new housing tracts and warehouses and apartment complexes, one with a huge sign that urged me to RENT A LIFESTYLE.

Looking for the desert instead of wanting to make time, I got off the highway at Red Rock Road, eased around the dust patch the drought had made of Silver Lake. After the congestion of Silver Knolls, the pavement turned to dirt and the road twisted up the mottled brown hump of Fred's Mountain, past new houses sitting in squares scraped clear of sage and juniper, past lots sporting realty signs.

More houses dotted the crest of the mountain. Then the road dipped into a damp-bottomed gulch, passed a pair of washed-out ponds and rotting stock pens and loading chutes, and ended at an old ranch house under old cottonwoods at the head of Red Rock Valley.

But I still hadn't found the desert.

The ranch house headquartered a realty company, the barn sheltered huge orange earth-moving monsters. The sage land that had once been transformed into pastures and alfalfa fields had been retransformed into square forty-acre "ranchettes" where only buildings grew and nothing grazed.

A dozen dirt roads headed off to the homes of those who would get away from it all by bringing it all with them—sagebrush and steel siding, desert vistas and satellite dishes. It took me half an hour to determine that the old McLeod road was now Buckaroo Lane.

At the last house, the road narrowed to a pair of dusty ruts, the ruts dropped into a narrow gully and climbed a brushy hill and brought me to the desert.

Not only desert, but, more and more, deserted. Everywhere the empty land bore the scars of inappropriate human aspiration, failed human enterprise.

Old roads wandered off toward the slump of abandoned ranch buildings, toward the squares of dust that cattle hooves had cut and cattle waste had poisoned the life out of, toward the fences demarcating rectangles of dirt and sagebrush and defeated ambitions, toward the shadows of holes that hadn't panned out and the tailing piles of mines that had played out.

Distant mountain ranges darkened as they rose into the haze like shadows of one another. The sky was as empty as the land.

I hadn't realized how depressed the agency's report had left me until in the desert, finally, finally alone, I began to feel better.

I rolled down my window, smelled the sage, listened to the silence deepened by the dull growl of the Wagoneer's engine. And gradually grew aware that I wasn't alone.

In breezeless gullies, dust hung in the stillness. In sandy spots I saw the recent tight-treaded tracks of a small car and the wider-patterned tread of a bigger, heavier car.

Ten miles from Red Rock, at the base of a low rocky hill, I realized that the wider, heavier tracks had doubled.

The road angled up the hill, and Zion Mountain appeared—gray rock faces, beardlike talus slopes, a thick collar of juniper and mountain mahogany above a sharp descent of buckled earth the color of buckskin. A thin line like a ragged knife cut sliced down a shoulder of the mountain, deepened, widened into wound, disappeared behind a long, low, brush-tufted dune.

Several ranges drained onto the broad alkali flat that was most of Beulah Valley. A lacelike ring of greasewood edged the alkali, dark dots in a precise water-conscious pattern.

As I trailed my dust cloud toward the flat, a sudden sun flash told me that one of the dots on the alkali wasn't greasewood. It was a car. As I came closer, I made out a black Geo with California plates.

A woman stepped out from behind it. Bone white dust veiled her short brownish blond hair, streaked her face like macabre makeup, clung to her yellow blouse and jeans and running shoes.

Martha Reedy, I presumed. She looked like a bride of nightmares.

I shut off the engine, climbed out, quickly read the story written in the dust. The big car had come at the Geo head-on and fast, forced it onto the shoulder, then off into the greasewood and alkali. Deliberately.

Leaning against the weight of a canvas purse slung from her shoulder, the woman drifted through the greasewood toward me.

When she stepped onto the road, I saw that she wasn't hurt, but her pale brown eyes were bright and blank, and under the white dust her skin was blanched. Sweat had soaked through her blouse under her arms and over her ribs.

"Could—could you give me a ride to the nearest phone?" The words scraped harshly in her throat.

"Sure," I said. "But first let me give you some water."

Opening the back of the Wagoneer, I took out a plastic gallon milk jug and a paper cup. "Take it slow."

She seemed puzzled, but she took the cup, sipped. "I'm ... all right."

"You're dehydrated."

"It's fall. It's not that hot. . . ."

I refilled the cup. "The desert doesn't pay much attention to the calendar. It's over ninety out here. And you worked up a lather. You've got to be a couple quarts below the add mark."

After she drank again, I handed her the jug. "Why don't you sit inside and sip this while I take a look at your car?"

"I appreciate . . . but I need a tow truck."

"Maybe, maybe not."

She didn't seem to understand what I'd said.

I put my hand gently on her elbow.

She flinched, jerked her arm back, dropped her hand onto her purse. It was a canvas and Velcro contraption I'd seen advertised in trade magazines as the latest in feminine pistol-packing fashion.

I moved around her to the passenger-side door of the Wagoneer, opened it.

She looked at the open door, started to speak, then stopped, as if she'd forgotten what she wanted to say.

I stepped back from the door, smiled, waited.

Then, as if she'd forgotten why she was hesitating, she tucked the canvas purse under her arm and slid past me onto the seat.

I shut the door behind her and went out onto the alkali.

I could see where the Geo had spun, then backed into a sandy mound at the base of a big greasewood ten yards from the road. Before it hit, a back tire had snapped a smaller shrub into sharp stakes that pierced a front tire. Trying to get out, she'd sunk the other front tire in up to the axle.

She'd tried to dig herself out, first with a large 7-Eleven coffee cup, then with a clipboard, then with her hands. She'd made a good-sized hole, must have been working at it for three or four hours.

I went back to the Wagoneer, opened the door. "We can get you out."

Her eyes looked better, but they still weren't really connected to her brain. "I . . . think I need a tow truck."

"It'll have to come from Reno or Doyle," I said. "That'll cost you a couple hundred dollars, and you won't be out till after dark."

"It's . . . really stuck."

I smiled. "I got stuck out in the Black Rock one time. It took me four hours to get out. When I mentioned it to the kid pumping gas in Gerlach, he told me that four hours wasn't really stuck. Four *days,* now, that's stuck."

"Four . . . ?" She wasn't ready for my jokes.

"Sip some water," I said, and shut the door.

From the back I took a trenching tool and a length of rope, carried it over to the Geo, took off my jacket and draped it over the branches of a large greasewood, and went to work.

CHAPTER SIX

Forty-five minutes later, I was digging under the side panel when Martha Reedy's shadow fell over me and I looked up.

She'd used some of the water to wash the dust and sweat from her face, had combed the dust from her hair. Her eyes looked human.

She held out the water jug. "You can probably use some of this yourself."

"Thanks." I drank from the jug, handed it back.

"What can I do?"

"It's about done," I said. "And we've only got one shovel."

"I can finish it," she said evenly.

"Not much point. You'd just get sweaty and filthy again. I'm already filthy." I shoved the tool into the alkali. After a moment her shadow disappeared.

I worked for another fifteen minutes, then got to my feet, saw her sitting in the shade of the big greasewood and my jacket.

She rose and came over. She didn't shuffle, didn't lean against

31

the dark weight in her canvas purse. She moved with the bounce of the natural athlete. "Now what?"

"Now we put on the spare. Then we tie onto the Jeep and tug it out. You'll have to steer. How are you feeling?"

"Better," she said. "Thank you for your help."

I grinned. "Code of the West."

She held out her hand. "My name's Martha Reedy."

"Jack Ross," I said, taking it.

The little Reedy girl, as Patsy McLeod had called her, was neither little nor a girl. In her mid-thirties, medium height, at once slim and sturdy—not plain, not pretty, with her pale brown eyes and brownish blond hair one of those women you see everywhere but never really see unless you really look.

She saw me really looking, withdrew her hand. "Let's do it, Mr. Ross."

Five minutes later the Geo sat on the road, grayed by the alkali dust but running smoothly. I checked the undercarriage, put the trenching tool and water jug and rope away, brushed off my clothes. Then I went out onto the alkali and picked up the clipboard and the scraps of the paper cup.

As I put on my jacket, I noticed the tight, heart-shaped depression that Martha Reedy's sitting had left in the sand.

She leaned on the fender of the Geo. "I really do appreciate this, Mr. Ross."

"You're not out of here yet," I said. "Those temporary spares are flimsy. Hard to tell how long it'll hold up."

She nodded calmly. "I'll have to chance it."

"Why don't you leave it here? We can take my rig up to talk to Royce McLeod. Then I'll follow you back to town."

Slowly she straightened up from the fender, her hand again coming to rest on the top of her purse. Her calm became a blank. "You . . . seem to have the advantage over me."

I took out my wallet and handed her one of my cards. "Patsy McLeod wants me to look for her daughter too."

She glanced at the card. "Why?"

I told her the truth. "She thinks investigation is men's work. And she's not sure you have her interests in mind."

"What interests?" Her voice too was blank, empty.

"Her only interest is her daughter."

"Are you also her attorney?"

"I don't practice law," I said. "It's on the card mostly to impress people who don't know any better."

It clearly didn't impress Martha Reedy. "Yesterday Mrs. McLeod told me that she thought Heather was dead."

I nodded. "I'd guess you know the syndrome. Her daughter has been missing for eighteen years, so she has to believe that. But she wants to know for sure."

Martha Reedy looked at me blankly. I understood why Patsy McLeod hadn't been able to get much out of her.

Then without speaking she climbed into the Geo and backed it onto the shoulder. I half expected her to turn around and drive off, but she parked, climbed out, stepped over to the Wagoneer and, still without a word, got in.

We drove toward the ranch in silence. Martha Reedy sat very still, looking at the desert. I couldn't tell if her silence came from a natural reticence or a feminine wariness or a professional caution or all three, but I didn't disturb it.

As I drove, I studied the road, and the double pattern of wide-treaded tire tracks in the dust. A hundred yards from the brushy dune that hid the ranch, the tracks turned onto a small rocky flat. I stopped, set the brake. "I'll be back in a minute."

In the brightness I could see the disturbed rocks where the car had turned around, the tiny fluid spatter where it had waited. A Coors can glinted in the sun; a crumpled paper sack clung to a golden clump of rabbitbrush.

I picked up the can and stuffed it in the sack, took it to the Wagoneer, tossed it in back. "This is where he waited for you. Far enough out so that you'd play hell getting back. If you got back."

"Why?"

"I'd guess maybe you'd know that better than I would, Ms. Reedy. And who."

What I didn't tell her was that, if I'd read the tracks right, whoever it was was still out there, probably close by.

She looked out at the desert, spoke without expression. "It was a big white car, new, American—a Lincoln, or a Chrysler. The windshield was glared. All I could see was that he was big. Like you."

I saw that she was serious. "Until two hours ago, I was in my office in town. Several people can confirm that, Ms. Reedy."

She didn't say anything.

"A hired hand, most likely," I said. "Who hired him?"

She gave me her blank look.

"Who knew you were coming out here?"

"The only person I told was Mrs. McLeod. Your client."

I didn't know what that signified, but it wasn't what she thought. "No other possibilities?"

She didn't answer.

I wasn't sure she really understood. "Bad things can happen to someone on foot out here, Ms. Reedy."

She looked out at the desert. "I know."

I wasn't going to get any more out of her. After a moment, I shrugged, released the brake.

"Well, let's go see if Royce McLeod will try to kill you too."

The road wandered toward the dune, slid along it and then turned into a gully carved by a creek that, until the McLeods had put in a series of ponds up the canyon, every few springs sent a rage of water roaring out onto the alkali. Now, in fall and drought, the creek was a series of shallow stagnant pools in a fluff of dead grass and weeds and dying sage.

On the other side of the dune sat the McLeod ranch.

Gone to ruin.

Alfalfa fields and pasture once wrested from the desert were desert once more, cut and channeled by runoff, rough with sage and bitterbrush. Up the long alluvial slope, near the mouth of the canyon, a small pond had washed out; the barn had collapsed, outbuildings sagged and leaned, corrals and pens were down. Like those I'd seen on the road out, the ranch house looked abandoned.

Just beyond the gully, a narrow pair of sandy, undisturbed tracks split off around a bluff to, I knew, an old mine. I took the fork to the ranch, stopped at the gate.

The fence on either side was long down, but the cast-iron pipe was chained and padlocked, festooned with dusty black and red NO

TRESPASSING signs surrounding a plywood square bearing the hand-painted black warning: KEEP THE FUCK OUT.

We got out. Martha Reedy studied the downed fence, the chained gate, the padlock. She nodded at the sign. "Symbolic?"

"Looks like it, doesn't it?"

"You could have driven around it."

"I know," I said.

We stepped around the gate and started up the road toward the ranch house. After a hundred yards of dust, she spoke again. "He's been shooting at people?"

"According to his ex-wife," I said.

Something had transformed her blankness back to quiet calm. "She said he was in prison for murder?"

"Manslaughter. Killed a drunk California deer hunter who'd busted down one of his fences and shot a cow."

She stopped. "Manslaughter? For killing a man over a cow?"

"And busting down a fence, don't forget that," I said. "But I know what you mean. Plumb bad luck. A few years earlier, before all the citified bleeding-heart liberals moved in and took over Nevada, he wouldn't of even been charged. Justifiable homicide. Especially seein' as how the victim was a Californicator."

I thought she was going to smile then, but she fought it off. "Code of the West?"

"Subsection three, paragraph eight."

She was struggling against a smile when a rifle report cracked the silence.

I wheeled, stared up at the house. Nothing moved. All I could see was a small shape that might have been a man sitting on the porch.

"This complicates matters," Martha Reedy said quietly. Her hand again rested on the top of her canvas bag.

I hadn't heard the whine of a bullet, hadn't seen dust fly. "I don't think he's trying to hit us."

"What if he does?"

"We duck," I said. "Or bleed."

Martha Reedy looked at me as if she were really seeing me. "You're just going to walk on up there?"

"Be pretty hard to talk to him from here."

A smile threatened her mouth. "What if he shoots when we get there?"

"You'll have to protect me with that gun in your purse."

Then her smile slowly spread, and her face opened like a flower. "You're not quite . . . *normal,* are you, Mr. Ross."

Her stress on the word "normal" wasn't, her smile said, accusatory. It turned the word into a shibboleth, a tribal recognition and greeting.

"I'd guess about as normal as you are, Ms. Reedy."

Still smiling, she turned toward the ranch house. "I don't really have much to worry about, do I? As big a target as you make, he'll shoot you first. I'll still have time to duck."

It was my turn to fight off a smile. I bowed, extended my arm in a chivalric swoop. "After you."

Her smile became a grin. Then she turned and started toward the house.

I caught her in a stride, and side by side we followed the ruined road up the slope toward the ruined house.

The rifle didn't fire again.

Beyond the barn, the canyon twisted up the mountain, narrowing through rock, widening in small grassy bowls, branching into brushy drainages. Rising, it changed in both texture and color, the dusty photographic green of willow and sage and cottonwood brightening into impressionist yellows and oranges of aspen that disappeared into the chiaroscuro of juniper and distance.

Martha Reedy stopped, looked at it. "It's beautiful, isn't it? Just sitting here in the middle of all this ugly nothing."

"It's pretty, all right," I said.

"It would be even prettier without all the junk."

She saw junk. But everywhere I looked I saw work, history. Rocks cleared from and bordering gardens and pasture, old rock-and-wire corner markers, barbed wire strung on peeled juniper poles and steel posts, dry irrigation ditches, rusted pipe and crushed culverts, worked-out tools and worn-out vehicles, the scattered bones of dead hopes.

We approached the house, such as it was—paint clinging in strips and patches to the rotting wood, ragged old curtains hanging limply in mostly paneless windows. The presence of the old man on the warped porch made the house seem more abandoned.

Never a big man, now Royce McLeod was dying-small and all bones, slumped inside a Marine staff sergeant's beribboned tunic like a child playing pretend in his father's clothes. A 30.06 lay at his feet. I wasn't sure he could even pick it up again, or lift the gallon of gin in his lap.

Martha Reedy asked quietly, "How do you want to play it?"

"I prefer it straight."

She gave me a small, odd smile. "I wouldn't be a bit surprised."

We stopped at the broken steps. Martha Reedy's face slipped into a folksy grin, her voice into a folksy drawl. "Afternoon."

His voice was a raspy whisper, his words like dead leaves stirring in the wind. "You see the sign?"

Before she could reply, his face suddenly set, his eyes brightened. Sweat beaded on his pale forehead as he hunched himself over his belly and grunted. He was in pain, big pain.

I found myself examining the double row of ribbons on his tunic. Most I didn't recognize—campaign decorations from a war I hadn't fought—but some I did: two purple hearts, a bronze star with cluster, a silver star. The ribbons should have made no difference—they might not even have been his. All the same, I looked at him with different eyes.

When the pain passed, he lifted the bottle, tilted it toward his mouth, splashed gin down his throat and chin and neck. Then he whispered, "Trespassers. Any reason I shouldn't shoot you?"

Martha Reedy grinned. "None that I can think of."

That stopped him. His gin-laced brain couldn't tell him what to make of her. Then he didn't care.

"Say your piece and git the fuck outta here."

She flinched, but she said her piece. "My name's Reedy. This is Mr. Ross. We've been hired to look for your daughter."

"Patsy put you on me, didn't she? Fuckin' whore. Fuckin' hippie kids, fuckin' half 'a Reno."

He lifted the bottle to his mouth, tilted it, let it fall back into his lap. "Not even any good at it. Goddamned useless bitch, killed my sons before they were born."

Martha Reedy took a half step back, her face expressionless. "All we want to know is if you've seen Heather recently."

"Look in the whorehouses. Street corners. Gutters. What her mother fit her for."

"When was the last time you saw your daughter?" I asked.

His eyes flared again with emotion. "When I went to the joint. Up to my ass in niggers after me with cocks and knives, she's fucking hippies like her mother, can't come see me."

Under the force of the whispered ugly words, Martha Reedy backed into the yard. She'd had enough.

I kept trying. "Is Heather alive, Mr. McLeod?"

He opened his mouth, but then the pain bent him over again. He gasped, poured gin in and around his mouth. "Who gives a fuck? You ain't fooling me. I . . ."

He waited out the pain, didn't drink this time. "This ain't about Heather. It's about this fucking bone orchard. Patsy wants it, wants to fuck hippies on my grave."

"Somebody will get it, whether you make a will or not."

"An' they'll die here too, like everybody else."

"May be," I said. Stepping forward, I reached out and grabbed the rifle and pulled it across the porch toward me.

Rage exploded in his eyes. "Bastard! You a thief too?"

"Just want to be sure I don't die out here."

"Leave it be," he said. "I need it."

"Why?"

But as soon as I asked the question, I knew the answer. What fueled his sudden rage was fear, fear that he wouldn't have the rifle when the gin stopped working.

I nodded. "Semper Fi, Mac."

It too was a shibboleth. He recognized it. "Marine?"

As I nodded, slowly the rage disappeared. He looked human. For the first time he looked at me as if I were human too. For a moment I thought he was going to ask me to use the rifle.

"She . . . tell her I never meant—"

The pain got him again, bent him over. When he straightened up, he wasn't human anymore. He'd forgotten what he'd wanted me to tell her he'd never meant.

"I'll leave the rifle in the yard," I said, and I turned and walked away, regretting my promise to tell Patsy McLeod how her ex-husband was doing.

CHAPTER SEVEN

Martha Reedy and I were halfway back to the Wagoneer before she shuddered, spoke. "What an evil old man."

"He's drunk. And he's in pain and dying and half nuts."

She looked at me, expressionless. "And that excuses him?"

"Explains him, partly."

She stopped, the skin pale around her mouth. "You think that explaining evil men explains away the evil?"

I stopped too. I could understand her anger; what I couldn't understand was why it was directed at me. "I didn't say that."

"But that's what you meant, isn't it?"

I shook my head. "No. I—you seem to have me confused with somebody else you've had this discussion with, Ms. Reedy."

"I . . . thought you sympathized with him."

I hesitated. "I guess I do, some."

Abruptly she started down the road again, then asked in a flat, toneless voice, "What was all that about hippies?"

"You run into it out here," I said. "The hippies showed up about the time things started going bad, the country started changing, people started losing their ranches. Some of them made a connection."

"There haven't been any hippies around for years."

"Twenty years ago, while he was in prison, some of them set up at an old mine over the ridge there. Mrs. McLeod got friendly with them. He heard about it, and it pushed him over the edge. He started on that stuff about her sleeping with the hippies."

"Was she?"

When I didn't answer, she looked at me, saw something in my face that made her look away.

"That wasn't all he started on. He told her she was ugly and stupid, that he had married her because she looked like a breeder who'd give him enough kids to help him build up the ranch."

She shuddered again. "Like something out of Faulkner. I—do you really think he's crazy?"

"I think everybody's crazy, Ms. Reedy."

She looked at me, then away, around at what she'd called the ugly nothing. "What were hippies doing out here, anyway?"

I shrugged. "What they were trying to do everywhere. Live a new way—or more precisely, live an old way but with what they thought were new ideas about love and chemicals."

She stopped, anger again mottling her skin.

"I'm grateful for your water, Mr. Ross, and your help. But that doesn't give you the right to patronize me."

"I . . . huh?"

"I grew up in Berkeley. I know all about love and chemicals. Precisely. Almost certainly more precisely than you do."

We stood about where we had been standing when Royce McLeod fired his rifle, where we'd recognized one another. If that had happened. I wondered if I'd imagined it.

"I didn't mean to condescend," I said. "I thought I was answering a question."

"I'll repeat it, then," she said flatly. "Why here?"

I'd never thought about it. "I . . . don't know."

"Thank you." She set off down the road, dust puffing under her heels. I watched her for a while, confused.

At the Wagoneer, she leaned against the fender. "You seem to have a talent for pushing my buttons, Mr. Ross."

It was an excellent time for me to keep my mouth shut.

"I saw it when I was a kid," she said. "Peace, love, flower power. When the scene got ugly, a lot of them left the city and started communes up in the mountains or out in the desert."

I'd seen it too, seen Woodstock turn to Altamont, flowers to needles, love to violence, the sixties' dream to the seventies' nightmare. But I didn't say so.

"Most of them straggled back, eventually," she said. "But not all of them. My sister died in childbirth in a snowy ditch in Oregon. Her 'old man,' as she called him, was so stoned he drove the car off the road and couldn't get it out of the snow. A dozen hippie-hating locals drove right past her while she bled to death. People like that evil old man up there killed her."

"I'm sorry."

She turned, looked back at the ruined ranch, the beautiful canyon, the brown mountain. "At least one good thing may come of all this. Once that old man is gone and Desert Conservancy gets the ranch, the land will be able to heal itself."

I didn't say anything.

"Can you imagine how it must have looked, how beautiful it must have been once, before men began to destroy it?"

All I had to do was nod. Not even that. All I had to do was keep my mouth shut.

"About as beautiful as Berkeley must have been once. Maybe Desert Conservancy can buy it, too."

She looked at me. Then her shoulders shifted in a subtle but certain gesture of dismissal.

We drove back to her car in silence. To break it, I turned on the radio, found Willie Nelson citing the subsection of the Code of the West that says you can't hang a man for killing a woman who's trying to steal his horse.

I looked at Martha Reedy, shut it off.

At her Geo, she opened the door. "You don't have to follow me back."

"We're going the same direction," I said.

"If you want to follow me, I can't—" She was quick. "But you aren't talking just about the drive into town, are you?"

I leaned back in the seat and gave it a try. It was probably going to be the only chance I had.

"I'm confused, Ms. Reedy. You drive all the way out here to ask Royce McLeod one question. That confuses me. Somebody tries to keep you from driving back out. That confuses me. You work for Desert Conservancy, which buys up land, and Royce McLeod says the fuss about his daughter is really about his land, which isn't worth enough to fuss over. That confuses me. And it takes two to fuss, but I don't see anybody else in this. I guess I'd just like to understand what's going on."

She gave it back to me, mimicking my tones and rhythms.

"I'm suspicious, Mr. Ross. You say you work for Mrs. McLeod as an investigator but not as a lawyer. That's suspicious. I get run off the road and then you happen along and happen to be working on the same case I am. That's suspicious. And the ranch may not be worth enough to fuss over, but Royce McLeod says that his ex-wife wants it. I guess that while we may be going in the same direction, it's not for the same reason."

I could see her point. "I'll be happy to share what I've got, Ms. Reedy. What would you like to know?"

"I'd like to know why I should trust you. And why you think that what you know would be of any interest to me."

I smiled, and quit. "Well, I'm a trained investigator, Ms. Reedy. Maybe I can find out what's going on. In any case, I'll follow you back to the highway."

"Code of the West?"

She was still mocking me, I knew. Maybe I deserved it.

"That, and the fact that it's the only way out."

She started to get out, then stopped. "If you want to know what's going on, ask Nolan Turner."

"The developer? What's he got to do with it?"

"You're a trained investigator. Maybe you can find out."

She got out. Before she could shut the door, I had a sudden impulse. "Did you come out over the mountain? If you turn right when you get to Red Rock Road, it'll get you back a lot faster."

"I can find my way," she said, and shut the door, climbed into the Geo, started it, turned it around, and headed back.

While I waited until she got to the top of the rocky hill and some of her dust had dissipated, I tried to think—about the name she had given me, about the way she had dismissed the significance of anything I might know. About the one question she had asked, the one mistake she might have made.

I also tried to think about the tire tracks, and the big white car that had made them and might still be close by, and what I might do about it.

But I couldn't really think about any of these things very clearly. Every time I tried, I found myself thinking instead of the heart-shaped depression that Martha Reedy's sitting had left in the sand.

CHAPTER EIGHT

I followed her out of the desert. Between the dust the Geo raised and the tracks I'd made and she was making, I couldn't tell whether the big car was ahead of us or behind us. I guessed behind.

At Red Rock Estates, she ignored my suggestion, as I'd thought she might, and turned south toward Fred's Mountain. I turned north. A few minutes later I was dipping into a pretty canyon and California, and a few minutes after that I was pulling onto 395.

If the man in the big white car was behind us, he couldn't follow us both. If he saw me take the shortcut, fine. If he followed me, fine. But I didn't think he would. I thought he'd follow Martha Reedy, and that was more than fine. There were too many people around for him to take another run at her, and when he got back to the highway, I'd be waiting for him.

Giving the Wagoneer the gas, I raced down the long brown valley to Bordertown and back into Nevada. By the time I got to the Red Rock turnoff, I knew I was ahead of her. And him.

Like a crumbling shadow, the old highway paralleled 395. I coasted over to it, doubled back fifty yards, and parked.

The engine ticked. Somewhere a dog barked. The sparse highway traffic shushed into the silence.

Finally the Geo nosed around Silver Lake, slid under the highway, and turned up onto the ramp. A few minutes after that a big white Chrysler Imperial came into sight.

Starting the Wagoneer, I eased it off the shoulder, then realized that I'd moved too soon, that he'd spotted me.

The Chrysler seemed to shudder itself free of dust, then surge forward. I stood on the gas pedal, raced the Chrysler to the ramp. He was still on the other side of the underpass when I screeched to a stop in the middle of the ramp entry, cutting him off.

The Chrysler didn't slow. For a moment I thought he was going to swerve around me and up onto the old highway. Then I sickened. Something about the hard charge of the big white car told me he wasn't going to swerve. He was headed straight at me.

The crazy bastard wasn't going to stop.

The big white car got bigger, whiter, the glass flashing, the grillwork shining madly in the sun, dulling bonelike in the shadow of the underpass.

I felt my bowels loosen.

Twenty feet from me the Chrysler somehow turned sideways.

Tires screaming, smoking, it slid, slowed, shuddered to a stop five feet from me.

The driver was a large shadowy blur. He eased his bulk out of the car. Trying to control the shaking of my muscles under an onslaught of adrenaline, I got out to meet him.

He wore his tan suit the way a pile of boulders wears dust. As he moved around the nose of the Chrysler, the shadow under his flat-brimmed Stetson vanished. Recognizing him, I shuddered under another jolt of adrenaline.

Linus Flowers's big body looked fat and slow, his round fleshy face stupid. In fact he was hard and fast and smart. He was as dangerous a human being as I knew.

He stopped, leaned his bulk on the fender. His tan jacket bunched open, exposing a dark shoulder holster.

I wasn't concerned about the gun. Linus Flowers was a man who enjoyed working with his hands. They were huge, thick, hard, with knuckles that made his fist a mace. His boots were cruel— toes sharp and tipped with silver.

His fleshy mouth moved under his soft voice. "I make just the tiniest little miscalculation, Ross, you're fucking history."

Sucking in air stinking of burnt rubber, I managed to find my voice. "You wouldn't wrack up Moby Chrysler on my account."

"I got insurance." His voice went even softer. "So what the fuck you think you're doing?"

"I'm keeping you from following the Geo."

"I want to follow her, I can have my dick halfway up her ass and she doesn't know it. You couldn't keep me from shitting in your ear, if I have a mind to."

At least he wasn't denying anything.

"May be," I said. "But I could slow you down some."

He tilted back his hat, smiled, said softly, "You want to fuck with me, Ross?"

"Not really," I said. "But when you run folks off the road in the middle of the desert, I don't have much choice."

An Isuzu Trooper came out of the underpass, slowed, and stopped ten feet away. The middle-aged woman behind the wheel looked at us, drummed her fingers on the steering wheel. Then she tooted the tinny-sounding horn.

Flowers ignored her. "Tell you what, Ross. As a matter of professional courtesy, I'm not going to stomp you into grease. You don't get that crate out of my way, I'll have to reconsider."

"The woman in the Geo's a PI too. You didn't feel obligated to extend her professional courtesy?"

The tinny horn tooted again. Flowers turned, looked at the Isuzu. With swift, surprising grace he moved his bulk to the driver's door, bent down, and said something. Even from where I stood I could see the woman's face pale. Frantically she rolled up the window. The Trooper jerked backward into the underpass.

I leaned against the fender of the Wagoneer and waited for him. "As a matter of professional courtesy, Flowers, why don't you tell me who hired you to run the Geo off the road, and how you knew where it was going, and what the hell is going on?"

He looked at me for a while, his huge thick hands slowly clenching, unclenching. With a sinking sickness I recognized as fear, I set myself. But he didn't come.

"Let's just say I'm protecting a business investment, Ross. Now get that crate the fuck out of my way."

There wasn't much I could do. Linus Flowers had run Martha Reedy onto the alkali, but I couldn't prove it, and the sheriff wouldn't do anything about it anyway. He hadn't been trying to kill her, because she wasn't dead. He'd been trying to scare her. He might have just been having a little fun.

"I'll do that, Linus," I said. "And since nobody got hurt, as a matter of professional courtesy I won't go to the sheriff. But if the Geo or its driver is involved in any other accidents, I'll know who to come see."

He smiled his smile. "That dyke give you a hard-on, Ross?"

I didn't say anything.

His voice went even softer, seemed a dry desert wind carrying words from a long distance. His big hands curled into big fists. "You want to settle the whole thing now?"

I didn't. For one thing, he had a gun and I didn't. For another, this sort of mindless testosterone-driven head butting was one of the things I was trying not to do anymore. For another, it wouldn't get me any closer to learning Heather McLeod's fate.

"I'll pass, Linus."

His small smile hardened; his voice became a whisper. "Wouldn't have figured you to pussy out, Ross."

I felt the flush creeping up my neck.

"But maybe all the stories are bullshit. Maybe you've been a pussy all along."

The back of my neck burned.

"Maybe in Nam you were a one-way motherfucker."

One-way. In Nam, the officer who would sacrifice his own men to save his ass or his career. It was the worst thing he could call me, and he knew it.

"Maybe," I said. I was trembling again. To stop it, I moved, opened the Wagoneer's door. "But don't count on it."

Linus Flowers smiled his steady sociopathic smile, turned his head and spat onto the dusty tarmac. Then he moved around the Chrysler and climbed in.

I backed onto the shoulder, sat there as he got the Chrysler headed up the ramp. He eased it forward, looked over at me, smiled, shook his head. Then the big white car leapt forward, up the ramp and onto the highway and out of sight.

I sat for a while, sweating, shaking. I tried to tell myself that what I'd just done—or not done—was intelligent, rational, mature. It was. But knowing that wasn't enough to dispel my sickness, my shame.

My mood deeply foul, I dawdled back to town, thinking about Linus Flowers, about what his involvement in whatever it was that was going on might mean. All I really knew for certain was that it meant trouble. Because Linus Flowers meant trouble.

Flowers and I had met in a downtown bar a couple of months after I had returned from Nam. He'd just returned himself, still had, as I did, the thousand-yard stare. We recognized each other, separated ourselves from the civilians who didn't understand, had a couple of drinks, talked.

It had taken me an hour and several drinks to realize what I was talking to. Linus Flowers had enjoyed the war, missed it. Smiling his small sociopathic smile, in his soft sociopathic voice he'd told me what parts of it he'd especially enjoyed.

I hadn't enjoyed any of it. I finished my drink and left.

Since then, I'd only heard about him. Rumors. Gossip. Somehow he'd wangled a PI license and had been using it as a shield behind which he disported himself with his fists and feet and penis and, sometimes, his gun. No one would sign a complaint against him.

Everyone who knew him was afraid of Linus Flowers. I was afraid of Linus Flowers.

I didn't want to think about Linus Flowers and my fear. Instead I tried to think about Patsy McLeod and her long-dead daughter. But when I did, again I found myself thinking of the heart-shaped depression Martha Reedy's sitting had left in the sand.

Dyke, Flowers had said.

I was surprised to discover how much I hoped that wasn't true.

CHAPTER NINE

At I-80, I stayed on 395, then took the Glendale exit. I'd managed to stop thinking about both Linus Flowers and the heart-shaped depression in the sand by thinking about Nolan Turner.

I knew him only by reputation—or reputations, for he had two. Depending on whom you talked to, Nolan Turner was either the Spirit of the New West or the Death of the Real West.

Starting with next to nothing, over a decade and a half Nolan Turner had managed to out-hardball the local good old boys and out-fox the no- and slow-growthers and develop housing projects all over Washoe County. Some thought this good, pointing out that he created jobs and homes and revenues; others thought it bad, that his developments destroyed land, used water, fouled air. Some argued that Nolan Turner had helped transform the small towns of Reno and Sparks into an economically sound and diversified metropolis; others felt that he and his ilk had ruined the Truckee Meadows, that the area was no longer fit to live in.

Both sides, I thought, were right. What I didn't know was if

50

there was anything new about the New West, or if the Real West had ever been real.

I also didn't know if Nolan Turner was just a wild goose that Martha Reedy wanted me to chase. But I decided to give finding out a quick, probably quixotic try.

Turner Development and Construction occupied several acres of dust that had once been a truck farm on Glendale Avenue. It was still a truck farm of sorts: behind a high heavy wire fence, construction trailers and piles of sand and open lumber sheds separated vehicles arranged in rows like carefully cultivated metal vegetables, huge machines fitted with rollers and scrapers, boxes and blades, jaws and claws.

Just off the street, the porticoed white office building sat on a landscaped patch of green within a parking lot filled with what might have been the same cars outside Rondo and Keene. In a slot marked "N. Turner" sat an emerald Ferrari.

I parked, walked through the heat, stepped into a cold air-conditioned world of High Slick—glass-encased scale models of developments, glossy brochures, glossy photographs of people with glossy smiles standing before new homes under the oxymoronic legend LIVE THE DREAM: FROM THE LOW $100,000s.

The receptionist was a young Madonna clone wearing congealed makeup, a fake beauty mark, and a blondly ambitious smile.

"May I help you?"

I played it more or less straight. "My name's Ross. I represent a party interested in a piece of property out in Beulah Valley. I'd like to talk to Mr. Turner about it, if he's in."

As she took in my dust-smeared boots and jeans and shirt, a faint fault line appeared between her waxed eyebrows. "I'm sure a sales representative can help you. Let me ring for one."

"Thanks, but I need to talk to Mr. Turner."

The fault line became a crevasse. "I'm afraid that Mr. Turner doesn't deal directly with . . . ?"

"I'm an attorney."

That impressed her. "I'm sorry, Mr. . . . uh, Ross? I—Mr. Turner doesn't normally—but let me see if he's available."

She was reaching for the phone when a red light blinked on the console. She hesitated, looked at me, tried to smile, picked up the receiver. "Yes sir?"

She listened, began to relax. "Yes sir," she said again, then hung up and smiled. "Mr. Turner will see you, Mr. Ross."

I wondered how he knew I was there.

She led me down a hallway past open offices filled with men— some in jackets and ties, some in T-shirts and hard hats—conferring, arguing, bending over drafting boards or computers or telephones, making plans, decisions, and money. The sweat behind the slick.

The large office at the end of the hall was panelled in walnut, thickly carpeted and darkly draped, dominated by a huge walnut desk on which neat piles of papers and folders lay in carefully ordered rows.

The man standing behind the desk didn't fit it. He belonged out in the slick. Despite hair the bone white of alkali dust, he was in his mid-forties, lean and deeply tanned, wearing designer jeans and a soft golden shirt, a thin gold watch at his wrist, a thin gold chain at his throat. His face was hawkishly handsome. His brown eyes were hawkish too, alert, probing, never quite still.

As I stepped inside, a connecting door opened. The man who stepped through it was nearly as big as Linus Flowers but dressed much like Nolan Turner, his red shirt swollen at the chest and shoulders and gut, his jeans at the thighs. Something about his square-jawed, ruddy face was familiar.

He leaned against the door, crossed his thick arms over his thick chest, might have smiled.

Nolan Turner dropped into the padded leather chair and gave me a grin that didn't reach his eyes. "Ross, what can I do for you?"

"Thank you for seeing me without an appointment."

"I was curious," he grinned. "I don't get a lot of private detectives in here, especially ones like you. Your reputation, as they say, precedes you."

Nolan Turner didn't really sound curious. He sounded like a man who thought he already knew all he needed to know.

"What reputation is that?"

The grin broadened. "Hey, you know. The last story I heard was pure Nevada noir. You and a dead man and a naked hooker in a casino bedroom littered with hundred-dollar chips and champagne bottles. Hot stuff, Ross."

I couldn't quite get a handle on him. The grin might have held a hint of sneer, the good-old-boy banter a hint of disdain.

"Is my reputation the reason your friend here is flexing his big mean muscles at me?"

Turner grinned again. "Mr. Mudd ensures my personal security and general well-being. He's flexing his muscles at you because that's one of the ways he does it."

I placed him. The Mudds were a Sun Valley clan of inbred uncles and cousins and brothers, all big, all mean, all—if the sheriff's department could be believed—dedicated to cooking crank and selling hot cars and perpetrating mayhem, when they weren't beating one another half to death.

I looked at Mudd. He might have smiled. "He's real good at it," I said.

Turner's grin broadened. "Very good, Ross. I used to get threatened—by competitors who couldn't compete, customers who couldn't read contracts, ecofreaks. Since I hired Mr. Mudd, I haven't been threatened."

"No threats from me," I said. "I just want to ask a couple questions. Your name came up in a matter I'm looking into."

"Sure," he said. "Glad to help. What matter is that?"

"A matter obliquely connected with the McLeod ranch."

He leaned back in his chair, as if to get a different view of me. "I know the property."

"Are you going to bid when the county auctions it off?"

He shook his head, grinning, but his eyes flicked, probed. "You really don't think I'd discuss my business plans with you?"

"Not normally," I said. "But you might want to in this case, in order to avoid having to discuss them with the sheriff. Another investigator was run off the road this morning in Beulah Valley by a man named Linus Flowers. That's against the law."

"Who's Linus Flowers?"

"The question is not so much who as what. Eighteen years ago he was a deputy sheriff they let join the Marines so they could avoid having to file extortion and battery and rape charges. Now he's a PI who never seems to have a client and always has a lot of money. They say he gets that money by doing unpleasant things to people for people who don't want to get their hands bloody."

"And you think I hired him to run this other detective off the road?"

"As I say, your name came up."

His eyes again flicked over my face. Then he shook his head. "Let me guess. Desert Conservancy hires a detective to look for McLeod's daughter so they can get her to sell them the ranch when he dies. Somebody runs him off the road, and he thinks I'm behind it because I'm the evil developer who wants the property."

He didn't know the private investigator was a woman. Which meant, probably, that he hadn't hired Linus Flowers to put the scare on her. I was wasting my time.

"Good guess. Mind telling me how you could make it?"

He shrugged. "It's what I'd do if I was Desert Conservancy, and they're the only other player in the game. Unless you're the one working for them?"

"I'm not."

"Or for somebody who wants in?"

I shook my head. "As I said, the matter I'm working on is only obliquely connected with the McLeod ranch."

He grinned. "What matter is that?"

I grinned.

He stopped grinning. "You're not telling me anything."

"I don't know anything," I said. "I'm just trying to figure out what's going on."

He looked at me, then rose and moved around the desk to a block of drapes that I'd thought covered a window.

"What's going on is exactly nothing, Ross. But why don't I show you why it's exactly nothing, so you won't waste any more of my time."

He pulled a cord, and the drapes slid back to reveal a huge relief map of Reno and Sparks and the desert and mountains for fifty miles around. City and county and state land was tinted green; Forest Service and BLM land yellow; developed private land was orange; all other private land was red. The geometric patches of color lay over the map like pastel flowers made by machines.

"I'm going to bid on the McLeod property," he said, "but it won't break my heart if I don't get it. Look where it is."

I saw what he meant. The city was spreading west to the Sierra, south to Washoe Valley, east to the Virginia Range, northeast to Spanish Springs and Palomino Valley. North, except for the places on Fred's Mountain and the Red Rock Estates, there were only odd bits of patented land locked inside BLM tracts. Other than the old mine where the hippies had camped, there was nothing within miles of the McLeod ranch.

"Half the homes in Red Rock Estates are already for sale. People get tired of the drive to jobs, services, schools. Beulah Valley is another fifteen miles. If anything happens out there, it'll just be vacation cabins."

He jerked shut the drapes. "I'll bid, and if I can get it cheap, I'll buy it. But I won't make any big money on it."

"A couple hundred thousand dollars is cheap?"

"I don't know where you got that figure, but yes, that's cheap. Plus what it'll take to get some kind of passable road in there. Bust it up into forty-acre lots and sell half of them and you've got your investment back, plus a few bucks."

I didn't know what a few bucks was to Nolan Turner, but it didn't seem to matter.

"Then why bother with it? That canyon is the only riparian environment for miles. An entire ecology depends on it. Why destroy it for a few bucks?"

He looked at me. "I thought you said you didn't work for Desert Conservancy."

"I don't."

"'Destroy' is their word," he said. "My word is 'develop.' I make the land useful, provide homes and jobs for people and revenue for the city and county and state."

"You're a humanitarian with a civic conscience."

"I'm a businessman," he said. He moved behind his desk, as if to indicate that the conversation had ended. But it hadn't.

"They say you do a lot of work for Wally Keene, Ross. He and I have talked about his firm taking over some of my legal work."

I grinned. "Is that a threat, Mr. Turner?"

He didn't grin. "Just an observation."

"So I won't have to worry about getting run off the road?"

His voice went flat. "Not over the McLeod property, not even if I were inclined toward that stuff. It isn't worth the risk."

Which was, essentially, what Patsy McLeod had said. I asked the only question I could think of. "Do you know who else might be interested in the property?"

"Not unless it's your client."

I didn't say anything.

After a moment, he said, "I've been honest with you, Ross. I'd like something in return. Do you know any reason why I shouldn't bid on the McLeod property?"

I thought about it, but not for long. "No."

He looked at me, then nodded, grinned. "Nice talking to you. Mr. Mudd will show you out."

"I can find my way," I said.

"Mr. Mudd will make sure you do."

Mr. Mudd did. At the office door he gave me a small shove. In the reception room he gave me another.

It told me something about him. It was gratuitous, the kind of bullyboy stuff you get from someone who wants you to think he's tougher than he is.

At the entrance to the building he put a thick hard hand on my arm. His deep-set eyes glazed as his mouth worked up a little speech. "You don't want to come back, asshole."

I felt another angry flush. "Back off, Mudd."

The glaze in his eyes hardened, told me that he was trying to think. His mouth worked up another little speech. "Fucking smart-ass liberals like you are ruining this country, Ross."

I felt my face spread in a grin. I'd been called a lot of things, but never a liberal.

He glowered. He was pretty good at that too.

Mudd was big, thick-muscled, but, I thought, there wasn't much else to him. His family's reputation, linked with his physical posturing and verbal intimidation, would be enough to dissuade most of Nolan Turner's enemies from taking action. He would puff and bluster, but he'd come at somebody for real only from behind.

He was a Linus Flowers wanna-be.

I turned and opened the door to the afternoon heat.

Mudd shoved me out into it.

CHAPTER TEN

As I pulled out of the lot, I mulled over my conversation with Nolan Turner.

Although he was capable of it, I didn't think he'd hired Linus Flowers to put a scare into Martha Reedy. For one thing, he already had a thug who could do that for him. For another, he didn't know the investigator hired by Desert Conservancy was a woman. And for another, as he and Patsy McLeod said, the Beulah Valley ranch wasn't worth it.

Somebody else was in this, whatever this actually was.

Unless Linus Flowers was working on his own. He'd said he was protecting an investment, whatever that meant. But it was much more likely that there was somebody behind him, and finally I didn't think it was Turner.

What I really didn't understand was why Turner had wanted to talk to me in the first place. He knew too much about me to be curious. That in itself was curious.

I was still thinking about Turner when I slid the Wagoneer into a parking slot shaded by an old two-story frame building that had once been a family grocery within neon range of B Street.

The window of Dormouse Books displayed an assortment of new fiction, old mysticism, deep ecology, feminism, and a row of New Age paperbacks titled with words like "child," "woman," "dream," "love," "goddess," and "crystal" in large letters and curious combinations. Into the entrance lintel, the store's owner had carefully carved not the Emersonian motto Whim but FEED YOUR HEAD.

Stepping into Dormouse Books was like suffering an acid flashback. Sunlight bounced off slowly revolving silvery mobiles that reflected bright book covers in a dusty, swirling, light-show rainbow. The air was thick with incense, quivered with the Fifth Dimension's invitation to ride in a beautiful balloon.

Stepping into Dormouse Books was also like stepping into one of its owner's dreams. Under the dead-eyed gaze of Janis Joplin and Aldous Huxley and Virginia Woolf and Jimi Hendrix, freestanding bookcases filled with novels and nonfiction provided perches for strange tableaux—stuffed Eeyore and Pooh peeked around *Trout Fishing in America,* a yarn Cheshire Cat smiled at *The Handmaid's Tale,* clay fertility gods propped up *Love Signs* and *Doors of Perception, The Tibetan Book of the Dead* faced Bradshaw's *Homecoming* over a plastic *Pieta.*

Like a dream, it all made sense if you could interpret the private symbols.

Behind the counter, the woman who called herself Gentle raised her fingers in a peace sign and the corners of her perpetual smile in surprise. "Jones!"

"How are you, Gentle?"

"In the embrace of the Goddess and at one with the All."

I grinned. She had gained some weight, which had dimpled her smile. "Seems to be a bit more of the All these days."

She glanced down at the new flesh that plumped up her wraparound denim skirt, lent a maternal lift to the tie-dyed T-shirt on which lay a crystal pendant and a set of love beads, billowed the open muslin blouse embroidered with red and yellow flowers.

"Good Karma and the Love of Gaea."

"More like tasty brownies. But it looks good on you."

"Maya, Jones, all is Maya," she said, but pleasure deepened, colored her smile.

As always, we had slipped into a playful banter. As always, I enjoyed it, enjoyed watching the subtle shifts of her smile.

"That's got to be the only tie-dyed shirt left in America."

She shook her head in delight. "You're so out of it, Jones. It's the Eternal Return—tie-dye, Day-Glo, acid, social consciousness, political awareness, Peace, Love—everything new is old. The nineties will make the sixties seem like the fifties."

She was teasing me. She was also, I knew, serious.

"Or maybe," I said, grinning, "between political correctness and AIDS, the nineties will make the fifties seem like the sixties."

Her smile feigned concern. "Still locked in the prison of individualism, Jones? If you would only abandon yourself to the All. By the light of the Goddess's love you will see the Truth."

"That would be the goddess Pollyanna?"

Her smile became serene, telling me what it always told me at the end of our little exchanges: It was silly—whatever she was into at the moment, Zen, astrology, female shamanism—but it was also all the same and all true.

"I saw a friend of yours today," I said. "Patsy McLeod."

"Iris Eyes?" Gentle had been the one to notice that Patsy McLeod's eyes were the color of the wild irises that grew in the big pond up the canyon. "She was such a beautiful person."

"She still is," I said.

As she nodded, the Fifth Dimension soared off into silence, to be followed at once by the clanging chord and sudden harmonies of the Mamas and the Papas and "California Dreamin'."

Above us I heard a shuffling male tread; the volume of the music swelled to fill the room.

"Phoenix loves that song." Gentle smiled lovingly. "He's a musician."

I didn't ask who Phoenix was, because I knew what he was—one more drug-fried, or booze-burned, or life-razed derelict male. They ended up at Dormouse Books the way starving cats end up at a widow's back door. Gentle shared with them her home, her food, her body—loved them—but they never stayed around very long. She was, literally, too good for them.

"You're into your detective thing, aren't you, Jones? Your aura's troubled."

I smiled. "It probably always will be, Gentle."

From the nape of her neck trailed a thick dark braid. She tugged it around her shoulder, began to coil it in her lap.

"You're looking for Heather McLeod."

After a stunned moment, I laughed. "I've asked you not to do that to me, Gentle."

She smiled again in delight. "I'm but a vessel, Jones, the instrument of Her Power."

Maybe. Or maybe her occasional near-clairvoyance was the product of logic, or intuition, or chemicals. But I'd always thought that that inexplicable prescience, along with the constant smile, was the psychoheritage of a lot of abused children.

She smiled eagerly. "Is that why you're here? Can I help her, Iris Eyes?"

"I don't think so." But then I thought again. I'd really stopped just to see Gentle and to tell her about Patsy McLeod. But I realized that she might be able to explain something for me.

"Tell me about Heather, Gentle."

She smiled, worked the hair in her lap into a tight coil. "She was a beautiful person."

"Right, you were all beautiful. But how was she beautiful?"

"Little Diva, the star freak. She was going to be a movie star, or a rock star. But . . . she didn't understand about Maya. She thought she was going to look like her mother, and she thought Iris Eyes was ugly."

"You know that she disappeared?"

Gentle smiled gravely. "I heard. But I don't know what happened to her. I was in the city by then."

"What did you hear?"

"California Dreamin'" ended. The volume subsided as the Rolling Stones began "Paint It Black."

Gentle looked down at the coil of braided hair in her lap, tugged at the strip of paisley cloth that held the final plait.

"Blake's trip went bad, and people left. Then the snow."

I knew about the snow, the cold, the winter. Patsy McLeod had helped get the hippies through it, but it had finished them.

"Blake was the one with the VW van with all the Day-Glo flowers on it?"

Gentle smiled brightly. "We all painted a flower on it, like signatures. The book of the heads, Leatherstocking called it."

I remembered the van, a Day-Glo chaos of color. I didn't remember Blake.

"What was his trip?"

"America," she said. "And God, and Love. You know, like being in Beulah Valley, on Zion Mountain, we were all the New Chosen, and America was the Chosen Land. We were going to live in Peace and Love and Joy, create a new America under the eyes of God. It was all sort of mixed up with the Prophetic Books."

"What prophetic books?"

"You know, Jones. 'Little Lamb, Who made thee?'"

I was confused for a moment, then connected. "This Blake, he was a William Blake freak?"

She smiled, quoted, "'Thou hast a lap full of seed, and this is a fine country. Why dost thou not cast thy seed and live in it merrily?'"

"What does that mean?"

"It was the First Commandment, Blake said, for us, and for America. The only commandment."

"Sounds more like—"

Gentle placed a finger to her smiling lips. The music had snapped off, and in the silence she listened to the footsteps shuffling across the ceiling and starting down the stairway.

Into the slow swirl of color in the room stepped a gray man—thin gray face, thin graying hair, brittle-looking body in a faded denim shirt and jeans and beat-up boots. He was probably in his late forties, but he looked seventy. He looked like a scrawny sprig of sage that drought had sucked the sap from.

He saw me, slowed the way a machine slows when you pull the plug, shuffled to a stop.

Gentle's smile deepened, glowed. She moved around the counter to meet him, placed a hand softly on his arm, led him toward me. "Phoenix, this is Jones."

He held out a diffident hand, as if doubting that I'd deign to touch it. I took it, found he had no grip.

He smiled through closed lips. "How's it goin', man?"

But his blue eyes confirmed how it went. He had the hollow gaze of the man who's been down so long he's not sure up exists.

"It doesn't go," I said. "You gotta push it."

He nodded seriously, barely moved his mouth as he mumbled, "Yeah, man. Keep on keepin' on. One day at a time."

"You remember, Phoenix," Gentle said, sliding her arm around his waist, "Jones is the one who took me to San Francisco."

"Yeah, right, man."

He looked at me, then glanced furtively around the store, as if searching for a place to hide. He didn't find one.

"Group time. I gotta go, babe."

Gentle raised her hand and drew it slowly down his face in a lingering caress, then stepped aside. Shuffling, he still seemed to run to the door.

When he was gone, I turned to Gentle, shook my head. "You picked a real winner there."

"You scared him, Jones." She moved back behind the counter. Her smile was maternal, and something else. "He's going to meetings, and he's working. He's working hard at being alive again, too. But he's still very delicate, fragile."

"Aren't we all," I said. But I didn't want to talk about his fragility. Or mine. "You were telling me about Heather."

She nodded, smiled helplessly. "I know what you want to know, Jones, but I can't help you. I loved her, we were sisters, but I wasn't there long. I really didn't know her very well."

I shrugged. "I just thought, you were closest to her in age, maybe you got tight with her?"

She recoiled the braid in her lap, tugged again at the paisley cloth. "I tried to get her to love her mother more."

"She had trouble with Patsy?"

"She couldn't see how beautiful her mother was." She smiled

sadly, wistfully. "I really don't know anything else, Jones."

"It's OK," I said. She'd told me more than I had a right to expect, even if I didn't quite know what to make of it.

She continued to smile sadly, disappointed in herself. "I wish I could help. Are you sure Iris Eyes is all right?"

I grinned. "Why don't you give her a call and find out? She's in the book. I know she'd like to hear from you."

Her smile brightened. "What a lovely gift you've brought me today, Jones. Thank you. I will."

I grinned, flashed her the peace sign, turned to leave. Then I stopped, turned back. "You said you heard what happened out there, Gentle. Who told you?"

Her smile took on a childish excitement. "Right, man. Cyclops can tell you."

"Cyclops?" I didn't remember him either. I remembered the camp, the mine, the pond, but I didn't remember any of the hippies. Over the years they had all blended into a single beaded, bearded memory. "Which one was he?"

"You know, always pointing a movie camera?"

I didn't remember a movie camera. "It was twenty years ago, Gentle. I was only out at the camp a couple times."

Her smile grew impish. "And you weren't paying much attention to the dudes anyhow, were you?"

I laughed. "Probably not. But I don't remember any of the chicks either." Faces hidden in hair, bodies in costumes.

She opened a counter drawer and began rummaging through its mess. "He was a teaching assistant in the art department at UNR, so he wasn't always around. He was tall, thinner then, always wore this cowboy hat because he was losing it on top."

For a moment I couldn't speak. Finally I found my voice, said as evenly as I could, "He wore a beard."

"All the dudes did, Jones, if they could."

"He drove a beat-up old Chevy pickup."

She looked up at me, her smile thickened with concern. "I think it was a Dodge, but—are you all right?"

"You wouldn't know where I might find him?"

"That's what I'm looking for. Sacramento, he comes over sometimes." Then from the drawer she pulled a small white card. Smiling like a child sharing a toy, she handed it to me. "Here."

I took it, stuffed it in my pocket. I wasn't ready to look at it yet because I didn't know what I should feel about it.

"Thank you, Gentle."

She smiled serenely, raised her hand, veed her fingers.

"Peace, Jones. Trust the Goddess to guide you."

CHAPTER ELEVEN

The Goddess must have guided me outside, for I found myself standing in the thinning heat and deepening shade, slowly beginning to feel. Elation—eighteen years before, I'd been right. And disgust—eighteen years before, I'd been wrong.

But I didn't look at the card. I still wasn't ready.

As I stepped toward the Wagoneer, a gray shape sidled toward me from the shadow of the building. The man Gentle had called Phoenix stopped, but his feet kept shuffling. He stared down at them.

"I—can you tell me something?" Again his thin gray lips barely moved; the effect was odd, as if he were both ventriloquist and dummy. "I mean, Gentle says you're her friend, man."

"That's right, man," I snapped. "Are you? Or are you just one more hustling, scamming, freeloading piece of shit, man?"

My anger surprised me, and scared him. His face went grayer as he shuffled backward, mumbled, "Not anymore, man, not with her."

"So what are you, man?"

"I'm a junkie," he said to his feet. Then he looked up at me. "But I'm sober, man, and I'm holding up my end."

"Or Gentle's holding it for you until you get well enough to rip her off and run."

There was some sap left in him after all; it flushed faint color into his face as it rose.

"I don't care what you think of me," he said softly. As he spoke his lips parted, revealed what he'd been hiding. His mouth was ruined, more gaps than teeth, less teeth than dark stubs.

"You couldn't come close to knowing what I've been, man. I've fucked over the universe, ripped off every friend I ever had for a nickel bag. See this mouth, man? I earned it. I've slept in my own shit and been glad for the heat."

I believed it.

"But not anymore, man. And I'm not going anywhere, except to meetings and to work, unless Gentle wants me to. And I'm not going to let you run me off."

It took all he had. His gaze dropped, his head drooped as he turned and shuffled off.

"Wait a minute."

I stepped after him, put a hand on his thin shoulder. He stumbled, spun, flattened against the wall, raised and crossed his thin arms as if to ward off blows.

"I'm sorry," I said. "I get protective of her."

He wasn't sure that I really was sorry. He hadn't been sure of anything for a long time. But slowly his arms dropped.

"I can dig it, man," he said finally, showing me again the burnt forest of his mouth. "I know I'm not the first bum she took in. But unless she says different, I'm the last."

He looked like he believed it. Or was trying to believe it. I was trying to believe him. "You wanted to ask me something?"

"I—" His eyes became less hollow. "You know about the scars? She won't talk about them, man, just spaces out."

"She has her reasons," I said.

"I know, man. But she has nightmares, wakes up whimpering, shivering, and I can't help her, man. All I can do is hold her."

"That's all anybody can do. That and love her."

"Naw, man," he said slowly. "That's just a word, man. Nobody even knows what it means. It's just a feeling. Feelings don't help anybody, man. I want to know what I can *do*."

All junkies are hustlers, and a straight junkie is still a junkie. But maybe not still a hustler.

"I can tell you what not to do," I said. "Don't ever show her a wire coat hanger."

Understanding altered his eyes. "Yeah, man, I can dig it. When I saw the scars, I couldn't believe it, it was like . . ."

Like a web of evil woven on a loom of madness.

"That's not all," I said. "She's scarred inside, too."

He nodded. "The nightmares."

"Not just that. She's physically scarred inside. That's why she doesn't have children."

"Love" was just a word, a feeling, and feelings don't help anybody, man. His didn't help him. They created the pain that twisted his gray face. "Ah, fuck, man . . ."

I gave him a three-block lift to his group meeting. From there, he told me, he went to a Winner's gas station and convenience store, where he clerked till midnight. Then he went back to Gentle.

"She said you were a musician. Still playing?"

"Naw, man," he said. "That was my scam. I was just a junkie with a guitar."

"Were you any good?"

It took him a while. "What it was, man, I couldn't do it the way I could hear it. In my head it was magic, but when I played it, it was just music."

I pulled to the curb in front of the old clapboard Methodist church, took out one of my cards and gave it to him.

"If she needs anything, give me a call, will you?"

He looked at the card. "I thought your name was Jones?"

I smiled. "You know Gentle. She's the new Adam, renames everything in creation."

He nodded, "Yeah, man, but how . . . ?"

"Remember the Coasters song about all the old-time Western

serials? Little Nell's tied to the railroad tracks, or to the buzz saw, and then, and then . . ."

He got it. His grin was ghastly. "'Along Came Jones.'"

"It's the same with you. You're Phoenix," I said, "rising from your own ashes."

"Yeah, man," he said. "That's what I'm doing. Except . . . that's really my name, Phoenix. Howard Phoenix."

I looked at him, then burst out laughing. When he saw I wasn't laughing at him, he laughed too.

I watched Howard Phoenix shuffle off to his group meeting. Then I headed home. I-80 was in full rush-hour crawl, but I took it anyway, crept to the Keystone Exit, spent ten minutes getting off the freeway.

I didn't mind. I watched the Sierra change in the slanting sunlight, watched shadows define the contours of the foothills, watched shadow pools spread through the high aspen thickets so that the splashes of gold seemed to float on dark water.

At home, I took a long shower and changed into clean jeans and shirt. I made coffee, made and ate an omelette, poured more coffee. Then from my shirt pocket I took out Martha Reedy's business card and the eighteen-year-old school portrait of Heather McLeod and the card Gentle had given me.

Dale Rutledge, his name was.

According to the card, Dale Rutledge owned and operated Intimate Moments Productions, which produced videotapes of family rites and rituals—weddings, bar mitzvahs, anniversaries, christenings, birthday parties. "Special Requests Our Specialty."

I picked up the phone and dialed, got a recording of a whisky-gruff voice telling me to leave a message, which I did:

"Mr. Rutledge, my name is Ross. I'm calling from Reno. I may need to speak to you on a matter of some import. If so, I'll be at your business in Sacramento this evening, or early tomorrow."

I dialed the number on Martha Reedy's card, got a recording of a calm voice asking me to leave a message, which I did:

"You were run off the road by a PI named Linus Flowers. He's not a nice person. If he shows, you don't want to mess with him. Unless you want to do the world a favor and shoot him."

I hung up, put the cards and photo back in my pocket, sipped my coffee, and found myself thinking again about the heart-shaped depression in the desert sand.

I took out my wallet, opened it to my daughter's photograph, looked at it. After a minute, I picked up the phone again and dialed a number and got no answer.

I frequently got no answer these days. My daughter was growing up, beginning, as teenage girls do, to lead her own life. She was growing away from me. It was inevitable, I knew, but I didn't know quite how to feel about it.

I put the picture away, took my coffee out onto the patio and sat and sipped and watched the shadows deepen on the desert ranges as twilight invaded the eastern sky.

After a while I realized that I was stalling. And why.

I didn't want to talk to Patsy McLeod, but not just because what I had to tell her would distress her. I was stalling because once I told her, I was probably going to have to stop pretending.

I'd been doing it all day, pretending. Pretending to be a private investigator on a pretend case, pretending to look for a dead girl I knew I couldn't find. Until Martha Reedy had made a mistake, maybe, and a sociopath in a white Chrysler Imperial had showed up, and in Dormouse Books I had found a tall thin bearded cowboy, and the pretend case threatened to become real, ugly.

I didn't want it to.

I wanted to pick up the phone and call Patsy McLeod and tell her that it was hopeless, that her daughter was dead, that I'd refund her money.

I wanted to spend the evening working on the house, making it a fit place for a normal human being to inhabit, making myself fit to inhabit it.

I wanted to go to sleep and get up the next morning and all next mornings and put on my suit and tie and go to my office at Rondo and Keene and play my little paralegal games and conduct my disinterested little investigations that touched no one that I knew or cared about.

The sound of the phone ringing jangled me out of my reverie.

Somehow certain that it was my daughter calling, I jumped up and hurried into the kitchen, picked up the receiver.

"Cynthia?"

"It's me," Wally Keene said. "Could you come down to the office for a minute? We need to talk."

"I can't, Wally. I'm working, remember?"

"This is important." His tone was curt, peremptory. And something else.

As evenly as I could, I said, "You're my landlord, Wally. You're not my boss, not yet."

There was a silence, then a sharp hollow laugh. "Jack, I didn't mean it that way. I'm sorry."

He sounded sorry. But then Wally was constantly playing to an audience, could sound any way he wanted to.

"I just got a call from . . . a local developer."

I wondered what he thought was going on that precluded him from using Nolan Turner's name. Or if all this was just more theater.

"What a surprise," I said. "And he wants to talk about your handling his legal affairs—if, that is, the PI who leases an office from you stops working on the case he's working on."

"No," Wally said. "He said talking to you reminded him he'd wanted to continue our discussion. But there were no threats. I—that isn't what we need to talk about."

"What is?"

When he finally spoke, it was in a voice I'd never heard him use. "Jack, I told him what you were doing, and who you were working for. I won't try to excuse it, or explain how it came to happen. Pure and simple, I fouled up. But I wanted to tell you face-to-face."

I expected to hear concern and contrition in Wally's voice about as much as I expected to hear him speak Shoshone. But it seemed genuine.

"Don't worry about it. Attorney-client privilege doesn't obtain anyhow. What did he say?"

"That he hoped you found her so he wouldn't have to involve himself in county red tape. I assume you know what that means."

"I do. But it's not that big a deal, Wally."

"He intimated that, but . . ." Wally seemed nervous, unsure of himself. That didn't make any sense if Nolan Turner hadn't pressured him. Or even if he had.

"So everybody's happy, Wally. No problem."

"Maybe," he said, but he didn't sound convinced. "The other thing, Jack, is that I wondered if you'd discovered, or maybe even already knew, something about him I should know before I talk to him."

"Like what?"

"It's not something I want to discuss over the phone."

The whole conversation was getting ridiculous. "Unless it can wait, Wally . . ."

He wasn't going to let it wait. "I know what this sounds like, Jack, but there have always been . . . rumors. That maybe he got too big too fast. That maybe there's too much money around him, too much muscle. That maybe he has friends."

I almost laughed. "Come on, Wally. You believe that?"

"I never did before," he said. "It always sounded like what he says it is, sour grapes. I've even heard him joke about it. With his white hair, like Steve Martin playing Don Corleone. It's just that it would fit. He lives the lifestyle, has that cretin Mudd as a bodyguard, owns a big flashy house in the foothills, collects fancy cars and fancy women, entertains big politicos, all the local movers and shakers. . . ."

I did laugh then. "Except for the cretin, you've just described your own lifestyle. Come on, what's got you spooked?"

After a silence, he said, "Do you have any idea what kind of billables a business like his generates? If he goes with us, it will make Rondo and Keene the top law firm in the city."

I got it. His dream was about to become real, but he wasn't sure what he was going to have to pay for it.

"You want me to tell you if it's clean money?"

"You know the streets," he said. "You talk to people I don't normally run into."

"I don't know anything you don't, Wally."

He didn't say anything, apparently waiting for me to say something else. I had nothing else to say.

"The other thing is . . . he doesn't seem to have a past. The story is he drifted around working construction, learning the business, then showed up in town about the time the boom hit, picked up a couple run-down rental properties and parlayed them into big money. I mean, there's no way to really check it."

"Of course there's a way, Wally. Hire me, or somebody like me, to look into it."

"I—there's no time now."

Again he waited for me to say something. Again I didn't have anything to say.

"Well, thanks anyhow, Jack," he said finally. "And I'm sorry about the slip. You coming in tomorrow?"

"Maybe," I said, "maybe not."

While I still had the phone in my hand, I called the number Patsy McLeod had given me. When she answered, I told her that we had to talk and that I was coming up. She gave me directions, then started to ask what we had to talk about. I cut her off, told her I'd see her in a couple of hours.

I didn't know where I'd be going from Tahoe or how long I'd be gone. I packed a bag with everything from a business suit to cutoff jogging jeans, cleaned up my meal mess, locked up the house, climbed in the Wagoneer, and pointed it toward the Sierra.

CHAPTER TWELVE

I met the night halfway up Mount Rose.

Getting there I'd played a few tail-losing games with side roads and dead ends; after them and the Reno traffic and the mountain switchbacks, I was as sure as I could be that Linus Flowers wasn't following me.

I could only hope that he wasn't following Martha Reedy.

In the darkness I reached the crest and began braking my way down into the Tahoe Basin. The air was cool, crisp with the scent of dying leaves and wood smoke, the scent of fall in the high country.

Then the highway bent around a pine-thick corner and Lake Tahoe came into view. Even at night, the lake came into view spectacularly.

The golden light of a setting moon splashed in a broad shimmering sheet far out on the lake; specks of starlight danced on the dark water, an eerie phosphorescent foam licked at the pale sandy beaches. Lights flickered in the little towns rimming the lake, sparkled and flared among the trees. Around it all the Sierra peaks slouched like shadowy primitive gods huddled over a dying fire.

As the highway descended, roads headed off toward ski runs and ritzy vacation cabins. Lower, the earth sprouted fewer pines amid the bright-windowed executive homes and flood-lit condos that spread from the golf courses. The pines thinned even more, the homes thickened, until the highway and the descent ended at Lakeshore Boulevard.

Tahoe at lakeside didn't look so spectacular. Piers jutted out over the sand to drying mudflats left by the lake's slow receding under the drought. In shallows at the water's edge, algae slime slicked mud and rocks, soured the chill air. The mountains seemed to lean inward, as if they wanted to collapse and bury forever what men had done to the lake and the land.

I turned west, toward Crystal Bay and the California line. Along the highway, storefronts were mostly dark, motel parking lots mostly empty, sidewalks deserted. Traffic was light, mostly locals drifting to the homes scattered along the lake and up the hillsides.

After a few minutes I spotted the unmarked turnoff that Patsy McLeod had told me to look for.

A narrow strip of new tarmac wound through big, evenly spaced timber to a wide meadow that sloped toward the lake. On my left, a huge barn and corrals backed against the darkness of the pines; from the barn, a path led past a badminton court and horseshoe pit to the green-shuttered white frame house on a low bluff overlooking the water.

As I had surprised Rosetta Draine, her home surprised me. The original two-story structure anchored a pair of new single-story wings, one of which, topped with a basketball backboard, seemed mostly garage used mostly to protect sporting and outdoor gear— mountain bikes, snow and water skis, a canoe, skates and hockey sticks, footballs, softballs and mitts. The red BMW and green Mercedes and white pickup parked before it said that money lived here, yet it was all fairly modest by Tahoe standards, bespoke not wealth and power so much as comfort and children and family.

Warm yellow light spilled from several windows, then briefly from the front door as Patsy McLeod stepped through it. Parking beside the pickup, I got out as she walked over. Behind her the door opened again, and a small figure slipped out and raced off silently across the grass toward the barn.

In boots, jeans, and an old Yale sweatshirt, with the night shadows smoothing her desert-scarred skin, Patsy looked like the woman I'd met twenty years before. "Patsy, I—"

"Not yet, Ross," she said. "Let's go meet the tribe first."

She led me inside, through a small foyer into a large family room warmed by thick pale-brown carpet, brightened by Sierra Club prints and glossy plants. The furniture—dark wood with flower-patterned upholstery—was expensive but well worn. An old golden retriever looked up from her curl in the corner, then dropped her head onto her crossed paws and drifted back into her doze.

From a sofa, Rosetta Draine smiled at me past a thick bound report. The others in the room formed a rough circle of which she was the center.

In a nearby chair a pretty dark-eyed teenage girl sat entranced by the soundless, stiff-jointed gyrations of Michael Jackson on the TV. Before a cold fireplace, a younger boy in horn-rimmed glasses and a Bart Simpson T-shirt studied the chessboard set up between him and the bearded man sprawled on the carpet.

I stopped, dizzied, disoriented by the sudden impossible certainty that I'd seen this room and these people before.

The bearded man got to his feet, tucked his shirttail into his jeans, adjusted his glasses, grinned down at the boy.

"Allow me to rest my brain a moment, my man. Then I'll wipe you out."

The boy grinned back. "Your brain doesn't need a rest to beat me. It needs a transplant."

Patsy nudged me forward, out of déjà vu. "Professor, this here's Jack Ross."

"Mr. Ross, Bill Draine. Nice to meet you."

Everything about William Draine—handshake, clothes, smile—was relaxed, casual, created the impression that he took very little seriously, including himself. It was an impression sharply at odds with the one I'd formed while reading his book.

Patsy nudged my elbow. "Mr. Smart-Guy over there's Charlie. And that's Claudette."

Under the affection that thickened her voice, the boy feigned concentration on the chess game, the girl turned and smiled her mother's small warm smile.

Patsy squinted at a low table covered with an open schoolbook and three-ring binder. "Where'd Lila get off to?"

"*Equus caballus,*" the boy said without looking up.

Patsy turned to him. "She finish her homework?"

The boy looked up then and grinned, but his sister answered. "Surely you jest."

Draine smiled. "Excuse me, Mr. Ross. We seem to have a minor situation here. Nana, you and Mr. Ross will want to talk in private. Would you like to use my office?"

Patsy shook her head. "My room'll do us. I—tell that young lady, she don't finish her homework before she goes to the barn, I'm gonna sell them nags for dog food."

All four of the Draines grinned at her.

"I'll tell her, Nana," William Draine said, "but I wouldn't bet the farm that she'll believe it."

Rosetta Draine put down the report, rose from the sofa. She wore a trim dark skirt, and a red silk blouse that softened, warmed her lovely skin. In her home, among her family, somehow she seemed smaller, at once more vulnerable and more sexual.

She moved to her husband's side, placed a hand on his hip.

"I'm going to make coffee. I'll be glad to bring you some, Mr. Ross. Patsy?"

Patsy smiled her cracked-playa smile. "That'd be real nice. C'mon, Ross."

We stepped through a door into a dim hallway. Patsy opened the first of several doors, flicked a switch. The light revealed a pleasant carpeted room centered by a large quilt-covered bed. Three walls were hung with blocky pencil-sketched horses and rough crayon flowers and pale watercolor lakescapes. A heavy bureau supported a gallery of photographs of the three Draine children.

Patsy shut the door, nodded at the round oak table before a window that overlooked the lake. "Take a load off."

Sitting across from me, she smiled proudly at the formal portrait of the Draine family on her bedside table. "So?"

I saw no pictures of either of the McLeod children. It was as if only her "pretend" family were real to her anymore.

"I don't run into a lot of happy families in my business, Patsy. It's nice to discover there are still some around."

She nodded, smiling with pleasure. "Happy is hard work, Ross. A lot of luck, too."

"I'd say you had some luck coming."

As she watched me, her smile slowly changed into her desert squint. "You seen Royce."

I told her what I'd seen, heard. Long before I finished, she had turned to stare out the window at the night. I stared out the window too. The moon had set behind the mountains; the lake smeared the reflection of the stars, seemed a second, troubled sky.

"It fits, I guess, him settin' there in his uniform an' all."

"The medals, they're—"

"His, all of 'em. He was a hero. That's why Mal went off to Vietnam, to be a hero like his dad was in Korea. He was, too, got his own medal, before . . ."

Slowly she turned to face me. "He should of looked at what they done to his dad when he got back. Told him he was a hero for fighting, then took away everything he was fighting for." That was a line from a bad country song. I didn't think she knew that.

"That's gotta be why he's setting there in his uniform, letting it all go to pieces. He's telling them. Worked his fool head off, but every time he managed to get a little ahead, they'd take it away— speculators, bankers, gover-ment, en-vi-ra-men-tal-ists. And he'd be worse off than before."

It was a refrain as common in the West as a coyote yowl. It was also true, even if it wasn't quite the truth.

"He's telling 'em what he thinks of this country, the one he killed people for. He's telling 'em it can go to hell."

"I don't think they're listening, Patsy."

"Never did when it mattered," she said, turning back to the star-smeared water. "He was a good man, an' they ruined him."

This about a man who had ripped holes in her heart. But her tense, I thought, explained it. She was not describing her ex-husband; she was eulogizing him. She was saying good-bye not to the man but to what might have been.

After a silence, she squinted again, said slowly, "There's something else, ain't there?"

I took a deep breath. "Martha Reedy thinks Heather's alive. She thinks she can find her."

As I watched, Patsy McLeod descended into the depths of her beautiful blue eyes, as if to hide from the dark visions that had plagued her for eighteen years.

"We talked to Royce together," I said. "The only thing she asked him was if he'd seen Heather recently."

When she didn't speak, I repeated the mistake Martha Reedy might have made. "Recently."

As if from a deep sleep, she said slowly, "A word."

"I know," I said, "it isn't much. But when I offered to share my information with her, she wasn't interested. I got the sense that she thinks she can find Heather on her own."

"A sense. A word."

"I know," I said again.

I withdrew the card Gentle had given me, placed it on the table between us. "And this."

She didn't look at it.

"His name's Dale Rutledge. The hippies called him Cyclops."

She didn't say anything.

I took another deep breath. "He was tall, thin, bearded, wore a cowboy hat. We had the pickup wrong. It wasn't a Chevy. It was a Dodge."

Her eyes glittered and smeared like the night lake as she surfaced. "Lord, I never even thought about . . . I mean, you kept talking cowboy, cowboy and me and . . . you never—"

At the soft rap on the door, she abruptly brushed at her eyes, turned away toward the darkness and the water.

I rose, opened the door for Rosetta Draine and her small warm smile. She stepped inside, set on the table a tray holding a coffee urn, cream and sugar, spoons and cups. "I forgot to ask how you take it, Mr. Ross."

"Black is fine," I said.

Something in my voice, or in Patsy's stillness, stiffened her smile. "Is something wrong?"

I didn't answer.

"I'm sorry," she said, "I'll leave you to your business."

"No." It came from Patsy, like a moan. "I—stay."

Rosetta Draine glanced at me. At my nod, she pulled a chair close to Patsy. Carefully she poured two cups of coffee. Then she sat down and took Patsy's battered hand in both of hers.

I sat back down, told her what I thought Martha Reedy thought, told her what I'd discovered in Dormouse Books.

When I finished, Rosetta Draine frowned uncertainly. "If I understand what you're saying, Mr. Ross, you believe that Heather might actually be alive, and that you have a lead, this . . ." One of her hands left Patsy's, picked up the card. "Dale Rutledge. But why isn't this good news?"

I took another deep breath. "Because in eighteen years Heather has never gotten in touch with Patsy."

"I see," she said. She put the card back on the table, straightened her back; her soft, clean features took on the in-charge expression they had assumed that morning in my office. "How would an expert in these matters account for that?"

"It doesn't take an expert, Mrs. Draine. Common sense says there are only two possibilities—she can't or she won't."

"That is, she's mentally incapable of it, or she's . . ." She glanced at Patsy, let the thought trail off to nothing.

Patsy again spoke as if from a drug-deep sleep. "No. She's dead. I'm her mother. I know."

I took out my wallet, removed the ten hundreds, dropped them onto the table.

Rosetta Draine frowned again. "You're quitting?"

"No. But I'm giving Patsy the chance to."

Neither woman spoke. So I had to.

"There are no happy endings to these stories, Patsy. You've been trying to find one for eighteen years, trying to think of a way to explain how Heather could be alive and not call you. You had to conclude that she's dead. You hired me to find her grave. But if I keep going, I might find something worse."

In the silence I could hear the muted laughing voices of the Draine children from the living room.

Rosetta Draine gave Patsy a deeply tender look, then rose. "Whatever you decide, dear, we're with you. All of us."

Patsy didn't answer. Her gaze fixed on the photographs on the bureau, as if they were the only real things in the room.

Then, with sudden energy she leaped from the chair, grabbed the bills. I felt a surge of hope. But she didn't stuff the money in her pocket. She held it out to me.

"Bring her home, Ross."

I shook my head in dismay. "She might refuse to come home."

"I—" Blindly she thrust the money at me. "Just find her."

When I didn't take the money, she dropped it on the table. Suddenly she reached out and grabbed my coffee cup. "Shoot, gotta be cold by now."

"Patsy," I said, "I—"

"That young lady ever come in to her books?" She put both cups back on the tray, picked it up, and strode to the door. "Her 'n me gotta have a little talk."

Then she was gone.

CHAPTER THIRTEEN

Rosetta Draine picked up the money, held it out to me.

"That was difficult for you, Mr. Ross. I hadn't realized that you . . . cared for her."

I took the money, stuffed it into my pocket, picked up Dale Rutledge's card and put it into my shirt pocket. "I still don't think she understands. . . ."

"She understands," Rosetta Draine said quietly.

"Mrs. Draine, if Heather's alive but incompetent, she's in an institution or on the streets, and in either case I can't find her. But neither can Martha Reedy."

She nodded. "And Ms. Reedy thinks she can, which suggests that Heather isn't mentally unbalanced or amnesiac. She's stayed away out of shame or guilt about what she's become."

I tried to shrug, felt my shoulders tight with tension.

"It isn't that simple. Runaway girls who end up hookers, say, or junkies, almost always contact their parents when they get older, to hit them up for money if nothing else."

She watched me. "Which means?"

"In a case like this, the explanation is usually grimmer. The girl either fears or hates her parents."

After a moment, she shook her head. "But that really doesn't matter, does it? Why she left, why she has refused to come back? What happened in the past has nothing to do with finding her."

She didn't seem to understand either. "But it has everything to do with what I'll find, what Patsy will have to deal with," I said.

She watched me, a smile playing at the edges of her small soft mouth, said softly, "If it were your daughter, Mr. Ross, what would you want?"

I hadn't thought of it that way. "I'd want to know, sure, but—"

"But that would be different, because you're strong enough to deal with it but Patsy isn't." Her smile deepened. "Some people would say you're a raging chauvinist, Mr. Ross."

I felt blood heat my face. "Patsy's had enough misery in her life. Some of it I brought on her. I don't want to bring her more."

Again she spoke softly. "Excuse me, Mr. Ross, but if there is a problem here, I think it's yours. Patsy's as strong a woman as I've ever known. She'll deal with whatever comes. You're the one who seems to be having the difficulties."

I was having difficulties, all right. I was also still having big trouble with Rosetta Draine.

She was lovely, warm. She said all the right things. But part of what had bothered me in my office was my awareness of how she had subtly controlled Patsy, had tried to control me.

I had that same sense now, even though I knew she was right.

I also had, in some murky, miasmic part of my consciousness, the same growing awareness of her body. I thought of the family I'd just seen, felt slightly sick, ashamed.

I tried to smile. "What you're telling me, Mrs. Draine, is that it's time for me to get my chauvinist butt in gear and do what I was hired to do, and let Patsy solve her own problems."

"I think so." She stepped to the door. "Except 'chauvinist' really isn't the word I'd choose to describe you, Mr. Ross. You're just . . . old-fashioned."

In the living room, the old dog still slept in her corner. William Draine sat browsing through a book, while the two older Draine children grinned at the television and each other as Woody Allen explained everything they ever wanted to know about sex but were afraid to ask.

Patsy sat at the low table, a tousled-haired blond girl on her lap. In her dirt-smeared hand the child gripped a pencil as if it were a knife. As the older girl had smiled her mother's smile, the younger squinted Patsy's desert squint.

Patsy glanced up from the book, scowled. "You know how to add in base five, Ross?"

It was as if the previous half hour hadn't occurred. "No."

"Know any reason why anybody in their right mind'd ever want to?"

I shook my head.

Her squint deepened, her arm tightened around the little girl. "All these smart people around here, an' what good are they? It's just you an' me, darlin'."

William Draine closed his book, rose from a chair. "Give it a few more minutes, Nana. If you don't have it by then, Charlie will show you how it works."

He stepped over to me, held out the book. "Mr. Ross, since you managed to wade through my first effort, I thought you might like to look at this. I've taken the liberty of inscribing it to you."

The jacket was blazing white, the crisp letters inky black. *The Last and Greatest Dream.* For some reason it reminded me of Royce McLeod's hand-painted sign.

"Thank you," I said.

His wife trailed her hand lightly across his shoulders as she stepped past him. Smiling, he watched her disappear through a narrow archway.

"I wonder," he said, turning back to me, "what you thought of *Squaring the Circle?*"

"I thought it was . . . well written."

"That's something," he smiled. "Tact, probably. I take it you didn't find the argument compelling?"

I didn't want to tell him how I'd found the argument, not in front of his children. Not after the last half hour.

It didn't matter; his question had been merely rhetorical.

"I know it's a difficult thesis to accept, since it overturns so many of our most cherished myths about the so-called winning of the American West—rugged individualism, Jeffersonian yeomanry, Emersonian self-reliance, industrious pioneers and visionary entrepreneurs and intrepid lawmen, all brought to us by John Ford and John Wayne."

"I'll read—"

"But looking it over, I found some weaknesses, passages in which the argument perhaps was carried more by assertion than by evidence. I think I've eliminated that problem from this one."

"I—"

"The title comes from *The Great Gatsby,* from that wonderful threnody in which Fitzgerald describes the Dutch sailors' first encounter with the continent. How does it go? . . . seeing for the last time in human history something commensurate to their capacity for wonder? But their vision was already dead, a part of their phallocentric and imperial European past, and it's destroying our present. . . ."

I glanced around the room. Only the boy, Charlie, was listening. He gave me a long-suffering grin, as if to suggest that the old man was at it again.

Somehow, and again stunningly, his grin told me something else.

It told me why I'd felt that I had seen this family before.

Because I had.

I'd seen it in the yearning fantasies of a small boy in the house of his grandparents, his mother gone, his father unknown. This was the family that the boy I once was had dreamed he would have when he became a man.

Shaken, I turned my attention back to William Draine. He hadn't noticed I hadn't been listening, hadn't really been there.

". . . their capitalist bourgeois ideology necessitated that to reify their dream they had to despoil all they saw, and in the bargain savage the indigenous populations and betray the promises made to their own people. Their vision wreaked havoc on the land, which we have to restore."

This was the William Draine I'd imagined while reading his book. He was smiling at me, but he wasn't really looking at me. Like some other academics I'd met, his focus was inward, on his ideas, on the working of his own mind, the popping of his own synapses.

"Fine," I said, suddenly, inexplicably angry. "You first."

"I . . . excuse me?"

Charlie grinned with delight.

"That lake out there is turning into algae soup, Professor— eutrophication, sewage, fertilizer are killing it. The only way to save it is if everybody packs up and leaves. But you probably won't want to do that."

He smiled, not at all troubled by what I'd said.

"You're oversimplifying an extremely complex issue, Mr. Ross."

My sudden anger suddenly vanished. "Maybe. I guess I'm just simpleminded." And old-fashioned. "I'll read your book, Professor. Then maybe I'll understand it the way you do."

I looked at the boy, Charlie. He grinned.

I looked at Patsy McLeod. "Good night, Patsy."

She looked up, and I saw then that the images of her eighteen-year-long nightmare had come back to haunt her.

Her face was uglied by anguish, her beautiful blue eyes muddied by shame.

I drove away from the Draine home thinking about the past, and the present.

Rosetta Draine had said that the past was irrelevant. Her husband had said the opposite. I didn't know which was true.

I was also thinking about *The Great Gatsby*.

As I drove through the darkness, I began to understand why I'd tried to get out of working for Patsy McLeod, why I'd stopped handling domestic and personal cases, why I'd leased an office from Rondo and Keene, with which I might soon be associated.

I began to understand what I wanted. I wanted never again to see a face uglied by anguish, eyes muddied by shame.

I wanted no more riotous excursions with privileged glimpses into the human heart.

CHAPTER FOURTEEN

At Crystal Bay I left Nevada, entered a California darkness littered with the lights from the tourist traps of King's Beach, the fancy homes and condos of Northstar, the slump and hustle of Truckee. Once on I-80 and past the Agricultural Inspection Station, I stepped on the gas for the run up to Donner Pass.

From there, the night was all downhill.

Ignoring the speed limit, for nearly an hour I drove down and west through a mountain darkness that warmed, thinned with each mile. Out of a weariness psychic or physical or both, my mind drifted through images from the day, somehow always swirling back to a heart-shaped depression left in the desert sand.

Martha Reedy had gotten to me. I wasn't sure why. About all I was sure of was that I hadn't gotten to her.

Finally the highway swooped out of the Sierra darkness. For as far as I could see across the Big Valley, lights cast faint grotesque shadows into the night sky.

Freeway traffic grew heavy, contentious, but seemed to be going nowhere. Roadside businesses dueled in neon of clashing colors, housing tracts bunched up in the middle of old fields as if for protection against both the darkness and the lights. The half-night teemed with cars in mindless motion. After the dark stillness of the mountains, I began to feel, as I often did in California, a strange dreamlike displacement, as if I were in a land occupied by creatures who had created a culture I couldn't understand as human.

Feeling myself sinking into depression, I switched on the radio and found a miracle, Mahalia Jackson singing spirituals about the River Jordan and the Promised Land.

By the time I slid off onto Auburn Boulevard in Sacramento, I was feeling almost human again. It was after eight, and I didn't think Dale Rutledge would be waiting for me, but I decided to check, hoping I might get it all over with quickly.

The street numbers led me to a section of the old highway that the interstate had strangled nearly to death—cracked pavement and crumbling curbs, weedy empty lots, hard dirt yards, ragged palms. In the old houses, open windows gasped for a breath of breeze. The cars at the curbs were old and primer patched. The few cars moving on the streets blasted rap drums and rock guitars and mariachi trumpets into the night. From every flat surface, graffiti in various languages sang songs of outrage.

Intimate Moments Productions occupied the darkened half of a double storefront on a corner lot. The lighted half was a movie rental shop, Videoscape. I nearly drove by; then, on the chance the businesses might be linked, I U-turned at the intersection and pulled to the curb.

The city night air held much of the heat of the day, smelled of caustic chemicals and eucalyptus. The air inside Videoscape smelled of caustic chemicals and sweat. The walls of the long room were plastered with gaudy movie posters, the floor scattered with flimsy wire shelving half-filled with black plastic video cases. Near the back, a short hall cut between two partitions marked ADULTS ONLY and EMPLOYEES ONLY.

A young woman sat on a stool behind the counter, her back to it all, her astonishingly black hair falling from between thin shoulders to a thinner waist.

As I came near, I saw that she was staring at a small silent black-and-white TV. Richard Crenna was, apparently, a marshal. Jo Ann Pflug, was, preposterously, a señorita.

Slowly the woman turned, showed me eyes even blacker than her hair, nearly all pupil.

"Sorry, *viejo*, . . . closing time."

"I'm glad I caught you then. I need some help," I said. "I'm trying to locate Dale Rutledge, from next door. I had a business appointment with him, but I got tied up."

A smile crept across her young, strong-toothed, rough-carved Indian face; her bright, blind-looking eyes couldn't stay focused on me.

"Tied . . . up. That your . . . business?"

I didn't smell marijuana, guessed barbiturates. "Figure of speech. But it's important that I get in touch with him."

"In touch?" She held out her hands. On one, L-O-V-E was crudely tattooed between the bony fingers, on the other H-A-T-E; the nails on both hands had been torn by teeth. "I got the . . . magic touch."

"Dale Rutledge," I said.

Slowly she shook her head. "Cop."

She wasn't totally gone. "Business," I said. "Money."

"Money . . . talks."

I took out my wallet, dropped a twenty on the counter. "Dale Rutledge. Business."

Her hand slowly spidered over the counter to the bill.

"Business. You got the . . . equipment for it, *viejo*? He'll like you . . . look like old what's his name . . . cowboy . . . used to stud for Liz Taylor, Lana . . . them. Star."

The hand holding the twenty-dollar bill rose, drifted in a slow arc around the roomful of posters and tapes. "I'm . . . in the business too."

"Dale Rutledge," I said slowly. "Where can I find him?"

Smiling, she stiffened her back, showed me crab-apple breasts under a worn Grateful Dead T-shirt.

"I buy . . . big boobs. You and me, *viejo*, we could be . . . hot. Big cowboy cop . . . petite Spanish princess . . . nothing but a mantilla . . . tie a bow around your nightstick. Stars."

I wasn't going to get anything from her. Still, I wasn't ready to give up. "I think I'll look around a minute."

She shook her head. "We're . . . closed."

I reached out, tapped a finger on the twenty-dollar bill. "You're open."

She looked at it, eyes like eclipsed moons. "Open . . ."

I walked toward the back of the room, to the door marked EMPLOYEES ONLY. When I turned to check, the Chicana was still looking at me, but I didn't think she actually saw me.

The knob turned under my hand, and I found and flicked on the light: metal filing cabinet, metal desk, chair, phone, adding machine, another door. A minute in the desk drawer told me that Dale Rutledge owned Videoscape, but it didn't tell me how to find him. The filing cabinet was locked. The other door wasn't.

The second office I entered was carpeted, with matching oak desk and filing cabinets; a pair of wing chairs sat before a window that opened onto a dark reception area outfitted with chairs and end tables, shadowy cardboard cutouts, obscure blown-up photographs.

I shut the door behind me, shielded the desk lamp with my body, and switched it on. Built-in wooden shelves held video cases marked with a pretty calligraphy—WRIGHT WEDDING, ASH BIRTHDAY; those in the locked glass case behind the desk bore only names. Brochures fanned across a small table, and several twine-tied packets of more brochures sat on a stack of old 16mm film cases in a corner. On the desk, an answering machine blinked.

Taking off my jacket, I draped it over the lamp, then sat behind the desk and started going through the drawers.

The first five told me that Dale Rutledge had adequate office supplies, few current projects, and many creditors. He owned not only Videoscape and Intimate Moments Productions but also the building, all of which he was trying to sell.

The last drawer was locked, briefly. The contents told me what kind of "Special Requests" Intimate Moments Productions specialized in. Each of the files contained a cover letter in which Dale Rutledge touted his credits in the "Sensuous Expression Film Industry" and offered to produce videos that transferred onto the permanence of tape the ephemeral beauty of lovers in their most cherished and intimately loving activities.

Strictly legal. Consenting adults. All orientations and pleasure styles. Absolute discretion. Fantasy costumes, props, and sets available. Taping in homes, on location, or at a private studio outside Davis.

In a file I found the address of the studio and instructions to get there. I copied them down.

As I closed the drawer, I realized that it was too heavy. I opened it again, found the false back and removed the two thick manila folders.

The first held newspaper clippings about incidents in what the media had labeled the West Coast Porn Wars. Over the previous few years, authorities from San Diego to Seattle had been finding bodies with the faces blowtorched to the bone. Each victim had been linked with the business side of the pornography industry. The blowtorch touch was a message, authorities believed, sent by what was euphemistically labelled the "traditional" distributors of hardcore films to those who had begun selling cheap video porn through ads in sleazy magazines.

The second folder suggested why Dale Rutledge was concerned about the contents of the first. The records were mostly numbers—invoices and bills—for a business called Amateur Orgies that sold films through a New Jersey distribution company. The few pieces of correspondence suggested that Rutledge had been editing and splicing some of his "Special Request" tapes into ninety-minute features.

I returned the folders to the drawer, then switched off the light and sat in the darkness.

Dale Rutledge was slime. The fact that I now had something with which to encourage him to be forthcoming about Heather McLeod should have cheered me up, but it didn't. It all left me depressed.

I punched the Play button on the answering machine.

There were three messages, three voices.

The first was male, unconvincingly apologetic, explained that J. T. Foote had received an "excitingly irresistible" offer from a "legitimate" producer and wouldn't be at the shooting.

The second voice was also male, sounded tired, angry. I hardly recognized it as my own.

The third voice was female, warm but businesslike, asking Mr. Rutledge to please call as soon as possible, leaving a number I didn't recognize.

I didn't know what to make of it. Why would Rosetta Draine try to go around me?

If that's what she was doing. Maybe she was just trying to help. But I didn't think so. I thought what I'd thought all day. Something else was going on, something that had nothing to do with Heather McLeod. Somebody else was involved in this something. And I didn't have the slightest idea what or who it was.

I reset the machine and left.

Videoscape was still brightly lit, the Chicana still perched like a scrawny stoned crow behind the counter, the movie still rolling soundlessly. Yul Brynner shot Leonard Nimoy as Richard Crenna bled against Jo Ann Pflug's heaving breast.

As she had when I'd come in, the Chicana slowly turned. "Sorry, *viejo*, . . . closing time."

"OK," I said. "Good night."

"Hey, man." She turned back to the movie. "She look . . . Spanish to you?"

"No."

"Not like . . . me." Slowly she lifted her arm, extended it toward me. Old needle scars traced her veins like a chain of flowers. "The King of Spain . . . lives in my blood."

"Why not?"

I walked to the door, opened it, released the lock, brushed my hand over the small bank of light switches, and went out, checking to make sure the door had locked behind me.

CHAPTER FIFTEEN

An hour later I was lost. I'd gotten back on I-80, over the Sacramento River, across the Yolo Causeway, into and out the back of Davis. Then it all got strange, my directions useless.

The city lights paled the darkness, turned the farmland into an eerily shadowed mechanical moonscape. Everything was straight, right-angled fields disced or furrowed and waiting for rain, rows of poplar and spruce, dry irrigation ditches. Dirt roads marked each quarter section. At the edge of the fields, rolling sprinkler racks stood like the skeletons of huge mutated insects.

Most of the scattered houses were dark; many were abandoned-dark, the homes of small farmers defeated by agribusiness. In the square sameness I quickly lost all sense of direction.

Approaching a lighted farmhouse, I decided to stop and ask for directions back to town. But as I turned onto rutted dirt, my headlights picked up the aluminum mailbox with the address I wanted stencilled in black letters.

A feeble lot light shadowed a big, newly sided barn. The old, narrow-porched white frame house leaked light. Before it, a gleaming new Jaguar and a grimy Plymouth Voyager sat in the dust.

As I pulled in, the door of the house opened around a large shadow. When it stepped into my headlights, I saw that what had once been a tall thin bearded cowboy was now a tall, swollen-gutted, meaty-featured man in a purple jumpsuit, pate gleaming through sparse hair. He pushed his paunch toward me as I got out.

"Where the hell you been! We were scheduled to shoot—" He stopped. His breath was sour with bourbon, his eyes bright with a sudden anxiety. "Who are you?"

"My name's Ross, Mr. Rutledge," I said. "I left a message on your machine that I needed to talk to you tonight."

"What message? I—" His anxiety became panic, raised his voice half an octave. "Who told you about this place?"

"Relax," I said. "I'm not interested in your business. I just need some information about a girl I'm looking for."

A slim male silhouette appeared in the doorway, pushed open the screen door, moved to the edge of the porch. Below a soft, fashionably rumpled jacket, his elegant trousers were as sharply creased as his thin, handsome, fortyish features.

"This won't do, Mr. Rutledge."

Rutledge wheeled his bulk toward the porch. "No, it's some mistake, this isn't—"

"This won't do," the man repeated curtly, staring at me. "I'm sorry, but this won't do at all. We specified young. This man is positively ancient. Totally unacceptable." He gave me a faint sharp smile. "No offense."

I gave him a positively ancient grin. "None taken."

"No," Rutledge sputtered. "This isn't J. T.! It's just some—what are you doing here?"

When a second slim male silhouette appeared in the doorway, I thought I might have a read on what was happening. The eagerly awaited J. T. Foote was apparently to be at least a prop, perhaps a participant, in tonight's film.

I decided to get rid of the two men. It wasn't difficult. "I'm a private investigator."

The man on the porch jerked as if he'd been slapped. The second silhouette materialized into another elegantly dressed man who might have been the brother, even the twin, of the first.

"I think we should be leaving now, Jerome."

"Gentlemen, please." Rutledge's voice again rose as the two men stepped off the porch. "J. T. will be here any minute now."

"I'm sorry, Mr. Rutledge, but I don't believe I'll want you to tape my parents' anniversary celebration."

"I—what?"

"I'm afraid . . ." Jerome shot a hard, sharp, superior look at me. ". . . that doing business with you would quickly cost us much more than we're prepared to pay."

The men got in the Jaguar, and the machine started with a lovely, throaty roar. Rutledge's big body slumped as he watched the car ease back into the lot, turn, and with another roar shoot forward and disappear in dust.

For a moment Rutledge breathed bourbon into the warm night air. Then he turned and breathed it at me. "Do you know how much money you just ran out of here? I ought to break your face."

His bourbon breath was more threatening than the words it carried. The quaver in his voice, the uncertainty in his glare, told me that Dale Rutledge was a small man in a big body.

"Sorry," I said. "I'm just doing my job."

"Your detective job? I have nothing to say. My attorney—"

"Ease up, Rutledge," I said. "You can videotape Elvis impersonators humping their hound dogs for all I care. I'm looking for a missing girl."

"Who?"

"Why don't we step inside and I'll tell you."

In the pale lot light his face and scalp had a greasy sheen. His fingers trembled as he made a study of pulling out a pack of Camel filters, lighting one.

Then he shrugged, forced a stiff grin. "What the hell? It's only money. And I need a drink."

I didn't buy the grin, but I followed him inside.

The living room of the old farmhouse was decorated with surprising taste—fine Navaho rugs on the worn hardwood floors, delicate maple and cherrywood furniture, Tiffany glass and old brass, an oak bar, glossy plants in beautifully glazed pots. The walls were lined with a collection of striking black-and-white photographs of nude women and stark deserts and stormy seas.

In the light I saw that Rutledge was decorated too, with rosettes of burst veins on his cheeks, booze blossoms on his fleshy nose.

"Can I get you one?"

His grin was still big, stiff. As he slipped behind the bar, he stubbed out his cigarette, reached with one hand for a half full bottle of Jim Beam. His other hand dipped behind the bar and reappeared holding a gun.

His grin became an arrogant sneer as he aimed the .22 Luger at my chest. "Don't fucking move, cowboy."

"I hadn't planned to," I said.

The Luger jerked. "Open your jacket."

"I can't. I'm not moving."

"Look, asshole—"

"I don't have a gun, if that's what worries you. Or a knife or a club or a cat-o'-nine-tails. All I've got are some questions."

His booze-ruined face went redder. "Open your jacket, wiseass, or—"

"Or what?" I smiled. "You'll shoot me, have me bleed all over this beautiful rug, because I want to ask you a question?"

The Luger jerked again. "I'm the one with the questions. Who are you? And how did you know about this place?"

"I told you," I said. "My name's Ross. I'm a private investigator from Reno. I know about this place because I'm good at what I do. And I'll tell you one more time. I have no interest in your business. I'm looking for a missing girl."

The Luger dipped slightly in his hand. "Who?"

I probably should have waited until he put down the gun. He wasn't going to shoot me, but he might have dropped the thing and put a messy hole in my shirt.

"Heather McLeod."

The color drained from his face. "I don't know any—"

"Sure you do," I said. "She left Sun Valley eighteen years ago with a man some hippies called Cyclops."

"I don't know what you're—"

"I don't want you, Rutledge. I want to know what happened to her. We can do it here, or we can go back to Reno and do it with the sheriff. But he'll want to talk about kidnapping, maybe the Mann Act, all those nice charges that have nice long statutes of limitation and nice long prison sentences. Do yourself a favor."

He was easy to bluff. Defeat settled in his watery pale blue eyes, looked comfortable there.

Shakily he set the Luger on the bar, grabbed a glass, half filled it, emptied it. I watched the booze thin his fear, waited while he dropped some ice in the glass, half filled it again.

"OK, yeah, ancient history," he said. "I knew her. I gave her a ride to L.A. A week after we got there she split."

"Split for where?"

His face set in his arrogant sneer. Dale Rutledge struck me as a man who needed to sneer, who needed to find people and ideas that he could feel superior to.

"Where else? The street. Where they all went, where they were going to get discovered by some hotshot producer or meet some rock star and live rich and famous and happily ever after."

It sounded like the truth. "You didn't look for her?"

"Why should I? It was what she wanted." He sipped again. "Besides, I had my own problems."

I didn't doubt that. "What happened to her?"

He took a quick pull from his drink, gave me the liar's confrontational stare. "I don't know."

He knew. The problem was how to get it out of him. Muscle would work, but I didn't have the heart for it. And bringing up Amateur Orgies didn't seem like a good idea; given his concern with the newspaper clippings, mention of his little side business might frighten him so much he'd actually use the Luger.

I decided to use the bottle of Jim Beam.

"Well, if you don't know, you don't know," I sighed. I took a stool at the bar, nudged the Luger with my elbow. "If you'll put that thing away, maybe I will have a drink."

He drained his glass. "I ought to run your ass out of here."

But he wouldn't. He knew it, and I knew it.

Finally, he slipped the pistol back under the bar, grabbed a glass, set it beside his own, filled both with ice and bourbon.

I took a sip of the drink. "You do the photographs?"

He nodded, sneered. "More ancient history."

"There's real talent there."

"Not that anybody gives a shit," he said. "Most people don't know enough about it to even notice."

"You that good with a movie camera?"

The look he gave me, I thought, summed him up. Arrogance and despair. "I'm an artist."

I nodded. "Tell me about Heather, Dale. I need something to give my client. Details. Your name doesn't need to come up."

"What details?"

I shrugged, waited, and slowly, as the bourbon level dropped in the bottle and rose in his blood, he began to talk. About Heather McLeod. About himself.

He'd run into her a year or so after the hippies had abandoned Beulah Valley, had hardly recognized her. Her gawky frame had fleshed out into a dynamite body, and she knew it, sauntered, posed, taunted as she half hid her not-quite-pretty face behind veils of hair.

She seemed different—not just older, but harder, angry. Her eyes, when he could see them, looked bruised and bitter, cunning and greedy. A weird chick.

She asked him for a ride home, directed him up a garbage-strewn gully in Sun Valley, gave him some dynamite dope, then dynamite head, then straddled him and rode him to orgasm.

Then she told him what she wanted. She wanted out—out of her mother's trailer, out of school, out of Sun Valley, out of Nevada. She wanted to go to L.A., and she wanted Dale Rutledge to take her there.

He laughed, until she informed him that because she was fourteen and he was twenty-five, he had just committed rape. With the dope, which she'd say was his, he'd be in jail for a long time.

He tried to laugh her off, but she told him that if he didn't want to go to jail, he had two choices: he could take her to L.A., or he could kill her.

Then she told him that if he didn't take her, she would kill him. She came, she said, from a family of killers.

He couldn't think, couldn't find a way out. All he could do was smoke more of her dope, get totally ripped.

But as was often the case, with dope came vision. His panic faded as he came to see that she was doing him a favor, forcing him to do what he should have done long before.

For his high school graduation, his parents had bought him a 16mm camera. He had lugged it to UNR, the only university he could get into, where he majored in beer busting and art-groupie coeds and dope doing and picking up hippie chicks, and he'd filmed it all, learning his craft, his art, fashioning images of the underside of student life in the late sixties and early seventies into a film that would stun the world with its savage, sensual beauty.

He managed to graduate, then took a teaching assistantship to give him time to finish his film. But it didn't get finished. It wouldn't, he had admitted to himself that night, not in Reno, not while he was surrounded by poseur and hag-fag professors who wanted to ruin his film with pedantic quibbles.

It could happen only in L.A. He should have been gone long before. Because he had talent, big talent. He had vision and style. He could discover and capture images of subtle beauty, imagine and create filmic narratives of powerful significance. He was, he knew, an artist. It was time the rest of the world knew it too.

He told Heather that he would take her to L.A. She gave him another blow job. They left two days later.

It was even fun, the trip. They had a little money and a lot of dope, they smoked and balled and made movies; he used the last of his film to get dramatic shots featuring Heather's body in the stark-ness of the desert.

The fun stopped at L.A.

How could he have known that, in the movie business, talent meant nothing, that all that mattered was who you knew or who you blew. The town was filled with cliques and gangs, assholes from the USC and UCLA film schools, networking faggots, the sullen sons of second-rate actors and the pseudointellectual daugh-ters of studio grunts. Insiders ran everything, from the mail rooms to the boardrooms.

Hollywood was a closed shop, closed to brains and talent and energy, to new ideas, to vision, to genius. In the film capital of the world, all everyone really did was look to score dope and get laid and do deals and, above all, to cover their ass. No one would see him, look at his work, give him a chance.

Heather waited a week, smoking all the dope and spending all the money on cosmetics she used to make up her face over and over again in their motel room.

After a week the money was gone, and the dope. Then Heather was gone too.

He saw her twice after that.

A few weeks later, when he too was on the street, sleeping in his pickup and living on ketchup tea, dodging faggots by night and beating on industry doors by day, he saw her one night on Sunset, in stiletto heels and pink hot pants and a string halter, separating herself from a clutch of teenage hustlers of both sexes and sliding into the backseat of a huge white Lincoln.

A few months after that, after he'd gotten a job as a gofer for a porn merchant, he'd run into her with another bunch of teenagers, scruffy and dirty. She was wired, muttering crazily, sported fresh bruises on her thighs and a livid scar on her recently broken nose. She'd asked him to get her in to see his boss. He'd told her he'd try, but he didn't.

He never saw her again.

The room had blued with his cigarette smoke, the Jim Beam bottle had nearly emptied.

I felt queasy, half sick, as if I'd ingested the ooze from Dale Rutledge's suppurating ego—the fantasies, the paranoia, the self-pity.

But he hadn't told me anything I could use.

"What do you think, Dale? Is she dead?"

Then he made a mistake. All he had to say was yes, or probably, or maybe. Instead, he sipped Jim Beam. "Who wants to know?"

I played my only other card. "That's privileged. But there's money in it. Enough for both of us."

Hope or greed or both slid into his red-veined, watery eyes. "How much?"

I shrugged. "My principals would reward anyone who can help locate her, or prove what happened to her. Reward generously."

He poured the last of the bourbon into his glass, didn't look at me. "We're talking . . . alive?"

"Either way."

His booze-flushed face had brightened with adrenaline. "I—might know somebody who might know something."

"Who?"

"Just . . . somebody. Somebody who knew her in L.A. But I'd have to check."

It might have been scam. It might have been booze fantasy. But it might not.

I nodded at the phone behind him. "Go ahead."

"Not now, not tonight," he said, suddenly uneasy. For no reason that I could perceive, he was afraid again. "I'll have to—tomorrow maybe. I—where can I find you?"

I slid off the stool. "I'll find you."

CHAPTER SIXTEEN

Dale Rutledge and his drink followed me out into the night. Around us the lights of the city dimmed the stars, pulsed like the glow of a metastasizing machine.

He started to step off the porch, then stopped.

"I don't get it. Where's the money coming from? Her mother works in the clubs, her old man's a jailbird. Nobody else would even notice she was gone. Especially after all this time."

Whatever else Dale Rutledge was, and that was plenty, he wasn't stupid. I had to give him something.

"I can tell you it has to do with the ranch in Beulah Valley. And with a real estate developer."

"You're working for a developer?" He frowned, bleary-eyed. "What's he want with that place? It's forty miles from nowhere."

"I don't know," I said, "but he knows his business."

He thought about it, nodded as he followed me over to the Wagoneer, again eager, greedy. "You think he'd be interested in film

of the place, for promotional use? I've got great stuff, lots of mountain and desert shots, the canyon, ponds, I—"

"I'll ask him," I said, opening the Wagoneer's door. Then I stopped.
"You were out there with the hippies—"

"No way, man. I wasn't with them." His face set again in his
arrogant sneer. "I didn't buy into Blake's crap. I'd just go out for the
dope and the chicks. And for my film. It was material, that's all."

His sneer turned hard, cruel. "That idiot Blake, he thought I
was documenting the birth of the New America, like I was some
kind of hippie PR hack. But it was all for my film."

"What was—"

"I got it, too. Great stuff, beautiful shots. The desert, the camp,
those dumb stoned kids. Fucking brilliant."

"What—"

"You ought to see it, see how I put it all together. Fucking brilliant. Dynamite images, a rock and folk sound track that gets more
and more ironic as everything goes to hell. Start with these chicks
naked in the iris pond, all that phony pastoral shit, finish with
Blake's VW van rolling into the pond and sinking. All intercut with
the campus stuff, the parties and hangovers and abortions, Joe and
Joan College going in the toilet. Fucking brilliant."

"What happened out there?" I asked when he paused to breathe.
"What finished it?"

The ego glaze faded from his eyes. He looked at me as if he'd
forgotten I was there.

"What always happened? The prophet decided he was really God."

His face set in his sneer. "Everything belonged to Blake—the
land, the food, the dope, the chicks. Especially the chicks. He got
like one of those mustang stallions, all the kids were supposed to
be his. Crazy bastard. The others didn't put up with it very long."

"Was Heather McLeod one of the chicks that belonged to Blake?"

He tilted his glass, dragged the back of his sleeve over his mouth.
"She wasn't supposed to be. That was part of the deal with old lady
McLeod. Nobody messed with her kid."

He almost grinned. "But somebody must have. She wouldn't talk
about anything out there, but . . ."

"But what?"

Then he did grin. "Hey, she didn't learn to give dynamite head in junior high."

I had to grip the top of the door to keep from hitting him.

I had to get out of there.

Martha Reedy stopped me. As I was sliding into the Wagoneer, I remembered the question she'd asked, the one I'd never thought of. "Why'd they pick Beulah Valley to commune in?"

He drained his drink. "When they first got there, Blake and Raven and a few others, Mrs. McLeod called the sheriff to run them off. The way I heard it, the deputy talked to them, then just drove off. I always figured Blake's family must have owned that old mining property."

Bits and pieces of the day started to settle into a pattern in the back of my mind. "Why Blake's family?"

"Hey, it was his show. And he's the only one who had any money, and he had a lot of it. He'd drive into Reno every month and pick up a check, buy supplies, score the dope."

I stared out into the city-paled night. "Ever run into any of them again?"

He shook his head. "Only this chick, Gentle. She—hey, that's how you tracked me down, isn't it? She told you."

"She told me you were in Sacramento. I did the rest," I said. "I don't suppose you know what anybody's real name was?"

"Pagan names, Blake called them," he sneered. "They never used them. The only one I ever knew was his. I saw one of his checks once. Draine. William, I think it was."

Sitting on the edge of the seat, I reached over and picked up my inscribed copy of *The Last and Greatest Dream*, opened it to the back flap, to the small, fuzzy photograph of the author. I held it up in the pale light.

Rutledge peered at it. "Let me see that."

I gave him the book, and he turned away from me, held it up to the lot light. He looked at the picture for a long time.

"I'll be a son of a bitch. A Stanford professor."

"Blake?"

He turned, handed me the book. "What about his old lady?"

"Who's she?"

But he didn't need to tell me. Suddenly I knew why Rosetta Draine had been causing me big trouble.

I'd seen her before, twenty years before, in Beulah Valley.

Fifteen minutes later I was waiting in the dark, parked on the edge of a side road a hundred yards from Rutledge's farmhouse, trying to think but mostly remembering.

I was trying to think about Dale Rutledge. He'd answered my few remaining questions, but he'd seemed antsy, as if he wanted to get rid of me. A mile down the road, I'd wondered why. I turned back, coasted to a stop on the crossroad, and waited.

And began to remember, watched a movie in my mind.

With Patsy McLeod, driving from the house up the canyon, past marshy pastures, through granite gaps, to the aspen line and the big pond, dark water frilled with thick reeds and cattails and the last late-spring flowering of the dark blue irises.

Parking, in the still chill early morning sunlight walking past the rusting floodgate crank, across the weedy face of the old earthen dam, listening to the meadowlarks singing their brief bright territorial challenge.

Following the recently worn path through the aspens up over the ridge, down into a sandy, sage- and juniper-studded drainage, past a dark empty hole in the hillside and an old tailing pile, following now not the path but the sound of bright young voices to the small grassy seep and tiny pool and camp.

Wandering through the cluster of Day-Glo-spattered tents and Day-Glo-garnished pole-and-brush lean-tos and Day-Glo-eyed young people costumed in bizarre combinations of skin and bead and bandanna and feather and leather and paisley and denim, tuxedo suitcoats and military fatigues and crocheted shawls and buckskin vests and granny glasses and aviator sunglasses and moccasins and wingtips and Keds.

Talking to them, suffering their monosyllabic psychedelic argot and sweet vapid smiles as we moved through the camp to a tent beside the seep and found the scarred girl who now called herself Gentle.

And at the edge of it all, always at the edge, the silent, watching, vaguely distracting presence of a young woman in layers of long skirts and shawls, the long dark hippie hair, the lovely skin, the face that even blurred by distance was beautiful.

Vaguely distracting because she was beautiful.

Vaguely distracting because, while she was always at the edge of it all, she was somehow also the center of it.

And I had forgotten her.

The Day-Glo-flowered VW bus hadn't been there that day. I must have seen it later.

And I wasn't sure that I'd ever seen Blake. I tried to remember, couldn't.

The other thing I couldn't do was figure out what all this meant. If anything.

Stanford Professor William Draine had once called himself Blake and led a hippie commune in Beulah Valley. So what? Most of the hippies I'd ever known were now real estate agents and shopkeepers and marketing executives and high school teachers and government bureaucrats. Most of the others were dead.

And yet . . . something was going on.

Then I thought I might be about to find out what it was. The farmhouse went dark. A large bulky shadow appeared on the porch, stepped off, got in the Plymouth Voyager. Its lights flicked on. It backed out, pulled out of the yard, turned and headed down the road, away from me.

CHAPTER SEVENTEEN

With my lights off I followed the Voyager back to Davis, then flicked them on and tailed it out onto I-80, west.

Rutledge drove with the drunk's exaggerated caution, carefully maintaining his position in a line of cars. I tucked the Wagoneer in a few cars behind him.

Like a thin sluggish river of red-flecked yellow light, I-80 flowed toward the sea, eddying at major intersections, pooling at the few small towns, trickling into bunched bare hills where it nearly died before draining into the sump of the North Bay. Then the warm darkness cooled, dampened with the breath of the Pacific.

Across the Crockett bridge, past housing tracts and shopping malls, along the bay under the hills of Richmond and Albany and Berkeley rising like light-strung Cubist bushes thick with plywood and stucco berries, and up onto the Bay Bridge.

At night, at a distance, San Francisco was beautiful, from soft dark hills its sharp geometrical skyline jutting into the city's night nimbus toward lambent wisps of fog.

As we exited into the area below Market Street, the city became less beautiful, dirty, cramped, dilapidated.

A few blocks after we turned onto Market, it became a sewer.

Concrete gulches drained waste into a litter-scummed flow between boarded-up stores and iron-grated discount joints, feebly lit groceries and neoned bars, bright porno bookstores and adult movie houses. On the sidewalks, hustlers harangued men who drifted through the yellowish mist past homeless shadows slumped on benches and homeless piles of rags in doorways.

In the light and the sparse midnight traffic, I dropped back. Then the Voyager turned onto a side street. When I reached the corner, the nearest taillight was five blocks up the hill, couldn't have been his.

Idling up the block past the gap-bulbed marquee of a porno theater, I checked the parking lots squeezed between buildings. No Voyager.

At the intersection, a flash of taillight turned a block to my right just as a set of headlights flicked on halfway up the hill ahead of me.

Other than a corner bar, only the theater was open. Playing a hunch that Rutledge was doing the California Square Dance in search of a place to park, I eased across the intersection and into the just-emptied space.

Rutledge circled the block twice. Then, after a long spell of anxiety-inducing nothing, I saw him walk around the corner from Market Street and slip inside the theater.

I locked up the Wagoneer. The damp night air smelled of sea and rot. My bootheels thumped into the dull hum of the city.

According to a pair of posters, Paradise Theater was showing *Lust Horizons* and *My Blue Heaven* and featuring Live Nude Dancers—including, a banner announced, a "Special Appearance" by the star of such adult film classics as *Naked Raunch* and the soon to be released *Hard Times,* the monomonickered Tramontane.

The lobby smelled of stale flesh and sweat and urine, was filled with scholars pursuing edification along the wall racks of books and magazines, warriors pondering the destructive capabilities of the implements in a glass case with the probably not misspelled label MARTIAL AIDS, onanists clinking quarters on their way to the Wackoffarama section of the outhouse-sized booths.

From behind the draped theater doors came the muffled tones of the rhythm of rut and a chorus of appreciative male yelps.

I didn't imagine that Rutledge was masturbating in a booth or howling in the theater. He was probably at whatever was at the top of a curved stairway. My problem was what was at the bottom—a squat, thick man with jailhouse biceps, tattoos, and stare.

I stopped at a turnstile below the skinny cashier. Under her tube top she was all skin and bone and breasts that wobbled like balloons on a stick. "Movie or quarters?"

"Browsing." The music and howls ended.

"Ten-dollar minimum."

I handed her a bill, waited for the click of the turnstile.

As I pushed through, one of the draped theater entrances opened before a thick stumble of damp-faced, red-eyed men.

Then, under a black hand the size of a shovel, the other drape jerked aside and a man who made the hand seem small moved into the lobby, holding open the curtain for a woman.

The silence in the room came so suddenly it seemed a gasp.

Under a short red silk robe, her body looked hard, strong, lithe— swoop of legs, swell of hips, bulge of breasts. Her sweat-streaked, heavily made-up face seemed carved of bone. Her hair was long, striking, the red-black of flowing lava.

Parading imperiously across the room past me and the other gawkers, she tugged all eyes to her and with her as she climbed the stairs. The mass of sharply defined black muscle in black slacks and a black T-shirt trailed her like a distorted shadow.

When she disappeared, a strange half sigh, half shudder swept through the lobby. Then the men in the room turned back to their fantasies. From the theater came the faint sound of organ music and voices in awkward artificial cadences.

I wasn't going to get past the tattooed biceps at the stairs. All I could do was wait and hope that Rutledge would show and that he wouldn't sic muscles on me when he did.

Because I had to do something while I waited, I browsed.

The first few minutes stirred a faint, involuntary sexual response in me, but it faded before the essential ugly sameness of it all. Cocks and cunts, mouths and hands, all somehow unattached to human bodies the way the forced expressions of sexual pleasure were unattached to human faces.

Under the onslaught of the images, my vision turned inward. I found myself seeing something real, the heart-shaped depression that Martha Reedy's sitting had left in the desert sand.

Even that wasn't enough. The California night caught up with me. Exhausted, depressed, I was about to give it up when from beyond the top of the stairs I heard girlish laughter.

Three young dancers dressed in various versions of very little started down the stairs. As they encountered the eyes in the lobby, their laughter died, their faces emptied.

When they reached the lobby, the tattooed chunk of muscle moved, clutched the behind of the tallest dancer. His fingers kneaded her flesh as she pulled him with her, toward the drape.

I took to the stairs, waiting for a shout that never came.

The small vestibule upstairs was empty. On the grimy, stained wallpaper, cherubs cavorted around chubby nymphs. A pair of locked doors led to the balcony, and between them the door to the projection room leaked dramatic organ tones and phony orgasmic moans. A door stood closed at each end of the hallway.

I moved to the one on my left, rapped my knuckles on it, heard nothing, opened it, found a small linoleum-floored antechamber and another pair of doors.

The one on my left was open, revealed a small makeshift dressing room of raw sheetrock lined on one side with cheap makeup mirrors and a counter littered with the gooey paraphernalia of beauty, on the other with a row of army-surplus lockers.

On the other door, a bent aluminum star hung by a nail above a smear of what had been a crude lipsticked drawing and caption that someone had tried to wipe away. The caption was illegible, but the drawing had been grotesquely female.

My rap produced an unintelligible response. I pulled open the door, leaned against its weighted wish to close.

She stood with her back to me, arms extended, lavalike hair trailing from under the white cloth that buried her head. She wore white high-heeled shoes and nothing else.

The body was a sculpture of flesh carved by iron weights and sweat, iron will and pain. As she burrowed her head and arms deeper into the cloth, muscles rippled the smooth skin the way a desert wind ripples a silent dune.

Oddly, it didn't stir me. Not a body but a thing, it seemed as unreal as her hair, with all the sensual appeal of a tattooed hula dancer flexed into sway on the biceps of a smirking sailor.

Then her head appeared, and the cloth became lovely and expensive lace and the lace became a dress, chains of white flowers swirling around small circles of nothing, and slid down her body to midthigh, covering little of what it covered.

Jerking her hair free, she half turned. "Monte, did you see what those cunts did to my door?"

She saw me, went still, her face set like a plastic mask. Her eyes were a dark, startling, angry green.

"Sorry," I said, "I didn't mean to barge in on you."

The room I'd barged into was carpeted in burgundy, painted eggshell white, and crammed with furniture too large for it—a white antiqued vanity and chair, an old cedar wardrobe, an oak-footed fainting couch with gray stains dribbling down the upholstery.

She stood unmoving in the middle of it, her angry green eyes flicking over my face like a forked tongue. "You better be a cop, asshole. Otherwise, you're fucking history."

"Sorry," I repeated, "I guess I got lost." I stepped back, and the door began to close.

"Wait a minute." She took a step forward. "Don't I—who the fuck are you?"

"My name's Ross," I said, stepping back inside.

"Vice?"

"I'm not a cop. I'm a private investigator from Reno." The door clicked shut behind me.

"Reno," she said slowly. Her face softened, and her voice. "Long way from home, cowboy. Big night in the big city?"

"Not so big. But long."

Her fingers were tipped with nails painted the lavalike color of her hair. With them she smoothed the lace at her hips, then arched her back and tugged the cloth taut over her breasts. The movement of her body under the dress created the illusion that the lace was shadow, that she wore nothing.

The performance was private, all for my benefit, although I couldn't imagine why. "You like this?"

"It's terrific. Tramontane your real name?"

"Like the wind, cowboy—hot." Her voice dropped into her throat, but not in seduction. She was taunting me, showing me what I could never have.

"You mosey on over the mountain, thought you'd come to my room and do a little private investigating?"

"I was looking for a man I thought came up here."

"A man. And you thought you'd see a free show? A little private action? You some kind of fucking Nevada hick freak?"

I didn't know what I was. But I knew what she was. She was a hard, tough, thoroughly nasty piece of work.

"Sorry to have troubled you."

But she wasn't finished with me. "Wait a minute. What man?"

Without her stage makeup her face was oddly beautiful—full wide mouth, bright white teeth, hollow cheeks under high bones, smooth-lined Nordic nose, startling green eyes. Oddly beautiful, for the individual features didn't quite fit together.

"His name is Rutledge."

"Dale Rutledge?" She spat the name. "What do you want with that drunken piece of shit?"

She knew him well enough to describe him. I wondered if I might have managed to dumb luck my way right around Rutledge.

"He told me he might know someone who might know something about a missing girl I've been hired to look for. I followed him here. I don't suppose he was coming to see you?"

She watched me the way a scaly coil watches a bit of desert fur. "What girl?"

"Her name is, or was, Heather McLeod. She ran away from Reno with Dale Rutledge eighteen years ago."

I might have seen a reaction in her eyes. Or not.

She turned, tapped a cigarette from a pack of Virginia Slims on the vanity, lit it with a gold lighter, shot dragony streams of smoke from her nostrils, then made the same mistake Dale Rutledge had.

"Who's looking for her?"

"I'm sorry," I said, "but I'm not at liberty to say."

She turned, stared into the vanity mirror. But she didn't seem to be looking at what it reflected, the oddly beautiful face, the body created by will and iron. She had the slightly lost look of someone gazing inward, and back.

She sucked in more smoke, spoke quietly. "I knew her, the stupid bitch."

"Heather?"

She turned on me. "Who the fuck are we talking about, anyhow, Hilary fucking Clinton? Big, ugly, stupid Heather McLeod! In L.A. She thought she was going to be a movie star. She was going to light up the silver screen, put Marilyn Monroe out of work, live in Beverly Hills, shop on Rodeo Drive. Dumb cunt."

Her anger was sudden, fierce—too fierce. I wondered if she might have been describing her own teenage fantasies as well as Heather McLeod's. And saying something else.

"She was your friend," I said.

Her wide mouth tightened as she tried to shrug that off.

"You cared about her."

"Dumb fucking Heather," she said slowly, in confirmation.

"What happened to her?"

She stabbed out the cigarette, fumbled with the pack, lit another, didn't look at me. "What difference does it make?"

"It makes a difference to some people in Nevada."

Her smile was angry, ugly. "There was nobody in Nevada she gave a shit about, except her brother, and he's dead. And it's a little late to be worrying about Heather McLeod now, isn't it?"

Again, I had the sense that she was talking about herself as well as about Heather McLeod.

"Why are you looking for her now, anyhow?"

Without really deciding to, I told her the truth. "Heather's mother hired me to find her when she ran away. I couldn't. Now she wants me to try again. She has dreams about her. Bad dreams."

"Bad dreams," she echoed. "Don't we fucking all."

She looked again into the mirror, her gaze probing her reflection as if she were searching for something—maybe for the girl she had been before she became Tramontane.

Or maybe not. Maybe I was projecting, trying to make her human. Being sentimental. Old-fashioned.

Then abruptly she turned to face me. Her smile was angry and ugly and perverse.

"You want to let her mother know what happened to Heather? She can see it for herself."

"See it? How?"

Her laugh was as perverse as her smile. "*X-Out 69.*"

"What—"

"Go find the sickest motherfuckers around, get a copy, take it back to Reno, show it to her dear old mother with the bad dreams. Let her watch what happened to her daughter."

Nausea gurgled in my throat. "We're talking about a movie, a film?"

"A special film." Suddenly she laughed again. "The great artist's first fucking film."

"Dale Rutledge made this film?"

"And stupid fucking Heather got what she'd been dreaming about all her life. She got in the movies. Her first, and her last. A starring role."

"Heather was in a . . ." I couldn't say it.

She could. "Right. A snuff film."

CHAPTER EIGHTEEN

"What's the matter, Ross? You don't look so hot."

I was trying to take in what she'd said without puking it back out. The obvious pleasure she took in my reaction made keeping my gorge down even more difficult.

Behind me I heard the outer door open, heard the hard clack of heels on the linoleum over the hard clack of young female voices, heard a door slam. Then the door behind me opened. I turned and found myself staring into eyes like the business end of a double-barreled shotgun.

The big black man smiled at me the way a wrecking-ball operator might smile at an old brick building. "Problem?"

"It's all right, Monte," Tramontane said. "Did Cleve get here yet?"

At his nod, she said, "Come on, Ross. Let's meet the Man."

Like Tramontane's, Monte's body had been sculpted by iron. But I didn't think he was a muscle-bound bodybuilder. I thought he was a pro.

He looked at me. His faint shrug suggested that he was just doing his job, his faint smile hinted that my body would appreciate it if I did as I was told.

Tramontane trailed her fingernails across Monte's chest as she stepped past him into the hall. I followed her. The movement of her body under the dress deepened my nausea. The silence behind me deepened my concern.

She pushed open the office door. From a chair before the big desk, Dale Rutledge looked up, startled, frightened. From a chair behind the desk, the man I assumed was the Man looked up with a small, kind-eyed smile.

He was older than I'd expected, a pudgily unprepossessing sixty or more. Damp-looking silver hair brushed close to his skull, smooth pink jowls, expensive chocolate-colored suit, pale green shirt. The large emerald in his brown tie matched the one on his plump finger, nearly matched Tramontane's eyes.

Tramontane sauntered around the desk, slipped behind the chair, draped an arm over its back, a hand over his shoulder. She smiled at me in angry amused anticipation.

The man avuncularly patted her hand with his emerald, then looked at Dale Rutledge.

"Is this the detective you were talking about?"

Rutledge swallowed, nodded. He looked worse than I felt—sick, terrified. Dark damp rings spread down the purple jumpsuit from under his arms.

"And you brought him to me."

"Mr. Culler, I didn't . . ."

"And now you've told him my name."

Rutledge's mouth opened, but nothing came out. He looked as dead as the women striking provocative poses in the adult movie posters that lined the walls. Three of the women, the posters announced in large letters, were TRAMONTANE. They didn't quite look like her. They didn't quite look like each other.

Culler looked at me, asked quietly, "What do you want?"

"He wants a copy of Dale's first masterpiece," Tramontane said with her angry smile. "He wants to take it back to Reno to show it to the star's mommy."

Rutledge paled even more, his watery eyes nearly glazing.

Culler's voice, his eyes didn't change. "That isn't what Dale said. He said you're working for a developer over in Nevada, that your interest is an old ranch and a lot of money. Which is it?"

I looked at him, trying to decide how to play it, trying to read him, the soft pleasant voice, the benign brown eyes.

He gave me a small pleasant smile, glanced past me.

The blow hammered into my kidneys, drove the air from my lungs, arched my body into a gasping bow. A stunning dull pain burst above my ear, spun me sinking into the thick flash of black handedge. A sharp pain shrieked from the broken bridge of my nose into my eyes.

I was on the floor, on my knees, gasping for breath between dry and violent retching, fighting the pain.

Through it I heard voices, an angry woman's, a frightened man's.

Gradually my body stilled.

Monte stepped in front of me, grabbed my jacket in his huge hands and lifted me to my feet. Through the flesh swelling around my eyes I watched him wipe blood from his hand onto my sleeve. My blood. He stepped aside.

Dale Rutledge was looking at me as if he were seeing his worst nightmare.

Tramontane was smiling with angry pleasure.

Culler was smiling pleasantly. "Which is it?"

It wasn't the pain that did it—the rage between my eyes, the throb of my kidneys, the fire above my ear. It was all of it, the darkness and light, the sickness and anger of the California night.

"Fuck you."

Culler glanced at the black man, and I tensed, waited.

Monte looked at me, then shrugged. "He's a Timex."

Culler smiled his small pleasant smile. "Monte's afraid he'd kill you."

I looked into the shotgun-barrel eyes. "Probably. But at least we'll do it face-to-face this time."

The black man smiled a sort of acknowledgment.

"That's not a problem, killing you," Culler continued, "but it wouldn't get me what I want. But we could trade. You answer my question and I'll let you stay alive."

"Fuck you."

He looked at me with something resembling interest. "You really don't care one way or the other, do you?"

"He wants the film," Tramontane said angrily. "Ask him."

Culler patted her hand. "If that's the case, then our friend Dale here hasn't been telling me the truth."

"Mr. Culler, I—"

"We have a special treat for him."

I looked at Rutledge. He seemed all eyes—red-veined, dead-pupiled eyes that floated in a sticky pool of pleading tears. Pleading with me, pleading for his life.

At that moment I hated Dale Rutledge and his pleading eyes more than I'd ever hated anyone or anything in my life.

"I want the film," I said slowly. "And the answer to your question is both."

"What does the one have to do with the other?"

"Not much." Through the taste of blood, I sketched the situation with the ranch—Desert Conservancy, Nolan Turner, the search for Heather McLeod.

Tramontane had angrily turned to the window, stared out into the darkness lit by the yellow bulbs of the theater marquee.

"So if the McLeod girl was alive," Culler said, "the ranch property would go to her. But what makes it worth anything?"

"It *isn't* worth anything," I said. "At least not enough to fight over." I described Nolan Turner's map, and his comments.

He nodded. "Something's missing here."

"I think so too," I said, tasting my blood, testing my pain. "But I don't know what it is."

"Why didn't you tell me this when I asked you?"

"Because it was none of your business."

He smiled at me, again with something resembling interest. "You're a confused man, Mr. Ross. You take one beating, ask for another, then waste the effort on a man like Dale Rutledge."

I tried to shrug, couldn't.

He smiled his pleasant smile. "I wonder if you know what you saved? Did Dale tell you what a great artist he is?"

"At length."

His smile brightened. "So great an artist he couldn't even shoot skin flicks, kept fancying them up with 'aesthetic significance' that nobody gave a shit about until he couldn't get hired to film a dog show. Did he tell you what a genius businessman he is, how he's going to save the adult film industry?"

"No."

"Oh, you need to hear this. Our auteur here wants to make big-budget productions, expensive actors, sets, everything. Wants to make artistic porn that men and women, lovers, husbands and wives will pay a fortune to watch together, even with their children, in the comfort of their own homes." His eyes twinkled kindly, his voice softened even more. "Family fucking porn."

I didn't say anything.

He turned his smile on Rutledge. "Did he tell you that he's so desperate for money to finance his family fucking porn that he makes cheap videos that cut into my business?"

This was, I realized, a performance not for my benefit. I was just an extra. The intended audience was Dale Rutledge.

And he was at the edge. His purple jumpsuit clung damply to his chest and gut and crotch, his eyes jerked wildly.

"If you knew that for a fact," I said, "he'd be out in the hills with his face under a propane torch."

"He denies it," Culler said softly, "but he does it. And we'll know, for a fact, soon enough."

That, I thought, was probably true.

Then the California night got worse.

"I wonder if you'd still want to save him if you knew what he did to the girl you're looking for," Culler said.

I didn't look at Rutledge. "What did he do?"

"He wanted to get into the movie business so bad he made a film of this girl, the only kind of film he knew he could sell. The film ends when she takes a bullet in the brain just as the man she's blowing comes all over her face. It's real artistic."

I didn't, couldn't, look at Rutledge. "If I knew that for a fact, he'd be in the hills with his face under a propane torch."

Tramontane turned away from the window. She was still angry. Angrier. "Let him have it, Cleve."

For a moment I thought she was telling Culler to kill me.

He smiled. "Tomorrow. You can pick it up downstairs, with my compliments."

I connected, finally. "The film?"

He smiled. "I imagine you can pick up a propane torch on your own."

It took me a minute to realize that it was over, that he was telling me to go. I turned toward the door, heard him say my name, turned back.

"Take the garbage out with you."

I ached my way out of the office. Movement freshened my pain, fighting it left me woozy. Vaguely aware that Rutledge was behind me, I bled and wobbled down the stairs, stumbled past the stares in the lobby and out onto the sidewalk.

The cool night air helped clear my head, sharpened the pain. Sucking in deep, damp gulps, I felt Dale Rutledge at my elbow.

"Ross, I didn't . . . it isn't like he—"

"Run."

"I—what?"

I turned, looked at him. I had to clamp my jaws tight to keep from screaming at him. "Run. Now."

He looked at me. Then he ran. And saved his life.

Three hours and a bunch of Patsy McLeod's thousand dollars later, I walked out of the emergency ward of the Herrick Hospital in Berkeley.

My face was clean of blood, my nose set and taped. The bone was cracked, the resident had told me, but should knit well and leave only a small lump. I'd notice blood in my urine for a while. When she'd asked what had happened, I'd told her I'd fallen down a mountain.

Behind the Berkeley hills, the stars were fading, the night ending. Dopey with pain pills and exhaustion, I couldn't remember why I'd come to Berkeley, but I knew I'd known I had to get there before I got treated or I wouldn't be able to get there at all.

But somewhere in my confused brain I did remember. As the night became dawn, I found myself parking in front of a small white stucco house a few blocks off Shattuck, behind a small black Geo.

I didn't want to wake her. Not that it mattered, since I knew I didn't have the energy to get out of the Wagoneer anyway. All I wanted to do was sleep. Easing my head back, I closed my eyes, worked to breathe evenly through my mouth.

But sleep didn't come. What came were images of the night, ugly, angry, in the swirling, shifting confusion of nightmare.

An Indian-faced, crab-apple-breasted young Chicana with the blood of the King of Spain in her veins coupling with a bloated, balding pornographer in a sweat-stained purple jumpsuit.

A sharp handsome face informing a pair of shotgun-barrel eyes that I was positively ancient.

A beautiful woman in a red silk blouse explaining to a benign-eyed man that I was really just old-fashioned.

A tall thin bearded cowboy aiming a propane torch at a distant beautiful hippie girl.

A lava-haired woman whose iron features didn't quite fit suffering the globular splatter of male orgasm as a small hole appeared in her forehead and the back of her head exploded.

Finally, mercifully, it all faded into near darkness, from which arose another image.

A room that a real family lived in, a family that should have been mine, a sleeping old dog and a trio of bright happy children and a gruff loving mother. A wife.

But there was no wife.

On the couch, at the center of it all, there was only a shadowy absence, a faceless female form, an emptiness to be filled.

The image began to fade, slowly tried to transform itself into a heart-shaped depression in the desert sand.

CHAPTER NINETEEN

Alone in a cave in the desert, I listened to the drought-ending rain. A bird sang against the faint rumble of far-off thunder as I watched the pale light throw obscure shadows on the wall. Somehow the shadows were messages, but I couldn't read them, didn't know who was sending them or if they were for me.

The rain began to fall more heavily, loudly, but oddly the light went brighter, the shadows thinner, until the sounds registered in a different reality: the rain became the shush of tires on pavement, the birdsong a fanbelt squeal, the faint thunder the low mumble of engines. Doors thunked shut, voices murmured, shoe soles scraped concrete.

Tugging open my eyes, I winced against the glare, gingerly fingered the swollen flesh under the tape on my nose and around my eyes. My head ached, and my kidneys; my mouth felt furry, my face gooey and scratched with beard, my hair stiff. I could feel the rankness the night had left on my body.

Still, the rest had helped. I wasn't exactly invigorated, but I felt better than I had any reason to expect.

Crawling out of the Wagoneer, I stretched the stiffness from my shoulders and back as I looked around.

The old residential neighborhood was one of the few in Berkeley that hadn't changed much, a quiet enclave of narrow, slightly slanting streets lined with small old middle-income family homes behind tiny front yards littered with the spoor of children and edged with neatly trimmed bushes under mature trees.

A huge old fir leaned against a corner of Martha Reedy's white stucco house, shaded most of the small, half-walled entry porch and all of the two women who sat watching me.

The brick walk was lined with the drooping heads of blue and white Lily-of-the-Nile in full and beautiful flower. I started up it, tucking in the tail of my bloody shirt.

At the step I stopped. "Morning."

"You're amazingly perceptive."

Her pale brown eyes danced with an arch amusement, and something else; whatever it was, it wasn't what I'd expected.

"But then you're a trained investigator."

"After the last twenty-four hours, there might be reason to doubt that," I said.

Her face was damp, heat-flushed. Sweat beaded becomingly at her hairline, dampened her Cal T-shirt at the throat and between and below the slow rise and fall of her breasts, stained the waist of her running shorts.

As I looked at her, something old, long still, nearly forgotten, slowly stirred somewhere inside me.

"You look like the Lone Ranger after a long weekend."

Realizing that I must be sporting a nifty pair of shiners. I started to grin, then ran into the other woman's glare.

A graying fifty, small and thin, she too had been running, in shorts and a Mills College sweatshirt that she didn't seem to have sweated into. Still she seemed exhausted, somehow seemed as if she had been exhausted for a long time.

I looked back at Martha Reedy. "I wonder if we could talk."

The other woman spoke as if through clenched teeth. "You don't need to do this, Marty."

Martha Reedy patted the woman's hand. "It's all right."

The low round wrought-iron table the two women sat at held a half pitcher of orange juice and two glasses, a thermal coffeepot and two thick ceramic mugs, a plate of muffin crumbs and a few cubes of melon. Martha Reedy nodded at a third chair.

As I stepped onto the porch, the other woman got up and placed her hand on Martha Reedy's shoulder.

"Hannah," Martha Reedy said, "this is Mr. Ross. Mr. Ross, this is my . . . friend, Ms. Fielding."

I held out my hand. "Nice to meet you, Ms. Fielding."

Her hand remained on Martha Reedy's shoulder. I looked at her hand, at her glare, then at Martha Reedy, and I understood.

Her use of the word "friend" had been another shibboleth, this one identifying not our similarity but our difference. My own hand dropped, as did my spirits. Whatever had been stirring to life inside me stilled.

Hannah Fielding stared me into the chair, then patted the shoulder under her hand. "I'll be inside, if you need me."

"Could you bring Mr. Ross a cup, Hannah, and a glass? He looks like he's a few quarts below the add mark."

When the screen door shut sharply, I grinned. "Thanks."

"Code of Berkeley."

"Your . . . friend doesn't seem bound by it."

"She's got you confused with someone else."

She was joking, I knew, parodying our conversation of the day before, but I didn't quite get it.

Hannah Fielding pushed through the screen door. The mug and glass clicked sharply against the iron table. Her glare was eloquent. Then she went back inside.

As I poured orange juice, Martha Reedy said, "You wanted to talk about Heather McLeod, I assume."

"Among other things. Heather's dead, Martha."

She didn't say anything. I drank the orange juice; cold, pulpy, it cleaned the grime from my palette. Then I started talking.

I went back twenty years, told her about finding the girl who called herself Gentle at the hippie camp in Beulah Valley. And about not finding Heather McLeod two years later, about the bearded cowboy and Patsy McLeod and what I'd made of it.

I told her about my conversation with Nolan Turner, about my uncertainties and suspicions.

Then I told her about the nightmare night I'd just spent and what I'd learned from a pornographer manqué and an adult film star, told her how I'd managed to get myself whipped in about ten seconds, told her about my conversation with an X-rated entrepreneur and about what he was giving me.

She drank her coffee and listened. When I finished, she was about to speak when the screen door opened again.

Her short hair feathered into wings that framed a face still exhausted looking but now also softened into a kind of gray attractiveness, Hannah Fielding wore no makeup, small blue enamel earrings, a light brown suit over a blue blouse, black flat shoes made of tightly woven wicker. A NO MOO BY 92 sticker blazed her cloth attaché case; on her gym bag, buttons urged the preservation of spotted owls and whales and dolphins.

She bent, kissed the top of Martha Reedy's head, patted her shoulder.

I rose. "It was nice to meet you, Ms. Fielding."

Her glare was fierce, as if she were trying with her eyes to drive me off the porch. Then she patted Martha Reedy's shoulder once more. "See you later, dear. Be careful."

We watched her stride down the walk, then down the street.

"Ms. Fielding doesn't seem to care for me."

"She worries about me," Martha Reedy said. "She worries about what I have to do sometimes to do my job, and the kind of people I have to deal with."

I rubbed a hand over my bristly chin, down my bloodstained shirt. "I can see why I might not have favorably impressed her. I— have you . . . been together long?"

She looked at me. Then, slowly, she gave me the smile that opened her face like a flower, even as she seemed somehow to hide behind it.

"Long enough."

Not plain, not pretty, Martha Reedy was actually, I began to see, lovely. Her features fit into a face that was like nothing other than itself. As with the desert, with Martha Reedy you had to know how to look to see what was really there.

But whatever was there, clearly it wasn't there for me.

"So what do you think?" I asked.

She shifted in her chair, reached for her coffee cup.

"I'd already accepted that you work for Patsy McLeod and that her only interest is in learning the fate of her daughter. As for the idea that someone other than Nolan Turner wants the McLeod property, that's possible. The rest of it, about the hippies and the Draines, is interesting but irrelevant."

I'd pretty much concluded that myself.

"And what Rutledge told you about Heather's disappearance may be true, but . . ."

She tilted her cup, emptied it, set it back on the table. "Heather McLeod wasn't killed eighteen years ago, or any other time. I talked to her on the phone last night. I'm meeting her in Oakland in an hour or so."

The sounds of the city whispered incoherently in my ear.

"The film they told you about is a simulation, Jack, a fake. Most snuff films are. They ran a con on a country boy. Rutledge knew about the fake film, because he made it. He thought he saw a way to get some money out of it. The rest worked itself out."

It didn't fit. "Tramontane told me about it first."

"If she was a friend of Heather's, she would know about it."

It still didn't fit. "But why would she want me to believe it was real?"

"Probably because she saw it upset you."

I remembered Tramontane's pleasure at my reaction. "Why?"

"Because you're a man."

It finally fit, made a sick sort of sense. "But Culler—he wanted to know about the deal for the ranch."

"He would," she said, her voice hardening. "Cleveland Culler has a dirty finger in every vicious pie in the Bay Area—drugs, prostitution, burglary, extortion, hijacking, murder for hire—and he pumps his money into legitimate business deals all over the West. If he thought he could launder cash through the McLeod ranch, he'd jump at the chance."

I couldn't argue with that. But I couldn't quite accept it either.

It wasn't that simple.

"What about Linus Flowers?"

She shrugged. "What about him? I appreciate your warning, but he hasn't shown up, and somehow I don't think he will."

I shook my head. "He will. Linus Flowers isn't just a thug, Martha. He's a tough, smart sociopath. He hurts people, and he's killed a couple the authorities know about but can't prove and probably a bunch they don't know about. He's in this, and he'll be back."

"He'd better hurry, then," she said. "It's almost over."

"If you found Heather, it is."

She didn't quite smile. "Does that trouble you? That I'm the one who tracked her down and not you?"

"No. Patsy McLeod won't care who found her, and Patsy's the only one I care about in all this. But I'd be interested to know how you managed it."

She smiled. "I'm a trained investigator."

She was enjoying herself, but I didn't think that this time it was at my expense.

"I don't suppose you'd want company when you meet her?"

She stopped smiling, shook her head. "I said I'd be alone."

"I don't suppose you'd mind telling her that her mother loves her and misses her and wants her to come home?"

"I'll be happy to do that." She pushed back her chair and rose. "But I won't be able to if I don't get out of here."

She picked up the empty cups and glasses and set them on the plate. I got to my feet. "Let me help you with those."

"I can handle it," she said quickly, evenly. "I'll be gone a couple of hours, but I'll be happy to tell you about it, so you can tell Ms. McLeod. How can I get in touch with you?"

I hadn't thought about it. But there really wasn't much to think about. "I guess I'll get a motel room, clean myself up. I could meet you back here."

She shook her head. "It's Saturday, big game day, Cal–Stanford. You won't find a motel room this side of Vallejo."

I shrugged, found myself noticing how healthy and attractive she looked in her cutoff jeans and damp T-shirt, wished I felt as good as she looked.

"Maybe I'll go for a run."

She laughed, shaking her head. "You wouldn't get a mile."

"True," I said, "but it would take me two or three hours."

She laughed again. "I'm beginning to understand why you think everybody's crazy. You think everybody's like you."

"God forbid." As she turned to the door, I said, "Martha, there's something I don't understand. Yesterday you drove off thinking I was some kind of corrupt macho reactionary idiot. My message about Flowers couldn't have been enough to change your mind."

She gave me a look I couldn't read. "One of the problems with men like you, Jack, is that you think you know what women think."

There wasn't much I could say to that.

"But in this case, you're reasonably close. When I got back last evening, I was convinced that you were a renegade lawyer at best, maybe a hired goon. Hannah thought we should find out for sure. She's an attorney, and she's worked with a lot of lawyers and agency people in Nevada, so she called some of them."

I nodded. "It's always nice to learn that people think well of you."

"Some people. They said you were honest and intelligent, Stanford Law, et cetera. But other people told her stories."

I could imagine—the same kind of Nevada noir story Nolan Turner had recounted. "What made her decide I was all right?"

"Hannah? Oh, she didn't. She thinks you're a corrupt macho reactionary idiot, and probably dangerous."

"But you don't?"

She smiled her wonderful smile.

"It was a little thing. Hannah was sure she'd heard your name before, in connection with Desert Conservancy. She thought maybe you'd been involved in trying to wreck another purchase, so she checked the files. She found your name, but not where she thought she would. Jack Ross has been giving money to Desert Conservancy for years."

"That doesn't necessarily mean anything," I said. "Serial killers tithe. Rapists support the symphony."

"So Hannah told me."

"So why don't you . . . ?"

"What's the matter, Jack? You don't want the world to know that under that hard-boiled Nevada exterior there beats a Stanford bleeding heart?"

CHAPTER TWENTY

I managed to change into jogging togs without scandalizing the neighborhood, then stretched, stuffed my keys and wallet in the pocket of my cutoff jeans, and shuffled off.

It was the stupidest idea I'd ever had. I'd dry-swallowed a couple of pills the doctor had given me, but they didn't do much against the pain that jackhammered between my eyes with every step.

I grimaced my way up toward UCB, forcing my legs to move, thinking of nothing but forcing my legs to move and breathing and pain. But once I was on campus, in the shade of the huge eucalyptus and fir, my muscles warmed up and the pain pills kicked in and I began to notice and to enjoy things—old stone buildings, old wooden benches under old trees, old walk bridges over tiny rock-bottomed drainages, old grassy flower-bordered quads.

I also enjoyed the stern scowls and occasional grins of the few Saturday students who did a double take at my T-shirt—in the center was a yellow smiley face with x'd-out eyes and a trickle of blood oozing from a bullet hole in its forehead.

I came out below Memorial Stadium, jogged past early-bird football fans and tailgate parties, then turned downhill and slowly zig-zagged my way toward Oakland and the bay.

Gradually the neighborhoods changed, from family homes to rentals mixed with small retail outfits and home businesses, then to near-slum shacks and warehouses. The trees went from leafy to stunted, the cars from gleam to junk. The elevation and the economic level decreased in inverse proportion to the pigmentation in the skin and the hopeless anger in the eyes of the people on the streets. Contemporary American Sociology 101.

Tiring, I turned and headed back toward University Avenue, stopped thinking about the things I saw and, slowly, stopped really seeing them. I began to feel strong, clean, healthy, free. I wasn't really aware that I was running. I was aware only that I was alive and that life was good.

A playfully insistent horn honk brought me out of it. In the Geo, Martha shook her head at me as she crossed Shattuck and headed down the hill.

I stopped and watched her until the Geo disappeared in the traffic. Then I started to jog again. I got halfway across the intersection before my body told me that the run was finished.

I didn't mind. I was surprised at how far I'd managed to get, at how good I felt. The morning was heating up, but I was comfortable, sweating lightly, breathing easily—especially for an old-fashioned, positively ancient private detective who'd gotten himself whipped in about ten seconds the night before.

Nearly flatulent with vanity, I was stepping onto the curb when something large and white slid into my consciousness.

By the time I realized what I'd seen, the Chrysler with Nevada plates was beating a red light a block away.

My runner's high vanished in a wash of anger and concern. Martha Reedy could take care of herself, but I didn't think she could take care of Linus Flowers, especially if she didn't know he was behind her. And there was no way I could tell her.

I hauled my suddenly foul mood up University, turned down Telegraph. The game-day sidewalk was packed with people, most dressed in what seemed to be Homeless Chic—army surplus drab and thrift store tattered, all self-consciously and profoundly PC. I couldn't tell the hang-on hippies from the artsy-craftsy vendors or the students from the panhandlers or the hard hustlers from the real homeless. That, I sourly assumed, was the point.

In the middle of it all, middle-aged alums in their sporty affluence looked on with the uneasily earnest approbation of liberal guilt.

Then I felt a twinge of guilt myself. Who was I to tell them what to wear, what to think? What the hell did a broken-nosed, black-eyed, corrupt macho reactionary Nevada idiot wearing a murdered smiley face over his Stanford bleeding heart know about anything?

I was so smart I didn't even know what the case I'd been working on for more than twenty-four hours was really about. I was so smart I'd spent the previous day weaving romantic yearnings around the image of a heart-shaped depression left in the desert sand by a lesbian.

My mood fouling even more, I got off Telegraph as quickly as I could, then slogged my way back to Martha Reedy's house. Martha Reedy and Hannah Fielding's house.

Naturally, I had a parking ticket.

I slipped it from under the wiper blade, felt its odd weight, then noticed that it was a ticket Martha Reedy hadn't paid yet. When I opened it, I found a key.

After I'd stretched, I moved up onto the porch and sat for a while, looking at the key. Finally I slipped it back inside the ticket and left the ticket on the table.

The patron saint of Nevadans—Luck—was watching over me.

As I drove down University, an overloaded Buick towed a U-Haul trailer out of a motel parking lot. I pulled in and managed to convince the clerk to rent me the vacated room before it was cleaned. Forty-five minutes later, I was showered, shampooed, and shaved, in clean jeans and shirt and hiding my shiners behind sunglasses. I was also easing the Wagoneer into the heavy stream of traffic on I-80.

In the bright sunlight, at a distance, San Francisco was beautiful, the beautiful city built by silver stolen from Nevada, silver for which Comstock tycoons had torn up the Nevada landscape and destroyed the Nevada forests.

My mood was still foul.

132

The area below Market was busy, but in the daylight it didn't seem so dirty and dilapidated. Market Street was thick with tourists and conventioneers, shopping and queuing up for the cable cars that would take them and their money to Chinatown and North Beach.

At the Paradise Theater I said the hell with it, popped on my emergency flashers and double-parked. The banner announcing the appearance of Tramontane had been taken down. I thought they should replace it with one reading ABANDON ALL HOPE, YE WHO ENTER HERE.

The lobby smelled the same, seemed filled with the same gray-faced men pursuing the same weary fantasies. The cashier was different, a husky blonde pounds and years past the baby face painted over her pulpy features. She said the same thing: "Movie or quarters."

"My name's Ross. Mr. Culler left something for me."

She reached under the counter, handed me a small paper sack.

"Thank you," I said.

"Fucking geek," she said.

Traffic behind the Wagoneer was backed up around the corner. In the first car, a red-faced man shouted obscenities at me as the woman beside him flipped me off.

A half hour later I was back in Berkeley, wondering what to do. I could rent a video player, but I didn't want to watch Dale Rutledge's first opus until and unless I absolutely had to. And if I went back to the motel room, I'd sleep, probably for days.

Instead, I drove in a fast-food circle, got a giant cup of coffee, and went back toward Martha Reedy's. And Hannah Fielding's. Sipping the coffee, I cruised the neighborhood trying to find where Linus Flowers might have been staked out. I couldn't.

But I did, maybe, fit something together. Maybe. Linus Flowers had been a Washoe County deputy twenty years before. Twenty years before, a deputy sheriff had been to the hippie camp in Beulah Valley. Maybe that deputy was Linus Flowers.

Maybe. And if so, so what? I didn't know. Maybe I was getting to be like Royce McLeod, fixated on hippies.

Back at Martha Reedy and Hannah Fielding's house, I sat on the porch and drank my coffee and thought about it. And worried.

The Geo pulled in behind my Wagoneer a half hour later.

As Martha started up the flower-lined walkway, I could see that she was upset. She stepped onto the porch, her mouth a stiff line, her eyes a troubled pale brown swirl.

As she reached into her purse, I held out the parking ticket. Tight-lipped, she jerked it out of my hand, slid out the key, opened the door, stepped inside.

She came out onto the porch five minutes later, a bottle of beer in each hand. She held one out to me. "You didn't use the key."

"JDFR." Just Didn't Feel Right.

"Why not?"

I shrugged. "Anyhow, I got lucky and found a motel room."

She gave me a long odd look, then sank into one of the chairs. I pulled up a chair across from her. "Heather McLeod. Bad?"

"She'll sell the ranch to Desert Conservancy. She'll sell it to the devil. But whatever she gets will go to her suppliers."

"Coke?"

She wiped the beer bottle on the sleeve of her 49er jersey. "Everything, I'd guess. There probably isn't a chemical substance devised by man that hasn't found its way into her system."

Given what Rutledge had told me, it could fit. "There's no question of identity. It's the right Heather McLeod?"

She nodded, depressed. "I'd told her to bring her birth certificate. Reno, Washoe County, Nevada, thirty-two years ago."

I took out the eighteen-year-old school portrait of Heather McLeod and dropped it on the table.

"I've got the same one. She's changed a lot," Martha said softly, an ache in her voice. "She looks sixty, Jack. She looks like she's been beaten half to death every day of her life."

After a minute, I asked, "What did she say about seeing, or calling, her mother?"

Martha sighed. "Maybe, after she got the money, and got straightened up. But Mrs. McLeod better not hold her breath. Heather— I couldn't get much out of her except her address, but it was clear that the only thing she cares about is the money."

If Martha was this depressed over the Heather McLeod she'd found, I didn't want to think about how Patsy was going to feel.

Distractedly she scraped the label off the bottle with her thumbnail. Something else was bothering her.

"What, Martha?"

She glanced at me, then out into the quiet street. "JDFR."

"How did you leave it?"

"I gave her some money to clean up with, and I'm going to pick her up Monday morning and take her to see Hannah and sign some intent papers for Desert Conservancy."

I watched her for a while. Then I smiled. "No you're not. You're going to hop in your car and drive back to Oakland and figure out what's bothering you. And I'm going along."

After a moment, she smiled faintly. "How did you know?"

I grinned. "It takes one to know one, Martha."

I squeezed myself into the Geo. By the time I had adjusted the seat so my knees weren't banging my nose and the seatbelt so I wasn't being strangled, we had crossed into Oakland.

By the time we got to the right street, I was as sure as I could be that Linus Flowers wasn't behind us. Martha Reedy had noticed me checking, but she hadn't said anything.

I'd lost all sense of direction, but thought we were somewhere behind the old naval shipyards. The neighborhood had deteriorated from slum to wasteland—oily vacant lots of dry marsh and damp mud, burnt-out or abandoned buildings, scattered squalorous shacks in the middle of muddy yards filled with the husks and skeletons and innards of planned obsolescence.

Over a CHECKS CASHED HERE sign, a beer sign glowed in the grimy window of a shack on the corner of a crossroad that ended at a muddy tide flat. A scruffy dog relieved himself against a utility pole. Nothing else moved. In the bright midday stillness, there wasn't a human being in sight.

Martha pulled the Geo to a stop in front of a house that had once been a boxcar. The roof was shingled with rusting flattened tin cans, the two small windows were covered with crinkled sheets of tinfoil. The front door was cracked, hung slightly ajar from hinges half torn from rotted wood.

We got out. In the heat, the sea smell was so heavy and rank that even I could smell it. But under it lay a heavier rankness.

The muddy yard was filled with junk and litter and mounds of old plastic trash bags, most of which had burst. More garbage had been dumped on the piles, trailed back toward the door. The garbage was alive.

As we picked our way through it, the stench grew thicker, made my eyes smart. At the door, Martha looked at me, blinking back tears, then knocked.

After a long silence, she looked at me again. Again we had a moment of recognition. We knew this kind of silence, knew what it meant. We had both opened doors like this before.

She took a deep breath and pulled it open. A wave of nearly palpable putrescence rolled over us. Draping my jacket carefully over my nose and mouth to keep from gagging, I followed her inside.

We didn't go in more than a couple of steps. In the utter human ruin of the room, the only spot not covered with filth was an old mattress on which lay an open-eyed woman.

From where we stood, we could see that she was dead. From where we stood, I could see that she wasn't Heather McLeod.

Martha turned, leaned her forehead against my chest, and nudged me back toward the door. I didn't resist.

At the car, Martha reached into her purse and pulled out her keys. "Take the car back to the house. I'll be there in a bit."

"Not a chance," I said. "I'm not leaving you—"

"Jack," she said evenly, "I'm going over to that bar and call the sheriff. I'll be home a half hour after you get there."

"I'm not going to leave you alone in this neighborhood."

"I don't need anybody to hold my hand," she said. "Go on."

I shook my head. "Martha, Linus Flowers is out there. He followed you this morning. He probably followed us here."

"So what?" she snapped. "If he shows, I'll deal with him."

"Martha, you don't—"

"If you're here when the deputies arrive, neither one of us will get untangled from this for hours."

"Martha—"

"Goddammit, Jack," she said, shoving me in the chest, "get the hell out of here!"

CHAPTER TWENTY-ONE

I had some trouble finding my way back, so I hadn't been on the porch ten minutes when the Alameda County Sheriff Department cruiser pulled to a stop beside the Geo. Martha got out, waved once as the car pulled away up the hill.

When she got to the porch, I stood up and handed her the keys. "Sorry."

She shrugged. "You can't help it, I guess. You want a beer?"

"Please."

She opened the door. "You might as well come in."

We stepped into a hallway with three closed doors on the right, one at the end. She showed me into a midsized room to the left of the entrance, a combination living room and office—worn but well-kept carpet, furniture from periods over the last forty years that somehow all fit together, a few old prints of High Romantic land-scapes, a desk and computer and file cabinet.

Something about the way she moved in it told me that this was the home she'd grown up in.

She pushed through a swinging door into a small kitchen, came back with two bottles of beer. I took one to the sofa.

Spinning the desk chair around, she slumped into it.

"I wonder how Mrs. McLeod will react when she finds out that her daughter was alive and we managed to kill her."

I tried my beer. It didn't cut through the taste in my mouth. "What did the sheriff say?"

"OD, probably on junk she got with the money I gave her."

I tried my beer again. "They get a positive ID?"

She shrugged. "Why? We know who she was."

"No we don't, Martha. We know who she wasn't. She wasn't Heather McLeod."

She slid farther down in her chair. "It really does bother you that I found her when you couldn't, doesn't it?"

"The dead woman's eyes were brown, Martha. Heather's eyes were hazel."

"Hazel, brown, it's a common—"

"It's pretty hard to tell what Heather would look like now based on that picture of her at fourteen, I'll agree. But whatever life did to her over the last eighteen years, it didn't shrink her by half a foot."

She jerked angrily up out of her slump. "You saw her for thirty seconds, Jack, and she was lying down. There's no way you could make that kind of determination."

"Maybe not," I said. "But you could. I met Heather McLeod twenty years ago. When she was twelve, she was already tall, five seven, five eight. You're what, five five, six? You must have stood beside that woman when you met her this morning. She was shorter than you are, by three or four inches at least."

After a while she shook her head. "It doesn't make sense."

"What does, in this mess? I don't even know what it's all really about. Nothing fits."

She slumped back down in the chair, laid the beer bottle between her breasts, stared at it.

"How did you get a line on this woman?"

She told me. She was a trained investigator.

She'd picked up the name at DMV, but the Sacramento address

was seven years old. With a social security number, she gleaned newer addresses from state agencies and traced her to Alameda County, worked county agencies for more addresses, none of them good. Along the way, she ran across the police record—solicitation, substance violations, suspended sentences or time served.

At a dead end, she had worked back through the addresses and the few phone numbers until she found an ex-roommate, a biker babe in Richmond who might know where Heather McLeod was living, who for fifty dollars up front and fifty later might find out. The morning before Martha had driven up to Tahoe to see Patsy McLeod, she had shelled out the fifty dollars and told the ex-room-mate what to tell Heather. When she got back from Nevada, she found a message from Heather and a number to call.

As I listened, I thought I might be getting a handle on it. "Did you ever go back farther than that first DMV record?"

She nodded. "There was nothing. She must have moved in from out of state seven years ago."

"Maybe." Then I told her about the investigation that the Draines had financed twelve years before. "They checked all over the coun-try, Martha. Heather would have been twenty at the time, she should have left some kind of trail. They got zip."

"So seven years ago," she said quietly, "this woman got a copy of Heather McLeod's birth certificate. Which means that she not only knew that Heather was dead but also where she was born, which means that probably she knew the real Heather."

I nodded. "Or knew somebody who knew."

She looked at me. "Dale Rutledge?"

"He'd be my first guess, since she surfaced in Sacramento."

She slumped back down in the chair. "Which leaves us with a woman we killed who isn't Heather McLeod and nothing else."

We hadn't killed anybody. But I didn't say so.

And there was something else. It was sitting out in my car in a paper sack. "You wouldn't happen to know anyone who can tell a real snuff film from a fake?"

She nodded, stared morosely at her beer bottle. "When I was still with the sheriff's office, we had a body that tracked back to a porn factory in Richmond. The perp tried to convince us that the movie our body had starred in was a fake. We brought in an expert who showed us why it wasn't."

I waited. After a while she sat up, drained her beer. "You might as well drive over and get it. The sooner you get back, the sooner we can get this over with."

"It's out in the car. No big hurry."

Her mouth set grimly. She'd thought she'd have time to prepare herself. "No. Let's find out."

In the Wagoneer the paper sack was sitting on the front seat in the sun. I almost hoped that the heat had baked the tape into mush.

Martha stood in the front doorway. "I'd rather do this alone, Jack. Do you mind?"

"I don't want to look at it if I don't have to," I said.

"This might take a while," she said. "If Hannah gets here, ask her to wait until I'm finished." She gave me a disconsolate smile and shut the door.

It was hot on the porch, but I didn't mind. I was better off outside, listening to the distant swell of sound from the football game, watching the breeze stir the trees, pretending it was just a normal Saturday afternoon in Berkeley, than inside watching what Martha was watching.

Twenty minutes later Hannah Fielding came walking up the street. She stopped at my Wagoneer, looked over at me, tried to glare.

She couldn't manage it. Even from the porch I could see the darkness under her eyes, the lines worn in her face. Whatever she'd been doing that day had deepened her exhaustion.

When she stepped onto the porch, I rose. "Ms. Fielding, Martha asked me to ask you if you'd wait out here until she's finished with what she's doing."

Concern softened, filled her eyes. "Is she all right?"

I nodded, sat back down.

She looked at me, at the door, then wearily set her attaché case on the table and slumped into a chair behind it, as far from me as she could get. Hannah Fielding, I saw, was afraid of me.

"Is it about the McLeod property?"

"In a roundabout way."

I told her what had happened, what Martha was doing inside.

When I finished, she shook her head. "If the film is real, we've lost all hope of acquiring the property."

A couple of hours before, a woman had been killed. Eighteen years before, probably, a fourteen-year-old girl had been killed. And Hannah Fielding was concerned about a piece of property out in the Nevada desert.

Only the haunted unhappiness in her eyes allowed me to keep my tone even. "Desert Conservancy can still bid on it."

"Not against Nolan Turner," she said through clenched teeth. "Even if we outbid him, with the connections he has with the good old boys in Washoe County, we wouldn't have a chance at the property."

She did manage to glare at me this time.

Martha, I thought, had called it. Hannah Fielding had me confused with someone else. She had me confused with Linus Flowers.

And I'd had enough.

"Martha said that Monday morning you were going to have Heather McLeod sign some papers having to do with the eventual sale of the property to Desert Conservancy?"

She picked up my tone. "You have a problem with that, Mr. Ross?"

I shrugged. "Were you planning to tell Heather to have a lawyer look the papers over before she signed them?"

A flush crept up her throat. "If Marty told you that, she also told you that I'm an attorney. I would have informed Heather of her legal options and rights before she signed anything."

"You'd see no conflict of interest in the matter?"

The flush deepened. She reached out and pulled her attaché case off the table and held it before her chest. Her voice was a rasp, sounded painful. "Are you questioning my ethics?"

Suddenly I regretted what I'd said. I didn't want to tangle with Hannah Fielding. She was tired and angry and didn't like me. And arguing the point was pointless.

I let it go. "No ma'am."

She didn't let it go. "Don't try that patronizing cowboy politeness on me, Mr. Ross. I know what you are."

All I had to do was keep my mouth shut. And of course I couldn't. "What's that, Ms. Fielding?"

Her smile was as thin as a knife blade. "You're a predator, a lone wolf who preys on his own kind, on the weak and the old, on the troubled and the trusting, on women."

Angry, I smiled. "Don't try to spare my feelings, Ms. Fielding. Come right out with it."

She flushed again, deeply. "Fortunately, you're also an anachronism, a figure from a childish dreamworld produced by the ideology of a morally bankrupt and withering patriarchal culture. The day of your evil, violent way is nearly past."

It was, I recognized, a piece of prefabricated rhetoric that had nothing to do with the reality of the moment.

She seemed to recognize it too. She slumped back into the chair. I wondered what she had been doing that would drain her to a hollow-eyed husk. I wondered something else.

"Why are you afraid of me, Ms. Fielding?"

She almost smiled. "You flatter yourself, Mr. Ross. I don't fear you. I despise you."

"I'm glad we cleared that up."

"Let me make it even clearer," she said, her voice again raspy. "If you weren't so dangerous you'd be comical, the way you amble up the walk wearing your tape and bruises like a badge of honor, expecting any woman you meet to swoon over you. Do you think it isn't obvious what you're really after?"

"What's that, Ms. Fielding?"

Her voice trembled with emotion. "Leave her alone."

"Leave who alone?"

Her sneer was profound. "Is your phallic arrogance so overweening that you can't see that she wants no part of you?"

I finally realized what she meant. "Ms. Fielding, you seem to be laboring under an illusion. I know what the situation is. I have no designs—"

"Men like you have nothing but designs. Leave her alone."

"Ms. Fielding, I—"

"You think we're all so stupid." Her smile got thinner, sharper. "You think I'm so stupid I don't know who you're really working for. You're supposed to do whatever it takes to make sure Nolan Turner gets the McLeod property so Wally Keene will get Turner's legal business and you'll get a well-paid sinecure at Rondo and Keene.

That's how good old boys do it, isn't it? Ethics is making sure your friends get a cut of the pie."

I wasn't sure how she could know about Turner and Wally, but it didn't matter. And if that was how she chose to read my part in all this, that didn't matter either.

What did matter was her supercilious smirk.

"And to you, Ms. Fielding, ethics is doing whatever it takes to force everybody to live and think and feel exactly the way you tell them to, regardless of who gets hurt—"

"Shut up, Jack!" Martha stood in the doorway, trembling.

Hannah Fielding jumped up. "Marty—"

"You too, Hannah! Just shut up!"

Hannah Fielding gasped as if she'd been slapped. Her eyes filling with tears, she stared at Martha the way a child stares at a parent who has betrayed her.

Then blindly she wheeled and half ran, half stumbled off the porch.

Martha tossed the paper sack at me and slammed the door.

Hannah Fielding hadn't returned by the time Martha came back out. She'd showered, drawn her hair back in a nub of damp ponytail, changed into shorts and a GIVE PEACE A CHANCE T-shirt.

She didn't look angry or upset. She looked exhausted. But she didn't sit down.

"You can tell Mrs. McLeod that her daughter was murdered eighteen years ago."

I got up. "You're sure?"

She shrugged. "As sure as I can be. It's either real or Dale Rutledge was a genius."

I nodded. "I'll tell her. And I'm sorry about my part—"

"Go away, Jack," she said wearily. "Just go away and leave me alone."

CHAPTER TWENTY-TWO

During the long escape from California, my mood thickened with shame at my asinine behavior with Hannah Fielding, darkened with the knowledge of what I was bringing back to Nevada with me.

As I drove past Davis, only a supreme act of will kept me from turning off and finding Dale Rutledge and beating him half to death.

Five hours after my banishment from Martha Reedy's porch, I pulled into the twilit parking circle before the Draines' house on the edge of Lake Tahoe. The big green Mercedes wasn't there. As I parked beside the BMW, I saw William Draine watching me from the garage, where he had been sorting through a box of toys.

When I got out, his affable grin tightened with concern. He stared at my nose, at the flesh puffing darkly around my eyes. "Are you all right?"

"I'll live. Patsy around?"

"No," he said. "She and Rosetta took the kids down to the waterslide in Reno. They should be back soon. I've got coffee going, or there's beer, or something stronger, if you want."

What I wanted was to hand him the paper sack and tell him what was in it and leave. Run.

"Coffee'd be fine."

He gave me another concerned look, then led me through the garage into a short hallway, opened a door into a large neat carpeted room filled with books and old maps and furnished with solid old chairs and a huge clutter-free desk. Feeble twilight seeped in through sliding glass doors that opened onto a small redwood deck overlooking the lake.

William Draine nodded at a pair of big leather armchairs. "Make yourself comfortable. I'll be right back."

While he was gone, I surveyed his carefully organized and labeled library. European political and intellectual history, and especially the Renaissance. American history, especially post–Civil War. The American West. He had, it seemed, most of the books ever written about the Great Basin—historical, technical, and fictional. He had more books about Nevada than I knew existed, from the accounts of the explorations of Fremont and Smith to the memoirs of miners and ranchers and sheepmen to biographies of Sara Winnemucca and Francis Newlands to muckraking studies of Vegas to hard-boiled detective novels about casinos, mafiosi, and showgirls.

What I found most interesting was what wasn't there.

Draine returned and handed me a mug of coffee. "I put a little bracer in it. You look as though you could use it."

"Thanks," I said, sitting in one of the big leather chairs. He was right. The brandy helped.

"You suppose it's true, Professor, that the tigers of wrath are wiser than the horses of instruction?"

He grinned, fit himself into a chair. "A lot of my students think so. Sometimes I wonder if they might be right."

I didn't say anything. He looked at me, and his grin slowly faded as he came to understand what my allusion meant.

"I don't read William Blake anymore, Mr. Ross," he said quietly. "It's too painful. It reminds me of a period in my life that I'm not very proud of."

"In Beulah Valley?"

"And all that led up to it." The dying light flashed on his glasses. "Some innocent people were nearly killed out there that winter. I . . . imagine Dale Rutledge told you about it."

"Some," I said. "Is that why your wife called him? To tell him not to?"

"No," he said, still quietly. "She wanted to talk to him about Heather. We thought that if he wouldn't tell you anything, maybe we could get information from him with money."

I'd been trying to fit things together during the trip back to Lake Tahoe. Somewhere in the middle of the Big Valley, I'd had an idea. Not a good one, it was turning out.

"You don't seem concerned that I know about it."

He gave me a small, pained smile. "It's not something that I necessarily want people to know, Mr. Ross. But neither is it something I would deny. I was young and foolish. Not that it excuses anything, but there were reasons. . . ."

"There always are, Professor. But reasons don't change the effects of actions."

"No," he said. "Nana mentioned, I think, that you were in Vietnam. Was the Jack Ross who returned the same Jack Ross who went there?"

I saw where he was going, could have stopped him. But I didn't. "No."

He nodded. "I expect that there were reasons you went. A sense of patriotism, perhaps the pursuit of glory, a need to test yourself? Would those reasons hold true for you today?"

In my case, as I'd only recently begun to understand, none of those reasons applied. But I didn't say so. "No, but it isn't an apt comparison."

"Perhaps not. But there were reasons. I—what would you expect to happen to a boy who simply could not be what he was expected to be by his family, a boy who . . ."

As he looked for the right phrase, I found it. "A boy who was a circle that his family wanted to square?"

He nodded. "You don't have to be much of a psychologist to perceive that most of the ideas and insights and obsessions of an adult have their roots in his childhood."

I wondered if that was true of my ideas and insights and obsessions, such as they were.

"The boy looks for a way out, an escape. In the sixties, the way out was obvious. War, or . . ."

"Peace and Love, Sex and Drugs," I said.

"Some went to war," he said. "Others chased a dream. All those lost and lonely and looking for love. That's what it was, Mr. Ross, under the fabricated sweetness and smiles and singing, the revolutionary politics and utopian visions. All of those people who had abandoned their families and gone out looking for love among each other."

He was trying to objectify his youthful self, distance the Stanford professor from the young man he once had been.

"When did William Draine become Blake?"

"When he'd been stoned so long he thought he'd learned why everyone was so unhappy. He thought he could fix it, that he could start everything all over again. He thought he possessed truth."

I remembered our conversation about his book. William Draine still thought he possessed truth.

He shifted in his chair. "He was lucky, Mr. Ross. No one died because of him. But coming close to death, realizing that he had been leading others toward it, was enough to shock him out of it, make him see what was really important. . . ."

He might have been describing my experience in Vietnam. Except that, in my case, all I'd been able to see as important was taking care of my troops.

"They didn't die out there because of Patsy," I said. "Is that why you found her and brought her up here?"

He nodded. "Rosetta had kept in touch, but Patsy never told us how bad it was, living in Sun Valley and working in the clubs. When we understood, we got her out."

I tried my coffee, savored the brandy. "What happened to Heather out there, Professor?"

He looked away, out the sliding glass door, to the lake and the gathering darkness. The room was graying, but neither of us moved to switch on a light.

"All that Patsy was afraid might happen," he said, and I could hear the pain in his voice.

"Everybody was doing drugs, having sex, and Heather couldn't understand why she couldn't participate. She and Patsy had terrible rows about it. Finally . . ."

His voice trembled. "Finally the point became . . ."

Whatever else William Draine was, he was a man who suffered. He was suffering then. And I thought I might know why.

"Heather got involved with drugs and sex. Did she get involved with them through you?"

The room was nearly dark before he finally answered.

"I know it doesn't make any difference, Mr. Ross. And I'm not trying to avoid—but it was Blake who . . . did that."

Maybe it shouldn't have, but it did make a difference. A small one. I should have been angry, but I wasn't.

Maybe because the young man he had described, the circle everyone wanted to square, was eerily close to the young man I had been. And I'd done the same thing—escaped.

But recognizing these things wasn't making what I had to do any easier. I stood up, handed him the paper sack. "You need to look at this before Patsy gets here."

He didn't look in the sack. "What is it?"

"If I were you, I'd forward it to the last couple minutes."

When I didn't say any more, he turned and left the room.

By the time he returned and sat in the chair, the room was dark. I listened to his ragged breathing. Whatever Blake had done, William Draine was paying for it.

"What are you going to do with it, Professor?"

"Tahoe is deep," he said.

It wasn't an environmentally sound proposal, but it was what I'd have done.

"Did . . . Dale Rutledge make it?"

"So I've been told," I said. "I—how did you know?"

"I saw a piece of his work once. This has the same clever camera angles, odd focuses."

"He told me about that film," I said. "He thought I worked for Nolan Turner and tried to sell it to me. Although what he thought a developer could do with shots of a hippie commune disintegrating and a VW van sinking in a pond escapes me. Most of what Rutledge thinks escapes me."

His breathing changed, but he didn't say anything more.

After a while we heard the soft murmur of the Mercedes, the bright chime of children's voices.

Draine got up and switched on a light. The flesh above his beard was old, ashen. Behind his glasses his eyes were red-rimmed and glittering. "What are you going to tell her?" he asked.

"Only what I have to," I said.

I went out the door, into the garage, onto the parking circle. Night had settled on the Sierra. Stars thickened.

Patsy was pulling wet towels and bathing suits from the backseat of the Mercedes. She heard my boots scuff the tarmac. "Seen your rig there, Ross. What's up?"

"Heather's dead, Patsy."

She stood without moving.

I waited for the questions, but they didn't come. She didn't ask how her daughter had died. She didn't ask how I knew her daughter had died.

Finally she stirred, spoke. "Is there a grave?"

"No." There wouldn't be.

"I . . ." She took a deep breath, shifted the load of damp swimsuits in her arms. "Could you do me another favor, Ross? I—you don't have to, but . . . Royce oughta know. You mind coming out there with me tomorrow so's I can tell him?"

I did mind. I minded a lot. But I didn't say so.

CHAPTER TWENTY-THREE

A hot ragged wind swirled across the desert, rasping at the land, scraping away dust that roiled up into the empty blue sky.

"Storm comin'."

It was the first thing Patsy had said since she'd backed the pickup out from under the mulberry tree shading my driveway. She had simply driven and, once in the desert, looked, her weathered desert face set in its deep desert squint.

Now, the closer we got to the ranch, the more things started to come out of her—questions, uncertainties, regrets, pain.

"Had the dream last night."

"You will for a while," I said. "It doesn't mean anything."

She looked at the land. "Suppose they're right, Ross, Rosetta and them? That people never should of tried to make a life out here?"

"I don't know, Patsy."

I too had been looking, at the dry land in drought, at the scars on the earth, the bones of dead ideas, the detritus of wrecked human hopes.

"They thought they could make their dreams fit the land, and it didn't work. But I don't think you can blame them for trying."

She nodded. "Professor says it's happening all over the West. People losing their ranches and farms and homes, all the little towns dying, everybody jammin' into the city. Gonna turn the Great Plains into a park for buffalo, the Great Basin into a bombing range, Nevada into a nu-ca-ler waste dump."

"Things change, Patsy."

"Maybe that's why we die. So's we don't have to see it."

We drove through the rabbitbrush and stunted sage, the rock and bitterbrush, the alkali and greasewood. In it all, nothing moved but the pickup and the wind-whipped brush and wind-stirred dust.

The pickup chewed gravel as it churned up the low hill, and Zion Mountain, then Beulah Valley, came in sight. At the crest Patsy slowed, eased down the other side, passed the spot where Martha Reedy had been stuck in the alkali, passed the spot where Linus Flowers had waited for her.

She turned the pickup into the creek-and-flood cut in the dune. On the other side, she coasted to a stop. As she looked at what had once been her home, her eyes began to glisten.

"The thing about it is," she said after a while, over the buffeting of the wind, "there's so much brown around it, the green looks like it oughta be somethin' special. But everybody who tried to make it something got killed for it. If the work didn't kill them, the water did."

In the desert, death by water.

She'd told me about it twenty years before. The canyon ponds weren't primarily for watering stock or for irrigation; they were for flood control.

Every few years, after a late snow or a big early rain, the runoff would drain into a watery death that roared down the mountain, carving more canyon, crushing everything and everyone in its path before it spread out over the alkali and stilled and thinned and slowly evaporated.

Paiutes had hunted and gathered there, leaving behind them work stones and obsidian chips and graves.

Mormons had given the valley its name and grown fruit and vegetables and hay and grain, built sod and timber houses, until a flood washed it all out and they moved on, leaving graves.

Various families had worked the land, and dug more graves, until the McLeods got the property.

The McLeods had ranched it for nearly a century, in good years hiring help to put in dams and fiddle with the irrigation systems, in bad years just hanging on. Most of the years were bad. More graves.

Now there was only one McLeod left, and he was waiting to die.

"Bone orchard, Royce called it."

She nodded. "We was always finding graves, bones. Mal used to . . ."

The memory of her son silenced her.

"The thing is," she said after a while, "we always tried to make too much of it. Alls I ever wanted—I mean, we could make a living, raise our kids, be a family, but that was never enough. He—we always had to make it bigger, get more land, run more cows, make more money. An' somethin' always came along to kick us in the head."

When I didn't say anything, Patsy let out the clutch and idled the pickup forward. As we crept past the old mine turnoff, I noticed the freshly broken sage, the tire tracks.

At the gate, Patsy stopped, shook her head at the lock, the sign. "Contrariest man in Washoe County."

We got out and walked through the wind up to the house. No rifle shots disturbed the silence. When we got to the yard, we saw why.

The thing that once had been Royce McLeod lay on the porch in front of the empty chair. The top of its head was a pulpy, congealed mess of brain and blood and bone. The barrel of the 30.06 trailed from a corner of its mouth down across the irregular row of ribbons on the Marine Corps tunic; the trigger guard sat in a stiff curl of fingers.

Above the wind, as if from a great distance, I heard an eerie, infantlike mewl, realized that it had come from Patsy. But when I looked at her, her beautiful iris blue eyes were clear, steady, if not quite focused.

"Too late," she said evenly, but not really to me. "But I guess it's been too late for Royce for a long time."

"We'll have to go call the sheriff, Patsy."

She took her keys from her pocket and handed them to me. "You go ahead, Ross. I'll wait here. Gimme a chance to . . . say good-bye."

I looked at her, thought that Rosetta Draine was right. Patsy McLeod was a strong woman. Within less than twenty-four hours, she had learned that her daughter was dead, as well as her daughter's father. What had been her family was gone.

Still, for Patsy, her family had been gone a long time.

It was that thought more than anything that raised the hand I placed on her shoulder. "I'm sorry, Patsy."

She put her own scarred hand on mine, as if she were in fact comforting me.

"Me too, Ross. Real sorry."

I left her with the body, walked through the wind-driven dust to the pickup, drove back to Red Rock Estates and called the sheriff.

I drove back to the ranch. At the turnoff to the old mine, I stopped, got out, and walked a few paces down the old pair of ruts.

The big, heavy, low-slung car had snapped a few sage sprigs on the way in, and on the way out stripped a rabbitbrush of its golden pods. The tire tracks in the sand were wide-treaded, familiar.

Climbing back into the pickup, I drove to the gate, around it, and up to the house.

The body still lay on the porch, but Patsy had carefully and discreetly draped a tattered piece of cloth over its face. I went over and removed it, then stepped back and studied the position of the body, the rifle.

Why was the body lying on the porch instead of sitting in the chair? The body hadn't fallen there, or the rifle barrel wouldn't still have been in its mouth.

Why would Royce McLeod have stretched out on the porch before he stuck the 30.06 in his mouth and pulled the trigger?

He wouldn't have.

Royce McLeod hadn't killed himself.

Linus Flowers had killed him, I knew, even if I didn't know why. But there was no way to prove it. Broken sage, tire tracks, a sense of some obscure pattern—that's all I had.

But why would anyone want to murder a dying man?

I replaced the piece of cloth. Looking around for Patsy, I noticed movement across the washed-out pond, at the top of a low knoll spattered with stubby piñon.

She leaned into the gritty wind, staring down at the earth. The site was high enough to be safe from whatever water might roar down the canyon, had been chosen because of that. I knew that Patsy was staring at graves.

Saying good-bye.

I crossed the low face of the pond, stepped across the trickle of creek. The narrow path that angled up the hillside, though it hadn't been used for years, was still hard-packed bare earth; it hadn't overgrown, as if the desert had decided that such a trail of grief should remain a permanent, natural feature of the land.

The wind swirled, snapped, stung. Patsy squinted through it, seemed not to notice it.

"Thought he might of at least tried to keep this up," she said as I approached.

Sage and rabbitbrush sprouted on the graves. Water had cut small courses through the sandy earth. The gritty desert wind had scoured small old marble McLeod headstones to blankness, had buried dark granite headstones in sand.

I could see where Patsy had brushed the desert away from two small granite markers. Steven McLeod. Carl McLeod. The stillborn sons between Malcolm and Heather.

"They gonna let me bury him here?"

"I don't know." Technically, legally, the property was now under the control of the Washoe County Administrator's Office.

She nodded into the wind. "He oughta be here with them all. With the boys. It was them boys . . . that started it."

I understood.

Like something out of Faulkner, Martha Reedy had said. Boys meant hands to work the ranch, to make it more than it really could ever be.

"An' I finished it."

I wasn't sure what she meant, but I knew she was going to tell me. It was part of her good-bye to what had been her family, her life.

"He still had some hope, long as Mal was here. Then I went an' let the kid talk me into signin' for him to go in the Marines when he was only seventeen, even knowing Royce figured . . ."

Her eyes were tearing, perhaps against the wind that swirled her words away into the desert silence.

"The thing was, Mal said it was the only way he could ever get away from this place. Go to war, be a hero, then he could stand up to his dad, do what he wanted with his life. He loved this place, but he never took to the life, the work. He was always wandering off, exploring, thinking. . . . If he'd of come back, he wouldn't of come back here."

Malcolm McLeod was not under the sage and sand. The North Vietnamese rocket hadn't left enough of him to bury. All that had come back was a piece of paper and a medal.

"When Royce found out what we'd done, he knocked me down. He'd never hit me before. Never did again. Never even . . . touched me again."

I had been wondering why Patsy had wanted me to come out with her. Now I suspected that she had known she would be saying her good-bye to a land and a life, had wanted someone to hear it. To bear witness.

"He started dying then, Royce, even though he didn't know it. He didn't kill that drunk hunter because he'd shot a cow. He killed him because he just didn't care anymore."

I didn't know if what she was telling me was the truth. But she thought it was. That was all that mattered. I bore witness.

After a while, I said: "If there's anything in the house you might want, you'd better get it before the sheriff shows up."

She shook her head. "I come out here more'n forty years ago with nothing but the clothes on my back. Left twenty years ago the same way."

She stared down at the graves. "Nothin' here was ever really mine. Took Royce knocking me down to get me to see that."

"You put twenty-odd years of your life into this place, Patsy."

She nodded at the two small granite stones. "An' all it got me was a pitiful alimony Royce never paid, and dead children."

In a sudden ebb of the wind, we heard a laboring engine. Patsy turned away from the headstones, and we watched the green and white Washoe County sheriff's rig bounce and dig its way up toward the house.

"You suppose they'd at least let me move these two, bury all three of them together in town?"

"One way or another, Patsy, we'll make sure that they're together."

CHAPTER TWENTY-FOUR

Late that night an arctic cold front shrouded the peaks of Sierra with snow, dropped the temperature twenty-five degrees, and brought a heavy frost to the foothills, fall to the desert.

The next morning, after a run along what was left of the Truckee River, I was back in my suit and tie and office.

Rondo and Keene was astir. Lawyers milled, spreading and assessing the word. The word was of such significance that no one bothered to comment on the muddying bruises around my nose and eyes. The word was that Nolan Turner had decided to retain the firm to handle all of his new business.

Ignoring the commotion, I got to work, did my nice little paralegal jobs, got on the phone and conducted my disinterested little investigations that involved no one I knew or cared about.

That night, to fight off a depression I could sense coming but could find no source for, I started to clean out my living room, piling on the kitchen table the bits and pieces I had, over the years, hauled in from the desert.

The feel of the old metal and wood and rock in my hands didn't
soothe me. Neither did Willie Nelson's rueful lament that his he-
roes had always been cowboys. I gave it up and went to bed.

The next morning, after another run along the river, I was back
in my office. I worked through lunch, dinner, into the darkness
that settled outside my window and the silence that settled inside
the building, until I had only one more thing to do.

After typing up an expense report, I made out a check to Patsy
for the balance of her thousand dollars, put both in an envelope,
addressed it, and put it in the outgoing mail.

Then, fighting off depression by listening to Schubert, I started
thinking about Patsy McLeod and her problem with graves.

Eventually I found myself thinking not like an investigator but
like an attorney. Eventually I discovered, maybe, a way not only to
solve Patsy's problem but also to end at least part of whatever it
was that was going on.

I let Schubert finish what he wasn't finishing. Then I shut everything off and locked my office, walked out the back door and
spotted Wally Keene's Lamborghini in his stenciled parking slot.
An emerald Ferrari gleamed beside it.

I went back inside. Walking down the hall, I passed a pair of very
junior attorneys slaving away in the library, their makeup gone pasty,
their voices tense. I went into the foyer, then climbed the thickly
carpeted stairs to a short hallway that led to what had once been
the bedroom of the love-besotted banker and his young Philadelphia dream girl.

The big man leaning against the door might have smiled. "No
sleaze allowed."

"That would explain why you're out here, Mudd."

He tried to glower. "How'd you like to have the rest of your face
match your beak?"

"No thanks."

"Candy-assed bastard," he sneered.

I took half a step back. "I don't have time for your silly games,
Mudd. Tell your boss I've got some information for him about the
McLeod ranch."

"He already knows."

"He doesn't know what I know. And he'll want to. If I don't tell him, it'll be your ass. Better cover it."

Confusion glazed his eyes. He wasn't very smart, but he finally figured out that I had him. He turned, rapped on the door, slid inside. A few seconds later the door swung open. Mudd stepped aside, gave me a stiff shove as I stepped through it, shut the door, leaned against it, might have smiled.

Although rumor had it that Wally occasionally used the sofa in it for activities similar to those engaged in by the banker and his bride and his bride and her florist, the room now looked nothing like a bedroom—thick carpet over old hardwood, a huge table-desk where the bed should have been, file cabinets, a mahogany-veneered bar, assorted plaques and framed certificates and degrees hanging from shadow molding over the fleur-de-lis wallpaper.

The two men sat in velvet-covered chairs at a small table before a window overlooking California Avenue.

His tie loosened, his shirtsleeves rolled up, Wally slowly set down his brandy snifter. "Jack, what's happening?"

I waded through the thick carpet, plopped into a chair. "All sorts of interesting things."

Turner set his brandy glass down beside the bottle on the table. He still wore casual clothes—designer jeans, a soft turtleneck jersey, a softer cashmere sweater draped over his shoulders. The outfit still didn't fit his raptorial eyes.

He grinned at my bruises. "You get run off the road, Ross?"

"More or less," I said. "I'm glad you're here, Turner. I have some information for Wally, but you'll want to hear it too."

"If it's about old Royce McLeod blowing his brains out—"

"It isn't," I said, then turned to Wally. "You still want to get a piece of the Mercer Foundation action?"

Wally glanced at Mudd leaning against the door, at Nolan Turner. "Jack, I don't think this is the appropriate time—"

"It's especially appropriate," I said, "because I can give you something that will make Rosetta Draine very happy. But it'll finish Turner's plans for the McLeod ranch."

Turner shook his head, grinned. "Ross, I told you, it's not going to break my heart if I don't get the McLeod property."

"Then you won't be upset when it goes to Patsy McLeod."

He shrugged. "If it did, I'd make her an offer. If she accepts, fine. If not . . . But I'd be interested to know why you think that's going to happen."

Wally's Dartmouth ring flashed as he adjusted the knot in his silk tie. "What's going on, Jack?"

"What you do, Wally, is tomorrow morning you check out the divorce settlement of Royce and Patsy McLeod. Then you call Rosetta Draine and tell her that if Patsy wants the Beulah Valley property, you can get it for her."

Despite Nolan Turner's presence, Wally was interested, even excited. "There's something wrong with the settlement?"

"A couple things. Royce McLeod was supposed to pay his ex-wife alimony. He didn't, so she has a claim on the estate. And a good lawyer could probably get the original decree set aside, given the way the courts view these matters these days. Whatever the property is worth, it still wouldn't compensate Patsy for twenty years of sweat. She'd get it all."

Wally glanced uneasily at Nolan Turner.

Nolan Turner again grinned, not at him but at me. "Son of a bitch, Ross. I got all this high-priced legal help and nobody thought of that. I could have talked to her and had the deal finished by now."

"I don't think so," I said. "I don't think she's going to let you fill up the land with plywood and concrete."

"Maybe not," he grinned, "but she sure as hell isn't going to sell it to Desert Conservancy."

As I was wondering how he could be certain of that, or even know it, Turner rose from the chair, nodded to Wally.

"I see now why you want to hire this guy. He looks like he's not much with his dukes, but he's got brains."

With slow, deliberate exaggeration, Wally smiled. Then he climbed out of his chair and trailed Nolan Turner toward the door.

"The papers will be ready tomorrow," Wally said.

Turner grinned. "Why not bring them over tomorrow night? I'm having some people over for a little fun. You might want to meet some of them."

He opened the door. Mudd let him pass, then looked at me. He might have smiled. The door closed.

Wally came back, pulled a brandy glass from a rack above the bar, brought it to the table and made an elaborate production of dumping in a dollop. He held out the glass.

"Do you mind telling me what that was all about, Jack?"

The brandy smelled, tasted, very good. "Not what I thought it was going to be about."

He sat down. "I—have you heard anything you think I should know?"

I shrugged. "You still spooked, Wally?"

He looked out the window at the darkness. "He's easy enough to read. What he wants is what everybody in the country wants, money, power, the best of everything. The question is just how far he'll go to get it."

"That's the question, all right."

"I've been trying to trace the rumors about . . . certain incidents. Accidents just before bids on property. Threatening phone calls. Two men disappeared. There are explanations, of course, and no one's ever been able to link anything to Turner. Or to his thug, Mudd. I . . . I'd just like to be sure."

"Before you sign the papers, you mean? I'm sorry, Wally, I don't know anything that can help you."

He picked up his glass, swirled the dark liquid. "Is it true about the McLeod divorce?"

"I think so," I said. "You can find out for sure tomorrow."

Wally swirled again. "I take it you didn't find Mrs. McLeod's daughter."

"She's dead," I said.

He watched the movement of the brandy. "I'll check out the decree tomorrow. If it's as you say, I'll call Rosetta Draine."

"There's a chance she may not want you to handle it," I said. "But if you want, you can tell her it was your idea."

"No." He grinned. "I'll tell her whose idea it was. If she wants her own people to take up the matter, that's fine. I'll already have what I want, which is Rosetta Draine's gratitude. And you'll have mine. I'll owe you one, Jack. A big one."

Wally finished his brandy with a theatrical flourish. "Where are you in all of this?"

"Nowhere. As far as I'm concerned, it's finished."

He studied his ring. "Are you sure?"

"Yes."

He sat back, folded his fingers around his empty glass. "Good," he said quietly. "Then there's no more reason for putting it off. Nolan called it, Jack. You've got brains. I can use them. What do you say?"

I wasn't sure what to say. All I knew was that, finally, I had to say something.

My life had come to crisis.

My job for Patsy McLeod was finished. The other jobs I'd left sitting while I went looking for a dead girl were finished.

All finished, all of it.

"The other day a woman told me I was, among other things, an anachronism, Wally. You suppose she might be right?"

Picking up the bottle, he tilted brandy into our glasses.

"I don't know, Jack. What I do know is that you leased the office downstairs not just because you needed a place to work but because you needed a change. You needed to get out of whatever it was that was always driving you crazy, or sending you out to hide in the desert."

That, I knew, was true. I'd been looking for a way to get my work out of my life. Not very successfully, as it was turning out. I wanted then to head for the desert.

"I also know that what I'm proposing is nothing more than what you threw away when you came back from Vietnam and set up as a PI—a law career, a life, a future."

Inexplicably, I was angry. "I didn't throw it away when I came back. I threw it away when I *went* to Vietnam. And a marriage along with it."

It was the first time I'd ever said it, or even admitted it to myself.

It was also curiously appropriate. The search for Heather McLeod eighteen years before was the final job I'd done before I'd left for the Marines. My life had been in crisis then too. I'd come full circle.

Wally watched me over the rim of his glass. "It never made sense, Jack. At Stanford, with all the antiwar stuff going on, you—you weren't burning your draft card, but you didn't support the war. I never quite understood why you went."

I hadn't quite understood either.

After I'd graduated from Stanford Law, I'd moved with my new wife back to Reno and helped my grandfather in his bail-bond and private investigation business while I studied for the Nevada bar exam. The day after I received notice that I'd passed, I joined the United States Marine Corps Reserve.

Hurt, my grandfather hadn't understood why I'd done it. Angry, my wife hadn't understood. Confused, I hadn't been able to explain it to them.

Finally, my grandfather had accepted it by invoking the old Code of the West platitude that, for good or ill, had ruled his life: a man's got to do what a man's got to do.

My wife had accepted it too, after a screaming burst of accusations about adolescent machismo and my refusal to accept adult responsibility.

Both of them were right.

"Poltroonery," I said.

Wally grinned. "If they taught me that word at Dartmouth, I forgot it."

"Cowardice. Base cowardice."

His grin faded. "That's not a word I'd have associated with you, Jack."

"Maybe not. But it's the right one."

I felt the heat at my throat and face, heat that hadn't risen from the brandy.

"I didn't *go* to Nam, Wally. I *ran*."

As I had talking to Wally a few days before, I found myself struggling to explain, to him, to myself.

"My life was all laid out, had been for a long time. My grandfather and I were going to go into business. I was going to be a criminal lawyer. He was going to be my investigator. He'd planned for it for years. But when the time came . . ."

I fortified myself with brandy. "I'd pretended to want it, pretended to him and to myself, because he wanted it and I loved him. But when the time came and I had to admit that what he wanted for me wasn't what I wanted for myself, I didn't have the guts to admit it to him. So I ran."

"What *did* you want?"

"I didn't know." I still didn't know, really.

He didn't say anything.

"The woman who called me an anachronism also called me a lone wolf. Everything that's happened since I got back from Nam seems to confirm that."

Wally watched me. "If I understand what you're getting at, you think the problem isn't what you want but what you are. I—you pretended in the marriage too?"

I nodded. "I went into it under false pretenses, led us both to think I wanted what she wanted—money and a house in upper suburbia and the kind of life that comes with it. But I didn't. Instead of admitting it, I lit out for the territory."

Wally nodded again. "But the difference between you and Huck Finn is that he didn't have a career and a family."

"No," I said quickly. "No family, just an essentially adolescent young man and an ambitious young woman who shared a powerful sexual attraction and not much else. My daughter was, it turned out, the result of our . . . furious farewell."

Ignoring his grin, I kept going. "I would have stayed at it, for Cynthia's sake, but my wife was smart enough to see it wouldn't work. She divorced me."

"And you never figured out," Wally asked after a while, "what it was you did want?"

"No," I said.

"Sometimes," Wally said, "I think that's what's wrong with this country. Whatever you think of the Vietnam War, it finished something in America. It showed us that the old dreams, the old ways, were dead, but it didn't show us what we should want or how we should get it or what we are. It left us . . . like you."

"May be," I said. "About the only thing I do know is that whatever it is I want, I haven't found it, and all the evidence suggests that if I keep doing what I've been doing, it isn't likely that I will."

Wally didn't say anything. There was nothing to say, at least for him.

The conversation, like my life, had come full circle. And Wally deserved—I deserved—an answer.

I stood up. "I'm going to take a few days off, maybe go out to the desert, let my bruises fade."

Wally didn't say anything.

"Draw up the papers. When I come back, I'll associate myself with the firm of Rondo and Keene."

CHAPTER TWENTY-FIVE

I didn't go to the desert.

I thought about it, thought about its huge, empty silence. But it wasn't, I knew, the cure for what ailed me.

The problem with going to the desert was that, finally, I always had to come back.

The next morning I went for a long run, steamed and sweated my way through the dawn chill up Peavine Mountain, jogged above the smog that was steeping to an ugly brown the still air hemmed in between the Sierra and the desert ranges.

I was high enough to see most of Reno and Sparks, the outlying valleys, the carefully engineered squares and rectangles of subdivisions and trailer courts and shopping malls, all the geometric jam and jumble overlaid on the swell and bend and dip of the Truckee Meadows.

It all seemed as ugly as it was inevitable.

Growth. Progress. Squaring the circle.

165

I could see, through an occasional gap in the cottonwoods, the feeble sun glinting off the Truckee River. What I couldn't see were meadows. There hadn't been meadows in the Truckee Meadows for years.

Things change, Patsy McLeod had told me, I had told her.

I jogged back, showered and changed, turned on the kitchen radio, dialed the oldies station, turned it up, and went to work on my house.

By midmorning, the Righteous Brothers were whoa-whoaing their way through "You've Lost That Loving Feeling" and my grandparents' heavy old furniture was stuffed into unused bedrooms and lining the hallway.

By noon, the Beatles were wandering through psychedelic "Strawberry Fields Forever" and the living room carpet was a stained, tattered roll in the driveway.

By midafternoon, Grace Slick was explaining how "one pill makes you larger and one pill makes you small" and I had stuffed chopped-up pieces of rotted carpet pad into heavy-ply garbage bags, had scraped and swept the hardwood floor until it was ready for sanding.

By late afternoon, the sheetrock walls were patched and taped and filled and textured and ready for painting. The room was an empty shell ready to become something.

Bob Dylan was announcing that he wasn't going to work on Maggie's farm no more. And I was angrily admitting to myself that I was pretending again. Or still.

Things change, Patsy McLeod had also said, but people don't. Apparently, I hadn't, at least not yet.

In a few days, I was going to be an associate of Rondo and Keene, doing disinterested investigations, preparing reports and briefs and making a lot of money as I sipped coffee and listened to classical music. That was what I wanted.

But because of what I was and what I couldn't manage to change, for those few days I had to continue to be a private investigator.

As I'd worked, I'd been thinking like one, getting angrier. I'd been angry, I discovered, for a long time.

Royce McLeod's death angered me. I still didn't know what had been going on, but I knew that he had died because of it. His death was no great loss to anyone, especially not to Patsy McLeod. And given his condition, his murder might actually have been a blessing. But it was still murder, a murder that somehow I'd played a part in.

The more I thought about it, the more I came to believe that Royce McLeod hadn't been the only one murdered.

I felt in my gut that Martha Reedy had been right, that we had killed the woman in the putrescent boxcar in Oakland, that she had died because she was pretending to be Heather McLeod. That angered me.

Still, it wasn't just the death of Royce McLeod or of the woman posing as his daughter that had kept me from hieing to the desert.

It wasn't just my sense that I'd somehow been both had and used.

It was also, mostly, what had been causing my depression—my sense that somewhere over the past few days I'd encountered something that was powerfully, profoundly wrong, something that violated everything I thought I was, thought I knew, thought I valued.

I had to find out what it was.

I ran it all back through my mind, trying to fit the pieces together. I made some connections, found some patterns, but I didn't know what they meant, didn't know whether I was piecing together a puzzle or creating a mosaic of my own design.

There was only one way I was ever going to find out.

I was going to have to come out from behind my rock and see who took a shot at me.

On the radio, prison inmates cheered as Johnny Cash growled that he'd shot a man in Reno just to watch him die.

CHAPTER TWENTY-SIX

By the time I'd showered and changed and packed a bag and loaded up the Wagoneer, the sun had lost its warmth, the foothills of the Sierra were deep in shadow.

I took the quick way to Lake Tahoe, I-80 to the California line and up the smoothly engineered concrete climb to Truckee, then over the snow-patched hill to the lake at King's Beach.

In the mountain cold, fast-fading sunlight danced on the water, glistened in the trees, glinted on the small patches of thin snow that had managed not to melt, glittered on whitened peaks. Smoke drifted from fireplaces and woodstoves through the pines and out over the lake. A pale moon waited for darkness.

Again traffic on Lakeshore Drive was light, again the little towns seemed nearly deserted. Crossing back into Nevada, I turned onto the Draines' road, followed it through the big trees toward the meadow and the house.

Smoke rose from the chimney into the graying sky, warm pale

light yellowed the windows. The garage door was closed, the BMW was gone from the parking circle. Over in the corral, Patsy McLeod and the youngest Draine child and a sleek young palomino mare moved in the deepening shadow cast by the barn.

I parked where the BMW usually sat, climbed out as the little girl led the mare into the barn while Patsy McLeod slid between the corral poles and walked quickly across the grass.

The happiness in her desert-worn, desert-cut face made her look beautiful, made me happy. Something in the shift of her raw-boned shoulders as she approached made me think that she was going to hug me. When she stopped, smiling, she swayed forward.

But they don't hug, desert folk. She stuffed her hands into her down vest. Her breath was a thin warm mist in the chill. "When you said you'd find a way, Ross, I never figured . . . I—thanks."

For nothing. But I smiled. "You're welcome, Patsy."

"Day after tomorrow, they'll all be together. That's good."

Somehow I sensed that whatever was going on would end with Royce McLeod's burial. I had less than forty-eight hours to find out what it was.

"Have you decided what you're going to do with the ranch?"

"Nothin'," she said. "Maybe take the kids and the horses out, camp at the big pond for a couple weeks in the summer. Just go out and be there. They'll like that—'specially Lila."

The smell of the smoke from the fireplace mixing with the crisp, clean scent of the pines nearly masked the odor of the beautiful, slowly shrinking, slowly fouling lake.

Maybe that was what made me think of it. "And down the road, Patsy, when . . . ?"

"When I'm bones six feet under, you mean?" She snorted, grinned. "I don't know. Leave it to the kids, I guess."

"You don't want to sell it, get something back for all that you put in the place?"

She shook her head. "I told you, Ross, never was my place. Alls I—besides, who'd buy it? It ain't worth anything."

"I know a developer it's worth something to, Patsy."

Her face set in its desert squint. "What's the matter with you,

Ross? You think I'd let them . . ." She didn't finish, didn't want to contemplate what would happen to the canyon if a developer got ahold of it.

"Eventually, though, it'll get sold. A developer will get it, and you know what that means."

"Well, it ain't gonna happen while I'm still breathing, anyhow." She shivered, perhaps against the chill, bunched the down vest tightly across her middle.

"Why don't you talk to Desert Conservancy?"

Her squint deepened. "You jokin' again?"

"No ma'am."

Her breath came in thicker clouds. "That's the last thing I ever thought I'd hear outta you, Ross."

I shrugged. "It's a solution, Patsy. My guess is that you could make a deal with them that would ensure that you and the Draine kids could camp there as long as you wanted."

"Not a chance," she snorted. "I—"

"You wouldn't even have to sell now. You could simply sign an agreement that if your heirs ever decide to sell the ranch, Desert Conservancy would have right of first refusal. If they took over the property, you'd know that the graves of your children would stay untouched."

"No way," she snorted again, shivered again. "Turn it into a little play-park so all them Sierra Clubber posey-sniffers from the city can go hiking around in their two-hundred-dollar boots and fancy backpacks like they own the place. No way."

I too was feeling the chill. "I know. But somewhere down the line, it's Sierra Clubbers or concrete."

The light was going fast, the gloam to gloom, the moon deepening to gold as it set. Patsy squinted up at it, down at me, turned and looked at the barn.

I could understand her difficulty. She'd spent a lifetime structuring reality according to a myth. It might once have been a good myth, but it no longer explained anything, and she had nothing to replace it with.

"It's not something you have to decide right now, Patsy."

She didn't look at me. "What're you sayin', Ross? That they been right all along, Rosetta and them? An' we been wrong?"

"No. I don't think there is a right or wrong, Patsy, at least in the abstract. But in specific cases, some decisions are better than others."

The moon brightened, sank, turned the snowy peaks a lovely gold.

"I'll think about it," she said finally. "I gotta get back to the barn."

I nodded. "Professor Draine's not here?"

"No," she said absently. "He's down to the university. Rosetta's here, though. I think she wants to talk to you. I—"

She turned to face me. "I owe you a lot, Ross. Heather. The ranch. But I don't know if I can . . ."

Patsy McLeod didn't owe me anything. In discovering that her daughter was dead, I'd at best paid my debt for the grief I'd brought to her eighteen years before. The ranch was something else again.

I reached out and put a hand on her shoulder. "You told me the other day that things change but people don't. That's all we're really talking about. Things changing."

She slid her hard-calloused hand from her pocket. As she had out at the ranch, she put it on mine. Briefly. Then she turned and walked slowly back across the grass toward the barn.

The night seemed darker, colder with her gone. I shivered as I moved through the chill air toward the door, which opened before I had a chance to knock.

Rosetta Draine smiled her small soft warm smile. "Mr. Ross, I'm glad you're here. Come in."

I stepped past her into the warmth of the house, catching a faint scent of something floral and lovely. In trim green slacks and a pale yellow sweater, with her glowing skin and glossy hair, Rosetta Draine seemed herself something floral and lovely.

In the living room, small flames danced in the fireplace. Before it the boy, Charlie, sprawled on the carpet reading a book. The older girl, Claudette, lay on her side, absently, dreamily, softly stroking the coat of the old golden retriever dozing in a curl between them.

Rosetta Draine looked at my fading bruises. "That must have been painful."

"It was."

She nodded, turned toward a hallway. "Do you mind if we talk in here?"

She showed me into a room opposite her husband's office. It wouldn't have been out of place in any city concrete-and-glass high-rise. Large and open, expensively carpeted, hung with small dark abstract etchings, furnished with pieces of pale wood furniture in modern style, and garnished with a rubber plant. A large desk stood before the window looking out onto the meadow, a computer work-station and modem and fax machine in one corner, a pair of filing cabinets in another—everything she would need to keep an eye on the activities of the Mercer Foundation and American Security Bank.

A pair of chairs stood before a low table. She gestured toward them, moved to a coffeemaker beside the computer, poured coffee into a pair of cups. "I was about to write you a note of gratitude, Mr. Ross."

I didn't say anything.

"Wally Keene called yesterday. Patsy should get the ranch. We've asked him to handle the matter for her."

I felt a slow flush creep up my throat. Anger.

Rosetta Draine handed me a steaming cup, then settled onto the edge of a chair, nodded me into the chair beside her.

"You didn't charge Patsy for your services. We think that you should receive your regular fee, plus a bonus."

"You're misspeaking again, Mrs. Draine," I said, my voice tight. "I wasn't working for you."

Her smile was soft, exuded a warmth that was faintly sexual but mostly just human. "As I'm sure you know from your talk with her outside, you have made Patsy very happy, Mr. Ross. That, from our point of view, deserves a reward."

"Fine," I said. "How about the truth?"

Slowly her smile tightened. "I—is something wrong?"

"Almost everything is wrong, Mrs. Draine. It's been wrong from the beginning."

Her smile tightened another notch. "I don't understand."

I set the coffee, untasted, on the table. "My brilliant idea about the divorce decree, for instance. It isn't brilliant. It's obvious."

"In what way?"

"Come on, Mrs. Draine, I'm not stupid, and neither are you. You would have known that Royce McLeod hadn't paid his alimony. Your own attorneys would have told you about the rest."

She looked at me, undisturbed. "And your point is . . . ?"

"You and your husband think things through very carefully, Mrs. Draine. You knew all along that Patsy would get the ranch."

Slowly her smile loosened, warmed. "Yes, Mr. Ross. We knew."

I was suddenly confused. "Then why . . . ?"

"Why didn't we just tell Patsy? Perhaps we should have. But we decided to wait. We thought—correctly, as it turned out—that if you were unable to find Heather, the fact that Patsy would get the ranch might be some consolation to her."

I was getting angrier, more confused. "But if I'd found Heather, she would have had a claim to the property as well."

She shook her head. "You don't understand, Mr. Ross. Hiring you had nothing to do with the ranch. Had you found Heather, then Patsy would have both her daughter and her ranch back."

I was getting a sense of how expertly she had orchestrated everything. And getting even more angry.

"When Martha Reedy was here, why didn't you tell her that Desert Conservancy would never get the place?"

She put down her cup. "Because we wanted Ms. Reedy to look for Heather, which she wouldn't have done if she'd known that Patsy would get the ranch."

When I spoke, my voice sounded strange to me. "So you used her, let her try to find Heather, knowing all the while that what she was doing was actually meaningless."

She finally saw my anger. Her smile tightened again.

"It seemed a relatively harmless ploy. Desert Conservancy has received a check far in excess of what the search cost them—Ms. Reedy was volunteering her time, of course, and charged them only expenses. She's received a substantial check as well."

"And you're letting Wally Keene handle the ranch affair because . . . oh, let's say because you have a lot of legal work and you could use another attorney and this is an opportunity to check him out, something like that?"

Rosetta Draine watched me. "Something like that."

"And you want to give me a check, pay me off too."

She folded her hands, composing herself, taking control.

"You think that we manipulated you. We didn't, really, but perhaps you're right to be upset. We might have told you about the ranch, but it didn't seem relevant to the search for Heather. It still doesn't. And we weren't sure what to expect of you."

She nearly smiled. "Patsy told us that you were honest, but she hadn't spoken to you in eighteen years. And, as I'm sure you know, you have a reputation in certain quarters for . . ."

Rosetta Draine still had an answer for everything. "You seem to feel we shouldn't have let Patsy believe that you were responsible for her getting the ranch. For that, I apologize."

Rosetta Draine still said all the right things. And I still had the sense that what she said was true but not the truth.

"Do you know, Mrs. Draine, that your little ploy, as you called it, nearly got Martha Reedy killed?"

Her gaze wavered. "How . . . ?"

"She was run off the road in the desert. If I hadn't come along, she might have died out there."

"I—I'm sorry. I didn't know."

I almost believed her.

"Do you know that Martha found a woman who was using Heather's identity and two hours later that woman was dead?"

"Dead . . . I—Mr. Ross, what are you . . . ?"

She couldn't be faking her confusion. She hadn't known.

I didn't know what it meant. I didn't know what any of it meant. I did know, finally, that there was only one way I was going to be able to find out. If it didn't kill me.

"Do you know that Royce McLeod was murdered?"

Her composure returned with her disbelief. Leaning forward in her chair, she again clasped her hands in her lap.

"Mr. Ross, that's preposterous. The sheriff has determined that Mr. McLeod—"

"Do you know that all of these things were done by a man named Linus Flowers?" It was the only way it made sense.

"I don't know what—" She stopped, stared. Something new rose into her dark eyes. "There was a man named Flowers, a deputy sheriff who . . . ?"

"Who came out to the camp where you and your husband were playing hippie twenty years ago."

"Mr. Ross, I don't . . ."

Suddenly she shuddered. The new thing in her eyes, I realized, was fear. "But why? Why would he do these things? Why would he kill a dying man? I don't understand."

"I don't either. But I'm going to find out."

"But what has he to do with . . . anything?"

"Linus Flowers isn't really important. He's a hired killer. What's important, Mrs. Draine, is who hired him."

As she watched me, her lovely skin paled, her face went blank. "You think we hired that Flowers person to . . . do these things?"

"Somebody did. And I'm going to find out who it is."

She shuddered again, looked down at her folded hands; under the pressure of her grip, her fingers were edged with white.

"I assume, because the sheriff has ruled Mr. McLeod's death a suicide, that you haven't told him of your . . . suspicions."

"No."

"I also assume that you haven't told him because that's all they are, suspicions. You can't prove anything."

"Not yet."

"And how do you propose to find that proof?"

I stood up. "I don't know. What I think, Mrs. Draine, is that somehow when I was looking for Heather I stirred something up, got too close to something. So I'm going to stir things up some more."

CHAPTER TWENTY-SEVEN

"Please, Mr. Ross," Rosetta Draine said. "Sit down."

"Why?"

"Because you're wrong." She nodded, grimly, at the chair. "Let me tell you why we would never hire that Flowers man to do anything."

Whatever she would tell me would be true, I knew, but it wouldn't be the truth. Still, there might be something in it that I could use. I sat down.

She picked up her coffee cup. It trembled slightly in her hand. "He was an evil man. He used to come out to the camp, pretending that he was checking for drugs, but that was nonsense. He did more drugs than anyone out there. He was really out there after the girls, after sex. He was especially after . . ."

The cup in her hand quivered, sent a spatter of coffee onto her green slacks. She didn't seem to notice. "He . . . caught me one day at the iris pond. He tore my clothes, had me on the ground. He was so big that I . . ."

She shuddered, violently, splattering more coffee onto her lap. She set down the cup, brushed absently at the stains. "Patsy came along. She had her rifle. Otherwise . . ."

She shuddered again. "She called the sheriff and told him that if that Flowers set foot on her land again she'd kill him."

I got her point. Rosetta Draine would never have hired a man who had tried to rape her.

She picked up her coffee cup again, sipped. Then she spoke so softly that I barely made out the words.

"You've made Patsy very happy, Mr. Ross. I would be very happy if I learned that Linus Flowers was dead."

It took me a moment to understand what she was saying. "Are you making me a business proposition, Mrs. Draine?"

She rose, went to the coffeemaker and refilled her cup, went to the window and looked out into the darkness.

"I was surprised that you didn't remember me, Mr. Ross." The words were addressed to me, but she seemed really to be talking to her reflection in the dark glass.

"I did, eventually."

She seemed not to have heard me. "I remembered you. I remembered your face when you found Gentle, when you discovered what had been done to her. You looked . . . murderous."

She turned away from her dark image, came back to the chair, sat.

"You aren't answering my question, Mrs. Draine."

She sipped her coffee. "Am I trying to hire you to kill Linus Flowers? No. But to be perfectly honest with you, if I thought you'd do it, I might."

I didn't say anything, waited to see where she'd go next.

"But you wouldn't. That's why meeting you the other day was such a surprise. The man I saw twenty years ago was capable of doing what we heard you had done, and more."

My violent, evil ways, as Hannah Fielding had said.

"You didn't seem to be that man anymore."

"I hope I'm not." If I ever was.

In the silence I heard the muffled slam of the front door, Patsy's half-stern remonstrance, a child's happy laughter. Then the fax machine blinked, began to hum softly.

"Excuse me," Rosetta Draine said, rising. She went to the machine, watched it. When it stopped, she took the sheet of paper from it, placed it on her desk, smiled.

"We've been negotiating with a group of church leaders in Las Vegas who want to establish a halfway house for runaway teenagers. I think we'll be able to help them."

"Too bad nobody helped Heather McLeod."

She came back, sat, picked up her cup. "We can't change the past, Mr. Ross. We can only work for a better future."

Her small smile went wry. "I sometimes imagine Bill's grandmother Felice rolling in her grave. All that money that old Claude extirpated from Nevada and bamboozled from Nevadans—we're giving it back, and more. Felice's only concern was keeping alive the Mercer name. She couldn't have dreamed we'd do it this way."

"Why don't you tell me how that happened, Mrs. Draine? How was it that an old-money Bay Area debutante found herself in a hippie camp in the Nevada desert twenty years ago and ended up controlling . . ."

I'd nearly said "everything."

". . . a bank and a charitable foundation? How did a rich hippie kid who was making a career out of sex and drugs and rock 'n' roll end up a Stanford professor who writes revisionist history of the West?"

Her eyes changed, lost their focus. "Not old money, Mr. Ross. Not any kind of money."

She sipped at her coffee again. "If you want to understand it, you'll need to hear it all. Although I'm not sure that you'll really understand."

"I'll do my best," I said flatly.

"No, I don't mean it that way," she said. "I mean, I'm not certain that I understand it all myself. It's all so remote from our life now, it seems like . . . something I dreamed once."

Rosetta Draine was definitely not old Bay Area money. She was Turk Street welfare, the illegitimate offspring of a San Francisco vice cop and an alcoholic part-time hooker.

Rosetta Greenleaf had grown up on the streets of the Tenderloin, she told me, dodging the grasping hands and boozy lunges of her mother's men friends, ignoring the whispered enticements from shadowed doorways and alleys, fighting off the advances of thugs and pimps, abjuring the consolations—sex, drugs, booze, fantasy, and romance—of the defeated and the despairing.

Rosetta Greenleaf, almost as soon as she knew anything, knew that she was beautiful and intelligent, as beautiful and probably more intelligent than the women who shopped in the boutiques at Union Square, who wore lovely clothes and lived in the lovely homes that hung from the San Francisco hillsides. Almost as soon as she knew anything, she told me, she knew she should, and would, be one of them. She just didn't know how.

But she prepared. She spent hours in the library, learning how wealthy women dressed and talked, analyzing what they thought and what they didn't think, charting the few things they knew and the many they didn't, assessing their ideas about decorating and clothes, about behavior, about love, about what was important.

She thought it was foolishness, the babble of the stupid and the deluded. These women believed that they wore lovely clothes and lived in lovely homes because they were inherently superior—when all they really were was fortunate.

She knew what was important—money. And she knew what wasn't important—love.

Love was the drunken groan and slap of flesh behind her bedroom wall, the flash of thigh in the backseat of an automobile, the hard anger in a john's eyes, the disdain in a hooker's hard voice.

Love, she told me, was a fantasy created by men and nurtured by cowardly women to protect themselves from the reality that they were being bred and marketed and sold like animals.

Intimate human relations were unavoidable but irrelevant to anything significant. Or so she had believed.

What mattered was money, and a woman who wasn't born into it got it with beauty, style, brains, courage, got it by controlling everyone and everything. Rosetta Greenleaf learned how to do it, how to control her mother, her teachers, men.

Then, just after she'd turned seventeen, Rosetta Greenleaf met

William Draine at a Grateful Dead concert. At first he was just one more stoned pseudohippie to her, until she learned who he was: a Mercer, of the Palo Alto and Mercer Foundation and American Security Bank Mercers. His parents had been killed in an automobile crash when he was six. His only relative was his aging grandmother. William Draine would someday be very wealthy.

Within a week she was a hippie chick and his "old lady."

It was easy. She was beautiful. And she was intelligent.

And while William Draine too was intelligent, he was also angry, confused, and usually stoned—so stoned that he couldn't see that his future and her destiny lay behind him, in the Palo Alto house he had fled, the lovely house he took her to one weekend after a private detective had tracked him down and informed him that his grandmother was dying and wanted to see him before she went.

"It was nearly Dickensian," Rosetta Draine said. "She, of course, wasn't dying. She was desperately trying to get her grandson away from all those disgusting hippies."

Once one of those beautiful, brainless women that rich men used to marry, Felice Mercer had withered into the image of Miss Havisham in *Great Expectations,* a calculating crone whose only concern was the family name. Her grandson was a source of despair, a nearly unrecognizable drug-muttering lout.

Felice Mercer had a talk with her grandson, but her carping and wheedling and threats to disinherit him couldn't pierce his dope fog. Then Rosetta Draine had a talk with Felice Mercer.

Perhaps because she had taught herself how to sit and speak, because she'd learned how women like Felice Mercer thought and what they thought about, Rosetta Greenleaf convinced William Draine's grandmother that the two were allies, that her hippie garb was merely a gesture of solidarity with William, who was a troubled but basically sound young man.

The young woman convinced the old that natural beauty and intelligence could substitute for good breeding. She convinced Felice Mercer that she would see her grandson through this unfortunate stage in his life, that she would make him into the kind of man the old woman could be proud of, a Mercer.

Felice Mercer agreed not to cut off her grandson and to give

Rosetta Greenleaf a chance to make him a Mercer. Neither woman used the word "love" in their conversation.

"It was a business arrangement, and we both knew it," Rosetta said. "Felice would get what she wanted—a Mercer—and I would get what I wanted."

I understood what she was saying. I thought I understood why she was saying it.

She sat back in her chair. "It's hard to remember the girl I was, so . . . cold. I can understand her, but I can't *feel* her. She's like a laminated photograph in my memory, untouchable."

William Draine and Rosetta Greenleaf, at his grandmother's insistence, were married a week later.

But despite her beauty and intelligence, Rosetta found that it was not easy to control and transform William Draine. Drugs and dreams had too strong a hold on him.

For a few months, she told me, she drifted with him through Haight-Ashbury hippie pads and Big Sur cabins and Grass Valley communes, faked frolic at the love-ins and be-ins, pretended interest at the revolutionary political meetings and the social consciousness–raising sessions, feigned sympathy with the worked-at weirdness of his friends who were his friends as long as he bought the dope.

All the while she subtly, intellectually, sexually, worked on him. But he did more and more drugs, more grass and LSD, washed down more uppers and downers with more red wine and Southern Comfort. And he drifted away from her, drifted away from everything.

Then he began to read Blake, and he began to think he had discovered what was wrong with America, began to think that he could change it, began to call himself Blake. Until, finally, full of dreams and visions and dope, he decided he had to go to the desert.

All the great civilizations that he knew about had begun in the desert.

His family owned abandoned mines all over Nevada, and he would go to one and start the world all over again.

Rosetta encouraged him. Because, she told me, she had begun to have a vision of her own, dark and terrifying, of her destiny turning back on itself. She began to have nightmares of living her now-dead mother's life in her mother's dead body.

But maybe the clean air and outdoor life of the desert would bring him back to reality, the reality of Palo Alto and the Mercer Foundation and the American Security Bank.

So she and Blake loaded the Day-Glo-flowered VW van with a few bits of clothes, a few cooking utensils, and a lot of dope. With another hippie, Raven, a small-time drug dealer who, Rosetta suspected, was leaving town one step ahead of the major dealers he'd been ripping off, they left San Francisco one damp and chilly April morning, heading for the dry warmth of Nevada and Blake's new world in the desert.

At first, she told me, that spring things went better than she could have hoped.

The thin, dry desert air did seem to clear Blake's mind. With another hippie who had shown up, a boy so at home in the desert outdoors that he quickly became known as Leatherstocking, they set up camp, laid out small garden plots and ran a drip system from Patsy McLeod's pond, made plans to drill a well the next summer and turn the desert into a garden. They explored the mountains and the desert, and Blake began to return to reality.

Patsy McLeod helped too. Her gruff, rough desert ways seemed to rasp off some of his delusions. They had odd conversations. She explained life to him; he explained America and love to her. Neither quite understood the other.

As the weather warmed, San Francisco people began dropping in at the camp, began staying. Good people, free and loving and joyous. They started more little gardens; with Leatherstocking they hunted rabbits and deer, scoured the mountains for berries and nuts and tubers, scratched the earth after turquoise and opal. They set up tents, built lean-tos, and decorated them and the desert with bright Day-Glo flowers. They played in the pond, she told me, made music around the night fires, made love in the desert sun and under the desert stars.

The summer was nearly as good. The desert heat seemed to suck out more of the toxins of Blake's anger. More people showed up and were free and loving together. Blake took new heart in his dream of the New America. His camp was the New Eden, he would make the desert bear fruit, he and his group would multiply.

Then, in the fall, the others began to wander off—those for whom the summer had just been a vacation from school, those who realized that spending the winter in the cold desert would make it hard to be free and loving and joyous, those who knew that only Blake's trust-fund check was keeping them fed, those who had endured his solemn campfire sermonizing in order to smoke his dope.

Blake saw it all start to fall apart, saw that few had ever believed in his vision, saw that he couldn't change them or the desert or America, and he started to fall apart.

He began to do more dope, got angrier, crazier, distant. And Rosetta grew concerned. He was going away from her again, she told me, where she could never control him. As his dream disintegrated, so did his sense of himself, of reality. As he disintegrated, so did her own dream.

Between the dope-induced paranoia and his sense of betrayal, Blake became convinced that he was more than a prophet. Gradually the hippie camp became the site of a trust-fund fascism, the spirit of loving became his insistence on sexual dominance, the joyousness became anger and fear and, finally, violence.

The first snow came in October, turned the camp to mud. By the time the snow had melted and the mud frozen, only a handful of people were left—Raven, Creole, Mahatma, Leatherstocking, Isis and Lavender Blue and Julie Star Eyes and her infant daughter.

The first big snow came in November. Then more snow.

By December, Rosetta said, the camp was snowbound—not that it mattered, since the flower-spattered VW bus was buried in the mud and snow where it had gone off the edge of the road at the creek cut in the desert dune. The only footpath they could keep open led over the hill to Patsy McLeod.

More snow. Patsy tried to get them to move to her place, if not into her house at least into the shelter of her barn. Raging, Blake refused. The others wanted to go, but Rosetta couldn't leave him. He was the only future she had. Then Leatherstocking said he'd stay too. They all stayed.

More snow. Patsy managed to keep them alive, butchering beef for them, hauling them firewood from town, driving Blake in to get his trust-fund checks and making certain that he bought food and blankets and clothing and medicine and not dope.

When Julie Star Eyes began coughing blood, Leatherstocking carried her, and Rosetta carried her baby, over the icy trail to Patsy's house. Patsy convinced the girl to call her parents in Lodi, then drove her into Reno to meet them.

The others stayed at the camp, ached with cold, with hunger.

With loneliness. Blake grew calm. Then the calm changed to an unsettling quiet. He was gone, lost in himself. More snow.

"Those last two months did something to us," Rosetta Draine said. "All of us. We didn't even want to go to Patsy's anymore. It didn't seem to matter. Nothing seemed important."

I didn't say anything, listened.

"It's hard to explain. The desert . . . the darkness, the cold, the awful silence. It was as if we were isolated on some icy uninhabitable planet where it would snow forever."

She was at the window now, looking through her dark reflection out into the night. Then she turned back to me.

"That's one of the reasons we decided to live up here, Mr. Ross. When it snows, sometimes, Bill and I look at each other, remembering. It reminds us . . . of what's important."

She picked up the coffeepot, brought it to the table. My cup was still full, the coffee cold.

Finally, Rosetta Draine told me, the snow stopped. In March, when the snow had mostly melted, when the first stalks of green began to poke up through the damp desert earth and the sage began to sweeten the air, two utterly astounding things happened.

Using Patsy's pickup, Blake and Raven and Leatherstocking got the VW van back onto the road. Blake drove it up the canyon to the iris pond.

Then he walked over the hill, collected all his pipes and hookahs, his tattered hippie finery, his leather-bound volume of William Blake, took them back and tossed them into the van, and rolled the van into the iris pond.

Rosetta Draine smiled faintly. "A rather grandiose gesture, but . . .

he was young. We all were. It's hard to remember how young we were."

But that wasn't the end.

They waited another couple of weeks. William Draine—no longer Blake, never again Blake—began to take long walks in the mountains, sometimes with Patsy McLeod, sometimes with Rosetta. He began to talk about what he saw on those walks, and what he saw was the history of men's misguided attempts to make the desert into something it could never be, as the McLeods had tried, as he had.

He began to talk about what he wanted out of life. He wanted to study history, to find out why human beings had done what they had done to the desert. And he wanted what he had discovered was the only important thing in life. A family.

Rosetta Draine smiled faintly again. "It was the first thing he'd ever said that I agreed with. A year before I wouldn't have, but . . . one of the things I'd learned that winter was that we don't have God anymore, people like us. All we have to give meaning to our lives is family."

I didn't say anything, listened.

As William Draine talked, Rosetta Draine told me, talked about history, about family, the second utterly astounding thing happened. She fell in love.

"I can't explain it, Mr. Ross. It wasn't something I wanted to happen. I would have been perfectly satisfied to go through life never loving anyone. But . . . I had changed as much as he had. That winter had stripped us to the bone. And I discovered that I wasn't quite what I thought I was."

I didn't say anything.

"We left soon after that. Bill wanted to get as far away as he could. We ended up in New Haven. The rest . . ."

"As they say," I said, "is history. William Draine becomes a Stanford professor, a Mercer his grandmother can boast about, and Rosetta Greenleaf Draine fulfills her destiny and begins giving the Mercer money back to those it was stolen from."

She detected my sarcasm, tightened her smile a notch.

"Felice never got to see it. We corresponded, so she knew what was happening, and when Claudette was born, I took her back to Palo Alto. But Bill was too busy catching up academically. He didn't get back before she died."

Her account had fascinated me. Not so much the details—some of it I had heard before, from Patsy, from Dale Rutledge, from William Draine. Some of it I'd gotten in generic outline from other disillusioned hippies. Some of it I'd guessed.

What fascinated me was the telling, the careful composition of her confessions, the neatly arranged sequence of events that became the moralistic and romantic tale of an exceptional girl emotionally stunted by the horror of her childhood, who to survive became a calculating young woman who through an act of the God she didn't believe in became a human being. All was designed to engage my sympathy with Rosetta Draine.

I got to my feet, and lied. "You were right the other night, Mrs. Draine. All that has nothing to do with the present."

"Or if it does, it can't change the present."

"Speaking of which," I said, "what did Dale Rutledge say when you talked to him?"

"He wanted money," she said, sighing. "He thought we'd pay him to keep silent about Bill and the commune."

"What did you tell him?"

"That he could shout it from the rooftops if he chose."

She too rose. "He wasn't very coherent, but it seemed he needed money to finance some film project. I told him to meet me at the foundation offices next week and we'd discuss it."

Clearly, Rutledge hadn't been coherent enough to explain what kind of film project. Family fucking porn, Culler had called it.

"Why would you want to do that, Mrs. Draine?"

"The foundation often makes grants to deserving artists," she said. "And while I don't know what his work is like now, what I saw of it twenty years ago was in many ways remarkable. I made no commitment, but I'll listen to what he has to say."

It was slick. She was not paying him off, but she was paying him off.

She looked at me, then went to the desk, sat, took out a checkbook. She looked at me again. Then she took out a pen and wrote out a check, rose and came over and held it out to me.

The check was made out to me, for ten times what Patsy McLeod had hired me for, drawn on Rosetta's personal account.

"I'd like to retain your professional services, Mr. Ross. If Linus Flowers killed Mr. McLeod, I'd like you to try to prove it. And to discover who hired him to do it."

I didn't take the check. "Why?"

"Because if you can learn who is responsible, you'll know that we weren't."

I looked at the check in her hand. I didn't think she wanted to hire me to learn who had hired Linus Flowers.

I thought she was trying to get me killed.

I grinned, took the check.

In the living room, Patsy McLeod sat on the sofa, the center of a sentimental tableau, the little girl on her lap, the older girl and boy on either side of her, the old dog at her feet. Four happy faces smiled at the television set and the amusing antics of another pretend family.

CHAPTER TWENTY-EIGHT

I stopped in Truckee for a quick hamburger and a cup of coffee, stopped again at the Donner Summit rest station to get rid of the coffee.

In the men's room I tore the check into small pieces and flushed them down the toilet. No grandiose gesture on my part. If I was wrong, Rosetta Draine could write me another. But I didn't think I was wrong. I just didn't know how I was right.

The night was cold, clear. I stood out in it for a while, getting colder, looking up into the night sky. In the endless darkness the thick stars hung huge and low. Venus and Mars pulsed. Love and violence.

When I was cold enough, I got back into the Wagoneer and headed down the mountain.

The night went from cold to cool, the crisp thin air to thick and damp. At Colfax, I managed to get something on the radio, the childish singsong chant of a song I'd never heard before. It seemed to sum up much of my life.

It was the end of the world as I knew it, but I felt fine.

Then the news came on. As I listened, it became clear that it was the end of the world as everybody in America knew it.

The hole in the ozone layer was much larger than predicted and imperiled the globe. The USSR continued to collapse, and the administration promised to send them money. General Motors had lost billions and planned to close plants all over the country. Half the farmers in the Big Valley would be without water next year. A Sacramento woman had shot and killed her husband in a dispute over the color of her nail polish. A Redwood family had abandoned the husband's senile mother at a bus station. Another arctic storm front was nudging the California coast, but it would bring no rain.

I shut it off.

The Big Valley blazed with light. Traffic thickened. By the time I got to Auburn Avenue in Sacramento, the sky had paled, the stars had dimmed behind high thin clouds. In the streetlights, the neighborhood looked to be in the last stages of abandonment, the graffiti brightening the shabbiness like mad makeup on a bag lady.

Intimate Moments Productions was dark, Videoscape lit.

The Chicana with the sharp Indian face and beautiful black hair was watching another movie. On the soundless screen, Raquel Welch heaved her señorita's breast at the tin star on Jim Brown's chest. For some reason I thought of Tramontane and her distorted black shadow, Monte.

"Hey . . . *viejo*."

I was surprised she remembered me, and, when I saw her huge dark pupils, surprised she could ever remember anything.

"You know why she . . . big star? Boobs."

She looked down at her loose halter top, at her crab-apple breasts. Then she gave me her strong-toothed, blind-eyed smile. "I . . . buy big tits. Be a . . . star."

"Good for you. Dale Rutledge been around?"

"Two days. Everybody . . . looking for him."

"Who?"

"Lady cop. An' . . . guys. Like you, *viejo*, big guys. You got the . . . equipment for it, you an' me, we could be—"

"Cops?"

Her head swiveled, sending bright ripples through her beautiful black hair. "Only . . . lady cop."

"How many big guys?"

She held up her tattooed hand. L-O-V-E. She raised two gnawed-nail fingers, then a third.

If I understood her, she was talking about, probably, Martha Reedy, and two big men, then a single big man.

"Who were they?"

She shook her head, dropped her hand and spidered it across the counter.

I took out my wallet and handed her a twenty-dollar bill.

"You play with fire, *viejo*, . . . you gonna get burned."

I might have understood that.

On the small square of screen, light and shadow formed unreal images. Again I found myself thinking of Tramontane.

The Chicana looked at the images. "Big tits . . . no soul."

I walked toward the back, past the racks of tapes and into the office. The drawers of the filing cabinet had been ripped open; the papers they'd held were scattered over the desk and floor.

I didn't need lights to see that the office of Intimate Moments Productions had been trashed. The window was shattered, as was the glass case behind the desk. Smashed plastic video cases lay over the desk and floor and chairs, twists and curls of tape trailing from them like the innards of huge black plastic bugs.

I couldn't tell if someone had been looking for something or just having fun. All I could tell was that the 16mm film cases that had been stacked in the corner were gone.

I went back to Videoscape. The Chicana studied the square screen. "Big tits. No soul . . . style. Not like me."

"Who trashed the place?"

She gave me her strong-toothed grin, held up two fingers.

"When?"

She shrugged, turned back to the screen. "She . . . Chicana. Tries to hide it. Buys a new nose."

"And you're going to buy big tits," I said. "I know."

"But not . . . to hide. I got . . ."

"I know," I said again, "you've got the King of Spain in your blood."

Again I shut off the lights, locked the door behind me.

Freeway traffic had thinned. Weaving my way through it, I got to Davis in half an hour.

The city lights collected in the high thin clouds, turned the night to twilight. In it the land around the city was just flat and furrowed brown earth waiting for the rain that wasn't coming, a man-made desert. I had no trouble finding Rutledge's place.

The dark old white frame house looked like most of the others that squatted amid the fields, empty, abandoned. The Plymouth Voyager stood before the house, its door open. No dome light glowed. The door had been open a long time.

Parking the Wagoneer partly out of sight beside the barn, I found my flashlight, got out and walked across the yard to the house. The front door was locked, but not very.

Once I was sure the house was empty, I turned on the lights and searched it carefully. I didn't find what I was looking for. All I found was Dale Rutledge's life.

The tastefully appointed living room, with its rugs and ceramics and photographs, was a sort of wish projection, an image of the life Dale Rutledge aspired to; the life he actually lived lurked in the rest of the house, which had the look and feel of failure, the smell of dead dreams and alcoholic despair.

The old-fashioned kitchen was littered with fast-food containers, the floor sticky and stained, the oven top crusted with charred slops, the countertops and table thick with dust.

The bathroom was filthy and infested, the shower stall dark with body grease, the stool thick-ringed and cracked.

The only used bedroom was a shambles of dirty clothes and dirty sheets, empty bottles and glasses, booze-stained copies of film magazines and sticky, smudged copies of skin rags. In the two other small bedrooms, dust lay thickly over the emptiness.

I found myself feeling some sympathy for Dale Rutledge. Or maybe just for myself. The emptiness at the center of his home and life reminded me of the emptiness at the center of my own.

I went back outside, over to the barn. The large door was se-cured by a large padlock. Around the back I found a small door secured by a small padlock. After a few minutes I had it open. Sliding into the dark silence, I fumbled, found a switch.

What had been a barn was a single, vast, concrete-floored, air-conditioned room broken only by a long sheetrocked rectangular room along a side wall. Across the open area, beds of various shapes and sizes centered sets that suggested variations on themes of sexual fantasy. On or around them sat or hung strange implements and objects, most of which were leather or rubber or plastic, most of which I had difficulty associating with any kind of human fantasy, sexual or otherwise.

Along the back wall, bits and swathes of colorful cloth hung from rolling clothes racks. Empty tripods and assorted tools of, I assumed, the cinematic trade sat in scattered abandon over the floor amid twists and tangles of cable.

Beside the sheetrock rectangle, a small enclave contained a couch and coffee table and a large television set and VCR. A rack of tapes below the VCR bore the same pretty calligraphy as those in Dale Rutledge's office; the printing appeared to designate the possibili-ties of each set—THREE-RING CIRCUS, TRUE ROMANCE, GLADIATORS, SERAGLIO, DESERTED ISLAND.

The door to the rectangular room was shut. Through it I could smell a foulness that the air-conditioning hadn't been able to suck away.

My sympathy for Dale Rutledge deepened. But it was too late for sympathy, or anything else. The foulness told me that nothing would help him now.

I took a deep breath, opened the door, found the light.

What had been Dale Rutledge lay on the concrete floor. What had been his face was charred flesh and grayish bone.

The walls of the room were covered with old film posters, most for porno flicks, most directed by Dale Rutledge. Two of them featured Tramontane. On a long wooden bench bolted to the out-side wall, machines whose purpose escaped me cast grotesque shadows.

I searched the room as carefully as I had searched the house. Then I shut off the light, stepped out of the room and shut the door, began searching again.

I didn't find what I was looking for.

Back in the farmyard, I searched the Plymouth Voyager. I found what I expected to find. Nothing.

I remembered the .22 Luger Dale Rutledge had pulled on me. I went back in the house and looked for it. I didn't find it either.

I drove back to town, stopped at a phone booth by the entrance to the UC-Davis campus, and anonymously called 911.

Then I called Berkeley and got Martha Reedy's recorded message. I nearly hung up. If she was asleep, or not at home, I'd have to do what I had to do some other way. But I left a message anyhow:

"This is Ross. It's a little past eleven. I'll be there by one. If you hear this before then, see if you can find out where I might find Cleveland Culler this time of night."

I hesitated, then added, "I'll pay you for your professional services."

"That won't be necessary," said a voice still thick with sleep.

"Martha?"

"Does this have something to do with the death of the woman in Oakland?"

"In a roundabout way."

"I know where to find Cleveland Culler," she said evenly. "But you can't get there from wherever you are. You'll have to start at my front door."

CHAPTER TWENTY-NINE

On the river of lights I drifted through the pale, not-quite-real California darkness.

In an odd way that I sensed but didn't understand, little of what had happened since I'd last made this drive seemed real. Fragmented by my anger, distorted by my depression, it all floated through my mind like scenes from an interrupted dream desperate to finish itself.

My discovery in Dale Rutledge's studio had taken a lot out of me. To dispel my weariness, I punched on the radio, found an FM station playing Randy Newman's *Sail Away* album, almost immediately began to smile—simple lovely chords, simple sardonic couplets. The world hates America and we don't know why. We aren't perfect but heaven knows we try.

The album was twenty years old. Some things don't change.

Under lowering pale gray clouds, San Francisco Bay at night was still beautiful. A sharp wind stirred the black water, tipped wavelets white. Around it the dark hills and the cubes and lines of city lights seemed to swirl like a galaxy around a black hole.

Berkeley was quiet, streets empty, aflutter with detritus driven by the wind.

The only light in Martha Reedy's neighborhood glowed behind her window. As I pulled in behind the Geo, the window went black. By the time I got out into the wind, she was halfway down the flower-lined walk, her purse swinging savagely from her shoulder.

On the drive from Davis, I'd concluded that what I was about to do was probably old-fashioned and chauvinistic and pointless. I did it anyway. "Martha, I really don't think you should—"

"Let's take my car," she said, stepping past me. She was angry. "I know where we're going. You don't."

"You don't even know why I'm going."

The wind tousled her hair, tugged at her bulky nylon jacket. Unlocking the Geo, she slid inside. "So you'll tell me, or I'll find out when we get there."

I didn't like it, but there wasn't much I could do. I went around the Geo and jammed and scrunched myself in beside her. "I hope you don't have a gun in that purse."

She gave me a sharp angry look but said nothing.

We were in the middle of the Bay Bridge before I spoke. "You're not still mad about that stupid little scene with Hannah and me on your porch. It's something else."

When she spoke, it was without intonation. "I got a note of thanks and a check from Rosetta Draine. A big check. What did I do to earn it?"

"You didn't find Heather McLeod."

"That's how I read it too," she said evenly.

She didn't speak again until we were on the City Center off-ramp. "Her name was Maureen Cody. They think. They had to run through seven separate identities, and Maureen Cody is the only one who hasn't been dead for years. She used the fake IDs to run scams on the welfare department, food stamps, mostly."

I'd assumed it was something like that. "You still think we killed her?"

Streetlights paled her face. "That was just . . . I get too personally involved sometimes."

"So do I," I said. "That's why I'm not doing it anymore."

She turned to look at me, expressionless.

"This is my last private investigation. In a couple of days I'll be an associate of the firm of Rondo and Keene."

Something came into her face, but I couldn't read it. She turned away from me, to the night and the wind and the city, spoke as if I hadn't.

"I made a mistake. Instead of concentrating on my job, I got caught up in a brainless competition with you. I wanted to find Heather myself, to show you . . ." She glanced at me, glanced quickly away. "I should have taken you along to meet her. You would have known she wasn't Heather McLeod, and Maureen Cody would still be alive."

"Maybe," I said. "What was the official cause of death?"

"Bad heroin. There's been a lot of it around lately, and a lot of dead junkies. They're still calling it accidental."

"Are you?"

We were in the city now, in the dim downtown canyons edged with dark shadows that might have been just shadows, astir with movement that might have been just wind.

"She still had the hundred dollars I gave her, so she didn't buy the bad junk. She either had it—but there wasn't any more in the house—or somebody gave it to her. I don't like the coincidence. She gets the bad junk an hour after talking to me."

We had started to climb, on wide streets terraced by cross-streets. The wind strengthened, buffeted the small car.

"After Linus Flowers followed you to the meeting."

"So you say." When I didn't respond, she said: "You seem to have a thing about this Flowers. Personal?"

The thought of my last encounter with Linus Flowers freshened my shame, my anger. Maybe it was personal. But that didn't mean I was wrong about what I thought he'd done.

"No. It's just that some people get me confused with him."

"If you mean, Hannah, that isn't—" She stopped, then said something different. "I thought about Flowers too. But we have to assume he's working for someone, and if he killed Maureen Cody he did it because he thought she was Heather McLeod. The question

is who would want Heather dead. And why. Do you still think someone else is involved in all this?"

"I don't know," I said. "But I know that Linus Flowers also killed
Royce McLeod."

"Hannah told me about—she said suicide."

I told her why it wasn't. Before she could ask, I told her I didn't
know why anyone would want to kill a dying man.

Then I told her how Nolan Turner had again insisted that the
Beulah Valley property wasn't especially important to him, and how
Rosetta Draine had explained that the search for Heather had noth-
ing to do with the McLeod ranch.

Martha's face didn't change, but I could feel the heat of her
anger. She didn't like being used either.

I told her how Mrs. Draine had explained everything else. I told
her about what she had almost hired me to do, about what she had
finally hired me to do, about what I had done with her check.

"You think she's setting you up? For Flowers?"

"I think I'll find out when I get back to Nevada."

"You're going after him?"

"No. Rosetta Draine is the only person I told about Flowers. If
he comes after me, then we'll know."

"You think she's behind all this?"

"I don't know, Martha," I said. "Maybe not behind. In the middle.
Rosetta Draine is always at the center of things."

"What does that mean?"

"I don't know," I said again.

"Mrs. Draine has made the Mercer Foundation a real force for
good, Jack," she said slowly, thoughtfully. "She's helped a lot of
people. It doesn't make sense that she could . . ."

I knew it didn't make sense. But that didn't matter.

We continued to climb. The streets stopped being straight, narrowed, began following the contours of the hills. The darkness deepened as the road we were on twisted through thick trees, edged
sheer precipices that gave scary and spectacular views of the city
lights. At the end of small lanes, sprawls and jumbles of glass-fronted
boxes dug into and cantilevered out over the steep hillsides like
handholds for social climbers.

"I went to Sacramento yesterday, looking for Dale Rutledge, on the chance that he might know of some other connection between Heather and Maureen Cody. All I could learn was that a lot of people are looking for him."

"Somebody found him." I told her what I'd discovered a couple of hours before.

Silently she slowed the Geo, turned onto a narrow lane bordered with huge old cypress and fir. The pavement ended at a retaining wall and another view of the lights and the deep and watery darkness at their center. From this vertiginous height the city looked like a distant and unfathomable universe.

The Geo coasted to a stop before a heavy wrought-iron gate in the center of a high block wall. "Is that why we're here, to establish that Culler had Dale Rutledge killed?" Martha asked.

"No," I said. "To establish that he didn't."

I told her what I hadn't found in Rutledge's house or studio or van.

"You think he was killed because of a film he made twenty years ago? What could be on it that—"

"I don't know. And never will. The film is gone."

The wind hissed in the trees, drove gray clouds across the sky, rocked the Geo. When Martha spoke again, her voice was different—droll, edged with excitement.

"And now you're just going to walk on in there and ask Culler if he had Dale Rutledge killed?"

I looked at her, slowly began to smile. As we had out in the desert, we recognized each other.

"Be pretty hard to talk to him from here."

Slowly she gave me her smile, the one that opened her face like a flower. Again she seemed to watch me from behind it.

"You really are crazy, aren't you?"

I didn't know about that. I did know that suddenly I wasn't tired anymore, wasn't depressed. "Takes one to know one, Ms. Reedy."

We climbed out of the Geo and into the wind. Through the gate I could see a courtyard designed like a cubist painting, with squares and rectangles of flower beds and grass, small square plots of skeletal citrus trees, a grid of brick walks. Behind it the house sprawled and jutted, it looked like something a two-year-old might have built of toy blocks.

Martha slipped past me, pressed the button on an intercom set into the wall.

We waited. Through the darkness the wind carried the scent of the sea. The darkness seemed to thicken even more. The silence seemed thick too, seemed not silence but muffled noise. I found myself glad that Martha was with me.

As she again aimed a finger at the button, a large shadow materialized on the other side of a gate. The shadow spoke, became the big, beautifully muscled black man Tramontane had called Monte.

"Timex."

In the shadowy night his eyes were even more like the business end of a double-barreled shotgun. "Lost again?"

"Not this time. We want to talk to Culler."

"Why?"

"To ask him if he killed Dale Rutledge."

He looked at me, shook his head, looked at Martha. She was grinning the way she had as we stood on the ruined road below the McLeod ranch.

Monte was again dressed in black—Air Jordans, two-hundred-dollar running pants, a T-shirt so tight he seemed naked from the waist up. He began to grin too, faintly. His hand disappeared behind the wall, and the gate swung open. "Be fun, Timex."

We stepped into the courtyard. Monte waited for the gate to click shut behind us. As we started toward the house, he said into the wind, "Bodyguard?"

"Ms. Reedy is also a private investigator," I said. "She has an interest in the case."

"Hardware, Timex?"

"No," I said.

With a small hop-step, Martha caught up with him. "Why do you call him Timex?"

"Takes a licking . . ."

"And keeps on ticking. Are you the one he took the licking from?"

He shrugged. "Nothing personal. What I do."

Just before we reached the front door, Monte stopped. "Let's check."

I opened my coat. He motioned for me to turn around, patted me down expertly, then turned to Martha.

She started to unzip her jacket. Monte shook his head. "Pistol purse, babe."

Her face went blank. Slowly her hand slid toward the strip of black Velcro. "I don't—"

"Hell you don't," he said quietly.

His huge hand shot out and grabbed a handful of jacket below her throat, jerked her up onto her toes, slammed her hard against the wall. Her small cry of pain scraped into the night.

His back was to me.

I could have done to him what he'd done to me.

I didn't.

"Let her go," I said, and set myself, waiting for him to turn on me.

He turned, but slowly, and gave me his shotgun-barrel eyes. "She play the game, play by the rules."

I looked at Martha. The blow had driven the breath from her, but she was all right. I started to speak, then saw her brief, surreptitious nod, telling me to stay out of it.

Weakly she held out the purse. Monte took it, eased her back to the ground, pulled away the Velcro and reached inside and smiled. "My, my."

The pistol was tiny in his hand, its plastic imitation-pearl grip dull in the pale light. It was a cheap, dainty little piece that was more likely to explode than to fire and not likely to do anyone much harm either way.

My estimation of Martha Reedy and her professional abilities dropped with my spirits.

"Cute," Monte grinned at me.

Martha gave me a swift pained grin. I thought I understood it. My estimation of her professional abilities rose.

"Jesus Christ," I said. "If you're stupid enough to bring a gun up here, at least you could carry something real."

She rubbed her lower back, grimaced, gave me a glare worthy of Hannah Fielding. "Shut up, you macho jerk."

Picking up her cue, I looked at Monte's grin, shook my head in disgust. "Goddamn broads."

He flipped the little pistol into the air, caught it, grinned. "Little penis envy. Real little."

He jammed the pistol into his pocket, opened the front door, half shoved Martha inside.

A short marble entry led to a split marble staircase that arched down to a vast marble-floored room. Large, mostly white paintings hung on the white walls. Geometrical chunks of marble that might have been sculptures or might have been just chunks sat on white pedestals. A bone-white sofa and chairs collected in a corner. Most of the back wall was glass, black with night.

The room rang with the scuffing of our shoes. As we made our way down the stairs and across toward a black wrought-iron spiral staircase, I asked Monte: "You the expert with the propane torch?"

He shook his head, grinned. "Field work. I's de house nigger."

From below I could hear organ tones similar to those that had oozed from the projection booth at Culler's porn house. As we descended the staircase, the music grew louder, more dramatic. Sounds that might have been human moans, or groans, sang a confused counterpoint.

The staircase ended at another large white room, this one carpeted, furnished expensively if more conventionally. The glass doors in the back wall opened onto a redwood deck and a big hot tub. As the room above had the feel of a museum that housed fake treasures, this one had the antiseptic air of a luxurious hospital for the wealthily insane.

On a large TV in the corner, what I assumed was Tramontane's latest epic rolled in garish color. It seemed a pornographic rendition of the stock Western theme of the Indian maiden being ravished by the lustful cowboy at the edge of the pond she'd been bathing in. Tramontane looked more like a hooker than an Indian maiden. Her companion looked like a dead man impaled on a fence post.

As the sound snapped off, I had a sudden vision of Rosetta Draine and Linus Flowers beside the iris pond.

From behind a bar, his smooth-jowled face pink with heat, his gray hair damp, his brown eyes benign, the sixtyish man in a silk robe watched Monte's face.

From her carefully posed lascivious lounge on a sofa, the lava-haired woman in a diaphanous pale blue dressing gown that clung to her fiercely willed and spectacularly unreal body watched me.

I met her eyes. They were still angry. But they were no longer green.

They were as blue as the movie rolling soundlessly on the screen.

Even as the thought that she was wearing tinted contacts slid across my brain, a stillness settled over me.

I forced myself to look away from her, found myself looking at the TV, forced myself to look away from it. Somehow it was worse, soundless.

I looked at Martha. She stared at the images on the TV, where the Indian maiden, in standard pornofantasy, was now the ravisher, then at the woman whose image cavorted obscenely in the big square of unreality, then at Monte.

Cleveland Culler smiled. "What do we have here?"

Monte shrugged. "His show."

Culler smiled at Martha. "Are you with our cowboy friend from Nevada, girlie?"

The skin around her mouth tightened, whitened as she faced Culler. She didn't answer.

Monte pulled out the tiny pistol he'd taken from her, let it dangle from a long black finger. "Lady dick."

Culler slowly shook his head. "What's your interest in . . . whatever is going on here?"

"I'm here so Mr. Muscles there has a woman to shove around," Martha said, rubbing her lower back.

Monte gave her his just-doing-my-job shrug. She grimaced, continued to massage her back.

Culler shook his head, smiled almost kindly at me. I tried to get my mind back on the business that had brought me—us—here.

"I found Dale Rutledge a couple hours ago. His face was blow-torched off."

"Good fucking riddance," Tramontane snapped. Her anger, like her profanity, seemed ingrained, permanent.

Culler's smile faded. "Who?"

"I wondered if it was you. You sent a couple of goons looking for him, and they trashed his office."

"They didn't find him."

"Somebody did. Why were you looking for him?"

Culler picked up a remote control from the bar. The images on the TV screen mercifully faded to black. "Not that it's any of your business, Mr. Ross, but I'll tell you. Dale called me. Drunk, of course. He said he had something so valuable that when he gave it to me I'd forget what he's been doing with his little side business with faggots and housewives. Then he didn't show."

"Fucking bullshit," Tramontane said angrily. "Drunk's scam."

I didn't look at her, watched Culler as he came out from behind the bar.

"Maybe. But maybe not," he said. "He was a foolish man, Dale was, but he wasn't stupid. You know what he was talking about?"

"Maybe," I said.

But I wasn't thinking about the 16mm film cases, or about Dale Rutledge. I'd gotten what I'd come for, and more. I was thinking about how I was going to get out of there.

Martha had managed to edge away from me, toward the wall. From where she stood, again massaging her lower back, everyone in the room was in a narrow field of fire. She was thinking about getting out of there too. I hoped.

I gave Culler a feint. "Whoever killed him wants the cops to think you and your friends did it."

He didn't fall for it. "What is it, Ross?"

I hesitated. There was no good reason not to tell him. In fact, there was an especially good reason to tell him at least that a woman had been killed because she had Heather McLeod's identification. But I couldn't quite do it.

"It can't be that ranch you were talking about," he said, his eyes and voice quiet. "I've looked into it. There's nothing there. So what's so important that Dale Rutledge gets himself killed over it?"

I shrugged. I still couldn't do it.

Culler looked at Monte. Monte put on his working face, waved the tiny pistol toward the door. "Outside. Less mess."

"Me too," Tramontane said angrily. "I want to see this."

Culler smiled. "We'll all go. It might be interesting."

Martha Reedy frowned, as if in pain, slowly stretched her hand behind her, massaged her lower back. When her hand reappeared, it held a gun. A real gun, .9mm Beretta.

"Why don't Ross and I go outside," she said evenly, "and the rest of you stay right here."

Culler's smile deepened. Monte's didn't. He looked at me as if I'd betrayed him, violated the code. I shrugged.

He looked at Martha. "How's it play?"

"That one doesn't have a firing pin. This one does."

"Thing is," Monte said slowly, "it's what I get paid for."

Martha trained the Beretta on the center of his chest.

"Takes balls," he said.

She smiled.

"Maybe you miss."

Martha didn't answer. Her hands were steady, her breathing even, calm.

"Maybe you need more than one shot to get me. Maybe I get my hands on you."

"And maybe we have your blood and brains polka-dotting this sanitorium." She almost smiled. "It might be an improvement."

Martha held the Beretta steady, glanced at Culler. "It's your call."

Culler's eyes were calm. "This is disappointing, Ross. I'd looked forward to seeing what you could do with Monte."

He turned to Monte, his eyes no longer benign. "But the way he's doing his job, maybe you could take him."

I grinned. "We ganged up on him."

Culler smiled at Martha. "You're pretty good, girlie."

She smiled at him. "You call me girlie again, I'll put a hole in your hot tub."

Culler stopped smiling. Martha jerked the Beretta, motioning Monte toward the bar. He looked at Culler. Culler nodded.

"Let's go, Jack."

We backed toward the staircase. Then I stopped, turned to

Tramontane. I now had an idea of what fired the anger in her eyes. And an idea about how to use it.

"The other reason I came up tonight is to thank you."

Slowly she sat up, managing to display most of her hard-muscled body in the process. Her now blue eyes glared, her not-quite-beautiful face paled to the color of bone.

"For what, asshole?"

"For telling me about the film that Heather McLeod made. I didn't show it to her mother, naturally, but she's at peace, now that she knows her daughter is dead. No more bad dreams."

Her face flushed, hardened, uglied. "Fuck her mother. Fuck you too."

I smiled. "As it turned out, knowing that Heather is dead rather than some kind of slime—a hooker or junkie or worse—was a real consolation to her. Especially since Heather's father just died."

She might have reacted, or not.

"She's burying him out at the ranch day after—well, tomorrow, now—beside her two children and the rest of the McLeods. Then it'll be all over."

Her not-quite-beautiful face became even uglier. "Who gives a fuck!"

"She's got a new family now. They love her, and she loves them. She's happy. You've done her a real kindness."

CHAPTER THIRTY

As we pulled away from the wrought-iron fence, I said, "Culler was right, Martha. You're pretty good."

"Not yet," she said wearily. The little scene inside had drained her. "I'm not ready to talk yet."

I didn't mind. The little scene inside had drained me too.

We drove in silence through the wind-whipped night, the wind-whipped city. The clouds had lowered, thickened, grown heavy with reflected light and the threat of rain. But no rain fell. It wouldn't.

At her house, Martha parked and got out. I stepped out into the wind, watched her head up the walk toward the porch. Halfway there she stopped, turned. "Are you coming?"

I moved onto the walk. "It's late, Martha, and I've got a long drive—"

"I know it's late. But I've got questions, and you seem to have all the answers."

She was angry again. Maybe with me. Maybe with herself.

I didn't want to talk. The time for talking was ended. I wanted to drag my bones over the mountain and let what was going to happen happen. I wanted it to be over with.

But she wanted something else. And whatever it was, I owed her. "All right."

Inside, a flick of a switch illuminated the hallway leading toward the back of the house, past the three closed doors.

"Out back," Martha said. I followed her down the hall, stepping softly. I didn't want to wake Hannah Fielding. I didn't think I could deal with her.

The hall ended at a small dining room. Beyond it an arch opened onto a square room that had been added on, the back and side walls lined with bookshelves, the other mostly window that looked out onto a small, flower-strewn yard. Before the window sat a pair of comfortable-looking chairs.

"Go on in," Martha said. "I'll be right back."

She stepped back into the hall, shut the hall door. In the semidarkness, I glanced at the books—recent psychology and sociology and criminology, most, if the titles meant anything, focused on women. Then I eased into a chair.

A pair of small floodlights cast shadows in the yard. Beds and bushes of perennial blooms, most of which I couldn't name, shivered in the wind; the pale light washed out the colorful blossoms to shades of pale darkness. Under the wind they tossed and trembled, creating a vibrantly grotesque dumb show of shadows on the redwood fence.

I was watching the shadow show when Martha came in. She was barefoot, wore a bulky terrycloth robe, smelled of soap.

She handed me a beer, sat in the other chair, sighed. When she spoke, her voice was slow, heavy with her weariness, and with something else. "Tell me what you meant the other day, about Desert Conservancy buying Berkeley."

It wasn't a question I'd expected. I had to think for a while before I answered. "I meant that it's easy for some people to tell other people what to do with their lives. It's easy to sit in a California urban blight and presume to tell people in Nevada how to use their land."

"You think the McLeod ranch isn't something worth saving?"

But she wasn't arguing. She seemed half-asleep.

"I think that what happens to the McLeod ranch should be up to the McLeods."

She settled back in her chair, sipped absently at her beer. "Tell me why this is your last private investigation."

I watched the shadow show for a while. "I could give you a dozen reasons, Martha. Let's just say I'm tired of opening the kind of doors we opened the other day."

"Then why are you still on it? You did what you were hired to do. And you tore up Rosetta Draine's check."

I didn't know quite how to explain it. "Something's wrong, bad wrong. I have to find out what it is."

I sensed her eyes on me, but I didn't look at her.

I heard a sound, thought it might be the wind, realized it was her sigh, deep, weary, and something else.

"How long have you known that . . . woman . . . was Heather McLeod?"

I thought she'd probably picked that up. "Not till tonight."

"Do you know, Jack, or are you just guessing? Wishing?"

It was the last thing I would have wished. "It fits. She had trouble with her mother. She thought she was ugly, wanted to change the way she looked. She wanted to be a star."

Martha nodded. "'Tramontane'—I looked it up. It's a kind of wind, but it's also someone who comes from the other side of the mountains, a barbarian. Like her father—symbolic."

"Seems like."

"The snuff film—apparently Dale Rutledge *was* a genius."

"There's a way to be sure," I said. "I've seen a couple of posters of her, for her movies, and she never looks quite the same. She created her body with weights and exercises. I think she's created her face too, with surgery. That's why the features don't fit together. If somebody went out to a dirty movie rental place and got copies of her films, he could trace Tramontane's face back to something pretty close to Heather McLeod's."

"Are you going to?"

"No," I said. "If I'm right, there's no point. If I'm wrong, there's even less."

"Her behavior toward you—that's because you're a friend of her mother?"

I nodded. "And, as you pointed out, because I'm a man."

"In my experience," Martha said, as if that experience were an oppressive burden, "women like that—on the one hand, she's a classic victim, the psychology is textbook. The hard-boiled act and foul language and arrogance is defensive, protection against pain. On the other, she's got the self-esteem of a slug. Years of victimization have convinced her that she must have deserved it."

"Yes."

"That may explain why she's involved with Monte."

I hadn't picked up on that.

"She thinks she hates her mother, but there's more there than that. She's deliberately not contacted her mother. She's punishing her, the way a child would. Do you know why?"

"No, not really."

"So," she said, "what are you going to do about it?"

I'd already done it. "Nothing."

"Do you expect me to do nothing too?"

"I expect you to do whatever you want to do."

The wind soughed, or Martha sighed. I looked at her. Her smile was slow, small, wry, seemed amused—not, I thought, with me but with herself. "Which is to say, it doesn't matter what I do, because you've got it all under control."

I had it all under such control that I was going to go back to Nevada and wait for Linus Flowers to try to kill me.

"I've set something in motion. Something's going to happen. I don't know what it is, and I don't know how it will turn out."

She looked at me. "What are you going to do now?"

"Go back to Nevada. Whatever happens will happen there."

"What if I decide to come along?"

"I can't stop you."

"But you don't want me to. Ain't no place for womenfolk. Code of the West."

I didn't argue the point. Maybe because I couldn't.

"Hannah thinks you're in this mess up to your . . ." Her smile became a mocking grin. " . . . eyeballs."

"Gosh. Last I heard, I was just trying to jump your bones."

"Are you?"

That question too surprised me. I looked at her, realized that since I'd left her porch the other day I hadn't been visited by the image her sitting had left in the sand.

It had been my own bad dream. One of them.

"They're nice bones, Martha. If the situation were different— but I don't covet my neighbor's . . . lover. I'd be very happy, though, if we could be friends."

I thought she was going to say something, but finally she didn't. She looked out at the yard, watched the shifting shadows.

I drained my beer. "I have to go. Thanks for the—"

"You think," she said as if she hadn't heard me, "that all of this has something to do with the McLeod ranch, and whatever is on the film Rutledge made, and that the film is now in the hands of whoever hired Linus Flowers to kill Rutledge."

"Yes."

"Do you know what it is?"

"No."

"Would the fact that Nolan Turner now owns that mine tell you anything?"

"No. There never was anything in that mine. It was just a hole Draine's great-grandfather dug to front a stock swindle."

When she didn't respond, I stood up. "I have to get going."

Martha looked up at me. "You'd be driving all night, then you'd have to sleep half the day before you could do anything."

I nodded. "I know, but—"

"There's a guest room, if you want to wait till morning."

It was, I thought, more than an offer of a place to sleep. It was also an offer of friendship. I didn't know what to say, how to reject the first without rejecting the second.

"Thanks, anyhow, Martha, but . . ."

She rose, grinned her weary, mocking grin. "JDFR?"

"I . . ."

"Don't worry about it," she said, and stepped into the hall.

As quietly as I could, I followed her to the door, stepped past her and out into the wind.

"Good night, Martha. And thanks again."

"I'm the one who probably should be thankful."

I didn't quite know what that meant, realized that I was too tired to try to figure it out.

CHAPTER THIRTY-ONE

I didn't drive back to Reno that night after all. As I pulled away, I suddenly felt limp, woozy with exhaustion. Martha had been right. Going back at that hour didn't make sense. Instead I checked into the same motel on University Avenue, showered, slept, didn't dream.

I hadn't requested a wake-up call, assuming that what I had to do would be enough to bring me back to the world early. But I was more tired than I thought, or less eager to get back to what I had to do. It was nearly ten before I climbed in the Wagoneer.

Even then I didn't go back to Reno. After breakfast I went looking for an address I'd found in the phone book.

Under the clear, cold, front-swept sky, the neighborhood I found myself in was in transition, for the better. Old Victorians that had been carved into flats for students and left to rot were gradually being reclaimed and refurbished by small businesses—clothing boutiques, art galleries, bookstores, private social service agencies, and professional offices of the sort that surrounded my own office on California Avenue in Reno.

Freshly painted gray, its blue trim the color of Patsy McLeod's eyes, the Victorian I wanted stood on a shaded corner.

The hand-carved wooden sign stuck in the grass listed the occupants: People's Legal Aid, the Committee to Aid Abused Women, the Gay and Lesbian Coalition, Desert Conservancy, Free Family Counseling, three psychologists, two attorneys.

The large young black woman at the reception desk met my inquiry with a pleasant smile and directions to the office of Desert Conservancy. Moving down the narrow hallway toward the back of the old house, past offices from which issued soft music and soft voices, I admired the restoration work done on the floors and woodwork and plaster, the polish of the old ceramic and brass fixtures. Unlike Wally Keene, the occupants hadn't found it necessary to destroy the building in order to use it.

At the back of the house, three offices lined a short hallway. On either side of an open door were the closed doors of Desert Conservancy and People's Legal Aid. The open door led to Hannah Fielding's office.

Inside it, a woman in silent if obvious distress sat on an old overstuffed Victorian sofa, not reading the magazine in her lap. Another young woman picked absently, savagely at her fingernails. In a corner, nearly shrouded in plants, a graying woman in a flannel shirt and granny glasses typed at a computer.

The office had once been a small bedroom. In the back wall, French doors blocked off what had once been a sunporch. Through the glass I could see Hannah Fielding move from behind her desk to place a hand on the shoulder of a woman sobbing in a chair.

I stepped past the door, tried Desert Conservancy's. A bell tinkled as I opened the door into a small room plastered with posters depicting before and after landscapes—barren and weedy ground transformed into fields of wildflowers, ruined and muddy creeks made fresh flows of clear water—and simpleminded exhortatory environmental slogans. A computer workstation sat in a corner. The only other piece of furniture in the room was a long cherrywood table stacked with glossy flyers and four-color pamphlets.

A window looked out onto the side lawn, where several small, shabbily dressed children played happily on a swing set and around a sandbox under the watchful eye of a smiling withered old woman.

Another set of French doors, these neatly curtained, blocked the entrance to what I guessed was the same sunporch that was now part of Hannah Fielding's office.

I suspected that in People's Legal Aid, French doors also opened to her office. If Hannah Fielding led three professional lives, that could explain her chronic exhaustion.

After a few minutes, the curtained door opened. Hannah Fielding stood in it, clearly not pleased to see me. "You don't seem to have gotten the message, Mr. Ross."

Naturally, I did exactly what I'd been telling myself I was not going to do. "My overweening phallic arrogance, no—"

I stopped. "I'm sorry, Ms. Fielding. That was uncalled for. So was my behavior the other day. I—do you suppose we could start over?"

"Certainly," she said, glaring. "You don't seem to have gotten the message, Mr. Ross."

So we weren't going to start over.

She wore another suit, brown, with a peach-colored blouse and tigereye and chalcedony earrings. She looked just as angry as she had the last time I'd seen her. And just as afraid of me.

"In fact, Ms. Fielding, I have a message for you. Desert Conservancy may still be able to get the McLeod ranch."

Uncertainty fissured her glare. "I—how? The property will go to bid, and Turner will use his influence."

"The property will go to Patsy McLeod." I began explaining the divorce situation.

Almost immediately her head was nodding sharply, grimly. "Of course. The alimony is a factor, but relative to the ethical issues it's insignificant. The courts have begun to demystify all the oppressive patriarchal assumptions that have prevented women from realizing their property rights. . . ."

She stopped, seemed suddenly to see me, seemed uncertain. I waited for more ideological jargon, but it didn't come.

"Who . . . determined that this was the case?"

"I did." It was true enough.

Her uncertainty deepened. "And why were you . . . interested in this aspect of the situation?"

"For the only reason I was interested in any of it, Ms. Fielding. Because Patsy McLeod was my client."

"I . . . see," she said.

I didn't think she did. I didn't know if she could. Hannah Fielding had a vision of the world, to which she devoted her life. It might have been a good vision. I didn't know. But I did know that, like Patsy McLeod's, it was essentially Manichaean, sorted everything into good and evil, black and white.

What she couldn't see was the world I lived in, where nearly everything real was a shade of gray.

"But Mrs. McLeod would never sell the property to Desert Conservancy. According to Marty, she holds environmental groups responsible for every ill to ever affect America."

I nodded. "I didn't say she'd sell. I said you had a chance at it. Talk to her. More than that, listen to her."

"I know what she—"

"You don't know anything about Patsy McLeod, Ms. Fielding. You've never met her."

She didn't say anything.

"She seems to be rethinking things these days. She might not sell, but I think she'll listen to what you have to say."

Hannah Fielding looked at me for a long time. Finally she stepped forward, extended her thin hand. "Thank you, Mr. Ross."

I thought I knew what the handshake meant. Not that suddenly we were friends, allies. Only that the question of whether I was good or evil wasn't answered, was still a question.

"You're welcome, Ms. Fielding." I held out my own hand.

CHAPTER THIRTY-TWO

It was after noon before I got out of Berkeley. For a while I fought the traffic, then finally, grimly, said the hell with it. Things seemed to be setting up on their own schedule.

I dawdled out of the Bay Area, through the bare and drought-withered coastal range and across the bare and drought-withered Big Valley, trying not to think about what I'd set myself up for.

To keep from thinking, I tried to listen to the radio—the ads a shriek of pseudosophisticated selling, the news a long litany of discouraging words, the music a mockery of adolescent love prattle. I turned it off.

I managed to keep from thinking until I got to the turnoff to Lake Tahoe. Then I had to think about Patsy McLeod.

I'd told Martha that I was going to do nothing about our discovery of the fate of Heather McLeod. It was difficult not to, but finally it would be less difficult than telling Patsy what I'd found and watching her face as I told her. Poltroonery.

The drought-shriven river trickled down the mountain to the desert. In the cold pale late-afternoon sunlight, Reno diced the natural fall drabness of the Truckee Meadows into dusty artificial green squares. The air was brown, thick, foul.

Less than an hour of daylight remained when I pulled the Wagoneer in under my mulberry tree. I went inside cautiously, searched the rooms, felt a bit foolish when I found only the same kind of nothing that I'd found in Dale Rutledge's house.

After unloading the Wagoneer, I went to my grandfather's desk and took out his old Smith & Wesson .38. In the kitchen, I cleared a space at the cluttered table and set to work cleaning and oiling the .38 as I waited for the coffee to cook.

Linus Flowers hadn't been in my home. Probably he wouldn't come for me here. Probably he was out there watching, waiting, would make his move in territory where he had an advantage, or at least where I didn't. Probably. If the pieces I had fit together were not simply a mosaic of my own design.

Amid the collection of desert relics on the table, I saw, I'd created another mosaic. In the center stood my daughter's picture. On one side of the picture sat William Draine's latest book, on the other my grandfather's .38.

I looked at the picture, felt less grim, picked up the phone and dialed and got no answer.

I looked at the .38, felt grimmer. I called Rondo and Keene and checked for messages. There was only one, from Wally. The papers were ready for my signature. Whenever I was ready.

I turned on the radio, found a country station, listened to Willie and Waylon advise mamas not to let their babies grow up to be cowboys.

Five hours later I was lying in the dark on my bed, the .38 on the table beside me, when headlights sent a rhomboid of yellow light splashing across the room.

I didn't need to look to know it wasn't Linus Flowers who had pulled in behind the Wagoneer. As a car door chunked shut, I got up, slipped my tattered old brown terrycloth robe on over my shorts, hesitated, then slid the .38 into the deep pocket.

Flicking on lights, I padded into the living room, had my hand on the doorknob when the knock came.

Outside Martha huddled into her nylon jacket against the cold. She looked tired. As she glanced at my robe, my bare shins and feet, a small odd smile crept over her mouth. "I got you up."

"I wasn't sleeping," I said, stepping aside. "Come in."

She nodded at the bulge in my robe. "As the woman said, is that a gun in your pocket or are you just glad to see me?"

"Both."

But I wasn't glad to see her. By showing up at my door, Martha had put herself in Linus Flowers's sights. On the other hand, I wasn't especially surprised. What I was, suddenly, was uncomfortable. I wished I'd put my clothes on.

She stepped inside the bare living room, looked around it. "You getting ready for a hoedown?"

"Getting ready for something," I said, starting toward the kitchen. "I can make some coffee. Or I might have a beer."

"A beer," she said wearily, "would be lovely."

I took out the .38 and set it on the table, nodded toward a chair. "Clear yourself a space."

I had three beers. I grabbed a pair, popped them, turned and held one out to her. She took a long swallow, looked over the desert detritus on the table, came to the photograph, smiled a question at me.

"My daughter," I said. "Cynthia."

As she looked at my daughter's smile, something went out of, or came into, her own.

"I wouldn't have guessed that about you, that you'd have children."

"Child," I said.

She slipped her purse from her shoulder, set it on top of William Draine's book, sat at the table.

"Hang on a minute," I said. "I'll get some clothes on."

Her smile gently mocked. "No point in bothering on my account, is there?" Before I could answer, or move, she opened her purse and took out an envelope. "I've got some pictures too."

As she sipped her beer, I sat across the corner of the table from her and went through them slowly. A series of Polaroids showing the square borders of the television screen—female flesh that was never quite the same body, female features that were never quite the same face—arranged so that the images on them descended into the past.

"It was a truly delightful experience," Martha said.

I could imagine.

"Once you get past the hair and makeup, it's rhinoplasty and dentistry, mostly. At least two different nose jobs, caps, molar extractions to hollow the cheeks, some tuck work around the eyes, maybe some work on the jawline."

I went through them the other way, watched Heather McLeod become Tramontane.

"One more victim of the American Beauty Myth," Martha said half wearily, half angrily. "She's spent a fortune, undergone the worst kind of pain, all to bring herself into conformity with some abstract idea of female beauty."

"If I make myself into something I'm not, maybe somebody will love me," I said, returning the pictures.

Martha nodded, put the pictures back in the envelope. They weren't the reason she'd driven two hundred miles. But she wasn't quite ready to tell me what the reason was.

Her gaze drifted over the scatter of desert relics on the table. Obsidian arrowheads and bone scrapers and half a feathered tule basket. A handful of Apache teardrops strung on a piece of rotting rawhide, a saw-cut chunk of garnet-dappled rock, bits of crudely polished turquoise, a fractured opal. A handmade iron knife, a hand-carved wooden spoon. Square nails, a piece of iron wagon-wheel cover. A shard of warped mirror . . .

She picked up the mirror, turned its expensively bevelled corner in her hands, stared through the patina of age and weather at her distorted image.

"Last night you said that you'd like us to be friends." She put down the mirror, picked up her beer, finished it. I hadn't touched mine, slid it over to her. "I'd like that too. But it means we see this thing through together. Can you handle that?"

Now that she was here, so far as Linus Flowers would be concerned, we were already together. But I didn't say so.

I met her pale brown eyes. "Together."

She looked at me for a long time, seemed to be looking for

something. I didn't know what it was or if she was finding it.

"You told . . . Heather about the funeral. You think she's going to show up there, don't you?"

"That was the idea. I don't know if it will work."

"What do you think will happen?"

"I don't know."

"But we're going to be there to find out."

"Be pretty hard to find out from here."

She didn't smile, didn't answer, picked up the mirror. "That means you'll wait for me in the morning? You won't go sneaking off without me?"

"I wouldn't go off without you."

She almost smiled. "You might think you wouldn't, but when it comes right down to it, you agree with Mrs. McLeod, don't you? That this is men's work?"

"You seem to have me confused with someone else you've had this conversation with."

"Maybe." Her smile was grudging.

"But it's easy enough to make sure," I said. "You can use my daughter's room tonight, if you want."

After a moment, she gave me another small odd smile. "That wouldn't violate one of those quaint cowboy scruples you haul around in your jeans?"

I shrugged. "Be my guest."

Her face went blank, expressionless. "I will. Thank you. I've got a bag in the car."

Abruptly she rose and went into the living room. I picked up the .38 and followed, turned off the light, stood in the door as she moved through the darkness to the Geo.

Not that I could do much. If Flowers decided to shoot her when she opened the car door and the dome light came on, he'd do it.

She opened the door and the dome light came on and Linus Flowers didn't shoot her.

As she stepped back inside, Martha nodded at the gun. "You really think he's out there?"

"If he isn't, he will be. He has to be. He can't take the chance that I—we—"

"It's hard to get used to, isn't it?" she said, smiling. "So hard it nearly chokes you, changing 'I' to 'we.'"

Before I could answer, she went on. "I feel like I've been swimming in slime all day. If you'll excuse me, I'm going to take a shower."

I showed her the bathroom, my daughter's bedroom. Tossing her bag on the bed, she glanced around—at the old teddy bear on the pillow, the rock music posters on the walls, the TV and VCR, the books in the shelves over the desk, the collection of desert rocks and dried desert flowers neatly arranged on the bureau.

Her eyes found, held the photograph beside the bed. In it a dark pretty woman in a stylish square-necked summer dress and a dark big young man in worn jeans and a Stanford T-shirt smiled into the Palo Alto sunlight. They seemed to be happy.

"Cynthia says that's the only evidence that my ex-wife and I ever smiled in each other's company."

She didn't smile, didn't look at me.

While Martha showered, I went into my bedroom and slipped my jeans on under my robe, then I went in and sat at the kitchen table, began working on the third beer. A few minutes later she came in, wrapped in the robe she'd worn the night before, her hair damp, her skin soft, glowing. She glanced at my jeans, might have shaken her head.

She sipped her beer. I sipped mine. Then, perhaps to avoid thinking about what would come with the dawn, we settled into the quiet, tentative, desultory conversation of people learning to trust each other.

She talked about the death of her sister, about which she was still angry, and from which neither of her parents had ever quite recovered.

She talked about the death of her mother, a high school science teacher, of cancer and guilt, and the death of her cop father of a heart attack and despair two years later.

We talked about music, she about her Al Stewart albums, about Bonnie Raitt and Mozart and the Police; I about Jimmie Rodgers and Bessie Smith and Mozart and Merle Haggard.

I talked about growing up with my grandparents, playing high school basketball, attending UNR and Stanford Law. She talked about living with her aunt, who moved in with her after her father died, and about running high school sprints well enough to earn a partial scholarship to Cal, where she majored in sociology with a criminal justice emphasis.

She talked about working part-time as a dispatcher for the Alameda County sheriff, about becoming one of the department's first women deputies, about the work, which she mostly liked, and about the chauvinism and bureaucratic nonsense, which she fought but which finally drove her to set out on her own.

Carefully, obliquely, she talked about her predilection for involving herself in relationships that always foundered on expectations she couldn't or wouldn't meet.

"Until Hannah," I said.

Martha looked at me for a long time. Then she said, with a sigh, "Hannah loves me. And she worries about me. But she lets me be what I am. Most of the time."

When I didn't say anything, she studied her now-empty beer can. "You stayed in Berkeley last night."

"I decided you were right."

"Hannah told me about your conversation. I—you made a point of making sure she knew that Mrs. McLeod would get the ranch. She's not sure why."

"It seemed like the thing to do," I said. "I guess I was trying to make peace with her."

"Did you?"

I shrugged. "More like a truce."

"I know," she nodded. "Hannah . . . she isn't really a zealot. It's just that she works so hard, much of it pro bono, and she has no . . . she hardly has time to keep up her flowers."

She smiled soberly. "If she'd lived a few hundred years ago, they'd have either canonized her or burned her at the stake."

I thought of the three doors, the three offices leading to one office. "She may be burning herself up, Martha."

"I tell her that, but . . ."

She began sorting through the things on the table. "You understand that it isn't really you that she's reacting to."

"I know. It's what she thinks I represent. The old ways."

"Partly. She deals with victims of the old way every day. Violence. Ugliness." She picked up a cruel-looking bit. "The victims are usually women and children. When she finds out what has gone on, and why, it . . . affects her."

Riotous excursions with privileged glimpses into the human heart. "It affects all of us, Martha. That's one of the reasons this is my last private job."

She put down the bit, again picked up the distorting mirror. "She could walk away anytime. There are several big firms that would jump at the chance to get her, for her expertise in environmental issues if nothing else."

I got the point. She wasn't talking about Hannah Fielding. "You disapprove of my decision."

She shook her head. "I don't have that right, Jack. I'm just trying to understand. You're good at it. Sometimes you help people. You make enough money to live on. What's wrong with it?"

I couldn't explain. "Why do you do it?"

"I'm good at it. Sometimes I can help people. I make enough money to live on."

I looked past her, out into the dark, empty living room. I didn't say anything.

Martha looked at my daughter's portrait, at me. She was back in her quiet calm. "You never thought about marrying again, or at least . . . ?"

Not recently. In fact, I suddenly realized that Martha was the first adult woman who had seen the inside of my home.

"I guess I'm not very good at it. A lone wolf, as Hannah said. I've been in a couple of relationships that held some promise of—but something always got in the way. My work, mostly."

She nodded, seemed to understand.

"The thing is, Martha, my work drives me nuts about half the time. I end up either wanting to kill somebody or to run off and brood in the desert. Either way I'm no good to myself or anybody else."

She put down the mirror, finished her beer. "You really like it out there, don't you?"

"Yes."

"Why?"

"Because it's beautiful, if you learn to really see what you're looking at," I said. "And because there aren't any other people there."

Martha finished her beer, slowly rose. "I don't know, Jack. I think you're confused."

Everybody I met seemed to think that. "About what?"

She waved her hand slowly over the things on the table. "You say you like the desert because there aren't any people in it."

"Yes."

"Then why do you only bring back things that have the mark of human hands on them?"

CHAPTER THIRTY-THREE

Martha laughed softly. "Maybe you're right, Jack. Maybe everybody is crazy."

Through breakfast and the drive out of Reno, she'd been settled in behind her quiet calm. Now she shook her head, smiled wryly.

"Here we are, a pair of private investigators without a client between us, heading into the desert so that another private detective can try to kill us."

We were finally beyond pavement and concrete and plywood, a mile past Red Rock Estates. The desert was still, silent, dun in the light and frosted gray in the shadows. The slanting morning sun was bright but without warmth.

I didn't smile. I was angry again, had been since I awoke. Angry at having gotten Martha involved in a situation that I'd forced. Angry at having had to force it. Angry at my fear of it.

Through my anger, I was watching—the road, the land, the rearview mirror.

The road was chewed up with tracks now. I couldn't tell if Linus

Flowers had been on it, but something big and wide and multi-wheeled had left tracks coming and going.

The land held opportunities for ambush at every gully and wash and outcrop of rock. I doubted that Flowers could have anticipated our being on this road, but I wasn't taking any chances.

The rearview mirror was a blur of dust.

"What am I supposed to be seeing out here that's beautiful? It's so . . . drab. Brown. Dead looking."

The dry land in drought in dying time.

"You want green," I said, checking the mirror again.

"I . . . suppose so."

"The trick is to see what's there, not what isn't, or what you think should be."

What was there was not green but greens, specks and splashes under the dust, subtle, subdued. Gray-green sage, deep olive bitterbrush, yellow-green ephedra. Shadscale and winterfat, greasewood and hopsage, mule-ear and rabbitbrush and desert thorn.

There was brown. Except when you really looked, the brown was shades of gold and yellow and red and lavender, ocher and umber, pale, quiet.

What wasn't there was people, man.

What was there was the brief history of man, written in the scars on the earth.

What was there was the long history of the earth, written in the strata of rocks and the shapes of hills, water traced, wind scoured.

What was there was silence, into which the desert silently spoke of deep time, eons and eternities, and the utter inconsequentiality of all life.

Yet what was also there was life, ignoring the message of the desert, struggling, surviving.

We drove through it. Martha looked at it.

"Oh," she said.

Then, finally, seeing what was really there, she said, slowly, "Aaah."

Zion Mountain. Beulah Valley. The dune and the drying creek and the McLeod ranch.

I stopped at the fork, where the big rig had unloaded something with huge hard tires that had rolled through the now-open gate and up toward the ranch house.

Martha saw it first. "At the barn, a backhoe."

It sat near the door of the collapsed barn. It could have been one of those I'd seen in Nolan Turner's lot. Or not.

Across the creek, on the low hill stuffed with McLeod bones, a small mound of bright artificial green rose from the dust.

"Fake grass." Martha shook her head. "Astroturf, out here in the desert. What's the point?"

I shrugged, still looking at the backhoe. It bothered me. It was too much shovel to haul forty miles just to dig a grave in the sand.

"We've got some time," I said, nosing the Wagoneer onto the dusty ruts. "Let's look around."

The old pattern of the Chrysler's tires still, if faintly, lay on the dust. The broken sage and crushed rabbitbrush had tried to heal itself.

The ruts tracked toward a low bluff, around it, and into a dry shallow wash strewn with boulders and bitterbrush. Above us, widely scattered juniper pocked the hillside.

"What are we looking for?"

"I don't know. Whatever's here."

The wash rose, the ruts narrowed and twisted into a water-carved gulch. Bitterbrush ended, sage began, juniper thickened as we climbed. Then the ruts became an old road that angled up toward a square opening that had been cut, a hundred years before, through a hump of mountain ridge. Beyond it, framed by it, the tailing pile of the old mine distended the side of the mountain like a yellowish tumor.

We ground our way up and through the cut, turned and eased into a broad sloping bowl. Juniper hung on the hillsides. Sage clung tenaciously to the tailing pile, trailed down and spread skimpily over the sand. Nearly leafless old aspen lined a narrow drainage down to what had been the spring, now just a patch of dead grass ringed by dark dead apple trees.

I eased the Wagoneer to a stop, shut it off. "Welcome to the American Eden."

"Here? Whatever possessed them to think they could . . . ?"

We got out into air tangy with juniper, into a cold the sun was beginning to soften, into a deep silence. The .38 was heavy in my coat pocket. Martha's bag hung heavy from her shoulder.

The desert had left little sign of the camp. A scatter of juniper poles, a scrap of cloth snagged on a sage, a rusty glint of tin can. The drought had dried the spring, but the pool had thickened with silt long before. Bits of charred wood, strewn ashes, a garbage mound feeding dusty-podded rabbitbrush. At the base of the tailing pile, old Day-Glo peace signs and American flags and crude flowers darkened the rocks like lichen.

A spatter of oil showed me where Linus Flowers had parked when he killed Royce McLeod. Nothing else indicated that human beings had been there for twenty years.

"This isn't too smart," Martha said calmly. "We're sitting ducks out in the open like this."

"He won't want to pick us off from a distance. He'll want to use his hands. And his boots." I looked at her. And his penis.

"Code of the West?" she said. "What happens when he tries?"

The taste of fear flooded my tongue. I didn't answer.

We wandered toward the tailing pile. Listening—only a burst of birdsong, a flutter of wings, disturbed the silence. Watching—only a scurry of fur disturbed the dust.

"What are we looking for?" Martha asked again.

"A reason to kill a dying man."

She looked around. "You think this whole thing has been about the ranch after all?"

"The ranch is part of it, somehow."

"But it wouldn't be here. We're not on McLeod property."

"Let's get higher, see what we can see."

We walked around the base of the tailing pile, started up its rocky edge. Listening. Watching. Hearing and seeing nothing we shouldn't have heard or seen.

The climb left a dampness on my back, a sheen on Martha's forehead. Brushing at it with her sleeve, she looked around: rock and rabbitbrush, scraps of rotted wood weathered to the color of the dirt, a few lengths of rusted metal, a boarded-up hole in the mountain.

Martha walked over to it, leaned, peered into the darkness.

"Somebody's been here."

As I approached, I could see the dust line where a timber brace and a pair of planks had been moved, could see the darkness where rocks had shifted under feet.

"We'll need a light," she said.

"We'll need more than that. These old holes are dangerous."

"But it doesn't matter anyhow, does it? If something was here, it's gone now."

I looked around, trying to see where whoever had been there had come from. Not from below. From over the ridge, from the McLeod ranch, from the iris pond.

Martha put her hand on my arm. "Look."

She was gazing through the cut in the hillside, far out over the dune and the distant corner of the alkali flat, to the rocky hill that edged it. Dust.

"That's too much to be Flowers," she said. "It's got to be the burial party. This can keep, Jack. If I've got the lay of the land right, the ranch house is down over the ridge. We can get there quicker by foot."

I didn't want to go down and over the ridge. I wanted to go up and over it, to the iris pond, where whoever had been at the mine had come from. But Martha was right. It could keep.

Watching, listening, we picked our way off the tailing pile, walked to the dead spring, up the drainage lined with nearly dead aspens, down the sandy ridge, finally around a dark clump of juniper two hundred yards from the bright fake grass on the low hill above the creek.

Under the thinning pall of dust, Patsy McLeod's pickup was parked in the shade of the old barn, beside the backhoe. Patsy and Rosetta Draine and a balding man holding a huge black book stood by a green Cherokee watching as William Draine directed a black panel truck to the edge of the creek bed.

Two men got out of the truck as the others collected in a small black cluster at its rear doors.

Martha's face was pink and glowing from the walk. Her pale brown eyes were somber. "No Heather."

I moved back to a juniper, squatted in its shade, waited while

Martha sat in the sand beside me. "As old Lodgeskins says at the end of *Little Big Man*—"

"'Sometimes the magic works,'" she grinned, "'and sometimes it doesn't.'"

Then she said, "No Linus Flowers."

I knew what she meant. He'd had plenty of time, plenty of opportunity to make his move. She meant that I'd fit all the pieces together into a mosaic of my own design.

"You wanted him to be out here. You wanted him to jump us."

I didn't want him to jump us. I wanted him to jump me.

I wanted things clear, simple. But they never were.

"Maybe I was wrong."

But as I said it, I knew it wasn't true. Flowers was out there, waiting. I just didn't know what he was waiting for.

The casket was small, plain. The four men slid it out of the panel truck, hefted it easily, stepped over the trickle of creek and started slowly up the hill. Patsy and Rosetta Draine, both in simple black dresses and jackets, followed.

When the casket had been centered on the nylon straps that would lower it into the earth, the two mortuary men stepped discreetly back behind the bright green mound. The minister opened his big book.

The three mourners, heads bowed as if searching for something in the grave, stood at its edge like a black blossom.

The minister spoke. The desert silence swallowed his words.

I looked down at the backhoe. I could see where it had eased across the creek bed and up the hill to dig Royce McLeod's grave. Then I saw the tracks it had made on the road up the canyon.

Martha put her hand on my arm again.

From behind the dune rose a rooster tail of white dust.

As the minister mouthed more words, the dust thickened, whitened, slid through the dune. Like a confused signal, the sun flashed on the chrome and windshield of a small gold Mercedes.

When the Mercedes was through the gate and scraping its way up the ruined ranch road, William Draine turned, looked at it briefly, then looked back down into the grave.

Martha rose. "This ought to be interesting."

I got up. "What it's more likely to be is painful."

We started slowly down the ridge. The minister's words became a meaningless murmur. The Mercedes bounced and teetered and crawled up into the ranch yard.

The minister stepped back. The two mortuary men came forward, pulled the artificial grass back from the mound of earth, began slowly cranking the casket into the grave.

The three people at graveside turned at the sound of the car door shutting, watched as the woman who had been Heather McLeod and a large black man stepped to the edge of the creek.

In his muscles and black leather jacket and bow tie, Monte looked like a headwaiter at a steroid bar.

In her wide-brimmed black hat and volcanic red-black hair and dark glasses and low-cut black dress, Tramontane looked like what she was.

They started up the hillside. Martha quickened her pace. I slowed mine, stopped.

Because I suddenly understood what Flowers was waiting for, what he wanted. Or maybe because I didn't want to have to see Patsy McLeod's face when she saw her daughter's.

Waiting until Martha had swerved around a stubby juniper, I half slid down the sandy slope toward the creek, stepped across the damp rocks and scummy pools, walked over to the barn.

I glanced back up the hill. At graveside, three black figures watched the approach of two.

Twenty yards from them, Martha looked back, didn't find me, looked around sharply, did. She stared at me. Then she shrugged her dismissive shrug, turned toward the grave.

The big tires on the backhoe were thick with dried mud. I walked around the barn, saw the muddied tracks on the canyon road, started up it toward the iris pond.

At my back I heard voices, then a sudden sharp, chilling wail.

I didn't turn around.

Poltroonery.

CHAPTER THIRTY-FOUR

Alone, I trudged up the dusty road, watching, listening. As I walked and watched and listened, something nudged the thought of Linus Flowers to the back of my consciousness.

Something in, or about, the canyon was wrong. But all I could see was what should have been there—dust, brush, rock; in small glades the ruined remains of old stock pens and fences; willows lining the creek, the dark shallow shine of the water.

Then the canyon opened up, and I saw what I'd been seeing all along. Several feet above the sluggish rivulets and still pools, the banks of the creek were dark, damp. Water, a lot of it, had washed down the mountain.

Up the canyon, I saw where the water had come from. The earthen face of the pond gaped. Behind the huge hole, mud dried. Reeds and cattails and irises—some long dead, some newly dying—yellowed in the sun. Sunlight glinted off the snout of muddy metal that nosed up from the bottom of the empty pond.

The broken concrete and twisted metal mechanism of the floodgate canted up from the mud. The backhoe had ripped the gate out and, after the water had drained, then dug out the earth from around the VW van.

The front windshield was shattered, the front tires rotted, the Day-Glo flowers reduced to streaks and smears of muddy color. Cable marks on the mud led to the front end. Deep human tracks cratered the mud around the front doors. Small piles of looser mud lay on the pond floor, pitched there by the shovel that had dug out the front seat.

Stepping onto the dam, I looked down at the van and tracks and signs of shoveling, tried to read it all.

The long-dead reeds said that the drought had lowered the pond, by ten feet at least. The front end of the van hadn't been silted over, might have been visible in the water. The cable marks said that they'd used the backhoe to try to pull the van free of the mud, had budged it a foot or so. Then they'd tried to lighten it, shoveling out the inside.

But the van was still there. Maybe that's why the backhoe was still down by the barn. When the funeral was over, they were going to come back and finish the job. But why?

As one part of my mind tried to fit it all together, another part began to whisper to me, urgently.

My hand was halfway to my pocket when, from behind me, the silence was broken by a voice like the desert wind. "Don't even fucking think about it."

I shuddered. Not with fear. With anger, a sudden swell of unreasoning rage I could barely control. Trembling, holding my hand away from my jacket, I slowly turned.

He wore his pearl gray Western-cut suit the way a pile of rocks wears frost. The fall sun flashed on the chrome of the .44 Magnum in his thick hard hand, the silver of his belt buckle, the silver tips of his cruel-looking boots. In the shade of his hat brim, his eyes flashed with their own light.

"Thought you'd never come out from behind that dike."

My voice sounded strange to me. "It took me a while to figure out you were afraid of the two of us together."

A small hard smile shaped his round face. "More fun this way. You first. Then her. She'll be more fun than you."

My anger sickened me past response.

He moved toward me, big, fast. His coat pocket sagged with the weight of another gun. I waited, looking for an opening, but he didn't give me one. Holding the Magnum steadily on a point between my eyes, he sidled close.

"Somebody softened you up for me. Bust that nose, did he?"

Gently he tapped the barrel on the bridge of my nose, smiled at my wince. Smiling, he lifted the gun barrel, jerked it down.

The crack of bone boomed into my brain. Pain shot up into my eyes. I stumbled sideways as my jacket pocket tore away and the weight of the .38 disappeared. Something hard slammed into the side of my head.

Blind with pain, I staggered, knew only that I couldn't go down under his boots, fought to stay upright. Then the earth beneath my heel slipped away.

Twisting instinctively, I smashed my shoulder into the soft slope of the dam face, rolled, slid, scraped down into the pond.

Then nothing happened.

My vision slowly returned. I was on my back. Above me, the sun flashed off the chrome barrel of the Magnum in Flowers's hand, off the silver in his belt buckle, the silver tips of his boots.

Slowly I pulled myself away from the suck of the mud, rolled onto my hands and knees, dripped blood as I struggled to my feet.

Flowers sidestepped toward me down the face of the dam. Now each of his coat pockets sagged with the weight of a gun.

"You're not much, Ross."

Adrenaline, anger diluted the pain in my nose and eyes, the ache in my shoulders. The light had a faint reddish cast, as if I were seeing through blood. I tasted blood, spat it.

"You want to toss the cannon and try me straight up?"

He smiled, spoke softly. "You figure it's the only chance you got. But there's no chance."

"I thought you were supposed to be tough, Flowers. This is a pussy play. I think you're afraid of me."

His voice softened even more. "That what you think?"

I took an angry step toward him. "I think you're real tough with junkie women and fat drunks and dying old men."

"Put it all together, huh? I wondered if you'd spotted me in Berkeley."

"I think you're a stupid slob who hides behind a big gun."

He smiled slowly, shaking his head. His voice was like the whisper of a cold harsh desert wind. "That isn't what you think. You think there's fucking rules, like we're gonna have some kind of showdown in the street at high noon."

"You and me, Flowers. Let's see."

"There ain't no rules, Ross. And you're fucking history."

I took another step toward him. I had to get close.

"One more and I blow your leg off."

Insanely, angrily, I took another step. "So do it."

He grinned again. "Don't want to have to haul your carcass out of here, work up a sweat, get my clothes all bloody."

I took another step. "Why should I care what you want?"

"Crazy bastard, aren't you."

Then he stopped grinning, trained the Magnum at the center of my chest. "You can live a few more minutes, Ross. Or you can fucking die now. Your choice."

My anger stopped me. I was burning with it, could feel its boil in the marrow of my bones. Anger at Flowers—at what he'd done to me, what he'd done to Maureen Cody and Dale Rutledge and Royce McLeod. But even more, anger at the people hiding in his shadow, those who had caused it all. They were the ones I wanted.

He jerked the Magnum toward the bank and the hillside. "Let's take a little walk."

Through my anger I saw that it was the only chance I had. The chance at a chance.

I slogged my way across the bottom of the pond. I could feel the flesh around my eyes and nose puffing. Behind me I heard mud sucking at his boots. Close, but not close enough.

In the distance, down the canyon, I might have heard the faint sound of an engine.

Climbing up the bank, I stopped, spat more blood. "This be about where you tried to rape Rosetta Draine?"

"Who the hell's—" Then he gave me his small hard smile. "That's the hippie chick? Christ, ancient history. But she was prime meat. Would of nailed her, too, if that old McLeod dyke hadn't come along with her rifle."

The whole mosaic began to split apart. Flowers didn't know who Rosetta Draine was.

He jerked the Magnum. "Climb."

I climbed, each step sending a bolt of pain into my eyes, as I followed the old trail the hippies had made, the trail Patsy McLeod and I had trudged twenty years before.

Watching—aspen, sage and juniper, sand stirred by recent feet—looking for an opportunity and not finding one. Listening—shush of the breeze in the warming silence, rasp of my breathing, and of his—close but not close enough.

The Wagoneer still sat where I'd parked it. Aspen leaves stirred, drifted down. Nothing else moved.

"Not there," Flowers said behind me, close but not close enough. "The mine."

I followed the recent tracks, slowly, to the top of the tailing pile. I was running out of time.

"Shaft's nice and deep," Flowers said behind me.

At the boarded-up mine entrance, I turned to face him. He wasn't holding the Magnum any longer. His huge fist clasped the .22 Luger that Dale Rutledge had waved at me.

"Magnum's too quick. I think a slug in the knees, elbows, let you try to climb out of that hole while you're dying."

It was a mistake. The Magnum would finish me, wherever it hit me. With the Luger, I might still get my hands on him.

If I could distract him. "Was Rutledge dead when you turned on the torch?"

He smiled, slowly shook his head.

"You tried to cover your tracks. In Berkeley, with the heroin. Not your style, but effective enough. And with Rutledge, you found the clippings, saw what he was afraid of, saw how to cover it up. But you didn't bother much with Royce McLeod."

"They bought suicide. Who gives a shit how a crazy desert hermit dies?"

"What confused me, Linus, was that I couldn't see how you fit in all this. This isn't just contract work for you."

"Told you I was protecting a business investment," he said. "A sort of silent partnership."

I didn't say anything. Being what he was, he'd have to tell me, show me how smart he was.

In the silence, I might have heard the soft click of rock on rock. I let my eyes slide past him, saw nothing that shouldn't have been there.

Flowers smiled. "There was this hippie out here had some big-time dealers after his ass, so he's been happy to give me what I wanted to keep quiet about it."

I remembered Rosetta Draine's carefully constructed tale. Raven, she'd called him.

"So I'm back from Nam, happen to get a line on him. Except now his hair's going white and he's not dealing, but he's still happy to give me what I want to keep quiet."

The mosaic in my mind became a pile of pieces. "Turner."

"Not just dope and pussy now. I got a piece of the action. Sweet setup. I handle minor problems. Everybody tries to put it on that pussy Mudd, and he's covered. Money keeps rolling in."

I listened, looked past him again. Nothing.

"The three people you killed, they were minor problems? In what? Why did they have to die?"

He shrugged. "Business. Who cares?"

He saw something in my face, took a cautious step backward. "Maybe the knee first, huh? In case you get any crazy ideas."

I spat blood at his feet. "Too bad you fucked it up."

"Fucked what up?"

"All of it. The woman in Berkeley, you stupid bastard. She wasn't Heather McLeod. Heather McLeod's alive, and I found her."

As the words hit him, stunned him, I moved.

The Luger blasted the silence as his mouth opened in a sharp soundless cry and the gun sagged in his thick fingers and the heel of my boot smashed into his knee.

He stumbled sideways, his face twisted with pain, and I kicked again, drove the toe of my boot into the center of his chest, heard bone crack, felt cartilage rip, slammed the heel of my hand into the base of his nose and felt bone shatter and saw his eyes whiten as the bone splinters pierced his brain.

He sprawled in the dust, twitched. As I stood over him, looked down at him, the world went red.

I kicked him in the head, as hard as I could.

I kicked him in the head again, again.

"That's enough, Jack," Martha said.

I kicked him again.

She grabbed my arm, turned me around, wrapped her arms around me, pushed her body against me.

"That's enough! He's dead!"

CHAPTER THIRTY-FIVE

Staggering to the edge of the tailing pile, I dropped to my knees and retched, spewing my stomach into the dust.

When the convulsions finally, mercifully, stopped, I raised my head and looked out at the desert. The autumn light was golden, the world was no longer red.

I got to my feet, weak, trembling. My chest hurt, and my throat. My nose was bleeding again, felt huge, heavy. My mouth was foul with blood and bile and death.

Martha was sitting on a rock, watching me. Beside her lay three guns—Magnum, Luger, Smith & Wesson—and a wallet. In her lap she held her Beretta.

The body lay gray and red in the dust. At the sight of the head, my stomach stirred painfully. Then I noticed the dark blood pooling at the right shoulder.

Trying to understand, I played it back through my mind. I had moved, the Luger had fired, Flowers's face had twisted with pain into a soundless cry, I had kicked. . . .

No. If the Luger had fired, why was Flowers bleeding from a shoulder wound? The Luger hadn't fired.

I wobbled over to Martha's rock. "Good shooting."

"Bad shooting," she said calmly. "I was trying to kill him."

"How did you—"

"Luck. I was in the aspens when you came over the ridge, but crawling up the rocks was slow going. If you hadn't kept him talking, I wouldn't have made it in time."

She slid off the rock. "But maybe it wouldn't have mattered. The first thing I saw when I peeped over the edge of the rocks was your face. I've seen that face before. One way or another, shot up or not, you were going to kill him."

She'd seen the face that Rosetta Draine had seen twenty years before. My face.

I was suddenly, profoundly weary. And feeling strangely empty. Somehow, over the past hour, I had lost something—lost it, I sensed, forever.

"Did you hear any of it?"

When she shook her head, I leaned against the rock and told her about Flowers and his silent partnership with a black-haired hippie who was now a white-haired developer.

She stared out over the desert for a while. "Now we know."

"Part of it. But Flowers didn't know Rosetta Draine, which means she didn't sic him on me. Turner did. But how did . . . ?"

But I was too tired to think, so I let it go.

"The problem is," Martha said, "we can't prove anything. With Flowers dead . . ."

I started to nod, winced against the pain in my nose, eyes.

Martha brushed at the seat of her jeans. "You look a couple of quarts below the add mark. And in need of a new wardrobe."

My jacket was torn, crusted with mud, spattered with bile and blood. My shirt was a red mess. My jeans were muddy, my boots bloody.

"And a bath."

"We can handle two out of three," I said.

We picked our way down the tailing pile. Opening the back of the Wagoneer, I grabbed a water jug, handed her my keys.

The water rinsed away most of the blood from my face, the foulness from my mouth. As Martha took out the bottle of Glenlivet and a pair of plastic glasses, I slipped out of my jacket, stripped off my shirt, leaned past her and took out a Raiders jersey and carefully slid it over my head past my nose.

Martha handed me a glass, raised hers. "To togetherness."

"Martha, it wasn't that I didn't think you could—"

"Forget it, Jack." She wasn't angry. "I told you that when it came down to it, you'd go off on your own. It isn't a matter of reasons. It's a matter of your being what you are."

The scotch burned the taste of death from my mouth.

"We could call the sheriff about the body," Martha said.

She looked at me. "Or not."

I nodded. We couldn't prove anything. The only way anything would happen now was if we did it ourselves.

"Why don't we put him where he was going to put me."

We finished our drinks, then I took out a flashlight and a length of rope, and we climbed the tailing pile, removed a couple of boards from the mine entrance. In the musty darkness we found a confused pattern of footprints and, after a few yards, the deeper darkness of the shaft.

It took us both to handle the body. We dragged it inside and nudged it over the edge. It hit bottom with a faint thump.

We went back out, replaced the boards, scratched out the trail the body had made, scuffed over the blood with dust.

It seemed as if we'd been in the desert forever, but the sun and my watch said it was barely noon.

Martha handed me the .38, gathered up Flowers's wallet and the two other guns. "His car's around somewhere."

"People abandon cars out here all the time."

"Not very environmentally responsible of them, is it?"

Back at the Wagoneer, we locked up the two guns, then had another drink while I told her about the iris pond and the VW van.

As she listened, she went through the wallet. It didn't take long. A driver's license, several fake cards identifying Linus Flowers as a member of law enforcement agencies, two foil-wrapped Trojans, $1,672 in cash.

"The drought lowered the water level. The van could be seen,"

Martha said, stuffing the cards back in the wallet. "They had to get it out."

"Why? It wasn't a secret. Rosetta Draine told me it was there."

She nodded. "It doesn't make much sense, does it?"

My weariness was hammering on me. I couldn't think straight. "Maybe I read it wrong."

Martha shrugged, handed me the cash. "You might as well let Flowers pay for your nose. Unless those scruples of yours tell you to climb back up that rock pile and toss this down the hole."

They didn't. I took the money. "I'll give you what's left."

"We'll split it, half and half," she said.

Then she gave me her odd small smile, held out the Trojans. "You can have my half of these."

She insisted on driving out. I didn't argue. The scotch had left me light-headed; the pain had worn me to the bone.

We eased down off the mountain, through the gulch and wash. At the McLeod gate, I looked back up the canyon at the ruined ranch. The black figures, the vehicles, the mound of bright fake grass were gone.

Leaning back in the seat, I closed my eyes, felt the flesh around them swelling. I tried to think, but all I could do was remember. The world going red. Linus Flowers and my boots.

After a while Martha spoke. "You haven't asked me what happened at the grave."

Opening my eyes, I blinked against the brightness. We were about a mile from Red Rock Estates, near where Martha had laughed what seemed years before. "How bad was it?"

"It wasn't. Whatever you were expecting didn't happen. She looked at her mother and let out a screech. Then William Draine saw me and said something I couldn't hear, and everybody just stood there looking at one another like they'd been lobotomized."

It hadn't been Patsy's wail. It had been her daughter's.

"It was pretty obvious that nobody was going to say or do anything while I was around, so I went looking for you. When I got to the top of the ridge I looked back. They were hugging. Or holding one another up. All of them."

We eased over a rise and houses appeared, the road smoothed.

"I've seen it before," she went on. "Especially with women like Heather. It's as if they suddenly awake from a nightmare. All the emotional ugliness they've nurtured for years vanishes once they see that they're really loved."

I'd seen them too, the reconciliations. Sometimes they held. More often they didn't.

This one wouldn't. Because something about it was terribly, profoundly wrong.

At the Red Rock Road, I told Martha about the shortcut. Soon we were through the canyon and on 395 in California and speeding back toward Nevada.

At Bordertown, Martha spoke. "About Turner. Any ideas?"

"You could shoot him and then I could kick him to death."

She gave me her calm, quiet look. "I take that to mean no."

At St. Mary's, Martha waited in the Wagoneer while I went into the emergency room, where I spent an hour and a half and much of Linus Flowers's $1,672 getting my nose set and packed and taped.

The break was bad. It would heal, the doctor told me, but I would never look quite the same.

When I came out, the Wagoneer was there but Martha wasn't.

Back in the hospital, I managed to find a harried nurse who might have seen a woman fitting Martha's description using the phone. Outside, I found an old man at a bus stop who might have seen a woman fitting Martha's description getting into a cab.

I drove over to Sparks, to Turner Development and Construction. The emerald Ferrari wasn't in Turner's parking slot. Mr. Turner was out of town. The Madonna-clone receptionist hadn't seen a woman fitting Martha's description.

I sat in the Wagoneer, trying to think.

Martha had gone off on her own, as I had in the desert. If she'd wanted me along, she would have waited for me.

She could take care of herself.

I could try to find her. Part of me wanted to. But that was the head part, the thinking part.

The feeling part, the heart and gut, told me to leave her alone, let her do her way whatever she was doing.

CHAPTER THIRTY-SIX

In the Rondo and Keene lot, I struggled out of the Wagoneer, tried to stretch the stiff ache from my shoulders. The peaks of the Sierra glistened cold and white in the sun. Below them the aspens had lost their leaves, the mountains their patches of color. Dark and still, they waited for winter.

I went in the back, slipped into my office. Neat, clean, stylishly appointed, the office suddenly seemed strange to me, as if it belonged to someone else. Only my daughter's portrait said it was mine.

A sheaf of papers lay on the desk. Beside them, fresh from the printers, sat a box of business cards identifying Jack Ross, attorney-at-law, as an associate of the firm of Rondo and Keene.

I called the receptionist and asked her to tell Wally that I needed to see him, preferably in my office, right away. She let me listen to Muzak for a while. About the time I determined that the stringy mush was supposed to be "It Ain't Me, Babe," she was back on. Wally would be right down.

243

I sat and looked at the portrait of my daughter until he got there. Holding bottles of Bacardi and Coca-Cola in one hand and a pair of glasses in the other, he stood in the door and stared.

"Jesus, Jack. Are you all right?"

"I'll survive," I said.

He stepped inside, shut the door, came over and set the bottles on the desk. "What happened?"

When I shrugged, he looked at me for a long time. Then he shrugged as well. He twisted open the Coca-Cola, the rum, slowly smiled his broad theatrical smile.

"I hope you'll indulge me, Jack. It's a little ritual I perform each time the firm does an especially significant piece of business. Your coming on board certainly qualifies."

"Rum and Coke," I said.

Pouring, he nodded. "I thought you'd get the symbolism."

He handed me a glass, with a dramatic flourish raised his own. "To your productive and profitable association with Rondo and Keene, Jack."

"Wally, I'm not here to sign papers. I just came in to tell you you'd better get free of Nolan Turner."

He set down his drink, made a production of tugging at the knees of his pants, easing onto the couch, shooting his cuffs.

"They're true, then, the rumors?"

"He's not tied to organized crime," I said. "But the rest of it—the threats, the nasty incidents, the disappearances—that was Turner, and a local thug named Linus Flowers."

Wally didn't say anything for a while. Then, slowly smiling, he raised his glass again. "Let's drink, then, to poltroonery."

It took me a minute. "You didn't go in with him?"

His smile faded. "I came close. But finally there was too much wrong about him. It was bad business."

I was surprised. And given what the decision had cost him, impressed. "That doesn't sound like poltroonery, Wally. It sounds suspiciously like simple, old-fashioned integrity."

"It couldn't be that," he grinned. "I'm an attorney."

I raised my glass. "To integrity."

He looked at me, but he didn't raise his glass. "I don't know if it's that. Maybe it's just that finally I believe we have to have standards of conduct, if for nothing more than to protect ourselves from ourselves. I don't know if that's integrity or cowardice."

I didn't either. I didn't know if what I'd done a couple of hours earlier was justifiable by his standards, or by mine.

"The problem is, Wally, there are different standards."

He hesitated. "I don't know what you mean, exactly."

I told him. "I killed a man this morning."

He paled, swallowed.

"I killed a man who had killed three people, and who was trying to kill me."

He worked moisture into his mouth, nodded.

"But it wasn't really self-defense. I deliberately set things up so he'd have to come after me. The whole point was to kill him. Because he needed killing."

Wally picked up his glass, drank deeply.

"One set of standards says I should notify the authorities, conform to the legal code—which as an attorney and member of the bar and officer of the court I'm sworn to uphold."

"Yes."

"But another, unwritten but so basic to me that it might be coded in my genes, says that I should dump his body in a hole in the desert and tell no one, because maybe by doing that I'll have a chance to get the man who is really responsible for those three deaths. Which should I follow?"

His color was coming back. "You're talking about Turner."

I didn't say anything.

"I don't think it's a matter of should. It's a matter of did. You've already done it."

He looked at his glass. "Not to put too fine, or perhaps sententious, a point on it—standards are abstract, guidelines designed to help us decide how to act. The decision to act and the responsibility for our actions are ours."

My grandfather would have put it differently, into a platitude. A man's got to do what a man's got to do. Code of the West.

"You're telling me something else, aren't you, Jack? You're telling me you're not going to sign those papers in front of you."

"I'm sorry, Wally."

"Can you tell me why?"

What could I tell him? JDFR? That it was a matter of my being what I was? That things change but people don't? That out on a desert mountain I had lost something forever? And maybe found myself?

Wally sat up, sighed. "I'm sorry, too, Jack. It would have been good for us both, I think. What . . . are you going to do?"

"About Turner? I don't know yet."

"No, I mean about you, your work. Doing what you do drives you crazy, sends you running out to the desert. That hasn't changed."

I remembered what Martha had observed the night before. Everything I brought back from the desert had the mark of human hands on it.

"A year or so ago I tried to quit, Wally. I went out and hid in the desert, but finally I had to come back. I went to the desert because there weren't any people there. But I had to come back because there weren't any people there."

He frowned, not theatrically but humanly. "I don't think I understand, Jack."

"My work drives me crazy sometimes, yes. But just listening to the news can drive me crazy. What gets to me, Wally, is just people, human beings and what they do to each other. But there isn't anything else."

He shook his head. "All you ever see is people at their worst. Why keep at it?"

All I could tell him was what Martha had told me.

"I'm good at it. Sometimes I help people."

We drank, finally, not to poltroonery or integrity but to each other.

When he left, Wally took with him the rum and Coke and the papers.

When I left, I took the photograph of my daughter.

CHAPTER THIRTY-SEVEN

I was lying in the dark on my bed, trying to find a way to breathe that would let me sleep, when headlights sent yellow light splashing across the room.

When I'd gotten back to my house, the small black Geo was no longer parked under the mulberry tree. Now it was. I got up and put on my robe, turned on lights on my way to the front door.

In the night's deepening cold, Martha seemed flushed, warm with an excitement that glittered in her eyes. A six-pack dangled from her hand.

She gave me her odd smile. "I got you up again."

"I wasn't sleeping."

Stepping inside, she held up the beer. "I'll drink my own this time."

In the kitchen she sat at the table with a beer as I put the remaining four in the refrigerator. When I sat down, she shook her head. "God, you look awful."

She didn't. She looked lovely, eyes glittering, flushed skin glowing. But I didn't say so.

"You don't want to run off and put some clothes on?"

She was having fun, I knew, at my expense. I didn't mind.

She took a long swallow, then set down the beer. "You're going to have to ask, Jack."

I asked. "What have you been doing?"

"Not much," she said. "It's just that we're supposed to be trained investigators, right?"

"Right."

"So I was sitting there waiting for you, and it struck me that one of us should try asking the kind of questions she'd been trained to ask. Like, what if that big beat-up Nevada redneck was right about Dale Rutledge being killed because of a film about a bunch of hippies in the desert twenty years ago?"

"What if?"

"And if the film was in his Sacramento office, why was his body found at his studio outside Davis?"

"I give up."

"Come on, Jack," she scowled playfully. "You Nevada good old boys are supposed to have gumption. Grit. Sand. You can't quit that easily."

I watched the dance in her pale brown eyes, the crinkle of the skin around her mouth, the glow of color in her face.

"You found it."

She shook her head, fighting a smile. "Not so fast, Jack. Think it through."

I thought it through. "The film was in his office. So he either told Flowers where the film was—"

"And Flowers went and got it," Martha said, finishing my thought. "But there's a simpler explanation. Rutledge—"

I finished her thought. "Took it to the studio himself, because he was—"

"Going to use it. Show it to Culler, maybe he was going to show it to Turner or the Draines, try some sort of extortion scam. But how was he going to do that, considering the form it was in. He'd have to—"

"Get a sixteen-millimeter projector, haul it around and—"

"And why bother when he could dub it onto tape, carry it around in his pocket. Everybody's got a VCR these days."

"So Linus got the original, but—"

"He didn't know about the tape."

Then, slowly, she smiled the smile that opened her face like a flower, the smile she watched me from behind.

"Where was it, Martha?"

She reached into her purse and pulled out the black plastic case. "'The Purloined Letter' principle. In the VCR."

"What's on it?"

Her smile didn't quite disappear. "I don't know. I only watched enough to make sure what it was."

That was hard to believe, but I looked at her and believed it.

"I thought about doing it alone," she said. "But it seemed as if all I've been doing for the past few days is sitting alone watching videos that you either brought me or pointed me toward. I thought it was time we watched one together."

"Together," I said.

"See, it's not that hard to say, is it?" Before I could reply, she went on. "Besides, I didn't want to make the mistake I made with Maureen Cody. You might see things that I don't."

"I doubt it, Martha."

Her eyes found, held mine. Then she rose, picked up the tape. "Let's do it, Mr. Ross."

Everyone, she'd said, has a VCR. I had two, both in bedrooms. "My daughter's room."

As the group America sang about "going to the desert on a horse with no name," the camera panned over the hazy desert mountains and down to the empty alkali flat in Beulah Valley, found and followed a tiny stream of white dust that swelled and billowed as the dark dot that raised it gradually became a Volkswagen bus splattered with hand-painted flowers.

Then, beneath Gale Garnett's carpe diem song about singing in the sunshine, a cut to the UNR campus and students scattered in lolling or flirting or Frisbee-tossing clusters over the ersatz Ivy

League quad; then another cut to the iris pond—the VW van parked on the earthen face, nude young people splashing in the dark, sun-streaked water.

A slow dissolve to Dylan exhorting everybody to get stoned and night and a campfire surrounded by a sprawl of toking, nodding, nuzzling kids in careful hippie costume.

A zoom in on the young man in boots and jeans and leather vest and love beads standing beside the fire, wild-bearded, wild-eyed, wildly gesticulating. The flames reflected in mad patterns on his rimless glasses as Gordon Lightfoot sang about catbirds and cornfields, daydreams together.

As I looked at him, most of what I'd learned and remembered in the past few days slowly shifted in my mind, rearranged itself into another pattern.

The pattern.

The young man was obviously making a speech. I didn't know what he was saying, but it didn't matter. He'd already told me what had been going on, told me what it was, finally, all about.

As I watched him rant, I suddenly understood something else.

I understood what it was that I'd encountered that was so powerfully, horribly wrong, what I'd found so threatening to everything I thought I knew, to everything I cared about.

It was that Patsy McLeod would live in the same house with, would become part of the family of, the man who had corrupted her daughter.

But it wasn't wrong.

Because Patsy McLeod wasn't living in the same house with the man who had corrupted her daughter.

CHAPTER THIRTY-EIGHT

Martha suddenly saw it too, froze the frame.

She'd taken off her jacket and shoes, was sitting cross-legged on the bed. Now she hunched over the beer in her hand and stared at the screen. "Blake."

"Yes."

"But not Professor William Draine."

"No." Before she could say anything else, I said, "Let's look at the rest of it first."

We watched it carefully, looking for people. Almost immediately we found a handsome young man in Indian drag, his hair as long and black and glossy as that of the star-struck Chicana in Videoscape, his raptorial eyes bright and never quite still.

Martha froze the frame again. "Nolan Turner."

"Raven, they called him."

She hesitated. "What it has to mean, Jack, is that it never has been Desert Conservancy fighting Turner Development and Construction for the McLeod ranch. The ranch has nothing to do with any of it, and the Draines and Turner are in this thing together. There never has been anyone else."

It didn't have to mean that, but it probably did.

As the film rolled, we found Patsy McLeod, twice. Early, leaning against the fender of her pickup, squinting into the glare reflected from the pond as she scowled at the two naked young women picking wild irises. Later, looking both foolish and pleased as she let the girl who called herself Gentle weave a garland of desert flowers into her hair.

Once, Heather McLeod, gangly and gawky under the burden of her burgeoning womanhood, dancing alone before a campfire and the heavy-lidded mad gaze of the hippie who called himself Blake.

Frequently, a beautiful dark-haired hippie chick at the edge of things but somehow at the center of everything.

Twice, fleetingly, shadowlike, always quickly moving out of camera range, another young man I could almost recognize.

But it was difficult to concentrate, or to think. I kept getting caught up in the images, in the story Dale Rutledge told with an almost savage finesse—softly focused ironic juxtapositions of desert desolation and manicured campus calm, of hippie frolic and frathouse high jinks; the inevitable change of the seasons on the land, change reflected in faces rendered almost lovingly by the camera as the focus became hard and grainy, the smiles became snarls, the pleasure became pain, hope became fear, love loneliness—all to the accompaniment of a sardonic sound track of rock and folk music.

The film was exactly what Dale Rutledge had said it was—fucking brilliant.

Martha and I watched silently as the VW van and its load of Day-Glo flowers rolled down the canyon. Across the pond a dark figure pointed. The sun flashed on the van's windshield just before it left the road in a long, slow nosedive, hit the water, floated, settled.

As it disappeared, Peter, Paul, and Mary sang "Where Have All the Flowers Gone."

Some small thing in the final scene seemed wrong, but I couldn't tell what it was.

Martha clicked the remote and the screen went black. She hit the rewind button, slowly shook her head. "How does somebody with that kind of talent end up making pornography?"

I remembered his paranoid explanation. "I don't know."

She uncrossed her legs, thrust her breasts against the circular design of her Cal sweatshirt as she arched the stiffness from her back. "So now we know."

"Yes."

"I need," she said, suddenly weary, "another beer."

Back in the kitchen, Martha slumped at the table as I got her another beer. Her pleased excitement was gone. She looked tired, angry.

Picking up *The Last and Greatest Dream,* she opened the back flap. "That's what Dale Rutledge had to sell Cleveland Culler that was so big. The Mercer Foundation."

"And American Security Bank. And Turner Construction."

She closed the book, put it down. "The kid in the film, Blake, at the end he was . . . I haven't seen eyes like that since Charles Manson. So they killed him—"

"We don't know that, Martha. He might—"

"Of course they killed him, Jack," she said angrily. "But even if they didn't, even if he just wandered off into the desert or got bit by a snake—"

She checked her anger. "We've still got massive fraud, to say nothing of three murders they're responsible for. Nolan Turner, Rosetta Draine, and . . . who is he, anyhow, the man posing as Draine?"

I remembered the shadowy figure in the film who kept moving out of camera range. "One of the other hippies, probably."

She picked up the book again, looked at the author's photograph. "How could they think they could pull it off?"

"They did pull it off, Martha. William Draine's only family was his grandmother, and she was old. They just kept him away from her, studying history in New Haven. Rosetta stayed in touch, sending her glowing reports of his transformation into a scholar and a gentleman. When the old woman died, Rosetta took over."

"It's still chancy, Jack."

"They thought it through very carefully. He stayed in the background, the cloistered historian who left business affairs to his wife.

They didn't socialize, hid out at Tahoe. It was easy."

Martha sighed wearily. "Until Hannah heard that Royce McLeod was dying and sent me looking for Heather. She would know that William Draine wasn't . . . William Draine. They couldn't take a chance that I'd find her, so they put Flowers on my tail."

I nodded. "I think they put me on your tail too, Martha. I was supposed to follow you, see what you stirred up, let them know if you found Heather."

She was angry again. "Then they sent him after Dale Rutledge and his film, because he tried to extort money from them."

I nodded. "Probably. I showed him that book, so he knew that Draine was a phoney, and probably who he really was."

"But why did he go to Culler with it first?"

I thought it through. "He didn't know about the Mercer Foundation, not then. Culler was onto his Amateur Orgy scheme, so getting out from under a propane torch was his first priority. He knew Tramontane was Heather, thought she'd get the ranch, thought that if a developer wanted it, it was valuable enough to get him off Culler's list."

Martha nodded. "Then Rutledge got Rosetta Draine's message, called her, told her about the film. And he was a dead man."

She sat back in her chair, picked up the distorting mirror. "The question now is what we're going to do about it."

That wasn't the question. Given what we'd done in the desert, there was only one thing to do, one place to go.

"Or," she said, "when we're going to do it."

"You found the film, Martha," I said. "That makes it your call."

She stared into the mirror, turning, tilting it. Then, she set it aside, stood up.

"I've been going for over eighteen hours. I stomped around the desert all morning, shot a man and lugged a body into a mine, then drove nearly two hundred and fifty miles. I'm more than a couple quarts below the add mark. And you look like you seized up hours ago."

"A few hours isn't going to make any difference," I said.

Martha nodded grimly. "I'm going to avail myself of your daughter's shower and bed and your hospitality again. We can do it in the morning."

I smiled. "We? You won't go running off without me?"
She didn't smile. "We."

Lying in the darkness, thinking about what we'd discovered and what we hadn't, drifting into something that was not quite sleep, I might have heard faint music, simple songs from a time of love and illusion, hope and horror.

CHAPTER THIRTY-NINE

After a night's rest and a healthy jolt of my caffeine-and-choles-terol breakfast special, Martha looked better—clear-eyed, refreshed, settled into her quiet calm.

I looked worse, my swollen nose darkly marbled, my eyes puffed half-shut and shot with blood. My sleep had been fitful, broken by pain and bizarre dreams.

But I was calm too, perhaps because I realized that it was over. We knew the important things. What we didn't know—why kill Royce McLeod, excavate the VW van, remove something from the old mine—was mostly just tidying up, fitting together the last few pieces. Then we would decide what we were going to do.

I wasn't too concerned about what was to come. In a way that I didn't quite understand, it seemed that from the beginning both Martha and I had been carried along on a deep current of inevita-bility. We would do what we had to do.

As I finished the breakfast dishes, I said, "You watched the film again last night."

Martha sat at the table, staring again into the shard of distorting mirror. She nodded, seemed to get quieter, calmer.

"You found something else."

"Not yet, Jack," she said.

I let it go. She'd tell me when she was ready.

Before we left, I put my .38 back in its teak box, the box back in my grandfather's desk.

The night had been very cold. The morning sun struggled to penetrate the already thick cloud of pollution in the Truckee Meadows, couldn't soften the heavy frost.

Martha nodded at the Wagoneer, exhaled gray clouds. "You know where we're going."

While she backed out the Geo and parked it on the street, I started the Wagoneer, got out and scraped the frost from the windshield, started to get in, then stopped, waited for her.

"You mind if we see somebody first? It doesn't matter much, I suppose, but there's a chance we can learn who he really is."

"Another hour won't matter," she said calmly. "There's no one left for them to kill. Except us."

The killing, I thought, was over. But I didn't say so. Instead I went back inside and got William Draine's latest book.

Morning traffic drained off the foothills, clogged the Keystone interchange, flowed in a steaming, sluggish stream onto the interstate.

I took the B Street exit into Sparks, into a downtown that had been "redeveloped"—brick and concrete and twiggy trees—so that now the old ranching and railroad town looked like every other "redeveloped" town in America.

A few minutes after turning off I pulled up in front of Dormouse Books. Martha studied the window display, the message carved over the door. She looked at me, nearly smiled.

I did smile. THE BEAT GOES ON.

Grabbing William Draine's book, I got out and ushered her into the incense-thick, rainbow-colored warmth. Through it wafted the thin sweet harmony of Simon and Garfunkel building a bridge over troubled waters.

Martha took it all in, the books and posters and symbolic tableaux, smiled a quiet smile.

My face sobered the smile of the woman behind the counter.

Beneath a beaded and quilled leather band, Gentle's hair cascaded
to her hips. Silver and turquoise at her ears matched both the
squash-blossom necklace that lay over her embroidered chambray
shirt and the belt at the waist of her squaw dress.

She held up two fingers. "Peace, Jones."

"Hello, Gentle," I said. "Or should I say 'How.'"

"You already know how, Jones. Trust the Goddess." She smiled
distractedly. "You look—"

"Maya," I grinned, "all is maya."

"Yes, but—" She looked at Martha, back at me.

"Gentle, this is my . . . friend, Martha Reedy."

Gentle lifted, spread two fingers. "Peace," she said.

"Peace." Martha said. Then she too gave the peace sign as she
slowly smiled the smile that opened her face like a flower.

For a long, still, silent moment the two women smiled at one
another, seemed to communicate in some private but profound
way.

Then Gentle looked at me. "You found her."

"Heather McLeod? Yes, we found her. With your help."

"And with help from Cyclops. And Raven?"

"Raven?"

She smiled excitedly. "I remembered the day after I talked to
you. I saw his picture in the paper once."

"Nolan Turner."

"Phoenix said you'd probably want to talk to Raven too. You'd
said you were going to see Cyclops, so I called him. He told me
he'd be seeing you again and would tell you."

What it meant was that Gentle had known all along who Turner
was. "You've never talked to him, to Raven."

Her smile wavered. "He—he was Raven. He was a beautiful person, but he . . . wanted."

Which was as close as she could come to saying she didn't like
someone. Gentle didn't like not liking someone. But in this case, I
thought, it might have kept her alive.

I also thought that Gentle's call to Rutledge might have gotten
him killed. I didn't want to think about that.

"We need your help again, Gentle." Placing *The Last and Great-*

est Dream on the counter, I flipped it open to the back flap. "Can you tell us who this is?"

As the music segued into Creedence Clearwater Revival's "Who'll Stop the Rain," she looked down at the photograph.

When she looked up at me, her eyes, her smile misted with emotion. "You bring me such wonderful gifts, Jones. Wonderful, beautiful people. Leatherstocking was such a beautiful person."

I remembered the name. "How was he beautiful?"

"The only way. He loved people. He helped them. He was very kind." She looked back down at the photograph. "You can see. He still is."

"I don't suppose you know what his real name was?"

She looked at the blurb beneath the photograph. "He isn't William . . . ?" Then her smile spread again. "No. He follows Thought-Woman."

I didn't get that. Martha did. "Under Her guidance, with Her power, think it, dream it, name it, and it becomes real."

Gentle smiled. "And good."

"And weaves the pattern that traces the pattern."

What followed was to me a swell of hippie-dippie New Age arcana, but I picked up some of it, partly because occasionally they were reduced to using the English language and partly because of what Rosetta Draine had told me.

The hippie Leatherstocking had known the desert, the mountains, what was edible and where to find it, what could be hunted and how to do it, the names of plants and flowers, where there was enough water to make things grow.

But for all his help, his kindness, he was solitary, lonely, disturbed. He didn't frolic with the others, wandered restlessly, appeared at the commune infrequently and never for long, sometimes seemed to vanish. He had a camp farther up the mountain, where only, sometimes, Lola, and, sometimes, Iris Eyes, visited.

"Lola?" I said.

Gentle's smile again faltered. "Blake called her Woman. She was very beautiful, but she was Lola."

Rosetta Draine.

"Why was Leatherstocking . . . disturbed?"

"He had lost his way, broken the pattern. He didn't know there is no pattern." She laid her finger on the photograph. "But he's found it again. You can see. He's back in Her embrace."

Something about his action in the film had stuck with me. "Was he hiding from something out there?"

Gentle smiled serenely. "From Her loving truth."

We'd gotten as much as we were going to get. I didn't know what, if anything, it was.

I picked up the book. "Thank you, Gentle."

She again raised and veed her fingers. So did Martha. The two women smiled at one another.

I fired up the Wagoneer, waited as the defroster worked on the thin film that had recoated the windshield. Then, under a sudden urgent impulse, I said, "I'll be right back."

Gentle still smiled. Chad and Jeremy explained that yesterday was gone. So, I'd sensed, was the gray man.

"He left, didn't he? Phoenix?"

Gentle nodded, smiled serenely.

I sighed. "I'm sorry, Gentle."

Her smile went impish. "He leaves every morning. Group."

My grin must have looked as foolish as I felt.

"You have to learn to have faith, Jones," she said. "Trust Gaea and those in Her loving care."

I laughed. "I'm trying, Gentle."

"Bud will help. You fit."

Bud. Martha. I got it.

"She's . . . " Martha searched for the word, didn't find it.

I wasn't sure the word existed. "She certainly is."

"Jones?"

Pulling onto the interstate, I told her why I was Jones.

"I like that. Jones." She smiled quietly. "She agrees with you about Rosetta Draine. Whatever Lola wants . . ."

Lola gets. Rosetta Draine.

As we drove toward mountains, through desert being buried under housing developments, I told her about Gentle—how we'd met, her faint old scars and her recurrent nightmares, what my grandfather and I had done when we had found her.

"I've seen it," Martha said, "but I've never understood it. How a man could do something like that to his own daughter."

"A man didn't do it," I said. "Her mother did it."

"Her mother. She must have been . . . "

"She was. She was a Vegas P.E. teacher who believed in True Love. It got her impregnated and abandoned. Then she didn't believe in it anymore. She believed that all men were evil and that it was her duty to make certain none of them ever touched her daughter. She made certain by whipping the girl with a wire clothes hanger whenever she so much as looked at a male human being, and she . . ."

I didn't go on. I could explain the evil, but I couldn't explain it away.

Martha sat as she had in the desert, silent, staring out the window.

"Where did Gentle get the money to buy a bookstore?"

"Her mother killed herself. Gentle was her heir."

Martha nodded. "Victims, both of them."

"Everyone's a victim, Martha."

"Of one another," she said slowly.

"And of themselves."

She looked at me, started to say something, then didn't.

Gradually I picked up on her mood—pensive, grave, nearly brooding. Behind her quiet calm, something was working on her. As we began to climb the Sierra, she looked out at it, not seeing.

She didn't say anything until we were pulling off at the Truckee exit. "You told Hannah that your only interest in this case was Patsy McLeod. Because she's your client, and because of what happened eighteen years ago?"

"That. And . . ." I had to think about it. Like Patsy McLeod, I was rethinking a lot of things. "The land isn't the only thing in the West that's being destroyed. A whole way of life is being bulldozed under. When I was a kid, half the people in Nevada were like Patsy McLeod. Now . . ."

I hadn't explained, knew it. "The other night you asked if the

McLeod ranch wasn't worth saving. I think the Patsy McLeods and what they think and feel are worth saving too. Their way might be old-fashioned, but it's real, and it's important that we don't lose it."

"Because it's the right way? They're right?"

"It's not a question of right or wrong," I said. "They're human beings with their own myths and values and history. They've developed their own way of dealing with life, their own ethos, culture. If we need to respect ethnic cultures, we need to respect theirs too."

"Theirs? Or yours?" But she didn't wait for an answer. "You think that because people like Patsy have a different set of values they should be judged differently?"

Truckee sat in the bright bare cold morning, waiting for the snow that would bring the tourists. If it came.

"I didn't say that."

We passed the golf course and condos, climbed up the man-made canyon through dark pines toward the summit.

"What you want to find out, when we get there, is why they would kill a dying man."

"Isn't that what you want?"

She didn't answer until we had crawled over the summit, started down, and Lake Tahoe came into view.

From the homes around it, woodsmoke rose thickly into the sky, hit the inversion layer, thinned and drifted out over the water, the pall dimming the brightness, dulling the blue.

"I want to know why Heather hated her mother."

CHAPTER FORTY

Sunlight whitened the thick frost coating the meadow. Smoke drifted up from the white house at the edge of the lake. Nothing else moved.

"She's here," Martha said.

The small gold Mercedes sat between the BMW and Patsy's pickup. The reconciliation apparently had held. So far.

"I imagine you'll want to play this straight, too."

I pulled the Wagoneer in behind the big green Mercedes. "It's your call, Martha."

She gave me her odd smile. "Straight's fine with me, Jones."

"Be careful with Mrs. Draine. If she tells us anything, it will be true, but it won't be the truth."

As we got out, the front door opened and Monte stepped out. He still wore black; standing in the doorway he seemed like a swollen shadow man.

As we approached, he smiled as he took in the new bandages. "Bodyguard blow it, Timex?"

263

264

"Ms. Reedy," I said, "is the only reason I'm still alive. And somebody else isn't."

"Lone Ranger, Faithful Companion."

"I thought you were the house nigger," Martha said quietly. "You're a long way from the house."

He shrugged his shrug. "Part of the job."

"The labor of love part? That Culler doesn't know about?"

His smile faded as he studied her, me. "We're bodies is all. Muscle and money to him. Nothing personal."

"But you'd prefer that Culler not know about how the two of you use your bodies together."

"When it's time."

It was a statement or a threat, depending on how we wanted to take it. Martha took it calmly. "I can't think of a single reason why he should have to know."

As he studied her, she said: "We're not here about . . . Heather McLeod. We need to see the Draines."

He continued to study her. Then slowly he smiled, turned, opened the door. "Be more fun."

Rosetta Draine stood just inside the door, as if she'd been waiting for us. In jeans and a green sweater over a green paisley blouse, she seemed more the hippie chick at the center of everything than the head of the Mercer Foundation. But her small body was tense, her lovely face stiff with strain.

It wasn't just Rosetta Draine. Tension, strain seemed to fill the house, deepen its silence.

At the sight of my bruises, she gaped as Wally Keene had.

"Mr. Ross, are you all right? What in the world happened?"

"I made you very happy."

Slowly she realized what I'd told her. Her eyes widened.

Monte stepped past us and into the living room. When he was gone, Martha said, "Mr. Ross has pronoun problems, Mrs. Draine. Not I. We."

"I . . . see." But she clearly didn't like what she saw. "You are working together?"

"Together and effectively," Martha said. "We've discovered all sorts of interesting things."

Rosetta Draine looked at us. She knew what we knew. But for all her tenseness, she seemed unthreatened, in control. She smiled her small wry smile. "My husband is in his study. Why don't we join him?"

"Let's," Martha said. The two women gazed at one another; then Rosetta Draine turned, and they started down the hallway. I took a step, then stopped.

The tension in the house hadn't been caused by our arrival. It, and the silence, radiated from the living room, from the mother and daughter sitting across from one another before the softly crackling fire.

Sensing my presence, Patsy looked up at me. The creases of her worn, weathered desert face were deepened with anxiety, her beautiful blue eyes red-rimmed.

She looked away, to her daughter. Heather wore jeans and a man's plaid shirt that was too big for her. Her artificial red-black hair tossed stiffly as she turned toward me. Her not-quite-beautiful face hardened into near ugliness.

The silence chilled the house. The silence of absence. What was absent was the Draine children, Patsy's pretend family, my dream family. What was absent was the McLeod family.

I turned away, went down the hall and into the book-lined, history-burdened office.

The man posing as William Draine sat at his desk. His wife stood, or posed, beside him, her hand on his shoulder. Both silently stared down at the black plastic video case resting on the table in the pale sunlight that flooded through the French doors.

When Rosetta Draine looked up, her eyes were steady. "This is a copy of the film Dale Rutledge made? You've viewed it?"

Martha nodded. "We have."

The man posing as William Draine sighed heavily. Removing his glasses, he leaned his elbows on the desk, placed his palms over his eyes, pressed.

His wife smiled faintly. "Please, Ms. Reedy, Mr. Ross, sit down. We know what you must think, how it must look, but we can explain, if you'll allow us the opportunity."

Rosetta Draine was going to explain away three murders.

Martha glanced at me, shrugged. She stepped over to a leather couch, settled onto it. I sat beside her.

Rosetta Draine smiled her satisfaction. She was in control. "Did I understand you correctly, Mr. Ross? That Flowers man is dead?"

"You may be happy to know that you helped kill him."

"I'm not displeased," she said evenly. "How did I help?"

"I told you I was going to prove he killed Royce McLeod. You were the only one I told. You told Nolan Turner, who told Linus Flowers, who came after me. Us."

"I told Nolan Turner," she said quietly, "but not for the reason you imagine. I simply made a mistake, Mr. Ross."

"You made a bunch of them, Mrs. Draine."

The sound of my voice surprised me. There was no anger in it, or in me. I wasn't sure why.

Rosetta Draine shifted her hand on her husband's shoulder, clamped her fingers into his flesh. He didn't seem to notice.

"After you told me about the . . . killings, I realized that Nolan had to be behind them. I informed him that if he didn't stop Flowers, he would get nothing more from us. He said he would, but . . . instead he must have sent Flowers after you."

"You also told Turner that I was looking for Heather," Martha said calmly.

"Yes, but—"

"And because of that Maureen Cody died. And you told him about Dale Rutledge's film."

"No, not Dale. I didn't tell Turner about the film."

Which meant that Gentle had told Rutledge about Turner, Rutledge had made the contact, then died under a propane torch.

"But you told him about me. Because if I'd found—" Martha stopped, looked at me. She'd just understood something, but I didn't know what it was.

Rosetta Draine took a deep breath. "We wanted you to find Heather, Ms. Reedy, if that was possible. And despite the . . . difficulties that have arisen, we're very happy that you did. But you're right about the woman in—about Maureen Cody. We are—I am—at least partly responsible for her death. I told Nolan what you were doing for Desert Conservancy."

There was a question to be asked, but Martha didn't ask it. She'd gone quiet, calm, seemed sunk deep within herself.

I asked it. "Why?"

"Because I was afraid that if he learned about it on his own, he'd panic, do something . . . unnecessary. As it turned out, he did anyway. He was afraid Heather might expose us and he would lose his . . ."

"His what?" Then I saw it. "He always had too much money around him, too much power. He got it from you, for his silence."

"Yes," she said, shifting uncomfortably. "We gave him money when he was starting his business. After that it was . . . our influence. It was a mistake, but once we'd started . . ."

Nolan Turner was to the Draines what Linus Flowers was to Turner.

"But," she said, regaining her composure, "we had nothing to do with the killing. I tried to stop it."

Something was wrong. As she had been in the foyer, Rosetta Draine was still tense, but she wasn't afraid, wasn't threatened. She was in control.

"You're telling us that Nolan Turner had Flowers kill the woman he thought was Heather and then kill Dale Rutledge and get his film, and you and your husband are completely innocent."

"I—we abhor violence, violence of any kind. Much of what we do with our funds is an attempt to eliminate violence from our society, and to assist its victims. I understand your incredulity, Mr. Ross. But we are innocent of—"

"No."

The word echoed softly in the silence. The man posing as William Draine stirred under her hand, dropped his hands from his eyes. They looked hollow, haunted.

"We are completely guilty. We—I—have been for twenty years."

Finally, the truth. "Since you killed Blake," I said.

He didn't answer. Leaving his glasses on the desk beside the video, he slid out from under his wife's hand, rose, slowly moved over to the French doors that looked out on the lake.

His wife watched him, her face twisting under a silent pain. Pain that was, I thought, an extension of his pain.

"And you killed Royce McLeod. Or are you going to put that on Nolan Turner too?"

Rosetta Draine took another deep breath. "I know this sounds self-serving, but it was Nolan who had Mr. McLeod killed. He felt that he needed to settle the matter of the property in Beulah Valley quickly, before someone found . . ."

Martha spoke then, finally, quietly, as if from a distance. "The body in the van."

As soon as she said it, I saw it was true, saw how I'd misread what I'd seen at the iris pond, saw what it was that was wrong at the end of Dale Rutledge's film.

"I had it backwards," I told her. "They didn't take something out of the mine. They put something in. The bones of William Draine, after they'd dug them out of the van."

Martha nodded. "We."

What was wrong in the film was the sun flash on the windshield. It wasn't the sun. It was a bullet hole starring the glass. The figure on the far bank wasn't pointing a finger but a rifle.

I started to say so, saw that Martha already knew that too, then saw that she knew something else. Uncertain, I worked it through.

"The drought lowered the water, and he was afraid that somebody might see the remains of William Draine in the van. But who would . . . ?"

Rosetta Draine looked at me. "You answered that question the other evening, Mr. Ross. He was afraid of you."

Maureen Cody had died because Rosetta Draine made a mistake. Dale Rutledge had died because Gentle wanted to help me. And Royce McLeod had died because I couldn't stop being what I was.

"Nobody had to die," I said.

"No."

"It was all a mistake."

"Yes."

"But they did die, Mrs. Draine. And we have to do something about it."

Rosetta Draine looked over at her husband, as if for help. In the silence, he must have heard her silent plea. But he didn't turn around.

She sighed, then sat behind his desk, folded her hands. "Mr. Ross, Ms. Reedy, everything I've told you is the truth. But this conversation never took place. If you go to the authorities, our lawyers will make you look very foolish, especially since you haven't a shred of evidence to back you up."

I remembered what Wally Keene had said about her. She could be as tough as she had to be. But I still didn't understand her confidence, her certainty.

"We have all the evidence we need. We have a film that proves that for twenty years you've been defrauding the legal heirs of Felice Mercer. And we know where the evidence is that will convict your husband of the murder of William Draine."

"You have nothing, Mr. Ross. What you'll find in the mine shaft is simply bones. Nolan took care to see that the . . ." She faltered, again seemed in pain. She fought it off. ". . . the skull was destroyed."

Simply bones. More bones.

"Beyond that, over the years we have seen to it that any evidence that might prove my husband is not William Draine has been altered or removed."

I started to object, then stopped. Given the power at her command, she could get it done.

"And there was no fraud. I am the heir of Felice Mercer."

"Not a chance," I said. "William Draine died before his grandmother did. It isn't the same thing."

"Legally, it's close enough that we could tie up any kind of challenge for years." She looked down at her folded hands for a moment. "But there will be no challenge, because there is no evidence on which to base it."

She was right. She was safe, had everything under control.

"In addition, Mr. Ross, we have not benefitted in any way. We have taken nothing from the estate of Felice Mercer. We live comfortably, but we do it on my husband's salary and what I earn as chair of the board of American Security Bank."

That was easy to check, had to be true.

"I'm telling you this, Mr. Ross, Ms. Reedy, because after what you've both gone through you deserve to know. And because you're both good, decent people. If you take the time to really reflect, you will see the justice of it all."

"No," I said. But I still wasn't angry. "You're telling us because there's absolutely nothing we can do about it."

Rosetta Draine looked at me, but she didn't answer.

Beside me Martha stirred, said quietly, "There is one thing we can do, Mrs. Draine. And it will put you in prison for a long time."

Rosetta Draine went very still.

"We can't prove who your husband isn't, but we can prove who he is."

Slowly Rosetta Draine stiffened, paled.

In the silence, the man posing as William Draine turned to face us. His smile was as pained, as haunted as his eyes.

"It was what happened at the grave, wasn't it?"

Martha nodded. "I didn't understand it then."

I didn't understand it yet.

Martha told me. "Heather didn't cry out when she saw her mother. She cried out when she saw her brother."

CHAPTER FORTY-ONE

For a moment, Rosetta Draine sat rigidly, her body still as death. Then she gave up control, sagged back into the chair.

Professor William Draine—Malcolm McLeod—moved behind his wife, placed his hand gently on her shoulder. Reaching up, she grasped his hand in her own, lay her cheek against it, closed her eyes. The act was that of a child—the child, I sensed, that somewhere deep inside herself she still was: the beautiful, intelligent Tenderloin waif who thought she wanted money and power but who really wanted only to be safe.

Maybe. Or maybe, as I had with Tramontane, I was projecting, trying to make her human.

Her husband, as he had to, began to speak.

Only half listening, I wrestled with the knowledge that I should have seen it. It had been there all along, in the darker currents of Patsy McLeod's beautiful blue eyes, in the photographic display in her bedroom, in her real love for her pretend family.

It had been there in the calculated tale Rosetta Draine had composed for me, in the account that Professor William Draine had suffered through a few days before in this same room.

I should have seen it, and I hadn't. Because I had been seeing instead my own childish dreams, my own obsessions.

He was talking about Vietnam, about the encounter of a seventeen-year-old's idealism with the horror of a reality that transformed dreams of heroism into a living nightmare from which there was no escape. Until the rocket and the confusion and the opportunity that, without thinking, he simply took.

He was talking about returning to America under a different identity, deserting before anyone could discover it, fleeing to Nevada and hiding in the desert mountains he had grown up in as he tried to come to terms with what he had seen, what he had done.

"You were there, Mr. Ross. You know."

I was there. I knew.

"I finally understood that what we were doing in Vietnam was exactly what we had done here, in America. Under a banner of moralistic slogans that masked our real motives, we were destroying a land and a people. And ourselves."

It hadn't been that simple. Like the entire history of his country, it had been complex, confused, morally ambiguous. As he did with the history of his country, he was revising, simplifying his own history, so that he could live with it, and himself.

But I didn't say so. Because I'd done both myself.

"So you stopped killing Vietnamese and came home and killed William Draine and took his identity and his wife and his money—real motives that I'm sure you'll mask with moralistic slogans."

But I wasn't angry. I seemed beyond anger.

He shook his head. "I know you won't believe me, Mr. Ross, but the money had nothing to do with it. Rosetta and I fell in love, yes, but we were just going to . . . I was going to turn myself in. She was going to divorce Blake. We . . ."

He seemed to hear it as I did, to hear the preposterousness of it. But he still seemed to believe it.

In the silence, I looked at his wife. As if feeling my gaze, she slowly lifted her head, opened her eyes.

I couldn't read her. She might have been confirming the truth of what her husband said. She might have been asking if I accepted it as truth. She might have been asking me if it was the truth.

I began, then, vaguely, gropingly, to understand why I wasn't angry. For some reason I didn't really care what Malcolm McLeod told us, or what the truth was.

Beside me, Martha sat silent, still. Perhaps she didn't care either.

But I played it out. "If that's the case, why did he die?"

As he hesitated, I saw in his pain another face, saw another suffering man looking out of his eyes. I saw his father.

"Blake died because of what he did to my sister," he said lifelessly. "She was twelve years old. And . . . I killed him."

"And then ran off to Yale, abandoned your mother to the clubs and your sister to . . ." I couldn't say it.

"Yes."

"And lived happily ever after."

His pain was deepening, freshening. And his guilt. "We only had the trust fund, barely enough for school and . . . But we came back for my mother as soon as we could. We looked for Heather. You had looked for her. We thought she was dead."

Martha had been still, silent for a long time. Now, still silent, she rose from the couch. She put her hand on my shoulder, briefly, then turned and left the room.

I played it out. "So you murdered William Draine—"

"No," he said sadly. "It wasn't murder. It was justice."

I didn't say anything.

"There are certain evils that can't be accepted, acts that can't—if it had been your sister, Mr. Ross, your twelve-year-old sister who had been filled with dope and dreams and violated body and soul . . . what would you have done?"

I found myself remembering how, less than twenty-four hours before, the world had gone red. I didn't want to think about it.

I didn't want to think about any of it anymore. But I had a couple more questions I had to ask.

"Why leave the body in the van?"

He nodded, seemed weary, dazed, seemed not to care anymore

either. "We tried to get it out, but the water was too deep, too murky. But we thought it was safe. When my father came back, he'd tend the floodgates, and he'd never know it was there."

"You didn't think about a drought." But now I had only one more question, the question Martha wanted the answer to. "Why does Heather hate her mother?"

Gently he slipped his hand from his wife's, picked up and put on his glasses. "She doesn't hate her, Mr. Ross. She loves her. If she didn't, three people would be alive today."

I did get angry then. "So now you're blaming—"

"No," he said, angry himself. "I'm not blaming anyone but myself."

His anger checked mine.

"Blake told Heather he'd help her become a movie star, live a life of glamour and excitement. She believed him."

"And?"

"And she thought that my mother killed him."

I didn't see it, didn't understand.

"Mr. Ross, all she had to do was tell the sheriff that my mother killed Blake. But she didn't do it. She's angry. She's been angry for a long time. And hurt. But she wouldn't send her mother to prison, because finally she loves her."

"Why—" I struggled with it. "How could you let her believe that Patsy . . . ?"

He took off his glasses again, rubbed at his eyes. "We had to, or thought we did. We've—I've made mistakes, Mr. Ross. But the biggest mistake, the one I'll never be able to atone for, is the one I made by not letting Heather know I was alive."

"Out at the ranch, she didn't . . . ?"

"I was hiding from her too. We—I couldn't take the chance. She was only twelve, and she loved me. She might have said something to someone, let something slip."

Whatever he saw in my face took the heart out of him. "At least that's what I told myself at the time."

I shook my head wearily. "So, Professor, what do you tell yourself now?"

He put his glasses back on. "What I've been telling Heather for most of the last twenty-four hours. That I loved her and that I didn't want to hurt her. That I didn't want her to know I was a ... "

I waited, but he didn't say the word. I didn't either.

"How much does your mother know about her, about the life she's led?"

"All of it," he said. "Heather spent most of the night making certain we all knew. In detail."

"And your children?"

"No. At least—Claudette and Charlie, they know, I think. Not the specifics, but they . . . know."

"Do they know that Patsy really is their grandmother?"

"No. We can't—"

"Take a chance? The way you couldn't take a chance with your sister? The sister you couldn't trust with the truth, even if it meant letting her live with a lie that destroyed your family and turned her life into a nightmare?"

He didn't say anything.

"So that's all of it," I said.

He put his hand back on his wife's shoulder. Again she grasped it in hers, slowly sat up.

As they looked at me, I understood that they were making one final stand. There was one final truth that they weren't going to tell me.

I thought I knew what it was.

I got to my feet.

Rosetta Draine slipped her hand from her husband's, sat up straighter. "May we ask, Mr. Ross, what you and Ms. Reedy are going to do about all of this?"

She was afraid now, threatened. She always had been.

"I can't speak for Ms. Reedy, Mrs. Draine. But I'm not going to do anything about it."

She folded her hands, thought she understood. "For which you want . . . ?"

"Nothing."

Her husband understood. "That isn't true, Mr. Ross. You're not going to do anything, but you want something. You want us to do it, what we should have done twenty years ago."

I turned and left the room.

Martha sat where Patsy had, across from Heather and Monte. The silent tension in the room had changed to silent confusion.

As I stepped into the arch, Martha looked up, gave her head a short, sharp jerk.

I left them there, went looking for Patsy McLeod.

Her tracks showed dark against the silver of the frost.

The barn was warm, sweet with the smell of hay and horse. With a curry brush, Patsy was working to a soft gloss the coat of the young palomino mare. The other two horses, a gray gelding and an older bay mare, stomped and snorted as if impatiently awaiting her hands.

As I came in, Patsy started, then turned her head away from me.

Moving over to the stall, I leaned against a post, watched her work, watched the hands that would caress her daughter caress the horse.

I hadn't known what I was going to say to her. As I waited, I discovered that there was only one thing I could say.

Finally, her hands on the horse slowed, stilled.

Finally she turned, showed me her desert-torn face, her beautiful blue eyes, showed me her grief and guilt, her anguish and shame.

Finally she gave me a privileged glimpse into her hopelessly human heart.

I told her the only thing I had to tell her.

"Good-bye, Patsy."

CHAPTER FORTY-TWO

The Wagoneer was warm by the time Martha and Monte came out of the house. For a while they stood in the pale sunlight. Martha talked. Monte listened.

I could see his face changing, see his anger. He said something, and Martha nodded. She held out her hand. He took it. Then she came over and got in the Wagoneer.

For our own reasons, neither of us spoke on the drive back to Reno. My reason was that I had nothing to say. I didn't know what her reason was.

As I pulled in under the mulberry tree, I saw that while we were gone the tree had, as they do, lost all its leaves at once. Broad, dead, pale green, they lay in a thick loose layer over the driveway.

I shut off the Wagoneer. "We could have some of my coffee or finish your beer. Or I could fix us some lunch, or we could go out for some."

"Or you could go in your house," Martha said, "and I could get in my car and drive off into the sunset."

"Be a little hard to do, since it's only noon," I said. "But...what's your pleasure, Ms. Reedy?"

She gave me her small odd smile. "What I'd really like, right now, is a run. Are you up to it, Jones?"

"I don't know, Bud. Why don't we find out?"

"Bud?"

I grinned, climbed out, crunched across the leaves to the house.

Twenty minutes later, dressed and stretched, we crunched back across the leaves to the street. Martha nodded at my sweatshirt, at the red legend that proclaimed me WORLD'S GREATEST DETECTIVE.

"How modest of you, Jones."

"My daughter's opinion," I said. "Let's do it, Ms. Reedy."

As we trotted away from the house, almost immediately I perceived that Martha's stride was shorter, quicker than mine. I shuffled, skipped, trying to adjust, just as she shuffled and skipped.

She laughed. "If we just let it go, it'll work itself out."

It did. We turned into Rancho San Rafael Park, followed the dirt track around it. By the time I'd broken into a sweat we were comfortably in stride.

Jogging over to McCarran Boulevard, we crossed, went up and around the Sports Complex, past the Basque Monument and onto the nature trail, then took an old dirt road up Peavine. Going nowhere in particular, we took cross tracks as we came to them, wandered over the trail-scarred desert mountain.

Sweat loosened my shoulders, deep breathing cleared my chest. Other than a dull ache in my nose and eyes, I felt good, better than I had in, it seemed, years.

Martha felt good too. I could see it in the color of her skin, the glow in her eyes.

I soaked up the smell of the sage and the dust, the pale yellow of the autumn sunlight, the faint sounds of the city, the sound of our breathing, our feet. I felt strong, light, clean, seemed to be sweating away psychic as well as physical toxins.

Finally we came to narrow drainage that twisted back down to the nature trail. By unspoken agreement, we took it, soon were back on McCarran.

Martha slowed. "To the house? Loser admits his gender inferiority? Winner gets the first shower?"

"I thought you were through competing with me?"

"I am," she said. "This won't be any competition at all."

It wasn't. I gave it all I had, but I couldn't come close to matching her sprinter's speed. With a sudden spurt she pulled away, quickly opened up a fifty-yard lead, glanced back, grinned. Easing off, she held the interval. I was just coming out of the park when she turned the corner and cruised into my driveway.

Sweating, grinning, she watched me slog my way to the house. As I walked up the driveway, she said, "You run like you're still wearing your boots, Jones."

"It's the burden I carry," I said between gasps of breath.

"All that testosterone," she grinned. "And that useless Y chromosome."

"Or all those cowboy scruples you were talking about."

She laughed. "I'll expect a victory beer to await me upon completion of my ablutions."

As I waited for her to shower, I examined my living room, began to plan. Sand and polish the hardwood floors, paint the walls and ceiling a soft white, the trim dust brown. Bring in my grandfather's desk, the filing cabinets, a pair of comfortable chairs and a low table and a bookcase, the sound system and speakers. Place the things I'd brought in from the desert on the walls and over the shelves where I could look at them.

It wouldn't be a normal living room, but it would be mine.

I heard the water go off, went back into the kitchen and grabbed two beers and sat at the table.

Barefoot, wrapped in her terrycloth robe, Martha came in, her face still flushed, her hair damp. She picked up her beer. "Your turn, Jones."

The dried sweat had left a salty crust over my body, but I still felt clean. "No hurry. I'm not going anywhere."

Her mouth settled into a soft, strong line. After a moment, she sat, sipped her beer, set it down. "Who goes first?"

"You should, probably," I said, "given the fact that you're the one who did everything that mattered. But it might simplify things if I did."

"All right," she said, "go ahead."

"As far as I'm concerned, Martha, it's finished. I'm not going to do anything. You can do whatever you want about it."

"That's it?" But she didn't seem surprised. "If I take the film to the authorities, you'll . . . ?"

"Do nothing."

"And when they come to you to confirm what I've told them?"

"I'll tell them the truth as I understand it."

She picked up her beer, but she didn't drink. She looked at my daughter's portrait.

"I keep thinking about Maureen Cody. I know why she died, but I don't know who, finally, is morally responsible for her death. Legally Flowers, of course, but somehow trying to hold him morally responsible is like trying to blame a coyote for killing a chicken. Turner, certainly. The Draines, partly, before the fact. And partly I'm responsible."

Liberal guilt. The illness of the age.

"And I'm partly responsible. And Gentle. And Heather McLeod. And General Westmoreland and Timothy Leary and General Custer and George Washington and Columbus and Adam and Eve. It gets meaningless pretty quick, Martha."

But I was afflicted by it too. Everyone's crazy, everyone's a victim, everyone's responsible.

"So who pays, Jack, besides Flowers?"

"We're paying right now. So, in their way, are the Draines."

"And Turner?"

I tried my beer. Nolan Turner was, as he'd been all along, the real problem. "I don't know. All I can think of is that if I wait long enough, watch him carefully enough, somewhere along the line he'll make a mistake and I'll get him. Not for murder, probably, but one way or the other, I'll get him."

A small smile quivered at the edge of her mouth. "So you are going to do something. At least about him."

"I guess so."

"I've already done something," she said. "I had a little chat with Monte. Interesting fellow. There's more there than I'd expected."

"There usually is."

"We agreed that Cleveland Culler might be interested to know that twenty years ago Nolan Turner ripped off some big-time San

Francisco dealers. Culler might have been one of those dealers, or a business associate of one of them. Their draconic little code of business ethics might demand that Turner pay."

"Lots of might's there, Martha."

"I know, it's chancy," she said. "But we agreed on some other things too."

She was going to make me ask. "Such as?"

"Such as, when Culler knows that Turner hired a man to kill the star attraction of his movie business, he might want to send out a field hand with a propane torch."

"More might's."

"Monte didn't think so," Martha said. She tilted up her beer. "He thought that Culler would be more than happy to oblige Tramontane, if she were to ask him for help in dispensing justice to the man who had her father murdered."

I sat back in my chair and looked at her. "You're a deeply perverse woman, Ms. Reedy."

"Thank you, Mr. Ross."

For a moment she stared down at her beer. "If there were any other—you understand what all this amounts to?"

"It amounts to your shooting him and my kicking him to death."

"Does that trouble you?"

Maybe it should have, but it didn't. "If it starts to, I'll just think about what we found behind that door in Oakland."

For a moment her gaze went vague, distant. She was seeing what we had found behind that door in Oakland.

"About the Draines," I said.

"I know, Jack," she said, sitting back in the chair. "I can go to the authorities, and eventually they can prove who he is—if in their politically determined wisdom they decide they want to—and it will cost the Draines a lot of money and maybe some grief, but finally they can buy their way out of most of it."

"You don't need to go to the authorities, Martha. They're going to go to the authorities themselves."

That surprised her. "They told you that?"

"No. But they're good, decent, honest, liberal citizens. And they've got to make sure no one else can ever get to them, that they're safe.

They'll take their lawyers and their checkbooks along. As you say, it will cost them a lot of money and maybe some grief, but they'll get out of it. He'll go on revising history, and she'll stay in control of everything."

Martha put down her beer, began absently sorting the desert relics on the table, rock with rock, metal with metal.

"If it were just the money business, the Mercer Foundation and the bank, I—the fact is, Jack, Rosetta Draine has done a lot of good with all that money."

"Yes," I said. But of course it wasn't just the money business. I waited for her to get to the rest of it.

She didn't. "Do you know why Heather hates you, Jack?"

"Because I didn't find her eighteen years ago."

She nodded. "There's a lot of ugly stuff there, but most of it's old. Old anger. Old scars. Monte's helped her, I think. For one thing, he's been able to make her see that her career is nearly finished, that she's old meat in the porn business. He's convinced her that they should go into business on their own."

"What business?"

"The gym business. Bodybuilding, aerobics, all that."

She looked at me, shook her head. "Can you picture the two of them, those two bodies strutting around . . . ?"

"That takes money," I said.

"Monte thinks they won't have much trouble getting a loan from American Security Bank."

I was still waiting for her to get to it. I nudged her. "Did you learn the answer to your question?"

She continued to sort. Feather with feather, wood with wood.

"It's complex, Jack. It's not really hate, it's hurt. And way down at the bottom, buried beneath all the scar tissue, it's love. Heather doesn't know that yet, or at least she can't admit it to herself, but only love could cause that much . . . ."

"That's what her brother says too."

Martha picked up her beer again. "Maybe you have to be a woman to understand. . . . She was twelve, entering puberty, which is a risky time for women. Everything is changing, their bodies, the way men look at them, treat them. They worry about how they look and what their life is going to be like and who, if anybody, in the world beyond their family will love them."

I looked at my daughter's portrait. "Yes."

"Then suddenly her father goes to prison and her brother goes to Vietnam and, she thinks, dies, and her mother doesn't have time for her because she's desperately trying to keep the ranch going...."

She was right. It was complex.

"What she's doing now is what she did by staying away. She wants her mother to suffer the way she did. But she doesn't want to ..."

I nudged her again, told her what I'd been told a couple of hours before. "Heather thought that her mother had killed Blake. All she had to do was tell somebody. But she didn't."

Martha looked at me, calmly. "Yes."

Slowly I smiled. "Thanks, Martha. You're a good friend."

"I—you're right. And you're welcome."

"And you're making the same mistake Malcolm McLeod made with his sister. You can't really protect people from the truth."

She didn't say anything.

I did. "Patsy killed Blake."

"Yes," she said.

"And you've known it since you looked at the film again last night."

"Not for sure. But it was the only thing that made sense."

I nodded. "And all of it, everything they've done—letting you look for Heather, hiring me, telling us this morning things they didn't have to tell us—all of it was to protect Patsy."

She looked down at the small, neat piles she had created on the table.

"And that's what you're doing, Jack. That's the real reason you're not going to do anything about it. You're protecting her too."

"I'm protecting myself," I said.

She looked at me again.

"I'd have done the same thing she did," I said.

We finished our beers, opened the last two. Martha was still behind her quiet calm.

"That face is apt to cause quite a stir at Rondo and Keene."

"Not for long," I said. "I'll be out of there when my lease expires."

It took her a moment. "You're not joining the law firm?"

"Hey," I grinned, "if Hannah can tough it out on her own, so can I."

She didn't grin. "What's the real reason?"

I hesitated. I didn't want to sound foolish.

"I was suffering from the same bad dream that turned Heather McLeod into Tramontane. If I make myself into something I'm not, maybe somebody will love me."

She didn't seem to find it foolish. She gave me her small odd smile.

"There may be hope for you after all, Jones."

"May be. Especially if I can take Gentle's advice and learn to trust the Goddess."

She laughed. "That I gotta see."

"She said you'd show me how, Bud."

Martha laughed again. "Bud? Is that her name for me?"

I grinned. "All closed in tight on yourself, until you open up and smile and bloom and become beautiful."

She laughed again, shook her head. "She's . . ."

"She also said we fit." I drained the last of my beer. "I think she's right, Martha. We work pretty well together. I don't know about your business, but more and more, mine takes me over the hill. It would be nice to know that I could contract out part of it to some-one there I could trust."

She considered it. "The arrangement would be reciprocal?"

"Makes sense, doesn't it?"

She didn't answer right away. Then she sighed, sat back in the chair and gazed steadily, silently at me.

"The only thing that doesn't make sense, Jones, is you."

"I don't—"

"Out in the desert the other day, you told me that the trick to seeing what the desert really is is to look at what's there, not for what isn't or what you think should be."

I nodded.

"Well, Jones, why don't you do that?"

As I looked at her, slowly she smiled the smile that opened her face like a flower, the smile she watched me from behind.

But she was no longer behind it.

"Oh," I said.

Then, finally, seeing what was really there, I said, slowly, "Aaah."